PRAISE FOR LUCY SCORE AND
MAGGIE MOVES ON

"Lucy Score always delivers on the laughs, expert storytelling, and full-body swoons."

—Tessa Bailey, *New York Times* bestselling author

"Fast-paced, fun, and full of *Gilmore Girls*-worthy banter! Silas is head over heels for Maggie out of the gate, and with his playful wooing that's equal parts sweet and sexy, readers won't be far behind. MAGGIE MOVES ON combines the signature charm of a small-town romance with blush-inducing starbursts of heat."

—Rosie Danan, author of *The Roommate*

"Lucy Score proves why she's such a powerhouse with this smart and sexy, head-over-heels, laugh-out-loud comedy!"

—Lauren Landish, *Wall Street Journal*
and *USA Today* bestselling author

"A delightful laugh-out-loud small-town romance with that special Lucy Score touch. An absolute must-read."

—Meghan Quinn, *USA Today* bestselling author

"Bursting with sizzling chemistry, charming characters, and heartwarming small town feels, *Maggie Moves On* is rom-com gold. I can't stop smiling!"   —Melanie Harlow, *USA Today* bestselling author

Maggie MOVES ON

LUCY SCORE

FOREVER

New York Boston

Forever
Hachette Book Group
1290 Avenue of the Americas, New York, NY 10104
read-forever.com
twitter.com/readforeverpub

First Edition: June 2022

Forever is an imprint of Grand Central Publishing. The Forever name and logo are trademarks of Hachette Book Group, Inc.

The publisher is not responsible for websites (or their content) that are not owned by the publisher.

The Hachette Speakers Bureau provides a wide range of authors for speaking events. To find out more, go to www.hachettespeakersbureau.com or call (866) 376-6591.

Library of Congress Cataloging-in-Publication Data
Names: Score, Lucy, author.
Title: Maggie moves on / Lucy Score.
Description: First edition. | New York, NY : Forever, 2022. |
Identifiers: LCCN 2021053940 | ISBN 9781538707081 (trade paperback) | ISBN 9781538707098 (ebook)
Subjects: LCGFT: Romance fiction. | Novels.
Classification: LCC PS3619.C637 M34 2022 | DDC 813/.6—dc23/eng/20211105
LC record available at https://lccn.loc.gov/2021053940

ISBNs: 978-1-5387-0708-1 (trade paperback); 978-1-5387-0709-8 (ebook)

Printed in the United States of America

LSC-C

Printing 4, 2022

To Binge Readers Anonymous, my found family—this one's for you.

Maggie
MOVES
ON

1

"DID YOU CONSIDER just setting a pile of money on fire instead?"

"Har har, smart-ass," Maggie quipped over Aerosmith wailing through the speakers.

She was used to Dean's overprotectiveness toward her home renovation budget and his consistent mistrust of her ability to turn nightmares into dreams.

The house rose in front of them through the rain-slicked windshield as the truck squeezed through the overgrowth on both sides of a rutted lane. Three stories. A massive porch that disappeared around one side. Shingles and carved wood with several layers of peeling paint battled it out to draw the eye first.

But nothing could compete with the turret. Part of the porch on the first floor, it became a balcony on the second. The third and final level was closed in with rounded windows and a needle point–tipped roof. The view from up there was one she predicted that even the pragmatic Dean would get excited about.

He flopped back in his seat and shook his head. "This better be the first and last time you buy a property sight unseen." His voice was its usual morning rasp when Maggie dragged him from his beauty sleep.

The property wasn't exactly unseen, but she doubted the truth of it would make her business partner feel more confident. "I saw pictures," she argued instead.

"I saw the same pictures and distinctly recall trying to talk you out of it."

"Whine later," Maggie told him as they got out of the truck. The ground was soft and wet beneath her work boots.

What had once been an elegant, tree-lined drive was now an overgrown trail. The neglected trees and shrubs seemed determined to force the property's surrender to nature.

But the house? Well, there was magic here on this bluff. She could feel it shimmering just beneath layers of rotting wood and what was most likely lead paint. Like a buried treasure waiting to be unearthed.

Maggie cocked her head and studied the exterior. Rain pattered off the bill of her cap.

Whimsical maybe. Dilapidated definitely.

"We're not in Oregon on the beach anymore, Toto," Dean said, eyeing the monstrosity.

"No, we're not," she agreed, tucking her hands into her coat pockets and wishing she had the keys. She'd closed the deal on her last flip, a charming beach bungalow, a handful of days ago. With the largest check to date burning a hole in her pocket, she'd packed up and hit the road, heading east for the new adventure.

"What the hell is it even?" he asked, zipping his vest to his chin. "What's it doing here?"

The fact that the once-grand fever dream of a mansion didn't fit was precisely what she loved best about it. This part of Idaho was full of timber cabins, smart lakeside cottages, and a tidy downtown of kitschy brick and clapboard buildings. But here, surrounded by mountains and aspen and river, the Queen Anne Victorian reigned over it all.

Proudly, unashamedly different, the Old Campbell Place had claimed this spot on the bluff without regard to any other outside forces for well over a century. She'd have bought it even without the house tangling up briefly in her own history.

"It was originally built by Aaron Campbell for his wife, Ava, allegedly a romantic at heart," she said, warming to her topic.

"Oh goodie. A lecture."

"Mr. Campbell's family owned jewelry stores and a timber operation in the area."

"Must have been a lot of money in murdering trees," Dean mused as he tested the first step leading to the porch.

"Actually, Campbell's money came from the fifteen western novels he wrote."

He groaned. "I hate it when houses have backstories. It makes you spend more."

"Mr. and Mrs. Campbell spent four years building this place, making sure every inch of it was perfect."

"And then they died tragically of typhoid and lead-based paint?" he guessed.

Maggie gave him a playful shove and danced up the steps onto the porch. "No. They lived happily ever after for forty-plus years, giving generously to the town. Raising a family. Throwing spectacular parties."

"And *then* they died."

"And then they died—romantically—a few months apart. The house was passed down through the generations—some with better taste than others. When the family money ran out after a few generations, the house was donated to the town in the 1980s."

"What did the town ever do to them?" Dean quipped. He gave the porch railing a shake and shot her a smug look when two of the spindles fell to the ground.

"I can fix that," she said with confidence.

"The town turned it into the Campbell House Museum and ran it for just over a decade. Which is why the place comes chock-full of family artifacts."

"Don't even ask me to run the cash box at the yard sale, Magpie. I'm busy that day."

"Come on. It was cute when you haggled with the church bingo lady in Aberdeen. The viewers loved it."

She cupped her hands to one of the dingy front windows and

peered inside. Wallpaper. Gloriously hideous pheasants in blue and gold climbed the walls of the study like an invasive ivy. Her fingers itched to touch it. It was so aggressively eye searing it might actually work. There were a few pieces of art, including what looked like a portrait hanging above a blackened fireplace. She gave the glass a swipe with her wet sleeve but only succeeded in smearing the layers of grime.

"Speaking of, when are you announcing this new 'guaranteed to bankrupt you and lose all of your followers' project?" Dean asked, clomping down the steps.

In Maggie's opinion, the man spent entirely too much time thinking about numbers. Budgets, YouTube subscribers—all 900,000+ of them—and advertising dollars. But that was why they worked so well together. Dean obsessed over numbers on the page while she turned disasters into dream homes.

She followed him around the side of the house to the uneven stone terrace. The whole thing needed to be relaid. "We've still got three episodes banked on the beach bungalow. But I'll start teasing this place on Instagram."

He tripped, stumbled, and then kicked at the offending stone that had caught his shoe.

"Wait until tomorrow when the place is ours and there's insurance before you fall and break your face," she advised.

"What the hell is that?" he demanded, gesturing toward a concrete monument.

Maggie grinned. "A fountain."

Four nearly life-size stone horses stood in the center of the base. One pawing the air, the others frozen midgallop. "That looks like the four horses of the apocalypse guarding a communitywide West Nile virus infection waiting to happen," he said, eyeing the foot of black, murky water and debris clogging the fountain's pool.

Despite the snarky, uncaffeinated grump show, she could tell he was starting to thaw...marginally. Dean had a soft spot for the quirky. Which was why he'd tolerated Maggie for so many years.

"Tell me they piss water."

"I'm sure it can be arranged," she mused.

He grunted and continued across the terrace toward the backyard.

"That's a sizable problem," he observed, coming to a stop.

She ducked around him and eyed the fir tree that leaned lazily against the back of the house. That hadn't been in the pictures.

"I can fix it," she chirped, already picturing a bench or chair reclaimed from the wood.

And she would. Maggie Nichols had yet to meet a challenge that she couldn't conquer. Her real estate picks had gotten progressively more dilapidated, and while they briefly gave Dean bouts of acid reflux, he always came around. Especially at closing, when keys were exchanged for big, fat checks.

"The whole budget's gonna go to landscaping," he complained.

"Dean, Dean, Dean." She sighed. "When are you going to start trusting my vision?"

Identifying potential had never been in the man's skill set. But she didn't hold it against him...at least, not anymore.

"This is going to be the one, Magpie," he insisted, nudging a damp fern with the toe of his boot.

She flashed him a smirk. "You think this place will be the one I can't finish?"

"I am absolutely certain you've bitten off more than you can chew. Eighteen rooms. I read the listing. There are outbuildings, which, judging by this wreck, are going to be hovels. There's no way you can do this. And none of those rabid followers of yours are going to tune in to a project this big. It'll be weeks of just hauling out god-awful carpet and scraping wallpaper. How the hell are you going to keep their attention?"

"You do realize you say that about every house, don't you?" She nudged him in the direction of the bluff.

"Seriously. I have concerns about your decision-making. Are you having some kind of midlife crisis? Couldn't you just buy a convertible and get a new haircut? Maybe date another guy who still lives with his mom?"

"You're mean when you haven't had enough coffee," she complained as they stepped over a log into a small thicket of briars and brambles. "Besides, I told you Bobby looked older than he was when he turned his hat around backward."

"You and the backward-hat thing," Dean groaned. "Ouch! Thorn!"

"It's not a *thing*. I just happen to find cute guys in backward ball caps attractive."

"And how old was Backward Hat Bobby again?" he pressed, feigning a faulty memory.

"Twenty-four." A mere decade younger than herself. "And don't even get started on the robbing-the-cradle bit. Men date younger women all the time. Besides, it was fun while it lasted." *Fun while it lasted* applied to all of Maggie's relationships. That particular one had lasted exactly as long as it had taken her to realize her cute California flirtation lived in his parents' basement while he "figured out" what he wanted to do with his environmental science degree.

"I have no problem with you dating guys ten years younger... if you were fifty and they were employed and had their own place. And knew what dryer sheets are for."

"I never should have told you about that," she grumbled.

"You know what I think?"

"No. But that's never stopped you from telling me before."

He paused dramatically. "I don't think you believe in love and romance and happily ever after."

She eyed him. "Oh? And you do, pot?"

"Listen here, kettle. I am a jaded man. A realist. A cynic, if you will. You buy hovels like this and turn them into castles. You *should* believe in romance. You should be dating and falling in love and settling down and giving me weekends off."

"Ah. *Now* I get where this is going. You're Danny Kaye–ing me," she said, referring to *White Christmas*, a holiday movie she'd tried to dislike over the years and never quite succeeded.

"I always thought of myself as more of a Bing Crosby than a Danny Kaye." Dean sniffed.

"Listen, Bing, Danny, or whoever the hell you are, I'm not in one place long enough to even learn a guy's favorite beer, let alone sexual position or 401(k) balance."

"But you could be. You could take time off between houses. You could take a vacation and fall in love with your scuba instructor."

"Or here's a thought. I could renovate this house, make it beautiful, and we could make an obscene amount of money." It's what they did and how she earned the freedom and financial stability she'd always craved.

"You already have an obscene amount of money," he pointed out.

"I think our definitions of *obscene* are pretty far apart."

"Check your statements and get back to me. You've leveled up and haven't noticed yet."

"Do you want a raise? Because I'll give you a raise if it stops you from whining all the time."

"I don't want more money—I mean, I wouldn't say no to it. But I want more time. You should, too. What's the point of making all this money and running your own business if it means you can't enjoy it?"

"I do enjoy it," she argued. "I love what I do."

"Well, you better, because it's going to take you six years to finish this place."

"Three months," she insisted. Then caught his skeptical look. "Fine. Four tops."

"You pay me to be practical," he reminded her as he carefully removed a briar that had attached itself to his sleeve. "It's impractical that your only days off are the ones you take driving between houses. You can't keep this up forever."

"Practical concerns noted. In the meantime, you trust me to have vision," she said, blazing a trail through underbrush toward the one thing that would shut him up.

"Vision. Not hallucinations."

She said nothing and pointed to the rocky edge of the bluff.

His brown eyes widened. "Oh. Shit."

"Yeah. Oh, shit."

They stood shoulder to shoulder and looked across the rolling foothills and canyons spread out before them. The Payette River zigged and zagged below, green and fast with snowmelt. The town, compact and cozy, was tucked into a hard bend to the north. The lake beyond fed the river and the tourism that coaxed travelers off the beaten path, away from the jagged mountain peaks and ski resorts and into Western Idaho.

"Figured we'd open up the view a little bit," she said, still looking out over miles and miles of rugged country. "Thin out the vegetation. Maybe take down a couple of the trees."

"The budget isn't big enough," Dean said, recovering himself quickly. He wasn't a romantic who could be charmed with breathtaking views and historical charm. But at least she knew he was willing to flirt with the value of a multimillion-dollar view.

"We could double our money here," she said, tempting him with his language of love.

"Double? Ha. First of all, you have to decide what's the absolute minimum to get this beautiful and market-worthy. Then you being you, you have to decide how much over that you're going to run amok. *Then* we'll have to pull a buyer who wants a seven-figure mausoleum in Where the Fuck Are We, Idaho, out of our asses."

She clapped him on the shoulder. "That's the spirit. Oh, and Kinship."

"Kinship what?"

"Kinship, Idaho. That's where the fuck we are. Now, if I promise to buy you two huge coffees when we go into town, will you be a good boy and get your fancy drone out?"

Grumbling, he left her there and picked his way through nature. "I hate thorns!" he called over his shoulder. "Son of a—"

She snickered when his dark head disappeared into a wet bed of tall ferns.

"Watch your step," she sang out too late, following him to the front. "I'm not too fond of you right now!"

While her partner swore his way back to the backyard, drone in tow, Maggie faced the house. With her thumbs hooked in her pockets and rain dampening the short ponytail pulled through the back of her hat, she studied it. Three sprawling stories. Eighteen rooms. Four fireplaces. Not nearly enough bathrooms.

The paint, at least six different colors that she'd counted, was peeling. The yard had been eaten by weeds and overgrowth. What looked like a very healthy crop of poison oak climbed the north side of the house, which faced the detached carriage house.

The front porch looked like it was a good four inches lower on the right than it was on the left. The warped front door was way too small for a house so grand.

She felt the rev in her blood. The low hum of excitement of a new challenge, an adventure at the starting line. It was like finding a secret treasure in a ruin. Only, the ruin *was* the treasure. And her favorite part was excavating it piece by piece. Restoring old charm and adding new-world function. Every project was someone's dream house. And she did what she could to bring it into being.

But this place, the Old Campbell Place—capitalized like a proper noun, as it had been dubbed for over a century—would be special. It already was. And it was even better than she'd remembered.

She waited until Dean had grumbled his way around to the back with his toy before taking out her phone and lining up a selfie with the house behind her.

It was tradition. Every project. Just her and the house at the very beginning of their journey together. She'd never shared any of them. It felt too personal, as if she were standing in front of her own dreams and asking them to come true.

"Closing's not until tomorrow, Magpie," Dean said when he returned. "Still have time to change your mind."

She heard the hope in his voice and grinned. "Nice try. This is happening."

He heaved a heroic sigh. "Fine. I have a couple of local trades lined up tomorrow after settlement. Figured you'd want to get started on the estimates right away."

"You figured right. Come on. Let's get you some caffeine so you can be nice. Maybe they'll let us check in to the hotel early."

2

"LOOK, MAN. ALL I'm sayin' is, if it makes you yack, maybe think about not eating it next time." Silas Wright's passenger had the good grace to look chagrined...and a little nauseated. "I mean, seriously, Kev? A whole pack of bacon. Even I know better than that."

Kevin, a burly pit bull, whined a little, his wet nose twitching.

Silas hit the button and lowered the window a little more. "Don't you puke. I'm trying to impress a client that desperately needs my expertise. Dog barf isn't impressive."

His dog's tail gave a happy wobble as warm spring air rushed in.

Silas loved this time of year, too. As a kid, it had meant that endless summers of swimming, skipping rocks, and sleepovers were just around the corner. As an adult, the first sustained days of spring buoyed Western Idaho residents into thinking about mulch and weeding and retaining walls and patios for outdoor entertaining. And how much they didn't want to do that work themselves.

It was no coincidence that the mailers for Bitterroot Landscapes were landing in mailboxes in a fifteen-mile radius today. Not only had he highlighted the nice, clean look of fresh mulch and neat lawn lines, but he'd also made sure to hint at what a pain in the ass the work was.

After several years of steady growth, he'd predicted this season would be tougher. The plant closing had many neighbors hurting for those paychecks. So he'd been prepared to tighten his belt and do what was needed to keep his people working steadily.

However, he hadn't predicted a call about the Old Campbell Place.

Born and raised in Kinship, Silas was as familiar with the house on the bluff as the cold cuts cooler at Garnet Grocery and every kayak-swamping submerged rock on the five miles of Payette River he considered to be his.

Judging from the call, the estate's new owner was looking to do more than Band-Aid the grand dame of a house. And Silas was going to dazzle the hell out of that someone into letting him get his hands on those grounds.

The dog let out a sigh.

As long as a certain someone kept his breakfast down.

The road got skinnier and steeper as his truck climbed. He'd laughed when the client—Dean Jensen with those California vowels—had asked if he needed directions to the project. Everyone knew where the Old Campbell Place was.

He slowed and signaled for the turn onto the lane. Not even the camouflage of wild Rocky Mountain maple and chokecherry could hide the way.

Bumping along, he noted the fresh ruts in the mud. He wasn't the first trade on-site. A good sign that the owner was excited to get started. He could get behind excited, he decided as the quaking aspens that seemed intent on devouring the drive thinned and the house came into view.

He let out a low whistle that had Kevin perking up.

She'd been a grand beauty in her day. Now, crumbling and sagging. But beyond the peeling paint and broken windows was the kind of charm that never faded. The grounds—he'd had a look at the site map to refresh his memory—were five acres of hilltop roll. House, garage, barn, remains of a greenhouse. Mother Nature had been busy here in the years the property stood vacant. Trees and shrubs, weeds and thistles.

She needed love. A lot of it. But the potential was there. She could rise again, given the right care...and a sizable budget. And he wanted his hands on it. Not just for the job security and that influx of cash to his bottom line. No. He liked the idea of adding his mark to this piece of local history.

Kevin let out a bacon-scented burp that pulled Silas from his romantic reverie.

"Gross, man."

He spotted a Hines Contracting van out front and swung in next to a pickup the same make, model, and blue as his own.

"Stay put and, if you gotta puke, puke out the window," he told his dog.

The screen door on the front banged open and then shut, and he spotted his old Little League coach exiting.

"How's it going, Jim?" Silas called, getting out.

"Some place, Sy," Jim told him with a grin usually reserved for over-the-fence homers.

"Sure is. I'm hoping the pockets are deep."

"Deep and smart. Big job," he said cheerfully. "But the owner's got brains and vision. And best as I can tell, a decent budget, too."

Music to the ears of the Kinship small businesses, Silas thought.

The screen door creaked open and banged shut again, and he felt his world tilt a few degrees.

The work boots were scarred and not for fashion. Long legs seemed to go on forever under a pair of battered utility pants. Curves, subtle ones, revealed themselves through a dirt-streaked tank top. Hands in pink-trimmed work gloves tossed a long-sleeve flannel over the porch railing.

Silas was already in lust before he got to her face.

Categorizing as fast as he could, he took in the sight. Sun-kissed skin, leanly muscled arms, strong shoulders. There was a softness in the heart-shaped face beneath a fringe of bangs. Loose strands in the same chestnut copper shade had escaped a short ponytail at the back of her long, slim neck and framed sharp cheekbones and a straight nose. Her lips weren't painted, but they were lifted in the kind of smile that hinted at secrets.

"Wow," he said.

"You okay there, kid?" Jim asked.

Silas, like the rest of Kinship's athletic population, had been "kid" to the man since he was seven years old. "Okay doesn't even begin to cover it," he admitted.

Jim rolled his eyes and then turned back to the goddess on the porch. "Real nice meeting you, Ms. Nichols," he said.

"Maggie," the goddess corrected. She had one of those throaty voices, just a little rough around the edges. Like the rasp that came from shooting whiskey too fast. "I'm looking forward to your estimate."

"Have it to you Monday," he promised. Jim paused to eyeball Silas like he'd just shown up on a job site in a prom dress.

To be fair, it *had* happened once. A bet was a bet.

He clapped him on the shoulder. "Later, Sy."

"Later, Coach," Silas said without taking his gaze off Maggie Nichols of the strong arms and sexy voice.

They eyed each other for a beat, and then she was shucking her work gloves. "Sy as in Silas Wright? Bitterroot Landscapes?" she asked.

"That'd be me," he said, approaching the porch like a tractor beam had locked on and was dragging him forward. "And you definitely wouldn't be Dean Jensen."

They met on the steps. "Maggie Nichols," she said, offering a hand. Ringless. Long fingers. Calloused.

Silas closed his hand around hers and enjoyed the invisible sparks that shot out from the contact. Her eyes were brown, warm, and golden. They made him think of topaz in the sun.

"That's a long handshake you've got there, Mr. Wright," she observed, giving their joined hands a pointed look.

He grinned. "I'd apologize, but I don't want our relationship to start out on a fib because I'm not actually sorry at all."

"Ah, a flirtatious landscaper," she said lightly as she withdrew her hand.

Kevin let out a mournful whimper from the truck window.

"Pipe down, Kevin," Silas said, without looking back.

The quirk of her lips was a full-blown smile now, and he felt his stomach dip like it was on the rolling hills of a coaster.

"You named your dog Kevin?" she asked.

In response to hearing his name, the dog let out another pathetic moan.

"He named himself," Silas explained. "The shelter tried every normal dog name in the book before they started on the people names."

"Aw," she said. The softness in her eyes had him reluctantly dragging his attention away from her. He saw Kevin was doing his best depressed pet routine, with one jowl pitifully draped over the truck's side mirror.

"Don't fall for it," Sy said. "He's a diabolical attention whore."

On cue, the dog let out a howl.

"You can let him out, you know," Sy's future wife said, falling into the dog's trap.

"You say that now, but Kevin's a little burly, and while he has a heart of gold, he can look a bit intimidating. Plus, he just ate an entire pack of thick-cut, hickory-smoked bacon, and I've got concerns about his ability to keep it down."

"Better for him to lose his breakfast out here than in there," she advised. "If it gets in the vents, you'll never get it out."

Sensing an ally, the dog perked up.

"I can tell this is the first of many times that you two will be ganging up against me," Silas said as he left the steps and headed toward the truck. "I don't want you to think I'll always be this easy."

"Oh, my," Maggie said as eighty pounds of brindle pit bull celebrated his freedom with a zoom around the front yard.

The dog remembered that thanks were in order and plowed his way up the porch steps.

"No jumping," Silas yelled, jogging after his wayward wrecking ball.

Maggie was braced for the impact, but Kevin skidded to a halt, plopping his big ass on the porch boards at her feet.

Disaster averted, Silas slowed his approach. Sometimes his fat dog's brakes didn't work so well.

"Well, aren't you the handsomest boy in the whole world," Maggie said as she gave the muscly dog a rubdown. Kevin swooned over onto his back to provide better access to his tummy.

"Stop horning in on my business, dog," Silas complained.

Maggie straightened to her full height, putting her about a head shorter than his own six feet four inches. Good height for kissing without getting a crick in his neck, he noted.

"Business," she said. "Let's walk and talk."

"I'm all yours," he told her as he followed her off the porch.

"I won't insult your intelligence by warning you that this is a big job," she told him. "For starters, the trees are trying to eat the eight-hundred-foot driveway."

"I've got a tree guy. Gal, actually," he said, falling into step beside her. Kevin trotted ahead of them to begin his sniffing inventory.

"Good. Then we've got these prehistoric shrubs crowding in the front and around the east side. A bumper crop of poison oak."

"I'm immune," he told her. "It's one of my many superpowers. What's yours?"

"Built-in bullshit detector. All of this needs cleaned up," she said, gesturing at the tangle of underbrush and trees that had cropped up alongside the house.

"Agreed. We'll get a lot more light into the first floor if we cut all this back. What's your favorite holiday?" he asked.

"Thanksgiving," she answered without missing a beat. "Back here we've got another small issue for your tree gal."

The small issue was a seventy-foot fir that had decided to take a nap against the house.

He took a closer look. "Been here so long it's all dried out. We'll give you a nice stack of firewood, since I'm assuming you won't be converting all of the fireplaces to gas."

"I'm keeping the two first-floor fireplaces wood-burning," she said.

"Good. I'd hate for us to hit a deal breaker this early in our relationship," he said, lifting a branch of a crabapple out of her way as they picked their way through the backyard. She ducked under his arm.

The dog joyfully barreled past them, nose to the ground as he sniffled and snorted his way around the perimeter of the old iron fence.

"The fence kind of makes me think haunted cemetery," Maggie said, eyeing it. "I wouldn't be heartbroken if you said it needed to come down."

"Easy enough," he said, pausing to take in the backyard. The morning sun was behind them on the front of the house. The weeds already coming back to life had no problem with the shade. Rocky Mountain maples sprang up from waist-high grasses in a jumble of branches and buds. A pair of spindly looking hawthorn trees loomed too close to the house.

"Might take a few of these taller trees down," he advised. "You won't want a sequel to that one. Plus, a house this size needs a backyard kids and dogs can run around in. Do you have any? Kids or dogs?"

"Agreed. And no, I don't. But the next owner might."

"Big project for a flipper," he observed.

"Biggest I've tackled," she said, leading him out of the jungle to the north side of the house. "But scope doesn't scare me, and I don't want anyone on my team that's afraid of a little—okay, a lot—of hard work."

He stopped in front of her and placed a hand over his heart. "Maggie, I'm deadly serious when I tell you that Hard Work is my middle name."

She shot him a look that told him he was definitely charming the hell out of her. "No. It's not," she said.

"Okay. Fine. It's actually Andrew. But my motto is Work Hard, Play Harder."

"Now, *that* I believe."

"I'm your guy, Maggie."

"Hmm. We'll see. I'm less concerned about the backyard and more hopeful that a smart, challenge-embracing landscape architect can bring this area back to life."

What had been a stately stone terrace was now about 167 trip-and-fall lawsuits waiting to happen. The retaining wall at the far end had given up on retaining and leaned into, well, just plain leaning. And then there was the fountain. Four huge horses, stallions if their equipment was accurate, claimed the center.

Dark, soupy water from the rains puddled at the base around years of nature's seasonal debris.

In its current state, the fountain was a mosquito breeding ground at best. At worst, it would have to be completely dismembered.

"Wow," he said for the second time since he'd arrived. Unhooking the tape measure from his belt, he turned his ball cap around backward.

"Uh. I don't know how long it's been since it ran, but I'd love to get it in working order," she said, a hint of wistfulness in her tone.

Kevin bounded up to her, a tree branch clenched in his massive jaws. He spit it out at her feet and waited expectantly. Silas noted the tangle of roots and dirt on one end and hoped the dog hadn't actually yanked it out of the ground. He was dirty from nose to tail, the bottom half of his pudgy body obscured with dark, fresh mud.

"Did you fall in a well?" Maggie asked.

The dog gave a happy bark.

She snapped off a significantly smaller branch and gave it a toss in the direction of the backyard. She had a good arm, and the dog barreled after it, flinging wet mud in all directions.

"I apologize for my brute of a friend there," Silas said. "I would assure you he is not always an asshole like this, but then I'd be lying. This is exactly why he got the boot from therapy dog school."

Her sharp brown eyes darted to where the dog was rolling, stubby legs in the air. "Therapy dog school?"

"The rescue thought, since he was smart and affectionate, he'd make a good therapy or emotional support dog. He was a fast learner, but they underestimated the stubborn streak. They could get him to open drawers and refrigerators, but only when he felt like it. Nailed my shin just this morning on a dresser drawer he left open before he helped himself to all my bacon."

"Wow," she said.

"Speaking of wow, how about you show me this view?" he suggested, pointing toward the bluff.

3

MAGGIE DID HER best to not watch Silas Wright take measurements of the terrace, the front of the house, the back fence. She had plenty on her plate without adding a flirty, not-terrible-to-look-at landscaper to it.

Dean—who was on the second floor and wailing along to a Britney Spears classic—had outdone himself in the research department. Mr. Wright was exactly right for the camera.

Her followers would eat up the curling, dirty-blond hair that peeked out from beneath the hat. The crinkles around the gray eyes. His stubble beard toed the line between careless bad boy and hometown heartthrob who was too busy to shave.

He was tall with a rangy, muscled build that filled out his T-shirt, advertising more than just the name of his business. Broad chest and shoulders with tan skin. The peek of a tattoo just under the sleeve of his shirt.

He bent to examine the stone at the far end of the terrace, and she had to turn away before she started thinking too hard about that very firm butt he came equipped with.

The sunroom. Yes. She *should* be thinking about whether she needed to replace all of the molding around the windows, not about man-butt.

She peeked again and had no regrets before prying another piece of casing free. Some owner in the recent lineage had replaced the glass in the enclosed porch, and Maggie's budget cheered.

Satisfied that the casing needed to be replaced on only one of the dozen windows—thank you, baby Jesus—she added the item to her growing list on the iPad and then put her gloves back on and loaded rotted wood into the wheelbarrow on top of the orange shag carpeting she'd ripped out of the small hall closet.

With a short running start, she bumped the wheel over the threshold into the kitchen. No rest for the busy. Not with a mammoth project ahead of her.

But she could *see* the finish line even though it was miles and months away. She could see cups of coffee in the brand-new kitchen with its wall of windows over quartz countertops and glossy new cabinetry. On nice, bright days, someone would take that coffee onto the sunporch or terrace. In the winter, instead of the small collection of cheap empty beer cans and liquor bottles she'd found, there'd be a fire in the high-ceilinged library at the back of the house. Of course, it wouldn't be *her* doing the living after the work. But someone would be here, enjoying the treasure she reclaimed for them.

Pushing for the front door, she wheeled through the rotunda, past the Scarlett O'Hara–worthy staircase, and paused outside the study's pocket doors she'd popped off their tracks to get a look at their hardware. The portrait above the fireplace beckoned again.

Mr. and Mrs. Campbell made a dignified couple. Maggie couldn't help but wonder if it was her imagination or the talented hand of the artist that had her seeing the Mona Lisa smirk on Mrs. Campbell's lips.

"Don't worry, Campbells. It's only trash," she promised them before backing out of the open front door.

"Mags, Mags, Mags." Silas was standing hipshot at the foot of the porch steps. "Got a hell of a place here," he observed.

The man certainly wasn't shy. Getting him on camera with his doofy dog and crooked grin probably wouldn't take much more than a "please."

"I am aware," she said mildly, parking the wheelbarrow on the porch, above the dumpster. "Now, before you start working numbers and figuring out how to sweet-talk me into doing more than I want to do, let me give you the rest of it."

"I'm all yours," he said with that easy grin.

Silas Wright was used to charming the ladies. But this particular lady was more interested in his prowess *outside* of the bedroom.

"Renovations are just part of what I do," she began, stepping off the porch. "I also film everything for my YouTube channel. It's a weekly show. I started it a few years ago mostly to teach women how to tackle renovations, and it grew from there. If I hire you—"

"You will," he said.

"*If* I hire you," she repeated, "I'd want you and your crew to be comfortable being on camera. To talk about what you're doing. Tell the story of your business, your town. I have a feeling you won't be deeply offended if I tell you you've got a face for the camera."

"I've heard I'm not completely hideous," he said with feigned seriousness. "But that came from my moms, so they're biased."

"Moms?"

"Two moms. Two dads. Three sibs," he offered.

"Your moms might be biased, but that doesn't mean they're wrong."

"Why, Ms. Nichols, are you *flirting* with me?"

"I'm not flirting. I'm flattering you. Because if I do hire you, I'd want you to be okay with me using my sweaty, good-looking landscaper to keep the show interesting."

"Hmm." Silas rubbed a hand over his truly excellent beard of stubble. She could practically hear her female viewership—and a good percentage of the men—purr. "Is this the same pitch you gave Jim?"

She did laugh then. "No. I went more with the 'free advertising for his business' angle. I have a few thousand followers in Idaho, a few hundred that could be considered local. I'll get more with this project. The more viewers who see your business, who see the people and hear the stories behind them, the more customers you'll get out of the deal. I've got numbers on new sales leads after working with me. They're good and getting better. And with all of that said, I sure don't mind seeing a discount worked out here or there for my troubles."

"You're a very smart woman, Maggie. I like that about you."

"I'm no therapy dog school dropout, but I do okay."

His laugh—a genuine one—tickled something inside her. Something that required squashing because casually dating contractors was a hard *no* after both Maggie and Dean had made that mistake early on.

"This is a big job. And it's got cameras, but the work isn't for the cameras," she told him. "It's got to be real. Because at the end of the day, this needs to be someone's dream home, and they have to be inspired to pay me top dollar for it."

"I wouldn't be here if you or someone hadn't already done the research," he guessed. "My crew is good. Solid. Not just dependable, but we're damn creative, too. I'd be happy to drive you around and show you some of my projects downtown," he offered with a wolfish wiggle of his eyebrows. "You know. Prove my prowess to you and all."

"I'll keep that in mind. Though, full disclosure, you'd be driving my partner, Dean, around because I'll be busy demoing the hell out of every damn room for the next week or two."

He leaned in close enough that Maggie thought for a second he might be lining up to kiss her. Which would mean she'd have to find herself another landscaper.

She was relieved when he stopped just outside the edge of her personal space. "Maggie Nichols, I don't mean to scare you off, but I think you just might be the girl of my dreams."

She gave him the eye. "I bet you say that to all the girls."

"Never in my life," he said, making an X with his finger over his heart. "How do you feel about breakfast for dinner?"

She rolled with the change in subject. "I don't trust anyone who doesn't want pancakes and eggs every once in a while for dinner. How do you feel about being on camera?"

She heard the already familiar screech of the screen door behind her. This time the noise was interrupted by a clunk and a crash. The hinges gave up their decades-long fight and surrendered, sending the door crashing to the porch floorboards.

"Maggie, if you don't burn this hellhole down to the foundation, I'll do it for you," Dean bellowed.

"I'll fix it," she called back cheerfully. "Come over here and meet the landscaper before you make any more arson threats in front of witnesses."

Dean clomped over in jeans and sneakers that were too nice to do any dirty work. He had an iPad in one hand and a very large coffee in the other.

Juggling both, he freed a hand and offered it to Silas. "Morning," he said with slightly less grump.

"You must be Dean," Silas said, shaking hands.

"That's me. Has the tour of this three-story garbage dump scared you off yet?"

"One man's garbage dump is another's mountain of hidden potential," Silas responded.

Maggie grinned.

Dean shook his head. "Great. Now there's two of you." He looked pointedly at Silas's backward cap and then at Maggie and smirked.

She shook her head and mouthed, *Don't. You. Dare.*

"If you don't mind me asking, how old are you, Silas?" Dean asked.

Maggie elbowed Dean hard in the ribs.

The landscaper watched their exchange with interest. "Thirty-seven."

"He's thirty-seven, Maggie," Dean repeated with as much subtlety as Kevin the borderline-obese pit bull.

"I heard," she said dryly. "Don't you have some calls to make? Dreams to crush with your heartless budgets, Dean?"

"Sure do. And I'll be doing all of that from the comfort of the inn because a ceiling tile just missed my head by inches when it crashed to the floor in the hellscape you call a kitchen."

"After you finish the B-roll of the sunporch and library," she reminded him.

"Yeah, yeah. Silas, it was nice to meet you. Give us a good deal."

With that last demand, Dean squared his shoulders and stomped back inside.

"He's a mercenary at heart and definitely not a morning person," she explained.

"I bet he doesn't like pancakes for dinner either," Silas predicted.

She laughed because it was the truth.

"Couple more questions," he announced.

"Shoot."

"You married?"

"Not anymore," she said. "Do you have any problems using advertiser products for the job?"

"Not as long as it's a product that does what it's supposed to. I've never been married, by the way," he said when she didn't ask him. "Early bird or night owl?"

"Bird," she said. "How big of a crew do you need to get this done by, say, mid-July?"

"Bigger than I've got currently, but I know where I can find a few new recruits who wouldn't mind getting dirty. Are you seeing anyone?"

"I'm too busy to see anyone. Can you turn on the charm for the camera?"

"As long as there's someone to hold my hand, I think I can manage," he told her.

"I'll see if Dean is available for the hand-holding," she deadpanned. She tucked her hands into her pockets and studied him. "Can you do this job, Mr. Wright?"

"Call me Sy, Maggie," he said, his tone serious, gray eyes locking on hers.

"Can you do this job, Sy?"

"I can make this your dream home."

"I'm not in the market for a dream home. But what I *am* after is a dream payday and the satisfaction of bringing this place back to life."

"What I hear you saying is that there's a twenty percent chance that you'll fall in love with this place and your handsome landscaper," he said.

"Clearly your auditory processing leaves something to be desired," she shot back. "And I don't date contractors. So if a dented ego is a deal breaker for you, you might as well get in that pickup and head home."

"My ego can handle the dents," he promised. "Think you'd be annoyed if I checked in every once in a while to see if you changed your mind?"

"I won't change my mind," she said firmly.

"But it'll be real fun trying."

"Wow me with your deeply discounted estimate, and maybe I'll let you ask me out once a week."

He grinned. "Deal. What's the name of your show?"

"*Building Dreams with Maggie*."

He nodded in approval. "Nice. I like it. What social media thing is it on?"

Social media thing? "YouTube."

"Like the letter *U*?"

"That's adorable," she said. "*Y-O-U*. If you have any six- or seven-year-olds in your life, they can help you find it."

"I'll borrow one."

"Great. Well, Sy, I've got a lot of work to do. Do you have what you need to work up an estimate that won't require mass quantities of alcohol to review?"

"Let me collect my mud-wallowing partner, and I'll get out of your hair."

On cue, the dog came bounding around the side of the house. This time he'd managed to roll in whatever muck he found. His beautiful brown brindle was completely obscured under a glossy coat of mud.

"He looks like a swamp monster," she observed. A very-proud-of-himself swamp monster with a pink tongue lolling in pure doggy delight.

"Don't you dare do it," Sy said to the dog. He grabbed Maggie by the shoulders and, before she could decide if she liked it or not, swung her around, putting himself between her and the rampaging mud monster. Crushed up against his chest, Maggie felt the impact.

"Uh. You okay there?" she asked, tilting her head back to look at him. Those gray eyes were rolled skyward, as if praying for patience. She wondered if she was about to get a front-row seat to an explosion of temper.

"Kevin," Sy said on a long-suffering sigh, "you're officially dead to me."

She pursed her lips together and tried not to laugh.

"Maggie, I'd like to point out how heroic that was," he said. "And I feel like that should carry more weight in your hiring decision than the fact that I was stupid enough to bring this pig-dog with me to a job site."

"So noted," she said.

He released her and turned just as Kevin the pig-dog bounded up the steps of the porch.

"Kevin, no! Stay!" Silas yelled as the dog eyed the wide-open front door.

Maggie choked down the laugh that bubbled up. The man's back matched his dog. Slicked and splattered with a mud so dark that she was concerned there was a more sinister ingredient than just dirt.

"If you put one paw inside that house, I won't take you to doggy daycare this week, and you won't see your girlfriend, Tabitha," Sy threatened.

At the mention of Tabitha, Kevin sat.

"Uh, I'd offer you a towel, but I don't know if I have any yet," Maggie said.

"Not to worry. Always Prepared is my other middle name," the muddy landscaper told her. "I've got tarps, towels, and a change of clothes in the truck. I'll just—"

All of Kevin's fun seemed to catch up with him at once. He opened his cavernous mouth and barfed on the porch.

"Oh, buddy," Maggie said. "Is he okay?"

In answer, Kevin trotted off the porch, tail wagging, and shoved his head into a shrub.

"He's fine." Sy put his hands on his hips and studied his boots for a long moment. "I've got a hose in the truck," he said finally.

"I'll leave you to it then." She managed to get the words out. Barely. "I'll just be in there trying not to laugh too loud."

"Appreciate that," he said.

"It was, uh...nice to meet you," she said. "You make quite the impression." She didn't make it into the house before the laughter overtook her.

Kevin emerged from the bushes and trotted over to Sy.

"Don't even try to make up with me," he told the dog.

Kevin gave a happy bark.

"No. I'm not proud of you," Sy said, rooting around the bed of his truck and producing a garden hose. "Why would you think I'd be proud of you?"

"What are we watching?" Dean asked, coming up behind Maggie.

"Just a man hosing a half gallon of dog puke off the porch," she told him.

"Try not to hold it against him. The guy will probably earn you your millionth follower in one episode," Dean predicted.

"Don't even think about getting in the truck like this," Sy said on the other side of the glass. Kevin barked and bit at the spray of water like it was a game.

Dean snickered.

"I should get back to—" Maggie's intention to work flew right out the window when Sy stripped off his hat and muddy T-shirt.

"Oh, my," Dean said.

"Wow," she said in appreciation for the very fine male form that was now toweling off his dog.

"Pants. Pants. Pants," Dean chanted.

"He's not going to— Never mind," she said as Sy toed off his boots and shoved his thumbs in the waistband of his cargo pants. She turned her back on the window.

"Bright-red Calvin Klein boxer briefs," Dean reported with approval. "Just the one tattoo. Spare flip-flops in the back. Garbage bag for the clothes and towel. He's prepared."

Only Dean would find preparedness as attractive as a muscled man in nice underwear.

"He's telling the dog to get in the truck. Uh-oh. The dog basically said 'fuck you' and took off running. Now our landscaper is running," he said, continuing his commentary.

Maggie couldn't help herself. She crossed the hall and peered out the bay window in the...parlor? Living room? Den?

Silas, in fire-engine-red underwear that confirmed her assumptions about his very fine rear musculature, sprinted into the backyard after the dog.

"I almost don't care what his estimate comes in at," Dean announced. "You have to hire him just for the face and the comedy."

"He does make an impression," she agreed when Sy came back into view carrying eighty pounds of wet dog like a very large baby. "He's an outrageous flirt."

"At least he's an 'of age' outrageous flirt," Dean said.

"I'm not dating my landscaper," she said definitively.

"Is he too old for you?" he teased. "Oh, look. He's so flustered he's getting into your truck."

She pushed him out of the way and looked.

"Want me to go tell him?" he offered.

"I'll do it," she said. "Keep your trigger finger off the record button."

She headed outside, across the wet porch, and down into the gravel and weeds.

"Hi there," she said, approaching the driver's side. Sy was behind the wheel doing a mad search of the console, presumably for car keys.

"Miss me already?" he asked, pausing his search and looking not at all embarrassed about being practically naked.

"Haven't had the chance. I actually had some very important information for you."

"Your astrological sign? Your love language? Your newly discovered fetish for men with ill-mannered dogs?"

"My truck," she said.

"Your truck," he repeated, resting his elbow on the open window, the picture of casual flirtation.

"You're in my truck."

He poked his tongue into the inside of his cheek and looked around the interior of the vehicle. "Huh. Yeah. That explains the lack of mulch on the floor mats and keys in the cupholder."

"Yeah."

He opened the door, and she took a step back as tall, nearly naked man and wet dog got out.

"It's a hell of a story we'll have to tell the grandkids," he said. "Or nieces and nephews if you don't want kids."

The words barely penetrated. She was too busy admiring that long, lean body. The outrageous confidence and commitment to go-with-the-flow that made it impossible for the man before her to feel the slightest bit of embarrassment over his predicament.

"It was real nice meeting you, Maggie," Silas said, offering her his hand.

"Uh-huh," she said to his abs.

4

FRESH FROM A shower at the inn, Maggie went in search of a strong Wi-Fi signal and dinner. Her muscles were singing from a full day of heavy lifting. But she'd gotten a respectable jump on the initial cleanup on the first floor. The more dirty work she got done now, the faster she and the crews could dig into the real work.

It was past sunset and a little chilly, but Kinship's downtown was lit with charming gas streetlamps and tempting window displays. The general store with its well-stocked candy and bug spray sections and the big timber church on the corner were familiar. But the brewery looked new, or if not new, it hadn't caught the eye of her twelve-year-old self all those years ago.

Also new was the artsy café on Main Street that was still open.

She headed inside the white clapboard building and was delighted when it wasn't a bell that chimed, announcing her arrival. It was a set of spurs hung above the door.

There were a few patrons huddled around small, round tables over books and coffees poured in big, white mugs. The vibe was Wild West meets folksy hipster. She liked it immediately. Cacti and other less pointy greenery perched on rustic wooden shelves in white and copper pots. The counter was crafted out of knotty pine, and on top was a glass case of sinful-looking baked goods that Dean would never eat.

Maggie admired the man's dedication to his physique. She could appreciate the effort and ethic but preferred applying her own to different areas.

She ordered a peanut butter cookie with her roast beef panini from

Jun, the teenage barista, and settled herself at a corner table under black-and-white photos of mountain peaks and river bends.

She unloaded her laptop, tablet, camera, and phone onto the table and got to work. The contract from a new advertiser went to her attorney, and Maggie paused for only a moment to shake her head in wonder at the offer. She hadn't started her show to build a platform of soon-to-be one million followers. Or to leverage that platform to move products for multimillion-dollar corporations. Yet here she was, getting a check and a closet full of Cat King workwear—a brand she genuinely loved.

Sometimes life was downright weird.

While the day's pictures downloaded onto her laptop from the memory card, she rattled off a few dozen likes in response to comments on her latest Instagram post. Next, she called up her floor plan program and adjusted a few of the first-floor measurements. She needed to find space for a powder room and maybe even a full bath.

She was in the middle of creating a collage of her weirdest "finds" so far in the Campbell place when the barista delivered her dinner.

From beneath razor-sharp bangs, Jun eyed Maggie's pile of electronics. "Need a power strip?" she offered.

"Just the sandwich and the Wi-Fi," Maggie promised.

The door opened again on the jangle of spurs, and they both looked up. A boy in his teens sauntered in, hands in pockets, shoulders hunched in that gangly not-quite-comfortable way teenagers had. Jun raised a hand, and the boy gave her a too-cool nod in return.

Maggie hid her smile as the barista practically skipped back to the counter. Despite what Dean said, she did believe in romance. She just didn't personally have the energy to carve time out of her schedule for it.

And why would she bother? Her life was on the road with pit stops in three- and four-month increments.

As soon as the "home" was beautiful and sellable, she was on to the next one.

No time wasted.

What man in his right mind would decide that following her from state to state and house to house would be his kind of happily ever after?

The idea was absurd enough to earn a snort. Her life suited her just fine.

She just wasn't in a position to add a serious love interest into her schedule. Either he'd have to thrive on neglect or she'd have to stop doing all of the things. And if she stopped doing all of the things, she'd be letting down the people who depended on her. Dean. Her followers. The crews she paid. Small businesses and local artists who got a boost from her platform. And now advertisers.

She had a responsibility to them all. It fueled her.

Her stomach growled, demanding she return her attention to the food. There was a cup of pinkish sauce nestled into her mound of fries. She sniffed it and then tentatively tasted.

Not bad. She dunked a fry into it and scrolled through the comments on her YouTube channel.

YOLO14: Do you ever get tired of moving? Have you ever wanted to stay in one of your houses?

Maggie took a fortifying bite of panini before rolling out her standard answer.

Every house holds a special place for me, but they're all meant for someone else. I'm just the lucky one who gets to play matchmaker.

Typing and swiping her way through the meal, she ticked tasks off her to-do list. It hadn't been the most productive first day on the job. Not with the morning distractions of a mud-bogging dog and his incredibly well-built owner. Silas Wright was a distraction all by his handsome self.

Once the nearly naked man had left, she'd made a dent in the cleanup, managing to start parsing trash from treasure. The Old Campbell Place had its fair share of both. The front study alone had a complete set of A. Campbell's hardback novels, a delicate needlepoint, an antique topographic map, and that portrait. The pheasant wallpaper had already grown on her and was most definitely staying. At least on the fireplace wall. The tiny room behind it, the one that was the most likely contender to become a downstairs powder room, was filled to head height with stacks of phone books and old issues of fishing magazines.

Anything deemed treasure got tucked into the back study for further investigation and careful boxing. The trash went straight into the dumpster or recycling bins she found in the garage.

Tomorrow would be more of the same, and the next day. Which meant she needed to keep fueled and stay organized.

Her panini was excellent, and the pink stuff on the fries really was good.

She checked the production calendar she shared with Dean. They had the last three episodes left on the beach bungalow. Then they'd start fresh and introduce fans to the Old Campbell Place. Her goal was to work her way up to six weeks of episodes edited and ready to go. More lead time meant better quality editing and a more cohesive story, and eventually she might be able to take some time off here and there between projects.

Maybe.

Truth was, she liked the work. Liked waking up with a purpose. Juggling both sides of the business. Busyness was purpose. And she appreciated having a constant sense of purpose.

Her phone vibrated on the table. She wiped her hands on her pants and answered.

"What are you doing?" Dean asked on a yawn.

"Giving myself a facial and reading that new time travel novel," she lied, shoveling another fry through the sauce.

"Uh-huh. So you're working late with no less than three electronic devices in front of you?"

"Four if you count the camera," she said. "How about you?"

"I'm at a club." He yawned again. "Met a cute librarian. We're drinking wine and voguing."

"Translation: You're already in bed and wearing your cooling eye mask."

"These eyes need daily de-puffing," he insisted.

"I won't judge if you don't," she said with affection. This complete acceptance of each other was why they worked. At least now. "What dragged you from your beauty sleep?"

"You mean besides nightmares of being saddled with a monstrosity that will devour every dollar in your account and still not be marketable?"

"Yeah, besides that."

"Just my monthly plea for more bodies."

Maggie rolled her eyes ceilingward. "You have this scheduled in your calendar, don't you?"

"You're damn right I do. Every month on the twenty-third, I plead my case for one more production person."

"And what do I say every twenty-third?" she asked.

"Ask me next month." His impression of her was not the most flattering. "It's next month, and I'm asking. Nay, pleading! We need someone else, Magpie. We can't keep up as it is."

"We're doing just fine," she said dryly.

"Maybe you can work around the clock like some robot overlord with no need for things like sleep and food and sex—"

"Excuse me, I'm having food right now."

"But I can't," Dean continued, ignoring her. "A production assistant. Someone to shoot footage, schedule social media, bring me coffee."

"You just want the coffee," she joked. But on the inside, she wasn't feeling so funny. More help meant another person to be responsible for. She worked her ass off for Dean. For everyone else who depended on her. How much ass did she have left for someone else?

"Just think about it, robot overlord," he said on a weary sigh. "If someone else can handle more of the day-to-day, I'd have more time to focus on editing, to schmooze more advertisers. And it's not like we can't afford it."

"Another person is another expense," Maggie pointed out.

"Seriously, when's the last time you looked at the numbers?" he asked.

"I look at numbers all day every day."

"I don't mean tape measures and follower counts. I mean the income reports."

Oh. Those.

"I look at them," she hedged.

"Look at the specially prepared reports that our very nice accountant prepares for you every month, Maggie. Look at them and consider adding another person."

"I'll think about it," she promised.

"Just so you know, I'm upping my scheduled request to bi-monthly."

"Doesn't that mean every two months?"

He groaned. "Yes, but in this case, it means twice a month, smarty-pants. I honestly don't know how you would survive without me."

"I don't either," she admitted. Not only was Dean the numbers guy behind their partnership, but he also handled most of the filming and editing.

"Well, you're going to learn if you don't get me some help because I'll die of a dramatic aneurysm attributed to overwork."

"I'll keep that in mind. Hey, this pink sauce came with my fries. Do you know what it is?"

"Dear God, tell me you're not putting fry sauce in your mouth."

"Fry sauce?" she said, her mouth full.

"It's ketchup and mayonnaise mixed together to create a fatty, sugary, disgusting condiment."

"Huh. No wonder it tastes so good," she mused.

"You disgust me," Dean sang.

"You adore me," she countered.

"Ugh. Good night."

"Night."

She polished off the rest of the meal, including the fry sauce, scheduled the new project sneak peek posts, and organized the last of the beach bungalow pictures into their appropriate folders in the cloud.

Then, because Dean had brought it up, she opened up the latest monthly report. With as many numbers as she dealt with every day—follower counts, budgets, measurements, estimates—Maggie had drawn the line at accounting.

Instead of micromanaging the finances, Maggie had a very competent accountant in Seattle she'd never met compile a monthly report on income and expenses.

"Holy shit." She sucked in a breath and choked on her own damn spit.

Those were commas. Not decimal points.

How long had it been since she'd last opened one of these?

She knew down to the penny what they made off each property, was vaguely aware of what came in through advertisers or through her own small online merchandise shop. But to see it all together. To come face-to-face with the oats she'd spent years sowing. The fruits of her labor...

Maggie blamed Silas Wright for the random growing metaphors. Putting them aside, she gave herself a moment to bask.

She was flush.

And granted, with the new advertising partnerships Dean had negotiated and the higher dollar investment properties they'd been tackling, things looked like they were on an upward trend.

But.

She drummed her fingers on the tabletop. Just because the resources were there now didn't mean they'd always be there.

She remembered with a familiar ache in her belly the excitement she'd felt when her mom came home announcing she'd finally landed a "real job," a "big job." She'd twirled Maggie around their tiny living room until the downstairs neighbor had pounded on their floor.

They would move to a bigger place, maybe even a house. They'd have all the steak and hamburgers they could eat. They'd take a vacation every summer. Somewhere different every time, her mom had promised.

But then all those hopes and dreams that had finally been within her grasp were shredded and tattered, unrecognizable. And the fall-out from it—well, it would have been better to not have had the hope in the first place.

It had scared Maggie, seeing her mom's brave face crumble. Realizing that it could.

Now a worldly adult, she understood viscerally that, just because checks were rolling in now, it was no guarantee that they would continue. A bigger team meant more people she'd be responsible for. More people to provide for.

If she were being honest, it scared the shit out of her. There were ways they could do more without adding more people. There had to be. Best to keep things within her control. Dean would just have to deal with it, she decided.

Her phone vibrated again, and she frowned at the text.

Dayana: How's Idaho? What's the new place like? Weirdest thing you found so far?

It was ironic, hearing from Dayana just when Maggie had been lost in memories of her mom.

She decided to sit on the text for tonight. Sit on all of it and focus on the job at hand.

Maggie managed another few minutes of work before the spurs jangled again. A group of teens strutted inside. *Troublemakers* was the label she guessed they'd want. Piercings, too much eyeliner, ripped-up jeans, and the sulky slump of teenage shoulders. They were too loud and drew too much attention.

A couple of the other patrons shot them dirty looks before going back to their coffees and their chats.

One of the boys, taller than the rest, with freckled skin and a head of thick blond hair, stuffed his hands in his pockets and stood back while his friends ordered at the counter. She saw him surreptitiously eye the community bulletin board, and when he was sure none of his friends were watching, he tore off a phone number from a flyer.

"Yo, Cody. You want something?" Jun called, unflappable in the face of her rebel classmates.

"Nah, I'm good," he responded.

She watched as they took their drinks and snacks and boisterously made their way to the door.

They seemed to take the energy with them, and she decided to pack it up for the night. She had the entire weekend to get shit done. And hopefully by Monday, she'd have a nice stack of job quotes and she could start hiring, start the real work.

She packed up her devices, carried her dishes to the designated bins, and headed for the door.

Pausing at the bulletin board, she noted the flyer that had caught Cody's eye. Warehouse work. Nights and weekends. She frowned and wondered what would have a kid who surely was still in high school looking for night shift work.

Giving Jun a wave, she pushed through the door and out into the chilly night. Tomorrow it would be sunny and sixty-five degrees. She'd open the windows—at least the ones that weren't painted or nailed shut—and breathe some new life into the Old Campbell Place.

Vegan4Life22: Maggie, what's Idaho like? Are you missing the beach? When will the first episode air? I NEED TO KNOW!

HandyHarryGuy: Sound advice on the plumbing in this episode. It's great to see a real pro online! Keep up the good work!

DonnaMeagleIsMyHero: Maggie fans, rumor has it she and Dean are in Kinship, Idaho! That's only an hour from my house! Hmmm, roadtrip?

5

TOBY KEITH CROONED about Solo cups from the speakers on the outdoor patio at Dive Bar. The night was a little cool, but Kinship residents were the hearty, outdoorsy type and didn't mind layering up in sweatshirts and circling their chairs around the gas heaters near the outdoor bar.

"So, you and Michelle get back together yet?" Michael, Silas's stepbrother, asked over the rim of his snooty Shiraz.

Silas snorted. "I told you, man. We're done. Stick a fork in it. Call time of death. *D-O-N-E.* Done."

Michael shoved his glasses up the bridge of his nose and shook his head.

On the surface, they couldn't have been more opposite, and not just because Michael was Black and Silas was white. Michael was shorter, quieter, and always dressed like it was Sunday brunch. If he had to spend the day outside, he'd prefer it to be under an umbrella at a wine bar. Silas was bigger, taller, louder. He'd loved sports all through school and preferred his pastimes to involve some level of physicality.

"I'll believe it when I see it. You've been on-again, off-again for a hundred years."

"Five," Silas corrected him. "And it was mostly off. And it's been a month since we called it quits."

"I thought you two were going to end up married by default," Michael said.

Silas sighed. Dating Michelle had been easy. But a relationship based on convenience wasn't much of a relationship at all, they'd finally come to realize. Knowing all the same people for the same amount of time wasn't exactly a reason to march down the aisle.

"Not happening. She's a great girl. But she's not *my* girl. It's time we stopped wasting each other's time."

"Five bucks says you two are back to kayak picnics in a week."

"I'll take that bet," Silas said, raising his pilsner. "And you know why?"

His brother leaned back on his barstool, looking smug. "She finally wised up and met someone better than you?"

Silas gave a dry laugh. Razzing was the family's second language. "Don't forget that your love life is up next for scrutiny, Mikey. And no. But I might have finally met the one."

"The one what?" Beneath Michael's plaid, pressed button-downs lived the heart of a pragmatic man.

"Come on, man. *The* One. I heard wedding bells when I saw her for the first time."

"You sure it wasn't just low blood sugar, or maybe you were standing in front of the fire station?" Michael posited with a frown.

"Positive," Silas said. "She's funny without ever hitting a punch line. She didn't freak when my dog barfed all over her porch, and I do mean *all* over. She's crazy smart and wasn't suckered in by my expert flirting. She works with her hands and works hard." He thought back fondly to the dirt-streaked tank top. The light sheen of sweat on her skin. "If she hires Bitterroot, I get to spend the next few months asking her out while dazzling her with my dirty expertise."

"Dating clients is a shit idea, and you know it," the risk-averse Michael reminded him.

"You can't expect me to follow rules when the potential future Mrs. Wright is on the line. Or maybe she'll keep her maiden name. Or maybe we won't even get married. We'll be life partners like Oprah and Stedman."

"How strong is that beer?" Michael asked, eyeing Silas's glass.

"I'm not drunk. And I haven't lost my damn mind. I just met

someone who took one look at me and—you remember when Todd Whitecastle tackled you on the playground and the football knocked the wind right out of you?"

Michael winced. It had been the beginning and end of his attempt at being an elementary school jock. "A guy doesn't forget that feeling."

"It was like that," Silas said.

His brother's brown eyes widened behind his glasses. "Wow."

"Yeah." He nodded.

"So all that stuff Mama B has been saying about love and the right woman—"

"Person," Silas interjected.

Michael smiled shyly into his wineglass. "Person. It might actually not be bullshit? I thought that was just so we didn't let our hormones run amok in high school."

"One day we'll realize our mothers already know everything, and we could have just saved ourselves a hell of a lot of time by asking them," Silas mused.

"Hey, Sy!" a bubbly brunette with a tiny nose stud and a UCLA sweatshirt said from the end of the bar. "Hi, Michael," she purred, tossing her hair over her shoulder.

"Hey, Charisse," Michael said, sounding awkward as hell.

"How's it going?" Silas said with a wave.

She took her drink, a frothy orange something accessorized with fruit and an umbrella, and wandered off, shooting Michael a backward glance.

Silas slapped the bar between them. "You've got to do it, Mikey."

"Do what?" Michael asked, feigning innocence.

"Pull the damn trigger," he said into his beer.

"Well, if it isn't our two favorite bachelors." A voice so familiar it felt like his own came from behind them.

"Mama B and Mom," Silas said, getting up to give both women a kiss on the cheek and a hug each. He'd seen his mom and stepdad yesterday and had lunch with Michael's mom and his own dad the day before. But spontaneous run-ins around town still deserved a proper greeting.

"What are you boys up to?" Silas's mom asked, her cheeks pink from the night air. Dr. Blaire Thomas had her blond hair pulled back in a low, sleek ponytail. She was bundled up in the green wool sweater she'd gotten on vacation in Ireland two years ago. Tall, angular, and always put together. It was part of what made the patients in her therapy practice so comfortable.

She made grabby hands toward Michael's wine and took a sip.

"And what trigger are you telling my sweet baby boy to pull?" Mama B demanded. Breonna Wright wasn't so much pulled together as always exploding outward. She was shorter, softer, brighter. She wore yellows and oranges and reds that popped against her dark skin. Her nails were always painted and never in any color that someone could call sedate. Her hair changed drastically every few months. This month she'd cut it in a taper, leaving longer, kinky curls tipped blond on top.

If Blaire was the person in the family you went to when you had a problem you couldn't solve, Mama B was the one you went to with good news that needed celebrating.

Together the women had given Silas, Michael, and their sisters a foundation of unconditional love, healthy boundaries, and a deep, abiding fear of disappointing either one of them.

"Volleyball," Silas and Michael said together.

"Mmm-hmm," Blaire hummed, not believing it.

"Dirty liars. Both of you." Mama B sniffed.

"What are two lovely ladies like you doing in a place like this?" Silas said, turning up the charm to avoid trouble.

"We're meeting up with our girlfriends to talk about our sex lives," Blaire teased. She raised a hand and waved across the patio to a raucous group of women clustered around a heater.

"Our moms have sex lives," Michael groaned.

"And someday you boys will, too," Mama B promised, cupping his face in her hands. Her rings glinted under the string of lights above them. She gave Michael a smacking kiss before turning to Silas. "You, son, need to come over for supper soon."

"What weed do you need identified now?" he asked with a grin.

"It's got flowers. Weeds don't have flowers." Mama B approached gardening the way she did life. With an exuberant amount of energy, secure in the idea that everyone and everything was chock-full of inherent good.

"What's on the menu?" he hedged.

"Salmon with lemon caper sauce, greens, and cheesecake."

He grinned. "I'll be there."

"Bye, boys," Blaire called over her shoulder, blowing them a kiss as she and Mama B migrated toward friends and conversations neither son wanted to overhear.

"That was close," Michael said, dabbing at the nervous sweat on his forehead with a napkin.

"That's why you need to tell them sooner rather than later. You know it's not going to be some terrible disappointment," Silas prodded.

"I know, but it's going to be a 'thing.' And I don't know if I'm ready for it to be a thing."

"They probably already know," Silas predicted. "You told me a month ago, which means Mama B has had plenty of opportunities to read my mind. And my mom probably knew longer than you did."

"Soon," Michael promised. "I'll tell them soon."

"Good." Silas signaled the bartender and pointed to the group that had enfolded his moms. "Put a round for those ladies on our tab."

"Kiss ass," Michael coughed.

"Mama's boy," Silas shot back.

They grinned at each other.

"So tell me more about this woman," Michael said.

"She bought the Old Campbell Place. Renovating it top to bottom."

"No shit. Really? Big job," his brother predicted.

"Huge," Silas agreed. "Hey, do you know anything about YouTube?"

Michael blinked at him and then smirked. "You're lucky you're so pretty and no one expects you to know about things like YouTube."

"Educate me. She's got some kind of show on it."

"You're telling me you fell for a YouTuber?" Michael laughed hard enough that he had to reach for another napkin to dab at his eyes.

"You can laugh all you want if you show me how to at least find it."

Michael held out his hand. "Give me your phone."

Silas dug it out of his pocket and handed it over. He watched over Michael's shoulder as his brother navigated to the app. "Well, that was easy."

"I still don't know how you can exist in this world without being on some kind of social media."

"I prefer my socializing to be done in person," Silas said, raising a hand to his next-door neighbor, who pulled up a stool across the bar. "See? That was an acknowledgment of a fellow human being."

"On Facebook, we call that a like," Michael told him. "You can also send mad faces."

"Ain't technology a wonder," Silas said. "In the good old days, we'd just flip someone the bird."

"Oh, you can do that with emojis," Michael said, pulling his own phone out, thumbs flying over the screen at expert speeds.

Silas looked at the text that came in. It was a brown hand holding up a middle finger. "Ha! Is that new? How come you never gave me the brown cartoon finger before in a text?"

Michael sighed and looked like he was considering something.

"What? What's going on in that big brain of yours?"

"You're not going to be happy," Michael predicted. He didn't look too worried about it though.

"Then you have to tell me. Right now or I'll call up Todd White-castle and tell him you're ready for a rematch on the playground."

"There's a second sibling-text group," his brother said before blowing out a long breath. "Wow, I really do feel better not keeping that secret anymore."

"What do you mean a second sibling-text group?" Silas demanded, calling up the group message on his phone.

Michael slid his phone over to Silas on the bar.

"What the hell, man?" Silas was offended and impressed. He considered himself to be the glue of his generation. Checking in with his sister, Taylor, on the East Coast. Demanding daily pregnancy updates from their half-sister, Nirina. But here was evidence of an entire conversation with flashing pictures and cartoon eggplants going on without him. "What is this?"

"They're GIFs and emojis. The ones that don't move are memes."

"I feel like you just told me there's no Santa Claus," Silas said sadly.

"You're the one who told me there was no Santa. Your parents didn't want you believing."

"So you cut me out of the family?"

Michael was trying not to laugh. "You're so antitechnology, we didn't want to overwhelm you," he said.

"You put me in this message thing right now, and after you show me how to look up the love of my life on YouTube, you're gonna teach me how to put those moving pictures in shit," Silas said.

"I think we're going to need another round," Michael said to the bartender.

"And maybe some finger steaks," Silas added.

Over finger steaks and alcohol, the brothers walked carefully through the steps.

"Hang on," Michael said, looking up with wide eyes. "*Maggie Nichols* is the future Mrs. Wright?"

"You know her?"

"I watch her show. She flips houses. The one she's doing now is this beachfront place in Oregon." Michael scrolled through the long list of videos while he talked.

"Was. Now she's here," Silas corrected.

"You've got to introduce me, man."

Silas hadn't seen Michael this excited over anything since he'd scored tickets to the John Legend concert in Boise. "Okay. Sure."

Seeing his bafflement, Michael grinned. "You don't get it. She's a celebrity. You see this number here?"

Silas leaned in, peering at the screen. "Yeah."

"That's the number of people who subscribe to her channel." At Silas's frown, Michael rolled his eyes. "It's the number of people who want to watch every video she uploads."

"That seems like a lot," he guessed.

"A million followers is a big deal," Michael confirmed. "And she's close. Wait a second. Are you actually going to be on her show?"

Silas unwrapped his brother's fingers from where they'd clamped on to his arm. "I am if she accepts my estimate. I made quite the impression on her this morning, so it could go either way."

"What kind of an impression?" Michael looked like all his hopes and dreams were pinned on this moment.

"Well, like I said, Kevin rolled in mud and splattered me while I heroically shielded her. Then he puked up a pound of bacon on her porch. So I took my clothes off and hosed off—"

"You got naked in front of Maggie Nichols?"

Silas could tell he was dashing Michael's hopes. "Only mostly naked. Kept the underwear on. And then I tried to steal her truck, but that was accidental because we drive the exact same make and model. Same color, too."

Michael just stared at him for a long beat.

"Do you need a glass of water or something?" Silas offered.

Snapping out of it, his brother shook his head. "Okay, so you're not getting the job. Maybe I can get Niri to invite her to the shop."

6

SILAS SHIFTED THE paper bag he carried and raised a fist to rap on the frame of the newly rehung screen door.

AC/DC blared from somewhere inside before being briefly muffled by a loud crash and some colorful swearing. Deciding to do the neighborly thing, he let himself and the contrite Kevin inside.

It was a foyer of sorts with a dizzying green wallpaper with shiny birds-of-paradise climbing the walls, stained hardwood floors that had last seen better days a long-ass time ago, and cased openings under dingy transom windows on either side.

The room to his right had one pocket door hung on the track and another leaning against the wall. Beyond, the hall opened up into a rotunda with carved wood and a not-so-grand staircase.

"Everything all right?" he called.

"Peachy," came the response. The woman of his dreams poked her head out of a doorway on the other side of the rotunda. She had a bandanna covering her hair, a smear of blood on her blue tank, and a sealed bandage that she was trying to open with one hand and her teeth.

Maggie didn't seem to be pissed about it. She looked like she was in her element.

"Need some help?" he offered.

She hesitated. "You're not squeamish, are you?"

"The word isn't even in my vocabulary," he promised, approaching.

She held out a hand with a nasty, oozing cut just below the knuckles. "I had to check. Dean fainted and hit his head when I caught my leg with a box cutter once. He needed more stitches than I did."

"My stepdad is a physician assistant. I give good first aid," he promised.

"Have at it," she said, grinning as she handed over the Band-Aid. "Aw, Kevin, you shouldn't have."

On cue, the dog spit out the bouquet of flowers he held in his mouth at her feet and proudly waited for her adoration. It came with one hand and a lot of enthusiasm.

"Apology flowers for the porch puking. Hold still," Silas ordered, eyeing the nasty gash. "Did you clean this yet?"

She waved away the suggestion with her good hand. "Just put a bandage on it. It'll be fine. I'll take care of it tonight."

"My stepdad would rightfully slap me across the face if I allowed my potential client and the object of my affection to get gangrene and die," he insisted.

"Well, if it will save you getting slapped in the face," Maggie said, amused.

"Kitchen?"

She pointed, and he dragged her in the designated direction.

The room was big but cramped, he noted, as he put the bag down. Some joker with no taste had painted the mismatched cabinets a bumblebee yellow. Half the doors were missing, revealing a collection of original orange Tupperware containers piled on top of peeling shelf paper. The countertops were a faded red linoleum with a stainless steel edge. The floor was...well, sticky. That was the best adjective for it.

"This is exactly why no one should have been allowed to renovate in the seventies," he noted, pulling her to the porcelain farmhouse sink, the only thing in the room worth saving in his opinion. He cranked the hot water handle and reached for the new bottle of hand soap on the counter.

"Sixty-nine," she corrected. "At least according to the receipts I found stashed in the mousetrap drawer."

"The treasures you find. Kind of like that file cabinet full of carpet samples in the Seattle Craftsman," he said.

"You've been doing some research," she said.

"I have. Paid the neighbor kid five dollars to show me what the YouTube was," Silas joked, deciding it might not be the best time to tell her his brother had a *Building Dreams* T-shirt with her face on it. "I'll give you a lollipop if you're a good girl and don't cry," he said a split second before shoving her hand under the water.

To her credit, she only yelped. "I can't tell if you're kidding about 'the YouTube,'" she said through her teeth as he carefully cleaned the gash.

"I'm a funny guy. But I also know jack shit about social media. So I hope that's not a deal breaker personally or professionally. When was your last tetanus?" he asked.

"Last year. Carpet tack in my foot," she said. "How do you advertise your business?"

"Good ol' word of mouth and the occasional mailer. How'd you do this?" he asked, holding up her now clean hand and applying pressure with a paper towel. She had a dozen small scars on both hands, like he did. Like anyone who worked with their hands for a living did.

"Broken glass-front cabinet in what I'm calling the second dining room for now because I have no idea what it was used for. So to what do I owe the pleasure? Are you here to attempt more Grand Theft Auto or do you just drive around town on Saturdays offering first aid?"

"I've got estimates for you," he said.

Her eyebrows winged up. "Twenty-four hours later. That's either impressive or you did a shit job."

"Trust me. It's impressive. I can do a lot of things in a lot less time. But a respectable amount of time," he added. "Not like eight or nine minutes."

Her shoulders bounced in that suppressed-laughter way of hers. He wondered why she didn't just let it out. "Anyway, the flowers—" He snapped his fingers at Kevin, who had thankfully woken up feeling obedient that morning. The dog scampered off to find them. "Are an apology, and this is to butter you up." He pulled a cold six-pack out of the paper bag he'd brought inside.

"Ah, an alcohol-worthy quote," she said, eyeing the beer. "I had a feeling."

"Quotes," he corrected. "Are you a five-o'clock-somewhere kind of girl or do you need it to be a respectable drinking hour before you start on a Saturday?"

"It's eleven a.m. here, and I've been at it since seven. I'm due a break, and I have a feeling I'm gonna need one of those beers when I look at your numbers," she guessed.

"Smart woman," he said. "Let's take our happy hour outside."

She followed him, the beer, and his paperwork through the front door. Silas stepped off the porch and crossed to his pickup, which he'd backed in. He sat on the lowered tailgate and patted the spot next to him. "Come envision with me."

He tossed Kevin a chew bone, and when the dog settled down on the porch with it, Silas popped open two of the bottles of beer. "Estimate A is for the scope of work we discussed yesterday before the puke and nudity. By the way, I'm hoping those two things evened each other out when it comes to your hiring decision."

She didn't exactly confirm, but her small grin was enough for him.

He produced the first piece of paper from a folder and handed it over to her. "Nothing too fancy. The must-haves. The tree trimming and timbering, foundational plantings, redefining the beds around the front, mulch, trimming up the hedgerows, maybe a focal planting here or there to take advantage of the views. Cleaning up the existing beds around the house. Reseeding the lawn. Scrapping the creepy graveyard fence. Relaying the terrace, using as much of the original material as possible. Shoring up the retaining wall."

She skimmed it, and he considered it a good sign that she didn't immediately chug the entire beer when she hit the total.

"Uh-huh," Maggie said with a nod that gave nothing away.

"This is what Estimate Must-Haves could look like," he said, unfolding a larger piece of paper.

"You drew this?" she asked, studying the sketch.

He liked that she sounded impressed. "I did. I like sketches better than renderings. More feeling. Makes it easier for the client to say yes to the dream."

"I'm ready to say yes right now," she said, still admiring the sketch. There were hanging baskets of ferns on the porch. Colorful foliage along the foundation. Dark, rich mulch and bright pops of annual color in rivers of plantings.

"Hold your horses—literally, actually," he cautioned. "Because this doesn't include the fountain. Rescuing it from its current state would take more. A lot more. If that's a no, then we might be able to save the horses and use them somewhere else in the yard."

"But no fountain?"

"It's not necessarily the worst thing in the world. Without that fountain taking up so much of the square footage on the terrace, you could expand the outdoor living space here and here." He tapped the drawing.

"True," she said. But he heard the disappointment, and it gave him a spark of hope.

"Now, let's move on to Estimate Dream Home." He withdrew the next stack of pages from the folder.

"Hang on. Let me prepare." Maggie took a quick swig of beer and a deep breath. "Okay. Hit me."

He handed over the significantly longer punch list.

"Oh," she said as she flipped the first page and then the second. "Oh. *Ohhh.* Ouch. That's more—knock on wood—than the top-to-bottom rewire and the plumbing, Sy."

"Yeah. But it'll look like this." He unfurled a short stack of drawings and let her page through them in silence.

"You sneaky son of a bitch," she breathed. "It looks like a damn fairy tale."

And she was the queen.

He grinned. "You like?"

"Ugh," she groaned. "A circular driveway out front? Wait a minute. Is that a trellis draped in wisteria? What's it lead to?"

"The rose garden. Stole some space from the backyard for it.

Nothing too structured. This place feels more charming fairyland than manicured estate. Upkeep's easier, too."

"I hate you right now," she said, flipping through the sketches again. "A fenced-in vegetable garden? Oh, come on. A secret path of wildflowers and grasses that leads to a firepit? Wait. Where's this view?" she asked, looking up from the drawing and eyeballing the yard.

"We'd clear another twenty feet or so along the bluff through those woods," he said, pointing to the west. "It's mostly overgrowth right now. It would give you a damn good spot for campfires and stargazing."

She let out a heavy sigh. "Okay. Let me see it," she said, holding out a hand.

He opened the folder again and placed the last drawing in her palm.

She opened it and immediately folded it back up. Then opened it again. "Damn you, Silas Hard-Work-Always-Prepared Andrew Wright."

He took that as a very good sign. She'd been thinking about him. And not just because his dog vomited on her house and he ended up nearly naked in her truck.

"So you *can* make the fountain work again."

"I'm confident we can bring it back to its glory. And while we're there, we might as well add on to the terrace, do something interesting with the edging, string lights everywhere."

She closed the drawing and drew long and deep on her beer.

When she studied the house, he knew she was seeing his vision.

"It's official. You're a diabolical jerk," she said finally.

"That I am."

"You know exactly what I'm looking for with this project, and then you have to go and show me what's actually possible. I bet your ancestors were door-to-door vacuum cleaner salesmen."

God, she was cute.

"I look at every project as if it were my place," he said. "And I ask myself, what would I want?"

"This isn't my place," she argued, perusing the sketches again.

"It is right now. And if, for some reason, you don't fall head over heels in love with me...I mean this house, the grounds will go from a Band-Aid fix to a selling point. I did my research. You haven't really dug into the landscaping beyond basic curb appeal. Your fans might like to see what's possible outdoors."

She picked up her beer. "I need to think about it. I wouldn't even know how to break it to Dean. He'd curl up into the fetal position on top of a mattress of profit-and-loss statements."

"When's the last time you were wrong about a house, Maggie?"

She looked surprised and then stubborn. "Never."

"When's the last time Dean questioned the investment?"

Her laugh was quick. "Every single time."

"Some people have vision, and others can only see what's right in front of them."

"Aren't you the philosophical landscaper?" She turned and studied him for a beat. "You know, for a number that painful, you'd have to make yourself available to the camera constantly. Charm it, flirt with it."

"I'm very shy," he fibbed. "But I could *probably* work up the nerve."

"Hmm," she said, hopping down. "Okay. Go away so I can think."

"I won't let you down, Mags," he promised, sliding off the tailgate. "You can put your hopes and dreams in my hands, and I'll make them come true."

"Where's a camera when I need one?" she complained.

"My number's on the paperwork if you have any questions." He shut the tailgate and whistled for the dog.

Kevin bounded down the steps, chewy in his mouth like a cigar. He stopped for goodbye pats from Maggie before jumping into the truck.

"By the way, Mags, neither of those estimates includes the ten percent friends-and-future-wife discount you'll be getting," he said with a wink.

"Ten?" Her brown eyes took on a shrewd gleam. "Huh. Now, if you had said fifteen, it would have been a no-brainer."

He kicked at the dirt and put his hands on his hips. "Meet me at twelve, and you've got yourself a deal."

Her teeth sank into her lower lip, and he could all but see the calculations happening in her head.

"Maybe. Lemme think."

He winked and slid behind the wheel.

He was fishing for his keys in the cup holder when she called to him.

"Hey, Sy?"

He leaned out the window. She was standing on the porch just like the first time he'd seen her. Only now he knew just enough about her to make him want to know a hell of a lot more.

"How'd you know I'd be here today?" she asked, shoving her hands in her pockets.

"You just bought yourself a playground. Where else would you be?"

She grinned. And he thought of the football and Michael and Whitecastle.

Throwing her a wave, Silas headed toward town. Windows down, music on, Kevin's jowls flapping in the wind on the passenger side. He felt good about it. Good about her. And them. Now he'd just wait and hope.

He had a job he wanted to swing by to check the hardscape progress and a shit-ton of paperwork to catch up on. He was just entering town limits when his phone rang.

Unknown caller.

"Maggie," he said smugly.

"Make my dreams come true, Sy. And don't make me regret it."

SideHustler: That oceanfront bedroom is my dream! Maggie you're a genius with the soft green on the walls. Totally feels like a spa!

Windows95Luvr: Maggie needs a man. I nominate Idris Elba!

GamGamof7: Maggie, dear, you have such a lovely face. Why must you spend so much of your time wearing ball caps?

7

MAGGIE WOKE IN the dark. Disoriented, thirsty, and already revving to get up.

Idaho. Kinship. The Old Campbell Place.

Current location set, she reached blindly for her phone and found it on the floor next to the cot. Monday, 6:05 a.m. Half an hour before sunrise. She'd moved out of the luxurious digs the inn offered the night before. It was the best way to get a feel for a place. Living, sleeping, and working under the roof until she knew a house down to its bones.

She indulged in a full-body stretch and bounded out of bed. "Lots to do," she told Mr. and Mrs. Campbell's portrait, which she'd rescued from the first floor. Using a toe to flip the switch on the coffeemaker on the floor, she padded into the connected bathroom.

She grimaced as the hideousness of the bathroom fixtures startled her once again.

It would be a gut job in here. The volcanic-orange toilet and tub with its brass swan faucet and sticky seashell clings were most definitely not long for this world. She'd spent the previous morning ripping out the god-awful blue-gray carpet on the floor. Because while she could live with eye-searing fixtures, she could not in good conscience get out of the shower onto moldy carpet.

She dressed and pulled her hair back from her face with a clip and returned to pour her first cup of coffee of the day. Snagging a sweatshirt from a wire hanger in the closet, she took her mug over to the tall, skinny glass doors. It took some muscle and a few drops of spilled coffee, but she got them open and stepped out onto the covered balcony.

Cool spring air and the stirring of birds and squirrels met her as the night began its slow fade from the sky. The porch faced south and east, and she caught a glimpse of the sunrise through the trees.

She balanced on the half wall, back to a support column, and enjoyed the peace.

The crews would be here soon, eager to get started. Once they were done for the day, she'd shift gears and dive into the second part of her business. She had a new episode dropping today. The kitchen reveal of the beach house. Corresponding social media posts were scheduled with all the appropriate advertisers and vendors tagged.

She'd need to be available to like and comment. Plus, there was the Day One filming. Which was mostly Dean's responsibility. But there were the one-on-ones she'd do. And the introductions of the local trades that would be on-site.

She was looking forward to seeing Silas Wright work his magic on the camera.

Far below her perch, the river glowed pink with the sunrise. She wondered if the new owners would take their coffee here like this. Or would they be late-night stargazers who drank wine around the future firepit?

Would there be kids filling the seven bedrooms on the second and third floors? Or would some enterprising investor snap up the property as a luxury rental?

The forest around her was alive now. Wildlife greeting the day. It was time for her to start hers as well. On a whim, she plucked her phone from the pocket of her sweatshirt and snapped a picture of river and rock and mountain. She thumbed her way through a quick text.

Maggie: Idaho is interesting. Found a drawer full of mousetraps. This is the view. How's Keaton?

Task complete, she drained her coffee, stowed her phone, and officially started her day.

"It's time to go break some stuff! Welcome home," Maggie said to the camera with a casual flip toss of her hammer as Dean panned out.

"Got it in one," he said, chipper after his extra-large afternoon cappuccino.

She stepped off her mark and surveyed the work happening . . . well, everywhere.

To the untrained ear, the sounds of construction were a cacophony of chaos. To Maggie, it was a symphony. Teams working together to build something grand, something greater than the sum of their parts.

Old shingles rained down from three stories above in steady *thwap thwap thwap* into the dumpster. The roof was a priority. As was the electrical work.

The landscaping crew, six of them armed with trimmers and loppers and wheelbarrows and leaf blowers, attacked the worst of the overgrowth around the house and drive. She didn't mean to zero in on him, but Silas Wright certainly drew the eye.

Taller than the rest, he moved with a practiced ease, doing battle with a stubborn patch of thorns and brush where a storybook walkway would connect the front of the house with the expanded terrace.

His shirt was already streaked with dirt, and the grin he wore was wicked, as if there wasn't anything in the world he'd rather be doing. That was as attractive as the rest of him, she decided. And she was definitely not going to go out with him, she reminded herself.

With more effort than it should have taken, she tore her attention away from all six-feet-plus of sexy landscaper. Through open windows, she heard the joyous sounds of kitchen demo.

"How about you focus on the porch roof, Billy?" Lou, the owner of the roofing company, suggested. Billy was a long-limbed and scrawny twenty-something with a shock of corn silk blond hair and a pair of job site–inappropriate sneakers. He looked a little green as he clung to the bottom rungs of the ladder.

"He's so good-looking it's hard to hate him for ruining the budget," Dean complained. Maggie realized he wasn't looking at Billy. He was eyeing Silas.

"He didn't ruin it," she argued. "He expanded it."

"He *exploded* it. We'll be lucky to afford half a roof now. We'll only be able to shoot from the front because the back will be open to the sky," he predicted.

"You missed your calling. Have you considered a career in motivational speaking?" she asked.

Dean cocked his head, still watching Silas. "He looks like a sexy lumberjack with that beard. I bet he's got a closet full of flannel."

As if he'd heard them, the man in question lifted his head and winked at Maggie.

"You need a date," she muttered to Dean.

"*You* need a date," he shot back. Then, to her horror, he waved Silas over.

"What are you doing?" she hissed.

"I'm getting you a date," Dean said, all innocence.

She sputtered and took a step back. "We don't date contractors, dummy!"

"Relax, weirdo," he said, gripping her arm. "I'm getting him mic-ed up so we can do his intro interview."

"Oh. Right." Her cheeks felt hotter than the breezy sixty-six degrees called for.

"So stop acting like a seventh grader with a crush and— Sly Sy, can I call you that?" Dean asked, shifting his focus to the tall, sweaty landscaping god who ambled over with a red thermos in his hand.

"You wouldn't be the first," called a woman with dark hair and a sweatshirt tied around her waist as she passed them with a wheelbarrow.

Silas lifted his thermos in a toast. The man appeared to be hard to offend. "What can I do for you, Dino?"

Dean went a shade of pink that Maggie had never seen.

When Silas lifted the thermos to take a long drink, Dean slapped her shoulder. "The hot guy gave me a nickname," he whispered.

"Control yourself, lover boy," she said, under her breath.

Reining in his caffeine-induced giddiness, Dean rested the tripod and digital camera on his shoulder. "If you've got a few minutes, we could get your intro interview out of the way."

"I've got all the time in the world," Silas promised. He dropped the thermos, swept off his baseball cap, and shoved a hand through golden waves. "How do I look?"

They both stared at him for a beat too long.

"Um," Maggie said.

Dean giggled nervously.

"Fine. You look...fine," she said. "I'll just go check on the electrical inside."

"Hang on," Silas said.

"Freeze!" Dean said at the same time, snapping out of his flirt zone.

"I believe you promised you'd hold my hand," Silas reminded her.

She feigned a wince. "Ooh. Didn't get it in writing though, did you?"

"Workaholic Nichols will stand by and supervise," Dean said, resetting the tripod and pointing the camera in Silas's direction.

"That's a small camera," Silas observed.

"Small but mighty," Dean told him.

"I was expecting TV cameras and those cool folding director's chairs," Silas admitted.

"Our production's pretty lean," Maggie explained, nudging him to the right so the camera would pick up more of the chaos behind him. "We use this camera for most of the interview footage. I've got a smaller one for selfie videos and shooting on the fly. Sometimes we shoot on our phones. And Dean has a drone."

Silas was watching her with interest. It made her nervous all over again. She unhooked the lavalier mic from her shirt and held it out to him. But he made no move to take it.

"You gonna stand there and hold the man's mic all day or are you going to hook him up?" Dean asked from behind the camera.

She turned around, stuck her tongue out at him, and then clipped the microphone to Silas's T-shirt.

"This is just an introductory kind of interview. Dean or I will ask you questions, and you answer to the camera," she said.

"I'm ready when you are," he said with that trademark smile.

"Okay, Sly Sy," Dean said, hitting record. "We'll warm you up. Where's your barfing dog today?"

Silas grinned at the mention of Kevin. "Kevin's at doggy daycare today. I keep him at home during the early days of a job because he likes to take advantage of the chaos. He sneaks off and noses his way into everyone's lunches. Plus, I don't like to bring him along until the owner gives permission. Not everyone likes to find a fat pit bull napping in their recliner."

"Maggie doesn't have a recliner, so I'm sure Kevin's welcome here," Dean said.

"He is. And if you need to keep him out of trouble, there are plenty of places inside he can hang out."

Silas's gray eyes were warm and amused and locked on her face. It made her wish she had something to do with her hands.

"So, tell us about yourself," Dean said, directing them back to the task at hand.

Silas crossed his arms over his chest, little beads of sweat glinting in the sun in blue-collar perfection. "I'm Silas Wright, owner of Bitterroot Landscapes in Kinship, Idaho," he began.

Maggie could hear subscribers swooning right out of their seats.

"What does it mean to you to be a part of this project?" Dean asked.

"The Old Campbell Place is part of our history in this town. Anyone who's ever come to Kinship sees the big house on the hill and wonders about it. It's a dream come true to get my hands on her," he said, his gaze sliding to Maggie again.

She absolutely refused to think about the idea of him getting his hands on...anything.

"History's important to Idahoans," Silas continued. "We're part of the Wild West. We like to make our mark on things. And we're all proud that Maggie asked us to be a part of breathing life back into this landmark."

Swoony. Savvy. Smart. She couldn't wait for the world to get their first glimpse of Silas Wright.

When Dean asked him for an overview of what his crew would

be doing, Silas suggested they walk and talk. Maggie followed along behind them as Dean filmed and Silas charmed. She found herself getting excited all over again as he discussed the plans for the grounds.

"You're a natural," Dean said, finally turning off the camera. "Maybe I don't hate you so much for getting Maggie to say yes to your astronomical estimate."

"Maggie wanted to say yes," Silas told him. "I just gave her a good enough reason to."

"How about we do an interview with the two of you?" Dean suggested.

It was perfectly normal. Maggie did it all the time. But this was the first time it had ever felt like a setup.

"I think we've got enough footage, don't you?" she said pointedly.

"No such thing," Dean insisted with cheer. "Meet me on the front porch in five. I'm swapping out batteries and cards. You can talk about the first impression Sly Sy made."

"He's a lot happier in the afternoon," Silas noted as Dean bopped toward the front of the house.

"The man runs on caffeine and protein shakes," she said as they picked their way through the backyard and around the side of the house. She spotted Billy scootching carefully across the sunporch roof on his butt. "Has he been in roofing long?" she asked.

Silas followed her gaze. "Billy's fresh off the turnip truck," he joked. "He worked in payroll at Canyon Custom Cabinetry. Until two weeks ago."

"The factory that shuttered?" she asked.

"That's the one," he said, taking his hat off again and running a big hand through his hair. "Forty-eight years in business and then bam. Done. The executives hightailed it out of town and had the sheriff's department escort employees out of the building on a Friday afternoon."

"Wow. What happened?" she asked, kicking at a lump of earth that had been dislodged.

"Top-heavy organizational chart. Big, fat bonuses for the executives. Pay cuts and understaffing for the workers. Some joker figured out how to save money by messing with the quality of the product, and they all but killed the demand. Three hundred and fifty neighbors out of work in one day."

"So now Billy's a roofer."

"We do what we can, where we can, to take care of our own," Silas said. "Marta's new, too." He nodded toward the woman with the wheelbarrow. She had broad shoulders, narrow hips, a manicure, and looked like she was having the time of her life.

"She looks a little more confident on the job than Billy," Maggie noted.

Silas grinned. "I bet Lou first pick that the Broncs—that's the Boise State Broncos—would hire a new head coach in the off-season. I was right, so I got Marta and he got Billy. And now thanks to you hiring both companies, Marta can still afford to pay her sitter, and Billy doesn't have to decide between groceries and insulin."

"You should be saving this for the camera," she teased.

He paused and looked deadly serious. "I don't need to look like a hero if it makes someone else look like a victim."

"That's not what we do," she promised. "We just tell the story."

"I'll hold you to it," he said, turning her around to face the house. "Now, just picture how nice this terrace area will be as long as Billy there doesn't take a header off your roof."

Maggie could picture it. Cool stone under bare feet and strings of lights. Music. Drinks. Food. Laughter. Plants in greens and rainbows of color spilling out of pots. The tinkle of water in the fountain. Stolen kisses in the shadows.

Whoops. Rewind. Undo.

"Come on, you two. The world needs to hear the story of how you met," Dean called from the front porch.

"Kevin is gonna be so embarrassed," Silas quipped.

8

THE DAY WAS done. And in the grand tradition of big jobs, things looked worse than when they'd first arrived.

Half of the roof was stripped, and the east side of the house looked naked without the plantings that just this morning had crowded the walls with a tangle of half-dead foliage. There were piles of rock, debris, and weeds that would only grow bigger in the coming days.

It was a good start to the project, Silas decided, dropping the tailgate on his truck and dragging the cooler closer.

Tradition. It was valued in Kinship. The shared history of people who'd grown up together, raised their kids together, worked together. Generation after generation. Sure, there was new blood every once in a while. And every summer and winter brought with it an influx of strangers looking for fun.

But the foundation was the people who lived and died there.

"Gather round, Bitterroots," Silas called.

Elton, a scruffy, weathered guy in his forties who could run a forklift and lay pavers in his sleep, gave him a hand with the cooler. He'd arrived after wrapping up the next-to-last day on a hardscape job one town over. "Hell of a place," he observed.

"That it is," Silas said.

He heard the sound of a drill biting into wood and spotted her on the porch. Apparently the front door had given up, much like the screen door. Maggie Nichols worked just as hard as any crew member on *and* off camera. It was a surprise. A pleasant one. And not because he had sexist leanings. His mothers had relieved him and his brother of any of those misconceptions before either of them realized that girls did not, in fact, have cooties.

He'd assumed that since she was the money, since she was the face of her own show, she wouldn't be the one hauling cabinets out of the kitchen or opening up walls to get at a house's secrets.

And he'd been damn wrong.

Elton let out a low whistle. "Heard she was a looker."

"This time they weren't exaggerating," Silas agreed.

"You and Michelle on again or off again?" Elton asked.

The fact that Silas was used to the question confirmed he'd let things drag on for far too long. "Off. Permanently this time."

His friend grunted. "Good timing."

It hadn't felt like it a month ago when Silas had looked his sometimes sort of girlfriend of five years in the eye and finally said the words they both needed to hear. He hadn't known exactly why he felt like he had to do it then and there.

But he was a man who believed in signs. And now things were looking a little more clear.

"Hey, Nichols?" he called out.

She looked up from the hinge she was trying to secure. "Wha?" she said around the two screws between her lips.

"Want a beer?" he offered, giving the cooler a jiggle. "First-day tradition."

She considered for a beat and then dropped the drill and screws and stepped off the porch. "Why not?"

He felt something like hot chocolate in his belly as she walked toward him. Silas was a fan of things that made him feel. He chased deep, complicated feelings and wrung every ounce of pleasure out of them.

Leading the way around the side of the house, he found his crew lounging under the new leaves of a maple.

They pounced on the cooler when he set it down. He managed to fish out two beers in the melee. Twisting off the tops, he handed one to Maggie.

"Some place you got here, Ms. Nichols," Travis said. The kid was taking a gap year between high school and college. Judging from the moony eyes the kid was shooting in her direction, he'd already developed a crush on the boss.

Silas couldn't blame him.

They sprawled in the shade, half a dozen of them sitting on coolers or the ground. Maggie—at home with a crew of dirty, sweaty men and women proud of what they had accomplished—stretched those long legs of hers out in the grass and lifted her face to the sun.

The conversation ebbed and flowed, crisscrossing back and forth across their little circle. She wasn't quiet, but she wasn't a talker either, he noted. She asked more questions than she answered.

The more he saw of Maggie Nichols, the more he liked the whole package.

There had been clients who treated his crew like faceless labor, like the people doing the sweating and the work they'd been paid to do were somehow less than those opening their wallets. Those clients didn't earn new slots in Bitterroot's schedule when they called back for more work.

There was nothing shameful about physical labor. Maggie seemed to get that. She was someone who understood the satisfaction of a long day of damn hard work and appreciated others who did the same.

"I might not be able to move tomorrow," Marta groaned. She was lying on her back in the grass, icing her fresh blisters with the beer bottle. She was also smiling.

"You better be able to move," Silas teased. "We're just getting started."

"I'm old. I get second-day soreness after a good workout at the gym. Two days from now, you guys are going to have to help me off the toilet."

"My knees were knocking so bad up there I lost feeling from the waist down," Billy quipped. He'd lost the green pallor after managing to finally find his footing on the sunporch roof. They'd make a roofer out of him yet, Silas bet.

The remedies flew fast and furious.

"Best thing to do is stretch when you get home."

"Take an Epsom salts bath."

"Nah. Ibuprofen. A lot of it."

"You guys are complicating things. You just go home, open the biggest bottle of alcohol you can find, and drink it until you fall asleep."

"You did good work today, Marta. You, too, Billy," Silas said.

"Thanks, boss," Marta said. "And thanks for the opportunity."

"To a good first day," he toasted.

"To a good first day," they all echoed, raising their bottles.

"Wrap up those blisters for tomorrow with some Neosporin, Marta. Keep 'em wrapped and clean, and they'll callus in no time," Maggie told her.

"From manicures to calluses," Marta said wryly, examining the chips in her purple fingernails.

"No reason you can't have both," Maggie pointed out.

It was a tough transition for anyone to make from cushy office job to physical labor, Silas knew. But Marta wasn't complaining. He liked it when people were too busy making things work to feel sorry for themselves.

One by one, the crew members started to pack up and head home. Some to nurse sore body parts. Some to make dinners and check homework. Some to coach soccer or shower for date night.

They all had their own lives and stories, and Silas appreciated that they shared hours of their days with him, with each other. Kinship wasn't just the name of his home; it was their way of life.

Maggie stood and began collecting the empties. "Thanks for a hell of a first day," she told them.

Travis scrambled to help. "Hit the bricks, kid," Silas said, nodding toward the driveway with mock sternness.

"I don't mind," he insisted, shooting puppy-dog eyes at Maggie's retreating back. "I can stay and help clean up."

"I know for a fact that your mom is expecting you home for

your brother's birthday dinner," Silas said. "And that you're the one pickin' up the cake."

Travis winced. "Oh yeah. I forgot about that."

"You can stare at her all day tomorrow," Silas promised. "Your brother only turns sixteen once."

With his young charge on his way, Silas gathered the rest of the empties and followed Maggie around the front of the house to the garage.

It was a detached two-bay building with carriage house stylings that needed a little love and a lot of paint.

She hooked an elbow under the lid of the recycling bin and, in a slick move, flipped it up into the air before dumping the bottles inside with a satisfying crash of glass. The economy of her movements intrigued him. It was like watching an athlete perform.

"Hang on," he called. "Last load."

She held the lid for him, and he deposited his armful.

"Do you host happy hour at the end of every day?" she asked. "Because I might need a bigger bin."

"First and last day only. Unless the client requests it," he said with a wink. "Are you asking me out for drinks, Maggie?"

"Aren't you ever off duty, Sly Sy?"

"Not where you're concerned. You've got my number. I keep hoping you'll use it."

"I'm not anticipating any landscaping emergencies," she told him as she wiped her palms on the seat of her pants. "It was a good day."

"It was, wasn't it?" he agreed as they walked companionably back toward the house.

"I like what I saw from the crews," she told him. "You all take care of your own. Lou didn't have to hire Billy. You didn't have to hire Marta."

"Just being neighborly," he insisted.

"Fingers crossed the shower upstairs is up to this task," she said, looking down at her dirt-streaked arms.

"You're staying here?" That was news to him.

She hooked her thumbs into her front pockets. "Well, yeah. Why wouldn't I?"

She had a point. If he'd bought an eighteen-room mansion, he'd damn well be sleeping in it even when it was more haunted house than home.

But it did create a bit of a problem for him. "Now, Maggie. I need to say something, and I don't want you to take it in a misogynistic kinda way."

"Oh boy," she murmured.

"I sure would feel more comfortable about you staying here all by your lonesome if you had a damn front door." He pointed toward the front door leaning up against the wall.

"Silas, I hope you don't take this as me being a hard-ass bitch. But at this stage of the relationship, I'm not really concerned about making you feel more comfortable."

He slapped a hand to his heart. "While I'm thrilled to hear you acknowledge our relationship, you also wound me."

She gave him an amused once-over from boots to cap. "Something tells me you're a fast healer."

He grinned. "Let me put it another way. It's only neighborly if I offer to help you rehang the door."

Elton's pickup pulled out on a jaunty toot of the horn, followed by Marta and Billy in Marta's SUV. They were officially alone together.

"Since you offered to help me fix the door instead of insisting on doing it for me, I'll take you up on the offer."

"I am not a stupid man," he promised. "I was raised by two very intelligent, competent women and two men smart enough to listen to them."

"Uh-huh. You hold. I'll screw," she said, grabbing the drill.

"Look at me not going for the easy punch line," he said, lifting the wooden door, which was heavier than it looked.

"Just promise me you're not gonna barf on my porch or take your pants off."

"I hate to make promises I can't keep," he teased.

"Try, Sy. Try." She fitted a long-ass screw onto the bit.

He held the door in place while she muscled the screw through the hinge plate and into the wood.

"Sounds pretty soft," he observed.

"Rotted," she agreed, angling the second screw. "Whole jamb needs replaced. But this'll hold for a while longer."

When they finished, he gave the door a test swing from inside. It wedged itself into the frame and required a good kick to seat itself properly.

"Just a little swollen," Maggie called cheerfully from the other side. After a few good shoves with her shoulder, she forced it open. "More secure than a dead bolt."

Her optimism was adorable.

"Since I'm already inside," he began.

She was shaking her head. "Uh-uh. You're not scaring me into a sleepover. I don't believe in ghosts, and I've already done the research on Kinship's crime statistics."

He held up his hands. "First of all, I would *charm* you into a sleepover, not *scare* you. But since this is only our second date, I don't want you to think I'm too easy or too desperate. So I'm gonna check the rest of the windows and doors on this floor."

She crossed her arms and looked up at him. "That's funny. I don't remember us having a first date."

"Saturday. We had drinks in your front yard. We're taking it slow," he informed her, stepping into the front parlor and testing the windows.

"Kinship hasn't had a violent crime in forever, and over half of what does happen here is attributed to tourists having a little too much beer and too much of a good time," she lectured as she followed him into the next room.

This one was smaller, cozier, with shoulder-high, dusty wainscotting. He noted the window was unlatched and shot her a "see, I told you so" look. "You're obviously a highly intelligent woman who does her research," he said. "Which is why I won't insult your intelligence by pointing out that your fourth dining room in the back had quite the collection of empty beer cans and Mad Dog 20/20 bottles."

He winked at her as he stepped around her to cross the hallway. The dining room shared a wall with the kitchen. It had a massive table centered on a dingy bay window that—if not for the decades' worth of film on the glass—would provide a killer view once the dead trees and overgrowth on the bluff were cleared.

"So the locals don't have great taste in booze," she said with a shrug. "It was probably just kids hiding out from their parents."

"Bad things can still happen even if no one has any bad intentions," he said.

She followed him into the kitchen and then the sunporch. He flipped the lock on the exterior door and then jiggled the broken latch on the first window.

"It's painted shut," she argued, crossing her arms. Immune to flattery. Rather than discouraged, Silas liked to think he was narrowing down the best way to connect with her.

He gave her his best concerned male look.

"And I'll fix it," she said in exasperation.

"Good girl." He swung through the last two rooms on the first floor, noting that someone—most likely Energizer Bunny Maggie—had already cleaned up the evidence of Kinship teens' taste in shitty alcohol in the corner den. "What are you gonna do with all these rooms?"

"I have no freaking clue." She laughed. "There's so many of them. Every time I think I narrow down which ones are going to get the budget, I walk into another room and see something worth saving. Another killer view, another piece of trim that somebody carved by hand. Another chunk of history of a family who hasn't lived here in decades."

"Hard to walk away, leave things unfinished," he mused.

She gave him a good glare. "Don't think I don't see what you're doing."

They were back in the rotunda, where the once-grand staircase curved behind her, corkscrewing its way up through two more floors. Waiting to be made grand again. They were standing at the very beginning of something great. And he wondered if she could feel it, too.

"Fine, as long as you don't think you're going to get away without hearing my safety lecture."

"You already checked every possible entry point on the first floor. What are you going to do next? Scale the side of the house and try the second floor?"

"I'm merely going to point out that you should consider being more careful about ending up alone in a house with a man you barely know."

"*You* insisted on coming in," she argued.

"A bad guy would be pretty damn insistent, too."

"I appreciate your concern, Mr. Wright," she said, a pretty pink flush working its way over her cheeks. "But I did my research and not just on crime statistics. I looked into you, too. I look into everyone I hire. I'm careful. And just because you don't see my due diligence happening, it's always a safe bet that I've done it. I don't make snap decisions. I weigh my options. I do my legwork. So when I decide to do something, you can bet that I know what I'm doing. Second-guessing me is *never* in your best interests unless you enjoy wasting time. Got it?"

"My mom is going to love you," he told her.

The look she shot him could have frozen lava into an iceberg. "If your goal is to annoy me, it's working."

"I'm just trying to get to know you and look out for you at the same time. I'm multitasking."

She didn't look impressed. "Go home, Silas, so I can get back to work."

"I'll go. And I won't even comment on how you seem to do a whole lot of working and not much playing."

"I appreciate you not pointing that out." She gave him a shove toward the front door.

He gave the knob a hard jerk, unwedging the door from its frame. "Full disclosure, Mags?"

She cocked an eyebrow and crossed her arms.

"I believe in signs. A few weeks back, I ended a relationship that wasn't going anywhere no matter how many times we tackled it."

"I'm sorry to hear that," she said dryly.

"See, we should have worked. But something was fundamentally wrong."

"I don't need to hear the details of your love life. We're working together, not living together."

"Here comes the sign part," he warned. "I'm pretty sure we're meant to be."

Her eye roll was extravagant. "Now you're really making me regret letting you in."

"I'm not saying we should get married."

"Oh, good."

"Yet."

Her eyebrow-raise was perfection.

"But I am saying I see the two of us getting along real well. There's a hell of a lot of potential standing right here," Silas said, pointing back and forth between them.

Maggie tapped a finger to her chin. "Hmm."

"What?"

"I'm trying to remember the last time a contractor proposed marriage this early on. I'm going to have to update my background checks to include workers who are too easily dazzled into monogamous fantasies."

"See? That right there. Anyone who doesn't fall hard for you is a damned fool."

"I agree. Now, go home. And don't come back tomorrow all puppy-dog-eyed and mopey."

He leaned against the jamb. "I know I'm coming on strong, and I know a lot of it's just flirtatious fun. But when I look at you, Mags, I see something I've been waiting for."

"And when I see you, I see someone I hired to do a damn good job. Regardless of any personal feelings—one-sided or other—I expect you to deliver what you promised."

"Oh, I'll deliver," he promised. "You and me, Maggie. We see things the same way. You don't look at this place and see the flaws, the hundreds of hours of labor it's gonna take to make her shine again."

"Pretty sure I see all that. And how much it's going to cost."

"But you also see what she could be. And that's what makes the work worthwhile."

She followed him out onto the porch. "Do you make it a habit to fall in love with all your clients?" she asked.

"No, ma'am. I do not."

She was looking at him like she was trying to figure out how long the crazy would last.

"I can't do anything about you being dazzled by me or whatever the hell put those cartoon hearts in your eyes. But I can return the full-disclosure favor."

"I'd appreciate that."

"I'm going to turn this place into a damn dream home. I'm going to make it so beautiful that every person who drives into Kinship spots it on the bluff and hears about the Old Campbell Place. And once every detail is perfect, I'm going to sell it to a lucky buyer, and I'm going to move on. Because I *always* move on."

"Just because you've always done something doesn't make it a choice," he said softly.

"I'm not the settle-down type, Sy. And you're not the pick-up-and-go type. That potential you think you see doesn't actually exist."

"Maybe you just can't see it yet."

"And maybe you're miscalculating again and missing a big, glaring, fundamental problem. I'm not a 'spend your life with me' girl. I'm a 'let's have a good time while we have the opportunity' woman."

"I can work with that," he said, rubbing a hand over his chin.

Maggie feigned a wince. "Yeah, but now that I know you're

deeply, irrevocably in love with me, it would just be cruel to string you along. I'll have to date Travis instead. It's a shame, really. Could have been fun."

He grinned at her. "I'll see you tomorrow."

"Unless you scared me off."

"I don't think anything scares you off, Maggie Nichols. Which is why I bet you five whole dollars that when this house is done, you decide to stay."

She laughed. A real, genuine, belly-deep laugh. He felt like he'd just taken the gold medal in something awesome.

"That's adorable. Why don't you just pay up now? I don't stay," she said when she'd recovered.

"Five dollars says you don't leave because you fall in love."

"With the house or my deranged landscaper? Because let me tell you, Mr. Wright, the odds are not in your favor."

"I don't know, Mags. I'm feeling pretty lucky."

He was still smiling when she kicked the front door closed.

9

MAGGIE BACKED UP the clip again and hit play, keeping an eye on the time stamp when the music hit. If Dean shifted the clip half a second later, the music crescendo would strike when her sledge-hammer met ugly red countertop. She scrawled out the note on her pad and then pulled up her browser window.

The most recent episode of *Building Dreams* was getting an astro-nomical amount of attention. Live for only twenty-four hours, it had nearly sixty thousand views already. Viewers loved a new kitchen. Her subscriber count was inching higher, too.

She'd hit the million here in Kinship—Maggie was sure of it. Silas Wright's face might even step up the timeline.

Stretching her arms overhead, she rolled out the crick in her neck.

Day Two had been just as satisfying as Day One. The rest of the roof was stripped. Electrical work had officially begun that morning. The kitchen had been gutted down to studs. Dean hadn't blown a gasket over her kitchen appliance wish list. And Silas's tree gal had shown up and accomplished a hell of a lot of work on the trees eating the driveway.

Maggie picked the library at the back of the first floor to use as her office. It was quieter here, which made marching her way through her to-do list easier. Grabbing the rough sketch she'd started the night before, she headed into the kitchen to pace out the measurements. She was debating whether she could get another foot of quartz for the island when something that sounded like a creepy cathedral organ exploded overhead.

"What in the scary fuck was that?" Dean demanded from the stairs. He'd claimed a bedroom on the second floor as his on-site office space. They knew from years of experience that working in the same room wasn't the best idea.

Maggie poked her head into the hallway and saw a figure standing on the other side of the screen door on the porch.

"I guess we have a doorbell," she said.

"Not it," Dean said, shaking his head. "I haven't had enough coffee to deal with a disgruntled local today."

"You owe me," she hissed at him before heading toward the door.

The visitor was short, round, and bald except for the neatly trimmed ring of white hair that ended just above his ears and the thick mustache. His pants were hiked to belly button height and held in place with suspenders.

"Hi," Maggie said.

"You the new owner?" the man demanded gruffly. She heard Dean sneak back upstairs. *Chicken.*

"I am," she said, leaning against the doorframe. She'd been at this long enough to know the type. Either he was a local historian afraid she was an evil developer out to ruin a piece of town history or he was a self-appointed tattletale who wanted to make sure she was following the letter of the law.

"I'm Wallace Pfeffercorn. I was a volunteer here when it was the Campbell House Museum."

"It's nice to meet you, Wallace. I'm Maggie. What can I do for you?"

He harrumphed at her politeness. "I'm dropping by to give you a piece of my mind."

"Would you like something to drink while you do that?" she offered. "I've got water, lemonade, and beer."

His frown lines deepened into canyons. "Suppose I wouldn't mind a lemonade. But don't think you'll be winning any points with me, missy."

"Come on back," she said, waving him into the house.

He hesitated before stepping inside with his cane.

"I see you haven't completely gutted the place. *Yet*," he said, eyeing the intact wallpaper with terrifying ferocity.

"Some of it will have to change," Maggie said, heading down the hall to the kitchen. The refrigerator stood by itself on a now-empty wall.

"Good Lord, girlie! You owned the place for five days," Wallace sputtered. His heavy eyebrows lowered, obscuring his eyes.

"They weren't the original cabinets, which I'm sure you knew," she said, plucking two plastic cups off the rolling cart and grabbing the lemonade.

"Mrs. Campbell is rolling over in her grave," he predicted.

She had the feeling she was getting a glimpse of Future Dean. Maybe she should have offered the man coffee.

"I bet you didn't even keep the portrait. You probably just chucked everything into the garbage." He was working himself up into a good fit, and Maggie had concerns about whether or not his heart could handle one.

"Why don't we have a seat," she suggested and led the way back to her office.

Blustering about progress and the disrespect youth had for the past, Wallace followed. His tirade cut off abruptly when he stepped into the room.

She smiled as he eyed up the art she'd collected from the first floor and stacked up against the walls. Knickknack treasures found in built-in curio cabinets were half-packed in boxes with bubble wrapping. Framed photos were spread out on a second table.

"Where's the furniture? You chop it up for kindling?" he demanded.

"We moved it into the garage for safekeeping."

He didn't acknowledge her answer. "This must be your sorting pile for the trash," he said, eyeing the paint-splattered worktable that held a few treasures she was keeping unboxed so they could be photographed first. There was an exquisite crystal decanter, an old inkwell, a few antique glassware items, and the needlepoint she'd rescued from the front den. It said: WHERE IS THE ADVENTURE IN FINDING ONESELF IF ONE USES SOMEONE ELSE'S MAP?

"Mrs. Campbell stitched that herself, according to her granddaughter," he said, peering at the needlepoint. "Not that you'd care. It's hung on that wall in Aaron Campbell's study for over a hundred years."

"It will hang there again once we refinish the floor and fix the plaster ceiling," she told him.

"You don't even realize what you're sitting on," he muttered to himself, settling heavily in the metal chair opposite her.

"Then tell me. I don't just fix things up; I also tell the stories of what happened within the walls I'm fixing."

"Aaron Campbell put this town on the map," Wallace snapped. "His novels still to this day bring in tourism dollars because he was a master storyteller. Have you bothered reading even one?"

"Not yet."

"His books are still in print, you know. The royalties are paid into the trust the Campbells left to the town. You could use that fancy show of yours to encourage those screen addicts to pick up a book, put some money in the town's pockets. But you'll probably just turn all those volumes spine-in on the shelves for aesthetics."

"So the house and the royalties went into the trust," she noted. "The Campbells must have loved this town."

"They did," he said. "Mrs. Campbell always said it was the first place that finally felt like home to her. 'Course there's the mystery surrounding how they managed to build this house. But you wouldn't be interested in that."

"Wasn't Aaron Campbell a successful novelist?" she asked.

His eyebrows winged up at her as he took a sip of lemonade. "'Course he was," he said. "But his first book wasn't published until over a year after this place was completed."

Maggie's interest was piqued. "What about the family jewelry stores?"

"What are you asking me for? How should I know how two

jewelry stores in Idaho in the late 1800s run by a father and three sons could afford a place like this? Especially when the homes of the other partners looked like shacks in comparison."

Perhaps Aaron Campbell had taken more than his fair share, she mused. "What about Mrs. Campbell? Maybe she came from family money."

"Ava Dedman Campbell's family allegedly came from some wealthy European dynasty," he said.

"Allegedly?"

"No one's had any luck tracing the ancestry."

Interesting. She wondered if any of the Campbell ancestors had done DNA testing from one of the genealogy sites.

She interlaced her fingers on the table. "Mr. Pfeffercorn, things will change here. But not everything. I'm not going to knock it down and start from scratch. I want to bring it back to life. Maybe with a few modern conveniences, but without taking away the historical significance."

He didn't look appeased. "That's what you say now to get me out the door. Then the thick-headed hammer swingers start putting holes in walls."

"I am one of the thick-headed hammer swingers, and I only put holes in walls that require them," she said.

"Yeah, yeah. Women's lib. You can do a man's job. Don't get your petticoat in a twist."

She sighed and tried another tactic. "Mr. Pfeffercorn, do you know what YouTube is?"

"I don't give a good dog crap about YouTube. I care about what this place means to this town. Just because it's not a museum anymore doesn't mean it doesn't deserve some dignity," he grumbled into his lemonade.

"I'm here to bring the house into this century and make it into a home again. But I'm also here to tell a story. This house's story. I do that through a show on YouTube. I think viewers would be interested in your expertise."

"A home or one of them condominiums that rents out to hippies and yuppies that come here for a week to stink up our air with their giant SUVs and take up too many restaurant tables?"

She pressed her lips together and held back a laugh. Wallace might be the grumpiest grumpy old man she'd ever encountered.

"What did you do at the museum?" she asked, trying to steer to a safer topic.

"Gave tours. Cataloged Mr. Campbell's papers. Decorated for the holidays. Not that you care. You'd probably just as soon dump all of those ornaments in the trash."

Maggie rubbed at the spot between her eyebrows. "If I promise not to throw out anything of reasonable significance, maybe you could help catalog some of the family possessions?"

"So you can do what? Sell it on that *Antiques Roadshow*? I won't be a party to the gutting of the Campbell family's estate."

"I'd like to keep as much of the finds as possible with the house," she said, exasperated.

He leaned in, mustache twitching with suspicion. "What's your game, girlie?"

"Right now it's not having an aneurysm. How am I doing? Are my pupils the same size?"

"My great-uncle died of an aneurysm. You shouldn't joke about that kind of thing. He was walking from the barn to the house and then BAM!" Wallace slapped the table with his hand. "Dead as a doornail. Left a wife and seven hungry children. My great-aunt worked from dawn to dusk to keep the farm going and all those mouths fed."

Maggie's head was starting to throb dully, and she hoped it wasn't the ghost of Wallace's great-uncle. "I'm very sorry for your loss," she said.

"My loss? I didn't even know the man," he barked.

She cleared her throat. "Uh. Okay. Well, you clearly have a great respect for history," she began.

"Darn right I do. If we don't honor our history, we're nothing but a bunch of heathens running around not understanding consequences."

Consequenceless heathens. That was a new one.

"If I promise to honor the history of the Campbell house, will you be willing to share some of the stories about the house and the Campbell family?" she asked wearily.

His glare was shrewd. "Maybe. Dunno. I'll think about it."

She tore off a corner of a piece of drafting paper, wrote down a number, and handed it to him. "This is my partner Dean's number. If you decide you're willing to help out, give him a call."

Take that, Chicken Dean.

"Probably won't," Wallace huffed, heaving himself out of his chair. His gaze roamed the room. "But I might."

Maggie stood, too.

"I'm takin' this with me," he said, grabbing his lemonade and motoring toward the front door.

"Thanks for dropping by," she called after him.

Windows95Luvr: Okay. Apparently Idris Elba is married. Who is single and worthy of our Maggie?

ShakespeareWuzHere: Just found out that my 55-year-old dad has seen every episode of Building Dreams! We're planning a binge rewatch when I come home from college for the summer! #FamilyForMaggie

10

"WHO'S A GOOD BOY?" Maggie crooned to the chubby dog wagging his entire back end at her. "This is Kevin," she said for the benefit of the camera she was shooting with. "He's with the landscaping crew, and we didn't want him to feel left out, so we got him a little present."

She held up the green, squeaky hammer toy she'd picked up at Tanner's General Store.

"Sit. Good boy. Here you go." She handed over the toy, and he took it with a gentle mouth, his whole body quivering. "Now, go fix something," she said.

With a series of gleeful hammer squeaks, Kevin romped out of her office and barreled down the hall.

Maggie turned off the camera and eyed the giant whiteboard she'd set up in her makeshift office, mentally juggling timelines. Outside, the roofers were making progress. She didn't envy them clambering over steep pitches three stories up. Silas's crew had built a mountain of brush in the front yard and were in the process of laying out new and improved planting beds around the house.

Inside there was more chaos. Usually it was tricky having the electrical work and plumbing done at the same time, with people climbing all over each other in kitchens and bathrooms, but given the scope of the work and the good-natured relationship between both crews, the trades were juggling things nicely.

While Jim and company opened and closed walls and ceilings, the electricians started their rewiring, and Albert, the plumber, and his apprentice, Judy—his daughter and another of the plant closing's victims—roughed in the plumbing for the new powder room in the former fishing magazine room and the full bath behind the kitchen.

She needed to make tile decisions for the kitchen and downstairs bathrooms by end of day to get the materials ordered. The fixtures upstairs could wait a bit, which was good, since she was still trying to figure out the best place for a freestanding tub in the master bathroom.

Making a note to revisit the idea of stealing space from the bedroom behind the master, she moved on to the production schedule. She would film some stuff on the fly today, maybe creepy basement footage. As much as her subscribers loved a kitchen reveal, they also seemed to enjoy freaking out over dank, eerie spaces. The episode when Dean walked backward into a cobweb in a garage and started throwing punches at nothing was one of their most popular. It entertained her to no end and pissed Dean off.

She added *lighting?* to the whiteboard, grabbed her fat stack of tile samples, and headed into the kitchen.

White subway was a classic for a reason, but this room, this house, called for something with a little extra personality. She lined up the tiles on the folding table that was acting as a makeshift countertop and studied them.

Too simple.

Too busy.

Too green.

"Maggie, what have you drilled into my head from day one?" Dean stormed into the room and tossed his iPad case down onto the end of the table.

She sighed and turned her back on the samples. He was going to be dramatic about it. "That it's not my house," she said.

"Would navy cabinets be spectacular in this kitchen? Yes. No doubt. Would anything less be a travesty? Probably. Is it in the budget to upgrade from a nice, *reasonable* stain to paint? No, it is not." Dean, the ever-responsible dream killer, marched down the list.

She scanned the room and pictured it. Not with the walls missing the cabinetry that had already been ripped out and were on their way to a local nonprofit. But with the clean quartz countertops with the gray veining. The bright punch of navy cabinetry with glass fronts was exactly what this room needed.

"Mmm. Yeah. I think I'm gonna do it anyway," she said cheerily. She grabbed her thermos from the windowsill. Outside, the siding guys took measurements. She could hear the electricians debating fuse box placement in the basement.

A week into the job and things were already starting to look less bad inside and out.

"I know you are." He sighed, pinching the bridge of his nose in theatrical frustration. "I don't know why I bother opening my mouth. You never listen to me anyway."

"I listen to you," she argued, taking a swig of water. "When you're right."

"Look, all I'm saying is we just started bringing on some serious advertisers. They and your followers expect the Maggie Nichols formula."

"Which is?" she asked, eyeing the wall space where the new cabinets would end and a single full-light door would open onto the terrace. Double would be better. French doors with the built-in screens would bring in more of the view and make for easier access to alfresco dining.

"You buy a crappy house with potential no one else sees. You do the necessary renovations *without overimproving* the property. And then you sell it quickly for a very nice profit," he explained with strained patience.

"Why do you think I'd deviate now on this house? We doubled our return on the last place."

"It was ocean block on one of the nicest beaches in Oregon. You were selling the literal American dream. Who the hell is going to pay seven figures—which is what you're going to have to list this place at—for some million-room Victorian monstrosity on a hill in fucking Idaho?" Dean's strained patience cracked and then shattered. "God. You're giving me flashbacks to our marriage."

Maggie used a bandanna in her pocket to wipe plaster dust off her face. She hadn't told him, her best friend and partner, why this place. Why she'd been waiting what felt like a lifetime for this opportunity.

She tucked the bandanna back in place and put her hands on his shoulders. "You've spent the last year talking me into leveling up. We're knocking on a million subscribers. We've got real advertising dollars coming in. The finale for the last place hasn't aired yet, but when it does, it's gonna be big. I trust *you* to handle the leveling up. But you have to trust *me* to make the calls that I know are right when it comes to the work. That's why we work as partners."

He looked tired, defeated...uncaffeinated.

"Did the café accidentally switch you to decaf?" she asked with a frown.

Dean sighed. "It's not the coffee."

Now she was worried. "What is it?"

"Will." The name came out with equal parts pain and annoyance.

"What about Will? Did he call?"

He shook his head. "Worse. He's engaged."

She winced. Will had been Dean's longest relationship, beating their own marriage. "Oh. Shit," she said. "I'm sorry. You'll meet someone. Someone great."

His laugh was bitter. "How? We're on the road practically year-round. You expect us to work around the damn clock and give me shit every time I take a day off. I'm not going to meet someone who is either willing to stay home and wait for me to drop by once every two months or someone who is happy to tag along on the road. Neither are you."

"I guess that's why you and I work so well together. We like the road, the unroutine." She said the words lightly but inside felt long-buried anxiety stirring up. Like he was about to tell her something that was going to change her life all over again. If she could just keep him from saying the words, maybe they both could pretend everything was fine.

Dean took a breath, and she fought the urge to put her fingers in her ears.

"I don't know if I still like the road," he admitted. "Maybe I want routine. Maybe I want to wake up in the same bed for more than a few weeks in a row."

"Okay. What are you saying?" she asked cautiously.

His shoulders jerked toward his ears. "I don't know. Maybe I'm just tired. Or maybe I'm jealous or worried about missing out. Either way, I don't know how much longer I can do this." He didn't actually say the words, but she heard them all the same. He didn't know how much longer he wanted to do this *with her*.

"How long have you felt like this?" Maggie asked, her throat tightening up and making it difficult to get the words out. This was why she did what she did. Why she lived like she lived. So no one had the opportunity to do this to her again. And yet it was still happening.

He crossed his beefy arms over his barrel-like chest. "Awhile maybe. I'm not saying you need to start looking for a new me or anything."

"But..."

He nodded solemnly. "Yeah. But."

She stepped back from him, needing the distance, and fiddled with her tape measure. "I thought you were all in for life on the road since you and Will broke up?"

How had she missed this? How had she let herself get so dependent on him again?

"I thought so, too. But the thing is, we broke up *because* of the road."

She narrowed her eyes. That wasn't the story he'd given her a year ago. "What are you talking about?"

"He wanted me to choose."

"Choose what?"

"You or him. And you'd never ask me to choose. So I chose you. But maybe sometimes—like when he posts a picture of his hot new art history professor fiancé—I wonder what it would have been like."

She felt like the time she'd taken a backward header over a roll of carpet into an open stairwell. Free fall. No time to brace for impact.

Dean had chosen her over Will. A man he'd dated seriously for two years. A man who'd wanted the condo with a water view and the dog park on Saturday afternoons. Hadn't she and Dean joked about it? Hadn't she teased him about narrowly escaping the horror of farmers market mornings and Sunday brunches with the same faces every week?

She was an idiot. A big, stupid, self-absorbed idiot.

But she was an idiot with an old wrong to right.

"Listen, you know that I want you to be happy," she said, still fighting the tightness in her throat. "So whether that's flying drones and living out of a suitcase or buying a place in a town you want to live in long-term, I don't need to be part of that equation. I want you to have everything that you want. I'll survive without you."

"Will you?" He didn't say it with a nasty edge. He said it wearily, as if it were a legitimate concern that kept him up at night.

"What the hell is *that* supposed to mean?"

"It means it's too early, and I haven't had enough coffee, and maybe I'm just feeling sorry for myself, so let's forget I said anything."

She crossed her arms over her chest. "Let's not. Let's finish it."

"Fine. I'm your best friend," he said.

"Yeah. So?"

"I'm your ex-husband."

"I repeat. So?" she said stubbornly.

He took in a breath and blew it out. "Magpie, I'm your best friend, but that doesn't mean you're mine."

"Um, ouch. *Ass.*"

"That's not what I mean. Of course you're my best friend. But you're mine by choice. I'm yours by default. I'm all you've got. I've still got friends back in Seattle and San Francisco. I keep up with them. We see each other when I'm in town. I get kid birthday party invites and Christmas and Hanukkah cards. I send flowers for babies and surgeries."

"So you're a social butterfly. What's your point?"

"You don't."

Her tidy little organized world was tilting on its axis.

There was a ruckus in the hall, and she jumped back just in time as Kevin barreled in, a powdered doughnut hanging out of his mouth.

"Get back here, you mangy thief!" Elton—powdered sugar on his chin and shirt—shouted as he gave chase. "Your daddy's gonna kick my ass if you get a sugar high!"

The dog gleefully plowed into the hall with the doughnut's owner on his heels.

"I love you, Mags," Dean said. "I do. But I shouldn't be your one and only person."

She stood there sucker punched, tape measure dancing from limp fingers. This hadn't been in the plans for the day. She hadn't penciled in a meltdown between opening up a wall and going live to show off the newly gutted kitchen.

But again. She owed him.

"Okay," she said, keeping her tone light. "Keep thinking about it and let me know what you want to do. We'll make it work."

It was his turn to grimace. "Look, I'm sorry. Just forget I said anything. I just need a massage and a gallon of good wine and to stop looking at Will's Instagram."

She smiled, not because she felt like it, but because he expected it. "Go plan your spa day. I have things to hammer."

He nodded and started for the door. Then he stopped. "Don't you ever get tired of it?"

"Of what? The work? The travel?" It was her turn to shrug. "Nah. I like being rootless."

"There might be a happy medium between being tied down and being a tumbleweed," he said.

She didn't think so. "Maybe," she said brightly.

Dean gave the wall a rap of his knuckles. "At least put the cabinet conundrum up for a vote on the 'gram. Get your people excited about it."

And then he walked out, leaving her all alone.

11

A STRING OF curses volleyed out of the kitchen, echoing off the walls of the hallway. Silas proceeded with amused caution.

He found Maggie yanking a sledgehammer free from the wall and hauling back to take another swing. It wasn't the kind of deliberate, economical move that he'd come to expect of her. This was temperamental destruction. He recognized it as he, too, was a fan of physically exorcising a good mad when the occasion called for it.

She was winding up again when he stepped up and plucked the sledgehammer out of her grip.

"Hey!" She was not amused.

"Hey back," he said, leaning the hammer against the wall out of her reach.

She had a fine layer of plaster dust on her shoulders. There was a raw scrape on her forearm and a tear in the knee of her pants that hadn't been there that morning.

Her eyes, that whiskey-in-a-glass color, flashed with emotion.

Silas knew better than to ask what was wrong.

"What do you want?" she asked. It wasn't exactly a snarl, but it was in the neighborhood.

"Wanna take a walk? Look at some dirt?" he offered.

She frowned. "What time is it?"

"Just after three," he said.

Swearing, she glanced around the dust-covered room. Taking a stab at what she needed, Silas handed her the thermos he found under the table and watched as she drank deeply.

"Been at it a while?" he guessed. He'd been at another job—

an outdoor kitchen hardscape—and hadn't seen her outside when he returned after lunch.

Maggie tugged up the hem of her tank and swiped at the sweat dotting her brow, earning him a peek at her taut stomach and bright-purple sports bra. Her gaze slid to the massacred wall and then back to him. "Let's look at some dirt," she said with a marked lack of enthusiasm.

It had become their little tradition in the week he'd been on the job, dragging her out of whatever she was doing at quitting time so he could walk her through what his crew had accomplished. It was as much to show off as it was to get the woman to take a damn break. Maggie Nichols didn't know when to stop.

He started the tour on the north side of the house. Showed her the now deeper bed between house and garage, newly edged and ready for plants and mulch. Rather than being impressed, she took another long drink and swiped at her mouth with the back of her hand, her eyes miles away.

Leading her around to the back, he pointed out the plots where the sod had been removed to reveal rich earth. Each six-foot-by-three-foot section would be its own raised bed for roses. When she stepped right over the spot where the creepy cemetery fence had been only that morning without noticing, Silas knew there was trouble.

Changing tactics, he nudged her farther away from the house. "Let's take a walk, slugger," he said.

"I have work to do," she grumbled, obviously not realizing that they were exploring a new path that had been created with two passes of a brush mower and some enterprising chainsawing only hours before.

"I know you do. Watch your step," he cautioned.

She grunted an acknowledgment, and he squashed the testosterone-fueled impulse to ask what was wrong so he could tell her how to fix it. He kept one eye on her and one on the path as it curved and climbed until they got to their destination.

"I can appreciate a good mad," he ventured.

"You don't want to talk me out of it? Soothe the beast?"

It was a little bit adorable that she could refer to herself as "the beast" and mean it.

Silas pulled off his hat and shoved a hand through his hair. "They're your feelings," he said. "You've got a right to them."

The tension that was holding her shoulders up around her ears seemed to release. She frowned thoughtfully. "I do. Don't I?"

He caught it for an instant. Underneath the thin layer of mad was hurt. Maybe even the tiniest edge of fear. "Sure do," he said lightly.

Then he took her by the shoulders and turned her to face the view.

"Oh," she said. "*Oh.*" A brand-new panorama spread out before them. Lake. Town. Mountains. River. Silas kept his hands where they were and gently dug into the knots he found with his thumbs.

"Oh," she said again. Only this time, it was a sigh as he kneaded the tension, the muscle, the hurt. "It's beautiful."

"And it's all yours," he told her.

"For now," she said bitterly.

The new tension he felt in her shoulders was definitely not in his imagination. "Now is all anyone ever has," he said, shifting his thumbs lower. Her sweat-slicked skin was soft to the touch, and under that softness was the tense rigidity of anger.

"Said the philosophical landscape architect."

"I took my share of philosophy classes back in the day."

She was quiet for a beat before asking, "You ever realize that you don't know someone as well as you thought you did?"

"Every damn day."

"I'm serious," she said dryly.

"So am I. Mags, you're talking to the man who walked in on his father and stepmom watercoloring some damn duck by video tutorial last weekend."

"Watercoloring a duck?"

Clearly she didn't appreciate just how out of character this was for his biology teacher dad and financial planner stepmom. Their hobbies—as far as he'd known—were limited to drinking good wine while watching documentaries about how fucked the earth was. "Trust me," he promised her. "You'll understand when you meet them."

"That's another thing. How is anyone supposed to trust anyone else if they don't actually know them? If they just keep on surprising you every time you manage to get comfortable?"

They were digging down to the root issue, and Silas was more than happy to get a little dirty in the process.

"You don't have to know every single thing about a person to know you can trust them," he countered.

When his thumbs moved between her shoulder blades, she let out a little moan that had his blood stirring.

"But they can still let you down. They trick you into relying on them, and then just when you get used to the way things are, they change the rules."

"That's people for you," he said. "How long were you and Dean married?"

He felt her tense again before she turned to face him. Genuine surprise was written all over her pretty, sad face. "How the hell did you know that?"

He gave her a shrug, palms up. "I'm a pretty observant, intelligent, good-looking guy. Y'all have a kind of intimacy. Like a language that only you two speak. From the outside, it looks like it runs deeper than just 'friends from college.'"

She watched him. "And you're asking me about Dean because you know he's the one I'm pissed at," she surmised.

"You're not mad at Dean," he countered, stepping up onto a sizable boulder that had tried to take a chunk out of the brush mower. He shielded his eyes from the afternoon sun and drank in the view.

"Oh goodie. We've arrived at the part where you tell me not only what the problem is, but you flex your muscles and offer to fix it for me."

"You're not mad at me either," he insisted. Leaning down and taking her hand, he tugged her up on the boulder next to him. "You're good and pissed at yourself for getting comfortable, letting yourself lean on someone. So you're mad as hell that you put yourself into a position where you can get hurt, or disappointed, or let down. And judging by that mangled wall in the kitchen, this is a 'been there, done that, got a souvenir shot glass' kind of situation."

Her chin jutted out. "That's ridiculous," she snapped. "That's beyond ridiculous. It's bullshit. And you know what?"

He looked down at her, trying not to appear too entertained. His mom had always told them, "You can learn a lot more about a person on a bad day than you can on a good day."

"Dammit. You're right," she admitted, her breath coming out in a whoosh.

"Darlin', I'm Mr. Wright."

Her lips quirked. "You're saying your last name, aren't you?"

"Maybe."

She shook her head. "Ugh. Does that line actually work?"

"We're about to find out. Now, if you can get showered and changed in the next hour, we can catch happy hour at Decked Out before all the good tables are taken."

She blinked up at him. "Huh?"

He stepped down, and before she could protest, he picked her up and set her on the ground.

"I'm taking you out for dinner and drinks," he explained, amused.

"Why?"

Well, it wasn't a no.

"Because if you don't talk it out, you'll just end up grabbing that sledgehammer again. And there's only so many peanut butter and Marshmallow Fluff sandwiches a person's allowed to eat before it's against the law in this state."

"Idaho has weird laws," Maggie complained. "But I *would* hate to break one so early on in my stay."

He grinned. "You don't by chance know what chapter sixty-six, section three of Title eighteen says, do you?"

She crossed her arms and looked at him suspiciously. "No. Should I?"

"I wouldn't worry your pretty little head about it, especially if breaking the law would keep you from enjoying a healthy physical relationship with, say, a handsome, sensitive, tall landscaper."

She shook her head, and he saw another hint of grudging smile. "I thought the full-court press flirting would slow down since you caught me mid–temper tantrum."

"Are you kidding? I think I'm more head over heels now," he told her.

"You're so weird, Wright."

"I am a student of human interactions. And I can tell you that I witnessed 'balls-still-attached, blissfully unaware of Mad Maggie' Dean get in his car and drive off today, which means that, as mad or hurt or pissed off as you were, you didn't take it out on him."

"I took it out on a wall. Instead of talking it out or burying it down deep like a normal adult," she argued.

And that was the other part of it, he realized. She was mad *and* disappointed in herself for being mad. He wanted to wrap her up in his arms and give her something else to think about. But that wasn't what she needed.

"What?" she asked, looking at him.

"Just thinkin' how cinematic it would be if I kissed you right here. Right out of a damn movie."

"Yeah, until we lose our balance and fall..." She peered down, gauging the drop. "A hundred feet or so."

"But what a way to go. Come on, slugger," he said, slinging an arm around her shoulders and guiding her onto the path. "I'm going to introduce you to the best finger steaks you've ever had."

She was frowning but didn't pull away from his touch.

"Considering I don't know what a finger steak is, that probably won't be difficult."

Then she slipped her arm around his waist, and Silas decided life was pretty damn perfect.

"Do you put fry sauce on finger steaks?" Maggie asked.

Maggie Nichols: Finger steaks and fry sauce with a lakefront view! Have you tried them?

12

IT WAS STUPID to be nervous. This wasn't an actual, real date. Was it?

Maggie surveyed her limited wardrobe and wondered exactly what the hell she was supposed to wear. T-shirts, tank tops, work pants, and gym shorts mocked her. The meager space required to house everything she wore on a regular basis made the bedroom closet seem cavernous.

She used to own date clothes. She used to be a person who went places, did things, saw people. Those clothes were most likely packed away in the storage unit in Seattle along with the furniture from the condo she'd sold...God. Had it really been two years ago already?

After flipping properties in Seattle for a few years, she'd decided to take the show on the road, literally. She'd planned on finding another home base, then forgotten, finding it easier to shorten the time between projects instead. Time spent not working was time spent not bringing in money.

Had she been "homeless" for two years? Just a storage unit and a post office box that one of her—or more accurately, Dean's—friends checked once a month.

She unearthed a pair of clean jeans and committed on the spot. Remembering the ivory, off-the-shoulder sweater that she hadn't been able to resist in Portland, she pounced on her suitcase. Behind it was a mangled men's sneaker, a pink bandanna, and a sandwich wrapper. Kevin the therapy school dropout dog had been foraging again. Yesterday on the third floor, she'd discovered the bottom drawer of a heavy dresser open. Tucked inside was the dog's new squeaky toy hammer and three pencils.

She found the sweater still inside her suitcase, on top of her only matching bra-and-underwear set that she absolutely was *not* wearing on this nondate.

Dressing quickly, she decided on the stacked heel ankle boots over sneakers. She debated texting Dean to ask if she should cuff or not cuff but then remembered she was mad at him—or herself *and* him—and decided to roll the denim to the top of the boots.

Earrings, dangly.

Lip gloss, dark rose.

She stepped back, trying to see more of herself in the tiny mirror mounted above the bathroom vanity. But she could only see her face or her chest.

"I really need to move up the timeline in here," she muttered to herself before jogging out into the hall. There she found the heavy, gilt frame mirror angled against the wall between two of the back bedrooms and—after a quick cleaning with toilet paper—surveyed her efforts.

"Huh," she said.

She looked . . . not bad.

Strong and soft, she decided, running a hand over the sweater. Fun without trying too hard. A belt would have worked, but she didn't have one on hand. A curling iron would have been even better, but she'd been without one since she'd left hers in a motel between the Charming Cape Cod and the Beach Bungalow projects.

Still, this was the most effort she'd put into her appearance in . . . a while. She pulled her phone out of her back pocket and snapped a picture in the mirror.

"Showered and on the hunt for finger steaks," she said as she typed up the caption. "Annnnnd, post."

Duty to her followers performed, she hustled back into her bedroom.

"What do you guys think?" she asked the portrait. The oil-painted Campbells eyed her impassively as she grabbed a small clutch and tucked her license, cash, and lip gloss inside. "You should have seen me a few years ago. I would have dazzled you in a dress and heels," she told her roommates.

She felt like the spark-eyed Mrs. Campbell was curious about what had happened to *that* version of Maggie.

Ignoring the judgmental vibe from inanimate objects, she headed into town for her first nondate in her new temporary town.

She parked her truck a block away and strolled toward the restaurant, glancing in shop windows as she passed. Every gift shop in town seemed to have a treasure chest of fake gold coins and bars in their displays.

Decked Out was a one-story building with gray cedar shakes that backed up to the lake. She remembered it from before. Remembered her mom sitting out on the deck, eyes closed, face to the sun. Basking.

As she approached, a long-legged man in jeans and with a charming smirk pushed away from the wall. *Silas.* There was something about the way he looked at her. Proprietary. Appreciative. Dangerous.

"Uh-oh," she murmured as her stomach did a funny nosedive when he gave her a sinful once-over. She felt like she had as a flat-chested ninth grader when dreamy senior Javier Cooper winked at her in the hall between classes.

But if teenage Javier had been dreamy, adult Silas was downright edible.

His jeans were worn and fitted so perfectly to his body that she guessed it had to be from years of wear. The long-sleeve T-shirt hugged his broad chest and shoulders. He looked as good in clothes as he did out of them.

No hat tonight. His hair was…ugh. Damn delicious. Those golden curls should have made him look boyish, but there was nothing immature about the delectable man in front of her.

Okay. Clearly she was hungry. She'd raged her way through lunch and now needed finger steaks—whatever the hell they were—stat.

"Hey, Mags," he said with a warm kind of familiarity. He didn't touch her when she stopped in front of him, but she felt the sparks ping-ponging back and forth between them.

"Silas." She wasn't feeling mad or pissed or scared anymore, she realized. She was feeling . . . interested. Maybe there was something to that whole "talking about your feelings" crap?

"Did I ever tell you that my heart skips a beat every time you walk toward me?" Silas said, flashing her a slow, panty-melting grin.

"You should probably get that checked," she said lightly. "Could be something serious."

"Oh, I sure hope so," he drawled.

Oh. My. God. "Feed me, Wright," she ordered.

He opened the door and ushered her inside. Rough and rustic was how she'd describe the place. There was wood everywhere. Gray-washed oak on the floor and U-shaped bar. A more natural finish on the rafters and beams. The back wall of the restaurant was all glass with doors and windows that opened onto the multitiered deck bigger than the restaurant itself. Beyond the tables and umbrellas with their handful of patrons was the sparkling waters of Payette Lake.

"Hey there, Sy," the bartender called out as they passed.

"Hey, Pete. You got my five bucks?" Silas asked.

"How about first round's on me?" Pete offered.

"Even better," Silas told him. "Come on, Mags."

"Do you have a gambling problem?" she asked. "You sure seem to make a lot of bets."

"Life's more interesting when there's something at stake," he said, leading her to one of the deck doors at the back and opening it for her. The smell of lake water and citronella hit her, and for just a second, she was twelve years old all over again. Memories, short but sweet, swirled around her like a favorite sweater.

She stepped outside just as a breathy voice called, "Sy!" A woman—a girl, really—in an apron jogged up to him, her long, blond pony-tail swinging. Her flawless cheeks were flushed pink, and she had the biggest, bluest eyes Maggie had ever seen. This was exactly the kind of girl Maggie hadn't been in high school. No acne, voluminous hair, and an overflowing self-confidence that compelled her to bound up to the cutest guy in school and expect him to like her.

"Heard you and Michelle broke up." Bubbly Blonde hooked an eyebrow expectantly.

Silas looked at Maggie and then back at Bubbly. "We did," he said.

"You should have called me. Didn't I tell you to call me if you two ever split for good?"

"Well now, that wouldn't have been fair to Michelle," Silas said. He looked at Maggie again and then took her hand. "Or Maggie. Mags, meet Arabella. Bella, meet Maggie."

"Hi, Arabella. It's nice to meet you."

Arabella wasn't nearly as excited to see Maggie. "Oh. Hi," the girl replied flatly.

Score one for the late bloomer. Maggie Nichols had something the cool girl wanted. Being in such a position of power made her feel magnanimous.

"Don't worry," Maggie said with a wink. "I'm only in town for a few weeks."

Hope must bloom eternal in Arabella, she guessed, because the girl brightened.

"See you around, Bella," Silas said, dragging Maggie away.

"I like your shoes," Arabella called after them, pointing at Maggie's boots.

"Thank you."

It wasn't crowded on the deck. Just a few couples enjoying the early start to their evening and a group of twenty-somethings talking over each other about their white water rafting. Silas pulled her to a table on the upper section of decking. The lake, an unbelievable blue-green, stretched out before them in a bowl of gently rolling hills.

"Well, *that* was fun," she teased, taking a seat and snatching the drink menu out of its holder.

He shook his head. "I do not know what's gotten into that girl. I've known her since she was born practically."

The bourbon barrel porter on the list caught her eye. She slid the menu across the teak table to him and leaned back in her chair. "I could hazard a guess."

"I really don't want to spend our third date talking about other people."

"Third date? Things certainly seem to be moving along," she quipped.

"You're taking things slow and being respectful," he explained. "But if you play your cards right tonight, I might just let you kiss me."

Maggie's quick inhale sucked saliva into her lungs, and she started coughing.

"You all right?" he asked.

She nodded, still coughing.

"Totally. Fine," she rasped.

Well, the cool-girl thing had been nice while it lasted. It was good to remember that deep down she was still the kind of gal who would choke on her own spit in public.

"Can I get you a water?"

Her eyes were watering too much to make out the server who had heroically appeared. At least it wasn't Bubbly Arabella.

"Two waters, Sean," Silas said.

"And a bourbon porter," she managed to gasp between coughs.

"Make it two," Silas said.

Lungs finally spittle-free, Maggie dabbed at her eyes with her sleeves. "So, come here often?" She sounded as if she'd just escaped a serial strangler.

He was watching her in that curious, appreciative way of his that had probably been turning women into active members of the Silas Wright Fan Club for decades. "You're quite a woman, Maggie," he said.

Their drinks arrived, and while Silas ordered the mystical finger steaks, Maggie—carefully—sucked down some water to soothe her throat. When the teenage server left, she pointed an accusatory finger at her dinner date. "See. That right there is exactly why Bubbly Arabella actually believed you'd call her."

"Now, hang on a second," he said, looking wounded. "Just because I am charming and manly and a sensitive ally of the fairer sex doesn't mean I want to..."

"Let's go with 'date,'" she suggested, switching to her beer. It was awesome.

"Date," he agreed. "Just because I pay attention to another human being doesn't necessarily mean that I want to *date* them."

"That's a fair point," she conceded. "However, shouldn't it be a charming, manly, sensitive ally's job to read the room and understand that some recipients might take the attention more seriously than others?"

He leaned forward and linked his fingers through hers. She pretended not to notice the "wheeeee" her stomach squealed from its front-row seat on the roller coaster that was Silas Wright's attention.

"Mags, I think you're under the misconception that I'm a serial flirt."

It was her turn to laugh. "What part of that is a misconception? I bet you wink at baristas and that you've told at least four of those little old ladies at the table over there that you wished you were twenty years older."

He glanced over his shoulder at the table of ladies wearing matching Kinship Senior Bowling League shirts. "I think what you're trying to say is that you don't believe my intentions."

"I think that's exactly what I'm saying," she said. "You flirt like it's your first language."

"You don't take me seriously," he said, sounding surprised.

"But Arabella does."

"Bella takes nonexistent clues to feelings that definitely do not exist and cobbles them into false proof of attraction," he argued.

"I don't think she needs to *pretend* that people find her attractive. She's stunning and young, and did I mention bubbly?"

"She's also Michelle's—my ex-girlfriend's—first cousin. And she's nineteen. What the hell would I do, babysit her?"

"I don't think that's what she has in mind." Maggie laughed. "No one knows better at nineteen. And most of us have to learn the hard way."

"I feel like we should get back to the part where you explain why you don't think I'm deadly serious about my feelings for you," he insisted. His thumb was stroking the calluses on her palm. Back and forth like a sexy metronome.

"You're the boy who cried love."

"I am not. I'm the reasonably good-looking *man* who identified an attraction to his stunningly talented, interesting, beautiful client."

It was her turn to lean in. "Silas. Listen very carefully to your talented, interesting, beautiful client. I'm not into serious relationships. *Especially* not temporary ones. However, I might not be opposed to having some fun—schedule permitting—with the right guy."

"The *Wright* guy," he said smugly.

"You're saying your last name again, aren't you?"

His grin, lightning-quick, should come with its own DANGER signage, she decided.

He was still holding her hand as if it were the most natural thing in the world. Her fingers itched to get into those blond curls. The moment was fun. Romantic. And for a second or two, she wondered what it would be like if it were real.

"I'll settle for whatever you're willing to give me, Mags."

"You say that now, when things are nice and neat and flirty. But what's going to happen when it's time for me to go?"

"I'm willing to find out if you are." His grip was warm. His eyes were the bottomless kind of gray that seemed to sparkle like sterling silver. She felt an almost hypnotic pull and found herself leaning toward him, closing the distance between them.

"Finger steaks," Sean the server announced, reappearing to drop a plate of what apparently were finger steaks in front of them. The scent of deep-fried red meat tantalized Maggie out of her trance, and she leaned back, extricating her hand from his.

Deciding it was safer and smarter to go for the food instead of Sy's hair or mouth, she reached for a plate.

Thank God she hadn't gone with the matching underwear set or shaved her legs.

13

"WHAT ARE YOU thinking about?" Silas asked an hour later, pushing his plate away and studying Maggie. Her brown eyes shifted from some far-off point across the lake back to his face.

"Well, if you really want to know," she said, leaning forward conspiratorially.

He mimicked the gesture. "I do."

She made a show of looking over both shoulders before answering. "I was wondering if this sweater was long enough that I could unbutton my jeans without anyone noticing."

"Beats fluffernutter, doesn't it?" he teased.

"Oh yeah." She leaned back in her chair, eyeing her own empty plate with what looked like a mix of satisfaction and pride. She'd loved the finger steaks, rhapsodized about her trout club sandwich, and guzzled fry sauce like it was a beverage. It made him wonder why a woman who enjoyed food so much would waste so many of her meals on convenience foods and sandwiches eaten standing up.

"You know what I'd like to do with you next?" he asked abruptly.

Those brown eyes widened in hesitation and, if he wasn't mistaken, anticipation.

"Excuse me, Maggie Nichols?" They jumped apart, and Silas eyed the interrupter. "Deputy Mayor Kressley Cho." The woman shoved her hand in Maggie's face, knuckles up, as if she expected one of her very large, very shiny rings to be kissed. Maggie leaned back and performed an awkward handshake.

"It's nice to meet you, Deputy Mayor."

"I'm really the acting mayor, seeing as how the actual mayor is a cat. Don't ask me. It's a town tradition," she said with a roll of her eyes. "I just wanted to drop by and introduce myself. We're all just *tickled* that you chose Kinship, and if you need any help with anything at all, I'm just a phone call away."

Kressley reached into her bag and slid a business card across the table. "I've got several ideas on how you can best feature Kinship and its leadership on your show. I can pencil you in at my office Monday at, say, eleven?"

Maggie looked at Silas with deer-in-headlights eyes. "How about I have my partner call you and set something up? He handles the scheduling," she said.

"I'll alert my secretary to expect the call," Kressley said. "Oh, excuse me. I see the school board president over there. Must go!"

She flittered off like a colorful butterfly.

"You were saying?" Maggie said.

"I forget." Deputy Mayor Cho had that effect on people. She fluttered in, said a lot of bright and cheery words without taking a breath, and then vanished, leaving her victims shell-shocked.

"You asked if I knew what you wanted to do with me next," Maggie recapped.

"Ah. Back on track. As I was saying, Mags. Do you know what I'd—"

"Excuse me?"

They both jumped again at the new interruption. A man with a sunburned nose and a little girl in pigtails and a Kinship hoodie stood next to their table. Silas didn't recognize them, but both father and daughter were sporting the telltale exhaustion of tourists.

"We're so sorry to interrupt," the guy began, looking almost as excited as his daughter. "You're Maggie Nichols, right?"

"That's me," she said with a quick, bright smile.

"My daughter and I are huge fans of you—your show," he added quickly.

Silas realized he might not be the only man in Kinship smitten with the pretty, talented Maggie.

"It's no bother at all," she assured them. "What's your name?"

"Isabella," the little girl whispered, twisting her fingers in the pocket of her dad's cargo shorts. "This is my daddy."

"I'm Mateo," he said. "We watch your show together every week."

"We're subscribers," Isabella announced proudly, shedding some of her initial shyness.

"You are?" Maggie asked, clearly delighted.

Silas watched with something that felt a bit like pride as his date chatted with her fans and snapped a photo with them.

"I'm gonna build a house with a room for ponies to live in," Isabella said. "Daddy said he doesn't know if anyone's ever built a pony room before. Have you?"

Maggie frowned thoughtfully. "No, I haven't built a pony room."

"You can build it first if you want to," Isabella said graciously.

"Well, thank you. But I think it would be pretty cool if you built the very first pony room, since it was your idea."

"Are you on vacation?" Mateo asked, trying and failing to sound like he wasn't prying.

She saw right through him. "I'm actually working on my next project. This is my landscape architect, Silas Wright."

"Wow!" Isabella gasped. "Can we see your new house?" Excitement had her voice entering near shriek territory, and Silas chuckled.

Mateo clamped a hand over his daughter's mouth. "Maggie's very busy, kiddo. We don't want to slow her down. It'll be just as fun to watch it on the computer." Then he mouthed *so sorry* to Maggie.

Maggie leaned forward and rested her elbows on her knees. "Do you see that house way up there on the hill?" she asked, pointing over Decked Out's flat roof. The Old Campbell Place was visible on the bluff.

Isabella nodded, and her dad dropped his hand from her mouth. "It looks very, very small," she said.

"That's because it's so far away," Silas explained. "It's Maggie's biggest house and biggest yard ever."

Isabella's mouth fell open, revealing two missing teeth. "Even bigger than the Midtown Mansion?"

Maggie nodded. "Even bigger."

Isabella was impressed into silence.

"I tell you what," Maggie said. "If it's okay with your dad and if you have time while you're in town, you can come for a tour."

The little girl was dancing on her tiptoes, giving Mateo puppy-dog eyes that could have rivaled Kevin's. "Daaaaaaaaad?"

"Are you sure? We don't want to impose," he said, sounding more than a little excited.

"I wanna impose!" Isabella announced.

"I'm positive. I've been dying to show it off," Maggie promised.

"Well, if you're sure..."

"I'm sure."

"Can I go tell Mom?" Isabella begged, her eyes wide.

"Quietly," Mateo insisted.

"Mooooooom!" Isabella sprinted across the deck to a woman who was sitting at a table with three plated desserts.

"I can't thank you enough," Mateo said, after ensuring his daughter had made it back to the correct table. "It's been a tough year. Her mom, my wife, is sick. Cancer. She's winning, but it's a tough fight. The three of us look forward to curling up and watching your show every week. And now I'm babbling and embarrassing myself."

Maggie reached out and squeezed his hand. "Mateo," she said very seriously. "I choked on my own spit earlier and almost received the Heimlich from our server. *You're* not embarrassing yourself."

"This... this really means a lot. Are you sure? Because I don't want you to be under the impression that we won't act like rabid fans."

"I'm sure. I would love to have your family come see my new house. It's a construction zone, so no flip-flops," she warned.

Dad looked much like daughter when he jogged back to his table.

"You just made someone's day," Silas observed.

She beamed at him. "I'm trying to play it cool, but honestly, it still blows me away that people can recognize me out in the wild."

"Take a walk with me, Maggie," Silas said suddenly.

She cocked her head and considered the offer. "I really should be getting back. Early start tomorrow."

Tomorrow was Saturday.

"If you say yes, I'll buy you an ice cream," he offered, sweetening the deal.

"Okay."

After a brief wrestling match over the check, he paid, and they headed for the street.

The deck and restaurant were starting to fill up. Families with kids in sports gear coming in for a dinner parents didn't have to cook. Adults gathering at the bar for some laughs after a long day. Tourists looking for a good meal before turning in early for tomorrow's adventures.

He waved a thanks to Pete the bartender for the beers and then introduced Maggie to his ninth-grade science teacher and her long-time girlfriend. He ignored the looks tossed their way as he took Maggie's hand and pulled her out. Kinship was going to have to get used to seeing him with someone else.

Finally on the street, she turned to him. "Are you the mayor or something?" she asked.

"Me?" He slung his arm around her shoulders and tucked her into his side as the evening turned cool. "No. Our mayor's a cat. The last election was pretty contentious. She barely beat out the parakeet."

"Freaking Idaho," Maggie murmured with that half-smile on lips that he couldn't stop thinking about.

His phone vibrated in his pocket, and he knew before looking that it was one of the moms.

Mom: Heard from Alice May on the bowling team that it's a nice night for a date.

Silas rolled his eyes. "Mags, you mind posing for one more picture?"

"With you?" she asked.

"It's our third date. I think it's time," he said with great seriousness.

She laughed but snuggled under his arm as he framed in the

mountains and lake behind them. He looked down at her and snapped the picture.

"You weren't even looking at the camera," she complained.

"Sy." Ricardo, manager of the garden center one town over, gave him a little two-fingered salute as he strolled by with his teenage son.

"Hey, Rico," he called back.

He kept Maggie anchored under his arm and fired off a text.

Silas: Meet the future Mrs. Wright. Or maybe I'm the future Mr. Nichols. We haven't discussed name changes officially yet.

"Are you cold?" he asked Maggie. The sun was dipping low in the sky, taking its spring warmth with it.

"A little. I have a coat in the truck. How do you know so many people?" she asked.

He looked down at her, baffled. "I grew up here. Most of them did, too. It's not that unusual. And it's something you can look forward to when you decide to stay."

"You must really need that five bucks," she mused, leading him in the direction of her vehicle.

They stopped at her truck, and she shrugged into a sexy-as-hell leather jacket.

"Damn, Mags." Silas sighed.

"What?" She gave her hair a girlie fluff.

"You look badass."

"It's important to remember I also licked fry sauce off my plate. So I'm not that badass. Where to?"

He held out his hand and didn't bother to not look smug when she finally took it. "If you don't mind, we'll swing by my place—"

"I'm not having sex with you tonight," she interrupted, stopping on the sidewalk and facing him.

He gave in and finally slipped his arms around her. Locking his fingers together at the small of her back, he tried out the feel of her in his arms. It worked. They worked.

"Tonight?" He hung on to that qualifier and gave her his best lecherous look.

She bit her lower lip, and he lost his train of thought.

"Definitely not tonight."

"Hmm," he said.

"What?"

"I'm having a hard time thinking about anything but kissing you right now," he said softly.

"Silas." There was a hint of warning in her tone, but she didn't do anything to put more space between them.

"It's a kiss, Maggie. Not a commitment. One kiss won't cost you a lifetime," he coaxed.

"Well, since I'm here. And you're here, and we're definitely *not* having sex tonight," she said, sliding her palms up his chest to his shoulders.

Something in the back of his brain said "uh-oh," but he wasn't one to back away from a challenge. No, he dove into them headfirst.

He lowered his mouth. She met him halfway, and the world as he knew it ceased to exist. Part of him knew he was on one of Kinship's busiest streets, kissing the hell out of a woman he'd known for one week.

But the rest of his consciousness was consumed—by the softness of her lips and the deceptively delicate way they parted under his. Inviting him in to be devoured. Her tongue met and twined with his, sending every drop of blood in his veins to his groin. He slid his hands under her jacket and gripped her hips, dragging her against him.

Her arms tightened around his neck, and he saw fucking stars when her breasts pressed against his chest. She moaned or whimpered, and enchanted him.

The sidewalk under his feet, the one he knew by heart, shifted, and he was no longer sure what was ground and what was sky. She was consuming him in ways he'd never experienced.

When her fingers dove into his hair and gripped, he threw aside any attempt at controlling himself. She tasted like dark beer and mysteries. He didn't know exactly how—if she had led and he'd followed or vice versa—but suddenly Maggie's back was pushed up against the front wall of Angela's Butcher Shop. And then his hands were slipping under the softness of her sweater to find the heat of her skin beneath.

She breathed out another whimper when his fingers coasted higher, thumbs and index fingers finding the edge of her bra. Her flesh pebbled under his touch, and the tremor that ran through her body made him feel like a wild man.

They were nothing but breath and touch. Need. Want.

The flavor of her filled his senses. Drove him a little crazy.

Crazy enough to forget that they were standing on the street in full view of most of downtown Kinship.

A car horn followed by a cheerful "Get a room, Wright!" dragged him back to the present.

"Um." It was the best he could muster.

Maggie looked ravaged. Her hair was tousled, lips swollen and pink, cheeks warm, eyes glassy and bright. It made him want to dive back in. Instead, he took a very deliberate step back.

Her knees buckled, and she leaned against the butcher shop, palms flat against the red plank siding.

"Wow," she breathed.

Silas shoved a hand through his hair and willed his hard-on to go away before it got a zipper imprint. "Yeah. Wow," he agreed.

Slowly, she pushed away from the wall. "That was...something."

He couldn't look at her and not stay hard, so he focused his gaze down the block.

"We should probably not do that again. At least not for a while," she said.

"Darlin', don't take this the wrong way. But do you maybe mind not looking directly at me like that?" He tried to keep the request light, but the desperation he felt, the primal need to drag her into the nearest dark alley, was overwhelming everything his mamas had ever taught him.

"Oh," she said. "*Oh*." He didn't have to see her face to know exactly where she was looking. "Can you walk like that?" she asked, sounding both fascinated and amused.

"I can do a lot of things like this," he growled. "Sorry. Just need a few seconds."

Maybe a month. A month of icy swims in the river. That sounded about right.

"I realize you have a lot going on right now," Maggie said, gesturing in the general direction of his crotch. "But I hope you don't think this is getting you out of ice cream."

"No, ma'am," he promised. Then swore when his phone vibrated three times in rapid succession.

It was his siblings. All of them. In the group he'd only just been admitted to after promising to only respond in GIFs for one week to prove his fealty to technology.

Taylor: I heard from Maxine Fulsom that Big Brother Silas is making out with a stranger on Lake Street.

She'd included one of those GIFs with a couple kissing.

Michael: Bet he's going to date her and break up with her 47 times before they end up common law married.

It was followed with three diamond ring emojis.

Nirina: Silas Wright, if that's the Old Campbell Place owner whose throat you've got your tongue shoved down and you don't bring that girl into this shop in the next 24 hours, you are dead to me. Dead. To. Me.

God only knew where his half-sister had found the dancing-skeleton-in-the-cemetery GIF.

"Mags, I know I just kissed the hell out of you on a public street and all, but if you could do a guy a favor and help me find a middle finger on this keyboard thing, I'll buy you two scoops," he begged.

She took the phone and unashamedly read through the messages. Then laughed. "I've got a better one," she said, then handed the phone back.

"New phone, who dis?" Silas read out loud.

He hit send, and within seconds, his phone was vibrating. "Now you've gotta stay. My whole family just fell in love with you."

14

SILAS TALKED MAGGIE into swinging by his place to pick up the dog. It hadn't been hard to convince her, since her brain was a stew of lust hormones. Besides, Kevin would be mortally offended if he knew Silas went for ice cream without him.

Maggie didn't like disappointing anyone—humans or dogs—if she could avoid it.

It looked a bit like a storybook. The cabin or cottage, she couldn't decide which was more fitting, had dark-green clapboard siding, a navy-blue front door, and a gingerbread front porch just big enough for two rocking chairs and a pair of ferns overflowing from orange pots.

He'd tucked solar lights along the stone path and deeper in the yard of shrubs and ornamental grasses.

"Wow, Sy," she said, not for the first time that night. The kiss had been dangerous. It had been an assault on logic. Biology talking her into something she'd prefer to think on for a while. But the house was a new kind of sneaky charm.

"I'd invite you in," he said, still holding her hand. "But..."

Thank you, sweet baby Jesus, for the "but."

"Are you saying you don't trust me to control myself?" she teased.

"Yes. That is exactly what I'm saying."

"A wise move."

"Besides, I purposely left it a mess just in case things looked like they were headed in the direction they're most definitely headed in."

Maggie couldn't help but laugh. "I didn't shave my legs for exactly the same reason."

He paused at the gate. "Just so you know, that wouldn't stop me from enjoying you."

"Neither would your mess," she promised.

He gave her one of those soul-jarring, stomach-on-a-roller-coaster looks. "Wait right there."

She watched him jog up the path, onto the porch, and in through the front door.

The second the door closed, Maggie busted a move on the sidewalk.

That kiss with Silas Freaking Wright had finally dethroned her engagement as the most romantic moment of her life. Which, to be completely honest, only held the top honor by default. Not that there was anything wrong with a drunken, late-night proposal in a Burger King parking lot when both parties were too young to know any better. Or to know if they were both straight. She winced at the memory of her drunk twenty-two-year-old self getting down on one knee next to Dean's VW Rabbit. She should have known then.

"Maybe we should get married," she'd slurred, leaning hard to the right.

"Maybe we should," he had agreed, closing one eye to zero in on which Maggie was doing the proposing.

Looking back, that shiny, sickly expression on his face should have been another neon warning sign. But she'd been caught up in the moment. Not the romance of it. Or her feelings for the cute, nice, dependable Dean. She knew now it was more a by-product of the crushing loneliness she had felt after losing the mother she'd depended on and the father she'd learned not to. It had threatened to swamp her, to pull her under and never let her find her way back to the surface.

She'd put it all on Dean's barely adult shoulders. Made it his job to save her. To protect her from the loneliness. To give her a place to fit into. And he'd loved her enough to say yes.

Even after he'd found his voice, even after he'd whispered the truth she should have already known, he still loved her. He still protected her.

And she was still using him to keep the loneliness at bay.

"Well, shit," she muttered to herself. The truth of it hit her like a wheelbarrow handle to the solar plexus. Before she could chicken out, she pulled out her phone, opened her texts, and typed.

Maggie: I really do want you to have the life you want. There's someone out there who's been waiting for your surly, snarky ass their entire life. It's not fair for me to hog your sour disposition all to myself.

His response was quick.

Dean: No one will ever knock you off your shrewish pedestal in my cold, shriveled heart.

Maggie: Love you, shithead.

Dean: Love you back, weirdo.

On a long sigh, she stowed the phone back in her pocket. She felt sad. And turned on. And terrified. Things were changing again, and she had no control over them. Change in her life hadn't been good. It had been hard. Painful.

She needed to calm the eff down. She didn't get carried away. No matter how fine Silas's butt looked in a pair of jeans, she wasn't about to throw her career away and settle down with the cute landscaper from Idaho.

Shifting gears, she studied Silas's home.

The professional in Maggie approved of the curb appeal, the whole aesthetic. She hadn't made a mistake in hiring Mr. Wright. Unless, of course, being able to think about nothing but the feel of his erection grinding against her turned out to be a problem.

Whoops. And there she was thinking about it again. How instantaneous and overwhelming his reaction had been to the kiss. She'd never been pushed up against anything before. Damn if she didn't like it.

Joyful barking erupted inside, followed by a loud crash.

Then Silas reappeared on the porch in a white hoodie with Kevin on a leash. "I said *i-c-e c-r-e-a-m*, and he knocked the couch over," he reported. She wasn't sure if he was joking.

The dog pranced down the sidewalk to her, shivering with delight.

"Who's a good boy?" Maggie asked, squishing his giant face between her hands.

"Not Kevin," Silas said dryly. "You sure you want to walk? That bed in there looks awfully comfortable."

"Nice try. We're walking, and you're feeding us ice cream."

Kevin made a whimpery moan of delight.

"Hey," Silas said, his voice suddenly serious. "What's wrong? Something happen while Hercules here busted up my furniture?"

She shook her head. "Nothing."

He closed a hand around her wrist and squeezed. "Uh-uh. That's a hard line for me, Mags. When something's wrong, you either tell me what it is or tell me you don't want to talk about it. You don't lie. And you don't try to hide it."

"You've got a lot of rules for third dates," she joked.

"I'm serious."

"I...I actually don't know what to say," she said on a half laugh. "I don't know how to tell people things."

"Sure you do," he said. "You tell your YouTube people stuff all the time."

"That's different. That's not me being..."

"Vulnerable and real?" he supplied.

"Maybe that," she admitted.

"It still counts as putting yourself out there. You aren't showing them some kind of highlight reel in full makeup with studio lighting. You're putting your hopes and dreams out there and asking strangers to care about them, too."

"Geez. You've really been doing your research," she said, impressed.

"When something interests me—or when I find out I'm missing out on something great like my asshole siblings and their dumb GIF conversations—I make an effort. Now it's your turn. Talk, Nichols."

Kevin, sensing her hesitation, leaned against her legs and looked up at her with unconditional love. She took a breath, and then the plunge.

"I was too selfish to notice Dean was gay, and I all but forced him to marry me, and then when he got up the guts to tell me the truth, just shy of our first anniversary, I put all of it on him. Blamed him for it all when the only thing he'd tried to do was not hurt me. We came back to each other—as friends—eventually, but I swore I would never do that to him or anyone again.

"Yet here we are a decade and change later, and I'm doing it all over again. I haven't learned a goddamn thing. I'm still a broken twenty-two-year-old hanging on too tight to the pieces, hoping they magically fit back together."

He didn't ask her what broke her or if those shards ever cut her from holding them too tightly. He didn't tell her to go easy on herself or agree or disagree. Instead, he very deliberately cupped her chin in his hands and kissed her softly, steadily.

His mouth was firm and warm against hers, and this time, instead of stealing her breath, it felt like he was giving it back to her. The tightness in her chest loosened, and something light and bright bloomed inside. Like heartburn. Only nice.

She tasted him, breathed him in, and felt both lighter and more firmly grounded.

"Gah," she managed when she pulled back.

The smile that danced at the corners of his lips was soft and amused. He swiped his thumb over her lower lip.

"What was that for?" she asked, finally finding her vocabulary.

"When Kevin does something good, he gets a treat."

Maggie felt her mouth fall open in an O. "Are you *dog training* me?"

"I'm rewarding you for learning to do something that goes against your nature."

She poked him in the chest. "That's *not* a no."

He shocked the hell out of her again by slipping an arm around her shoulders and dropping a kiss on the top of her head. "Come on, darlin'. Let's get you some ice cream."

The dog let out a strangled kind of yodel and danced up on his hind legs.

"Heel, you muscle-bound jerk," Silas said, giving the leash a tug. Kevin jumped to obey, trotting at his heels.

"Look how good he's being," Maggie said, falling into step.

"Fancy dog trainers call it being food-driven, which is usually a great way to motivate during training. But if Kevin gets bored, he just decides to cut out the middleman and give himself the treats. Two weeks ago, I got a call from the ice cream place saying Kevin was waiting in line for his usual. Still don't know how he got out of the house."

They left the block of single-family bungalows behind them and crossed the street into a quiet section of the downtown. Brick row homes in cute paint colors and tidy front stoops crowded close together.

"Kevin has a very smart approach to life. Figure out how to get yourself what you want," she mused.

Silas gave her shoulder a squeeze, and she refused to acknowledge how good, how right, it felt to be touched by him. "You can't get yourself everything you want," he told her. "Otherwise you end up trying to do the jobs of a dozen people and running yourself ragged."

"Maybe I just need to simplify. Make my wants fewer," she hypothesized. She could do a whole year on tiny homes or smallish homes. Less square footage meant less to renovate. She could double the number of properties she normally did in a year.

"Or maybe," he said, interrupting her thoughts, "you should honor your wants as they are and accept the fact that no woman is an island. Get some help. Take a damn break once in a while."

"I see what you're doing here," she warned him.

"The metaphors about you letting people in or that I'm using your food drive to reinforce positive behavior?"

"Oh, you suck, Wright!" Another shop window caught her eye. "What's with all the gold bars and coins?"

Silas stopped in his tracks. "Are you telling me you don't know about the Dead Man's Canyon Stagecoach Robbery?"

"Maybe?"

"Maggie, as a property owner in Kinship, Idaho, you are required by law to know that, way back in 1865, a coach left Kinship on its way to Boise when it was robbed by three bandits about twenty miles south of here. The bandits took the coach and everything in it—except the people, of course."

"Of course," she said.

"They were gentlemanly bandits and didn't shoot a soul," Silas promised. "Anyway, the bandits took off. And a couple of hours later, the passengers and driver were found walking in the canyon. Turns out there was gold on board—a lot of it—heading to a bank. It was never seen again."

"So Kinship's claim to historical fame is a hundred-and-fifty-year-old-plus robbery that happened not here?" she clarified.

"It's the West, Maggie. Every drop of history is important." He guided them across the street and around the corner to the sunny yellow awning of Frosty Peaks.

The memory—her own drop of history—hit her hard and fast. Cones, chocolate-vanilla twist. The melt and drip, the race to not waste a single drop. Her mom's laugh, brighter than the summer sun. Being here, walking down these memory lanes, made her feel closer to her mom than she had in years.

"Do they still have the lemon cheesecake hand-dipped?" she asked.

Silas stopped and looked down at her. "You've been here before?"

"Once," she admitted. "When I was a kid. And that's one of the things I don't want to talk about."

"Then I guess I won't be pointing out the fact that that's one of those signs I was telling you about."

"Guess not," she said, fighting a smile.

He leaned in and peered into her eyes. "You didn't used to be a pretty eighteen-year-old snowboarder named Sun-mi, did you?"

"I think I would have remembered if I were."

"Best winter break of my high school life," he reminisced.

"Bet it was pretty great for Sun-mi, too."

"I like to think so. Anyone catch your eye when you were in town mysteriously?"

"Not that first time, but this time around there's someone I can't stop thinking about."

"Maggie Nichols, I swear to God, if you say Travis, I am going to ship him off to summer camp."

She laughed her way into the shop.

15

MAGGIE DROVE HERSELF home with Poison and then Pearl Jam blaring. It had been one hell of a night. She wondered if Silas and his siblings were texting about it. Then wished *she* had someone to text about getting recognized at the restaurant, learning what finger steaks were, and that kiss. Or was it kisses? Where did one kiss leave off and another begin?

Feeling philosophical, she gave thought to what it meant that one "almost fight" left her with zero people to talk to. Maybe Dean was right. Maybe she did need to make more of an effort to make and keep friends.

But real friends were so much work. And her followers and subscribers, well, they were happy with a like or a response. Something that only took a second. What kind of friendship could survive on that?

She parked the truck on the side of the house, wishing she had remembered to leave a light on. Or at least check the bulbs in the exterior lamps. It wasn't that she was afraid of the dark. It was more that few things cemented loneliness like coming home to a dark house. Knowing that there was no one there waiting, excited to talk.

Was it odd that she was thirty-four years old and, besides that brief attempt at marriage over a decade ago, she didn't know what it was like to come home to someone? To swap stories about the day, to fight over who cooked or who ordered out.

Maybe I should get a dog, she mused, getting out of the truck. She thought of Kevin and his couch-crashing affection. Then again, maybe not.

The night air was crisp. The wind was stronger up here on the bluff, making the trees creak. Maybe she was lonely. Or maybe she was happy. Either way, she didn't really have time to delve into her psyche. Lonely or happy didn't matter when up against deadlines.

She thought about Silas and his talk of fate and signs. Was she here because of fate?

Maggie snorted at the thought and let herself in the front door. She was here because she'd been fascinated by the big house on the hill and had wondered what kind of people would live there. If she could ever be one of those people.

That wasn't fate. That was drive. There was a distinct difference.

Phone in hand, she made a note to replace the bulbs in the exterior lights on the porch. After a night out with Silas, of interesting conversations and being surrounded by people, the three empty stories felt particularly tomb-like. So she cued up a playlist and went upstairs to change into her comfiest pajamas.

Okay, fine. Her *only* pajamas. They had hammers and saws on them and had been a gift from a viewer.

Deciding to squeeze in an hour of work before calling it a night, she headed back downstairs. She grabbed a tall glass of water and turned on the desk lamp in her office. It was a heavy thing with a huge stained-glass shade that cast an unnatural red and green glow around the room.

She had a power washer scheduled for drop-off in the morning, and Jim would be swinging by to do a few hours of wiring while the house was quieter. Maybe she could set aside a half hour or so to dig into the Campbell family research again.

Her phone vibrated on the table next to her, and she peeked at the screen.

Silas: Just in case there was any question, I'll be looking up at the ceiling and thinking about you all night.

"Ooof," she said, rubbing a hand over her heart. She needed to be a hell of a lot more careful where Silas Wright was concerned. The man could charm his way into places he had no right being. Including her pants.

Another message came in while she was still swooning. It was a GIF of Keanu Reeves in fake glasses blowing a kiss.

Silas: Shit. Sorry. Still figuring this GIF thing out. Meant to send this one.

A GIF of a teddy bear being crushed by hearts arrived next.

Maggie was debating whether or not to text the man back when she caught a glimpse of headlights as they shone through the glass at the front of the house. Instinctively, she turned down her music and then heard the crunch of gravel.

It was after ten. Too late for a neighbor dropping by. She turned off the light.

The engine cut out front, and she eased into the hallway. Regretting that she'd left her shoes upstairs, she ducked barefoot into the kitchen and grabbed the girthy flashlight she'd used to examine the innards of the bulkhead that the upper cabinets had been attached to.

There were footsteps on the porch. More than one person from the sounds of it. She debated for a hot second and then decided to go for the flank. She stole into the sunporch, unlocked the door, and tiptoed out onto the terrace.

If she snuck around to the front, it gave her the opportunity to scare the shit out of the trespassers. She was in the process of ninja-ing her way along the side of the house when she stubbed her toe on a hunk of slate.

It hurt. Badly. Hopping and flailing, she suffered in silence until the pain started to subside. This was why shoes existed. She lived in a construction zone, for Christ's sake. She knew better.

Cursing under her breath, she jogged with high knees to the far end of the porch and then remembered the short part of the porch's L didn't have its own stairs. A design flaw in her opinion. As quietly as she could, Maggie climbed up and over the railing, her toe still throbbing.

"Of course it's locked. Someone else owns the place now," a voice whispered loudly from around the corner.

She edged up against the house and hoped to hell none of the floorboards would give her away.

"It's not like they're living here now," another, more surly, voice whined. "This place is a shithole. You'd have to be a complete freak to move into it like this."

Maggie took offense.

"Guys, I told you I heard it's some big deal who bought the place," a third voice, deeper and softer, said. "She's probably got a security system. Let's just go someplace else."

Maggie chanced a peek around the corner, and in the scant moonlight, she recognized the small group of teens from the café during her first night in town.

Cody, the only name she knew, had his hands in his pockets and was still on the steps.

The rest of them were on the porch. Her porch.

Cody's flannel-wearing pal with homemade tattoos feigned a tap dance and held up both middle fingers. "Fuck off, security cameras," he sang. Maggie wondered if he'd had formal dance training as a kid or if he'd studied ironically for just such an occasion.

"Ugh! Why do we even come here?" a girl in jeans and a sweatshirt six times bigger than it needed to be pouted as she took out a tube of too-dark lipstick and started to write on the front window.

"It's our thing," Tattoo Boy insisted.

"We need to get a new thing," Lipstick Artist whined. "This place is so creepy. I bet it's haunted. There's probably chopped-up bodies in the basement." She looked like she was hoping Tattoo Boy would comfort her.

Ah, to be young and dumb again.

"I always expect some kind of zombie to climb out of the basement," said Girl 2, who had waist-length black hair and her face glued to her phone. Her thumbs moved so fast that they were a blur.

Tattoo Boy switched to zombie mode and approached her, groaning and hissing while he dragged one leg behind him.

"Stop it! You're creeping me out," Lipstick Artist whined.

He gurgled convincingly and then pretended to eat Girl 2's arm like it was a corn cob.

By this point, Maggie felt reasonably certain she was in no real danger and began plotting out the best way to terrify the little shits.

"Are we going in or not?" Girl 2 said, ignoring the zombie apocalypse and her impending loss of limb. "Because if we're not, my friend Madison just found her mom's Valium prescription."

"The door is locked, smart-ass," Lipstick Artist reminded her. "What are we supposed to do?"

"Then just break a fucking window," the bored girl said without looking up from her phone.

They wouldn't be so hell-bent on window breaking if they knew how much a plate glass window that size cost to replace. None of them looked like they'd be good for the cost of the window either. It was time to make her move.

"Yeah. I wouldn't do that if I were you," Maggie announced, snapping on the flashlight as she jumped around the corner. She shined it right in the bored girl's face. The kids froze comically. Except for Girl 2, who finished her text first.

"Zombie!" Lipstick Artist screeched.

"Fucking-A," Girl 2 said, putting forth the effort to sound at least moderately nervous.

The highest-pitched shriek came from Tattoo Boy, who was no longer proudly waving middle fingers or tap-dancing.

Cody stood frozen on the steps, both hands in plain sight, his face pale.

Maggie heard the clunk of something heavy hit the floorboards and then the clump of clunky, gothic boots as they sprinted for safety.

"Run, Tommy!"

"Don't say his name, Ashley!"

Amateurs.

"Freeze or I'm calling the cops!" Maggie said halfheartedly. There was no reason in hell why any of them would actually stop. And she didn't know what she'd do with them anyway if they did stop.

The engine of the little blue hatchback turned over, and three doors slammed.

Cody was still standing on the steps, holding his hands in the air and looking like he might vomit at any moment. A bottle of liquor lay on the porch in front of him.

"Please don't call the cops," he whispered.

She could barely hear him over the high-pitched rev of the car engine as it fishtailed away from the house, sending a shower of gravel in all directions.

Maggie sighed. "I'm not calling the cops. But I am confiscating this." She picked up the bottle and turned the flashlight on it.

Ugh. Mad Dog 20/20. Really she was doing them a favor. A plastic bottle of mango-flavored liquor was never a good idea.

"What's your name?" she asked, shining the light on the boy.

"Cody."

"Cody what?"

"Cody Moses."

The kid must have her confused with actual authority unless he'd given her a fake last name. Either way, he'd stayed to face the music. That was something.

"Well, Cody Moses. Your friends suck."

There was a hint of a smile curving one side of his mouth. "Yeah. Kinda."

She remembered that hungry look. The fact that he'd ripped off the phone number for a night shift job. "I'm Maggie. How old are you?"

He winced. "Eighteen."

Which made him an adult if she did call the cops. It didn't take much to ruin a life.

"Are you still in school?" she asked.

He nodded. "I graduate in June. Maybe."

She blew out a breath. "Look, I'm not calling the cops on you. But I also have to set an example so your zombie-fearing friends don't come back. So you're going to come back here tomorrow morning."

He looked at her with suspicion, and she wondered if she looked like the kind of stranger who would chop up teenagers and bury the pieces in her basement.

"Your trespassing punishment will probably involve something with manual labor that I don't feel like doing myself. How are you at scraping wallpaper?"

"Uh, I don't know."

"I guess we'll find out tomorrow. Do you need a ride home?" she asked. Her toe was throbbing worse now.

He shook his head. "Nah. Not supposed to take rides from strangers."

"Not supposed to break into their houses either," she pointed out.

"I'll text my sucky friends and meet them on the road."

"Good enough," she said, suddenly feeling exhausted. "I'll see you tomorrow. Be here at nine."

He nodded, hands in his jacket pockets, and turned to leave.

"Oh, and, Cody?" she called.

He turned around.

"If your sucky friends ask, tell them I cut off your pinkie toe with a hatchet and buried it in the basement."

MomOf4: Maggie, I just wanted you to know that my daughter and I have been watching your show for years and today she applied for tech school where she's going to learn to build houses! Proud mama moment. Thanks for being the amazing example you are!

FortyThreeBabe: OMFG, if MY ass were that big I'd never let myself be seen on camera. Maggie is so gross I can't stop laughing!

DallasDeelite: I am living for this beach house! Maggie is this the one you're going to finally keep?

16

SATURDAY MORNINGS WERE when Bitterroot's teenage part-
timers were dispatched in two pickups with trailers to do the mowing
and trimming jobs around Kinship. Silas had a few commercial
properties as clients, but most of the business came from families too
busy with spring sports to keep up with the lawn, or senior citizens,
who got the rock-bottom discounted rate.

The kids fought over the old folks because the snacks were great.

Silas liked to do a few drive-bys every weekend to make sure
everyone was on task and not fucking around with string trimmers
and leaf blowers like he and Michael had when they were put in
charge of the family lawns. He still had a scar on his shin from the
cord of a Weed Eater. Teenagers today seemed to be at least a little
more responsible when money and snacks were on the line.

There was no real reason for him to swing by the Campbell Place.
And if he got his drive-bys out of the way and spent an hour or two
on paperwork, he could take the paddleboard or the kayak out for
the afternoon.

If he stopped in to see Maggie, well, that would throw a wrench
in his whole day. Plus, he'd probably end up kissing her again. And
he wasn't sure how she'd feel about that. Seeing as how she hadn't
responded to his texts last night. Maybe that had given him a mild
case of nerves.

But if he *did* drop by, maybe he could test the waters, so to speak,
under the guise of preparing for the week ahead. It would just take a
minute or so.

"Wanna go see the pretty lady?" he asked his dog. Kevin cocked his head from his copilot position in the passenger seat.

"All right, then. Let's go." Silas steered the truck out of town and up into the hills. It was less than a ten-minute drive, during which he called his sister Nirina and got the 411 on her last doctor appointment. Five months along, and mama and baby were doing just fine.

"When are you bringing Campbell Place Girl into the shop? We need a heads-up so we can dazzle her with our wares," Nirina chirped in his ear after she'd filled him in on all things baby.

"Listen, I *just* talked her into kissing me, and it took me three dates. Meeting the family's gonna take at least seven."

"Damn, Sy. You're losing your touch in your old age." At twenty-six, Nirina was the baby of the family. To her, anyone over thirty was old.

He slowed to make the turn onto Maggie's lane and noticed the deep ruts in the dirt that turned to black tire tracks on the asphalt. "Hey, I gotta go, Niri. Call you back."

Kevin, picking up on his concern, put his front paws on the dashboard and let out a low growl.

The ruts fishtailed back and forth on the narrow lane the whole length of the driveway. There was a gouge taken out of one of the tree trunks. He bet the car looked worse. Grimly, Silas tightened his grip on the wheel.

He was relieved to see Jim's van parked out front. A power washer hooked to a hose sat at the bottom of the porch steps. The front door behind the screen was open, and there was music, Whitesnake, coming from somewhere inside.

Silas pulled in behind the contractor's van and shoved the truck into park.

"Maggie!" It was not a friendly call. It was a summons.

He was halfway up the porch steps when she limped through the screen door.

"Oh, hey," she said, giving him a smile that pissed him off.

"Oh, hey? What in the hell happened?" he demanded, closing the distance and grabbing her by the shoulders.

She looked puzzled. "I just took a break from power washing—"

"Your driveway, Mags. It looks like someone turned it into a slalom. And why are you limping?"

"I stubbed my toe. Some kids showed up last night, not realizing the place was occupied, and I tiptoed around the side to give them a scare. Ended up tiptoeing right into a rock."

"You best back that story up and start from the beginning."

When she merely looked up at him, annoyed, he bared his teeth. "Now, Nichols."

He heard Jim hoot from somewhere inside, "She got him good and riled!"

"Stay out of this, Coach," Silas snapped.

"Leave Jim alone," Maggie shot back, daggers in her eyes. "Who do you think you are, showing up here and demanding to know shit that's none of your business?"

He leaned in dangerously close. "You're my business, Maggie. Whether you like it or not. Accept it or not. That kiss last night makes you my business."

"Please," she scoffed. "You don't get to go all Idaho cowboy just because we locked lips."

"Darlin', welcome to the Wild West."

"Oh, I want to slap the crap out of you right now," she hissed.

"I can't decide if I want to shake some sense into you or kiss the hell out of you."

"Maggie? I'm running into town. You want some ice for your foot?" asked Jim's guy, Rudy, a recent tech school graduate with a baby on the way.

"No, thanks, Rudy," she said without breaking eye contact with Silas.

"Really should get that looked at." Jim added his two cents, appearing behind Rudy. "Could be broken."

Maggie rolled her eyes and blew out a breath. "It's a toe, gentlemen. Not a femur. Can we all get back to work now?"

"Get her some ice," Silas told Rudy. "There's a ten spot in my cup holder."

"Ice is on me," Rudy said proudly. "Maggie bought us doughnuts this morning since she couldn't sleep from all the excitement last night."

"Tattletale," Maggie muttered under her breath as Rudy trotted past them. "Hey!" She pulled against his grip when Silas started dragging her toward the steps. "Hands off!"

He shoved her down on the top step. Kevin, unaware of any betrayal, plopped down next to her and begged shamelessly for belly rubs.

"Which foot?" Silas snapped.

The look she shot him could have peeled bark from trees. But one thing Maggie didn't know about him—when his dormant ire rose, shit burned down.

Finally, she acquiesced and pointed to her left foot and then yelped when he attacked her boot. He felt his nostrils flare at the effort it took to steady his hands. Easing the boot off her foot, he worked her sock free.

"Fuck me, Mags," he said when her bruised and swollen big toe came into view.

"That's definitely not happening now, buddy," she snapped, sounding good and surly.

Gently, he held her ankle in one hand and traced the tendons and bones in the foot with his other.

"Wiggle it," he ordered.

She did, and he heard her sharp intake of breath. He rested her foot on his knee and dug his phone out of the pocket of his shorts.

"What are you doing?" she demanded.

"Hey, Morris," he said into the phone when his stepfather answered.

"Silas! What brings you to my ear on this fine Saturday morning?"

"Have time to make a house call? I've got a mule-headed woman with a potentially broken big toe." He closed his fingers around the arch of her foot when she tried to pull away from him.

"I don't need medical attention. It's a fucking toe," she argued in a low voice.

"Shut up," he told her, covering the phone.

"I've got nothing but time, especially since this will get me out of helping your mom reorganize the pantry," Morris announced.

"The woman loves her alphabetized canned goods. I appreciate it." He looked at Maggie. "I'm up at the Old Campbell Place. Oh, and don't bring any lollipops. The patient doesn't deserve any."

Maggie flipped him the bird as he hung up.

"This high-handed, 'I'm in charge' bullshit does not fly with me," she announced.

"You either tell me what happened or I go inside and get Jim to tell me, since you had no problem talking to him. And if you make me hear this secondhand, I'll be very, very pissed off."

"For Pete's sake. It was no big deal. Four kids—teens—showed up here last night and tried to get in so they could drink their cheap garbage liquor. The front door was locked, and they were having a debate about going someplace else or breaking a window to get in when I scared the crap out of them. Most of them peeled out like it was the zombie apocalypse."

"What happened to your toe?"

"Jammed it on one of the stones on the terrace when I snuck around the side of the house."

He looked up and counted backward from ten. It didn't work. "You confronted a gang of trespassing criminals in the dark when they tried to break into your house?"

"They were teenagers with a bottle of Mad Dog, not mastermind villains," she argued.

"Did you call the cops?" Her hesitation had his blood pressure skyrocketing again. "Did you call Dean? Me? Anyone to come over so you wouldn't be alone if they came back?"

"No. I handled it."

"You need to get it out of your stubborn head that every single thing has to be handled by you."

She yanked her foot off his knee. "I don't *like* being handled, Wright."

"Yeah? Well, I don't like you taking unnecessary risks just because you think you're safer depending on yourself."

She scrambled to her feet on a gasp of indignation. "This is *exactly* why I don't tell people shit. You open up to some good-looking, landscaping jerk one time, and he can't wait to throw it in your face."

He rose to his full height. "Get over it, Nichols. And sit your ass down."

"You sit *your* ass down. In your truck. And drive away from here. Far away from here."

He reached for her and caught her because she was off her game. Cupping her chin in his hand, he leaned in. "This is one of those signs from the universe I was telling you about. You tell me you feel like you can't depend on anyone when really you're too scared to ask for help. And now you're paying for ignoring that sign with a busted-up toe and a pissed-off boyfriend."

His dog wedged himself between their feet and grumbled about the lack of attention.

"You are *not* my boyfriend. I really don't like you right now," she seethed.

"Be as pissed off as you want to. You know I'm right."

"Go home, Silas," she said. "If you're lucky, your crew will be allowed back on Monday."

They turned at the crunch of gravel. Dean pulled in next to Sy's truck and hopped out of his snappy little Mini Cooper.

"You two should be more careful with those sparks. You could burn this dump down," he said, clapping his hands and calling Kevin to him. The dog joyfully barreled into the man, and the two exchanged enthusiastic greetings.

"What's with the one shoe?" Dean asked. "You playing Cinderella?"

"Oh, allow me," Silas told Maggie with malicious glee.

She growled at him.

"Maggie here decided to bust up her big toe while trying to get the drop on a bunch of trespassers that tried to break in," Silas informed him.

Dean straightened up from the dog and shook his head. "Yeah. That sounds about right." He eyed the power washer. "You cleaning the shit you scared out of them off the porch?"

Kevin let out a bark and trotted a few yards down the driveway, where he stood his burly ground against a visitor that had shown up out of nowhere.

He was tall and gangly. His blond hair was in dire need of a cut, as a cowlick stood straight up at the back of his head. He'd seen the kid around town. Cody Moses. Rough family. There'd been some gossip recently that he couldn't quite remember.

"Kevin!" Maggie and Silas said together. The dog trotted back toward them, throwing interested glances over his shoulder.

"Do you want me to come back?" the kid asked.

"You're right on time, Cody," she said. "Come on in. Grab a doughnut. I've got a couple of questions for you when I'm done here."

Dean and Silas exchanged shrugs as Cody made his way up onto the porch. Kevin trotted over, gave the boy's jeans a sniff, and, deeming him safe, demanded pets.

"Dean, meet Cody. Cody stopped by last night to volunteer his services around here," Maggie said.

The kid didn't so much as wince as look resigned to servitude.

Silas ignored the "I told you so" look Maggie shot him.

"Well, isn't that nice of him?" Dean said, clearly trying to decipher the unspoken conversation happening between Maggie and Silas.

"Can you get him started with the steamer in the dining room while I say goodbye to Silas?" Maggie asked Dean.

"Sure. Come on in. See you around, Sly Sy," Dean said, leading the way inside. "You know anything about making coffee, Cody?"

"I'm not going anywhere," Silas warned her.

Hands on hips, she scowled up at him. "I've got a to-do list as long as my arm. I don't have time to argue with you, let alone justify my actions."

"Where's the list?"

She frowned at him.

"The list, Maggie," he growled.

"It's on the whiteboard," she said.

He stomped inside and found a small whiteboard on an easel in the front room. The woman probably owned stock in the company. She limped in behind him, mouth open and ready to go another round.

"Uh-uh," he said, drilling his finger into her shoulder. "You will sit and be nice to my stepfather and do exactly what he says."

"I have work—"

"You *are* work. I'll start at the top and work my way down. Whatever doesn't get done is *not* an emergency requiring you to limp around trying to finish up. Dean and Jim will back me up."

They both heard the car in the driveway. He poked her again. "Behave yourself."

"You're not actually going to—"

But he was already shoving his way out the screen door.

Not only had the woman confronted a pack of teens hell-bent on troublemaking, but she'd made one of them come back to get punished. Two things were certain: Maggie Nichols was a hell of a woman, and he was still very, very pissed off at her.

17

MORRIS THOMAS WAS a mild-mannered man with a soft voice, softer middle, and thick glasses. He showed up in an Idaho State University T-shirt, chunky outdoorsy sandals, and a backpack full of medical supplies. He looked utterly huggable.

"I'm sorry to waste your time," Maggie said as he carefully examined her foot and toes. "Silas overreacted." She said that last bit louder to make sure the man who was muscling the power washer around to the side of the house would hear her.

"If Silas is overreacting, you must really have had him worried," he said with a smile playing on his mouth.

"He doesn't need to worry about me," she grumbled.

"Don't be too hard on him," Morris advised, noting the glares Silas and Maggie exchanged. "My stepson has a big heart and usually a very long fuse. How does that feel?"

She winced as he poked and prodded. "It's okay."

"I don't suppose you're going to let me talk you into an X-ray at the urgent care?"

"I don't suppose I will," she agreed with a small smile.

"My best guess is it's a sprain. Rest. Ice. Keep it elevated. Some anti-inflammatories to help with the pain and swelling. Take it easy this weekend. As long as the swelling stays down and you're careful and you take regular breaks, you can be back on your feet Monday. You can try buddy taping it to the next toe. It'll take a few weeks to heal."

"Okay," she said. She must have answered a little too quickly because the PA sharpened his gaze.

"Your body needs energy to heal," he cautioned her. "Don't force it to expend that energy somewhere else less necessary."

"I have a timeline," she complained. Ugh. She hated whining almost as much as she hated not getting things done.

"You remind me of my lovely wife. Very smart. Very good at what she does. And very, very bad at remembering that getting ahead of the to-do list isn't the only way to be successful."

"Your wife sounds like someone I'd like," she mused.

They heard a snarled curse as the hose attached to the power washer whipped off the porch.

"I imagine she isn't the only one in the family you'd like," Morris guessed. "If it isn't getting better, I want you to go in for an X-ray. Now, what are we going to do this weekend?"

She sighed. "Rest. Ice. Elevation. Anti-inflammatories. Pout."

"It's a beautiful spring weekend. Might I suggest enjoying the view with a glass of wine and a good book?"

She didn't know what was odder, the suggestion or the fact that she couldn't remember the last time she'd done anything like that.

"Sounds great," she said lamely.

He patted her knee. "If you don't mind, I'm going to go ask Silas for a quick tour of the grounds. His mother and I are very proud of his work."

She opened her mouth to volunteer to lead the tour—after all, it was *her* yard—then shut it again when her toe throbbed in protest.

"Of course. Make sure he takes you up the path in the backyard."

"It was delightful meeting you, Maggie," he said, producing a lollipop from his backpack with a flourish.

She couldn't help but smile as she accepted the candy.

After a long, leisurely pout, Maggie gimped inside, following the sounds of arduous labor into the dining room. There she found the determined Cody steaming a section of god-awful plaid wallpaper between the windows. She flopped down on one of the dusty chairs and, because physician assistant's orders, propped her foot on the mahogany table.

"How's it going?" she asked. He'd made good progress in the hour he'd been at it.

Cody looked up from the steamer, his expression guarded. "Okay."

His attention returned to the task at hand. He'd made some slow, methodical progress, she noted. His patience had him making steadier gains than she would have. She'd been known to get frustrated with decades-old glue and take a belt sander to entire walls.

"Good. Hey," she said casually as she shifted to dig her phone out of her pocket, "the lighting's pretty good in here. Mind taking a picture of my gross toe so I can post it?"

If the kid thought it was a weird request—and who wouldn't think it was weird?—he didn't say anything. Instead he took the phone, tapped the screen a few times, and angled the lens this way and that.

"That work?" he asked, handing it back.

She glanced at the screen and felt the urge to do her "I was right" dance. But it would only further anger her toe. "Yeah. That works."

He'd screwed up, showed up when he said he would, accepted a half-assed punishment without complaint, and was doing a decent job. It made the decision an easy one in her mind.

"Dean!" she shouted in the direction of the hall.

"What do you want, woman?" he hollered back.

"Can you come down here?"

He came down the stairs grumbling. "What's your problem, Magpie?"

She handed him her phone.

"Gross. But great shot," he said.

"Thanks," she said dryly. "Cody took it."

He looked up at the kid. "Are you into photography?"

"I guess."

"I scrolled through his Instagram account last night," she told Dean. "He's good."

He managed to look both suspicious and hopeful. "Are you saying what I think you're saying?"

Maggie turned back to Cody. "How would you like a job?"

Cody dropped the steamer to his side. "I have one," he said slowly. Then his lips quirked. "It doesn't involve wallpaper."

She grinned. "Wallpaper removal sucks. What do you do?"

"I work a couple nights a week at a gas station in town." He said it while looking her in the eye, as if daring her to judge.

She nodded instead. "Must make you tired for school," she mused.

He gave a jerky, one-shoulder shrug, as if it didn't really matter.

"Dean and I could use some help around here. After school. On the weekends. Not construction," she clarified. "Pays fifteen dollars an hour to start. You'd be helping out with the technical stuff. Videos, photos, social media posts. Maybe some editing."

She saw the hunger, the *hope* when she named the pay. It made her feel impossibly sad for the boy already used to not belonging. But she could do this for him. And while it would cost her a little, it would be worth far more.

"We'll be in town at least three months," she told him.

"Probably closer to five," Dean cut in.

He was probably right. And five months would give the kid a lot more pocket change than night shifts at a gas station. More options after they were on to the next job, too.

"I'll take it," Cody said quickly.

"Do you need to talk to your parents?" she asked.

He shook his head, but she didn't miss the hardening in his eyes. "Nope."

"Great. You're hired," she told him.

Dean punched his fist into the air. "Eighteenth time's the charm!" he said, most likely referring to how many times he'd asked Maggie for help.

"Yeah, yeah, smart-ass. Give Dean here your lunch order for later. He's buying for all of us today."

"I won't even make dry-heaving noises when you lick your fry sauce straight out of the container," Dean promised Maggie. He danced over to her, grabbed her by the shoulders, and kissed her on the mouth.

"Get ahold of yourself, idiot." Maggie laughed.

Even Cody cracked a smile.

Kevin bounded into the room, happy to find so many people in one place.

"Looks like I'm missing a party," Silas drawled from the doorway. His T-shirt was damp. His hat was on backward, and he had little chips of paint clinging to the hair on his arms.

"Tour over already?" Maggie asked, extricating herself from Dean's embrace.

"It doesn't take long for family to recognize my genius. Unlike some others," Silas said pointedly.

"Don't worry, Sly Sy," Dean assured him. "I'm not moving in on your girl. I'm just thinking about what I'm going to do with my free time." With another whoop and an "Eh, what the hell?" he grabbed Sy by the neck of the damp T-shirt and laid a smacking kiss on him.

Maggie barely managed to smother her laugh when Dean released a dazed Silas.

"I get why she married you," Silas mused, recovering from the kiss.

"Should I come back?" a tentative voice asked from the doorway. The stranger was dressed like he was heading to the office instead of a job site on a Saturday morning. His skin was dark, his hair cut in a precise fade. He pushed his glasses up his nose in what looked more like a nervous habit than a necessary adjustment.

"Maggie, Dean, this is my brother, Michael," Silas said. "Mikey, this is Maggie Nichols and Dean Jensen from *Building Dreams*."

"Wow. Hi. It's great to meet you." Michael's head bobbed and then bobbed again. "I watch your show. A lot. Like every episode. You're great." He said it to Dean. Then blinked. "Uh, you *both* are great. And yeah. I'm gonna go now."

"We're kind of a big deal," Dean stage-whispered to Cody and then winked at Michael, who suddenly became very interested in the toes of his shoes. "You're welcome to hang out. I'm buying everyone lunch later." The tips of Dean's ears were turning pink.

Well, well, well, Maggie thought.

"Oh, I just stopped by to see Sy, since he bailed on paddleboarding this afternoon."

"Sy is free to keep those plans," she said quickly. "He's not needed here."

"Nice try, Nichols. You're not getting rid of me that easily," Silas said, his tone edging into sinister.

"Clearly these two need to finish their fight," Dean said to Cody and Michael. "Why don't we turn lunch into brunch and the three of us can run delivery service. If we're lucky, they'll have knocked the place down by the time we get back."

"Let's maybe not freak out our new hire?" Maggie suggested, no longer as amused.

"You're the one who asked him to take a picture of your feet and then confessed to stalking him on social media. I'm rescuing him before we end up in some creepy harassment lawsuit." Dean turned back to Cody. "Come with us, New Guy. Leave the steamer. You're above that now."

"I want a breakfast sandwich," Maggie called as they headed for the door.

"Yeah. Yeah. Egg, bacon, cheese croissant." Dean rattled off her favorite order. "Sy?"

"Sounds good to me," Silas said, without taking his eyes off Maggie.

Cody followed the elated Dean and the starstruck Michael to the doorway. He paused. "Thanks, Maggie," he said, his voice low and earnest.

"You're welcome," she said with a smile. "Welcome to the team."

Silas laid a hand on the kid's shoulder. "Let's walk and talk for a second," he said.

"Silas." Maggie packed a hard-to-ignore warning into those two syllables.

"It's happening whether you like it or not. Stay there. I'll be

back," he said, guiding the nervous-looking Cody out of the room
and toward the back of the house.

"Of all the high-handed, annoying, arrogant..." Maggie muttered
to herself until she heard the door to the sunporch squeak open
and shut.

She jumped out of her chair, wincing when her toe reminded her
it wasn't ready for speed, and then limped to the bay window.

Silas faced Cody on the ripped-up terrace. The kid didn't look
terrified exactly, but his shoulders were hunched almost up to his
ears. It looked as though Silas was doing most of the talking.

It wasn't up to him to discipline her employees or take care of her
problems. She didn't need someone overstepping and taking charge.

Cody was nodding now, arms crossed in front of his chest as he
stared at the ground.

She watched Silas lay a hand on the boy's shoulder. It didn't look
overtly threatening. Still, she was surprised when Cody cracked an
actual smile.

It was a short conversation with none of the yelling she'd expected.
And when it was over, they shook hands before parting. Cody jogged
toward the front of the house, but Silas stayed where he was...staring
right through the window at her. They studied each other through
the glass, and Maggie was the first to break. She limped out of the
room, down the hall, and into her office.

She pretended she was deeply intrigued by a spreadsheet when
Silas appeared in the doorway a minute later.

"Now it's your turn," he said.

She kicked back in her chair and crossed her arms. "On top of
all of the things that aren't your business, let's add disciplining my
employees without my express permission."

He strolled into the room and studied the whiteboard in the corner
and the boxes of half-packed treasures. He looked much too casual for
her liking. The man should be adrenalized and pissed off and feeling
ready to boil. Like she felt.

"I didn't discipline the kid," he told her. "I had a conversation with him about expectations and how you just handed him one hell of an opportunity and he'd better not blow it by doing something stupid like last night."

"That's a conversation that didn't need to come from you," she pointed out.

"Tough shit. It did. I also reminded him that it would be in his best interests to make sure his friends never show up here again without an engraved invitation and that if he even hears a whisper of them thinking about it, to call me."

"Don't you think this protector routine is over-the-top? We kissed. I'm not something you ordered online and now own."

"I'm looking out for you, for him, and for the work all your crews have done and will do. It's not a win for any of us if a couple of bored kids show up and cause trouble. And it's certainly not in Cody's best interest to get caught doing petty shit at eighteen, when the consequences are a hell of a lot more serious."

He prowled toward her, and Maggie felt her pulse rate jump. She wasn't sure if it was nerves or lust. Because while easygoing, good-guy Silas was sexy, pissed-off Silas was dangerously attractive.

He placed his hands on the worktable behind her, caging her in between his arms. "Now, let's get back to the 'you not being my business' thing. I don't know how many guys you've kissed like you kissed me, but to me, it means something."

She opened her mouth to argue but then thought better of it.

"The way you reacted to me last night has me thinking about nothing but your mouth. You gave yourself up to that kiss, to me." There was fire in his gray eyes, turning them to silver. "You woke up something in me, and I gave you something you needed. We're going to see where this goes. As soon as you apologize."

The last word finally drilled through the cloud of lust that had all her attention focused on the firm mouth that was just inches from hers. "Apologize? For what?"

He brought his hand to her face, fingers skimming along her jawline, setting her skin on fire. The way he tucked her hair

behind her ear seemed gentle, but there was an underlying threat
of...possession. She wanted to hate it. She wanted to smack him in
his smug face. She wanted to grab him by the front of his damp
T-shirt and kiss the hell out of him.

"For taking unnecessary risks with something that's important to
me." His voice was low, but she could feel the heat of his breath
on her face.

She thought he made the move, but somewhere in the recesses
of her mind, Maggie realized that it was her fist closing around his
shirt. Her dragging him down.

And then, as their mouths crashed into each other, it was him
lifting her out of the chair. Picking her up like she was a bag of
cement, wrapping her legs around his waist, and pressing her against
the wall. Pinning her there with his hips. He smelled like sunshine
and water, tasted like salt.

She knew she was supposed to be mad. Should be kicking him in
the balls right about now, but she was having a hard time remembering why she'd want to do anything but let him kiss her like this.

His tongue was working some kind of magic in her mouth.
She couldn't quite catch her breath—it seemed as though he were
stealing it.

One of them growled. She couldn't tell who because she was too
busy shoving her hands into his hair, knocking his hat off his head,
and wishing away the layers of clothing that separated her core from
the hard-on he was sporting.

Then suddenly she was flying or falling or floating. And his mouth
was gone from hers. She felt the metal of the chair under her as he
put her back with care.

She was panting and dazed. He looked...hungry.

"Scared the hell out of me, Mags," he breathed. "Don't let it
happen again."

She blinked up at him, trying to find her way out of the
lust fugue.

He straightened and took a deliberate step back, shifting gears despite the impressive bulge in his shorts that she couldn't quit staring at.

"Power washing's done. I'll get started on the next item on your list before the guys come back with the food. You're in charge of the paperwork while you rest, ice, and elevate."

He started for the doorway but then paused.

"Oh, and, Mags? If I catch you stomping around, trying to tackle some job you're already paying someone else to do, I will tie you to your chair."

LeafBritneyALoan: Maggie's toe legit looks like it's going to fall off. SO GROSS!

FlowerGurl4Life: OMG! The pics of Maggie with the little girl she met in town. Dying! The cutest! Maggie Nichols is the NICEST HUMAN EVER. Also so excited to see the first episode of the new house!

DaaaaaamnGirl: That toe is definitely broken. You need this new healing paste from Organiks For Life. It's lifechanging. DM me for a sample!

18

FOR THE REST of the weekend, Maggie followed physician assistant's orders and rested, iced, and elevated. Besides giving the promised tour to Mateo, his wife, and Isabella from the restaurant, she'd used the unscheduled downtime to crack open A. Campbell's first novel. Historical western fiction had never made it onto her To Be Read list before. But she'd found it entertaining all the same, even going so far as to put a plug for *Sunset on the Horizon* up on Instagram.

May began, and the cure to a Silas Wright Lust Fugue, Maggie found, was to never be alone with the man. To be fair, it wasn't difficult, since he was still just as mad at her as she was at him. It had been over a week since their fight-kiss. And Sy's stupid ultimatum.

They glowered at each other whenever the job required them to be in the same vicinity. Though Maggie wasn't sure how much of it was mad and how much of it was a ridiculous desire to rip each other's clothes off. Either way, it seemed safer to avoid the man.

Elton, Bitterroot Landscapes' second-in-command, had taken over the daily walk-throughs, since his boss and Maggie couldn't seem to get along long enough to not take a few swipes at each other.

Thanks to her jacked-up toe, she'd had a lot of downtime to think about all the wild and wonderful ways Sy could use those big hands and hard mouth on her. She couldn't remember the last time she'd ever been this hung up on a guy. They weren't even dating. It felt like an out-of-control teenage crush. On steroids. In an inferno.

Even when he wasn't on-site, she was thinking about him. It was fucking annoying. She wasn't going to apologize to him for looking out for herself. Not even if an apology meant Silas would get off his high horse and into her pants. She had morals. She had ethics. She had...lady blue balls.

That afternoon, Maggie waved off the last of the tradesmen and debated whether she should shower first before heading into town to the inn.

The debate was put on hold when a yellow SUV crawled toward the house. Beyoncé carried through the open windows until the driver cut the engine and stepped out of the car.

She was fitness-model lean with a sassy, messy bob haircut. Athletic, attractive. She took off her sunglasses and eyed Maggie with curiosity. Then she squared her shoulders and approached.

"Maggie Nichols?" she asked.

"That's me," Maggie answered, leaning against the porch post.

"I'm Michelle."

Uh-oh. Michelle as in Silas Wright's ex Michelle?

"I dated Silas Wright."

Yep. That's the one. Well, this should be interesting. And hopefully not terrifying.

"What can I do for you?" Maggie asked.

"Don't worry. I'm not here to hack you into pieces or hurl insults and tell you to stay away from 'my man,'" she said, adding air quotes.

"Well, that's a relief," she said to Michelle.

"I was just dropping by to say thank you."

People sure drop by a lot around these parts.

"Thank you for what, exactly?" Maggie asked.

"I know Sy's told you about us and our on-again, off-again...thing."

"He may have mentioned it."

"And I know he's interested in you," Michelle added.

Maggie wasn't sure how to respond to that.

"I also know my boy-crazy cousin made a pass at him in front of you," Michelle continued. "She's nineteen. Anyway, I guess I'm dropping by to say thank you and apologize for my idiot cousin."

"Do you want a drink or something?" Maggie asked, hooking her thumb toward the house.

"No. Thanks," Michelle said. "I'm actually hitting the road. You're my last stop."

Maggie noticed that the SUV was full. Suitcases. Boxes. *Dear God.* Had she somehow accidentally chased this woman out of her hometown?

"Anyway," Michelle pressed on, sticking her sunglasses in the scoop neck of her T-shirt. "Silas was my dream guy in high school. I had the biggest crush on him. It seemed only natural that we'd end up together as adults. Both being single. Both still here in Kinship. But it never quite worked. And I think I held on for too long because of that teenage fantasy, you know?"

Maggie nodded. "I am familiar with that particular experience."

"We just never fit right. But we were convenient, and part of me thought that, if we just tried a little harder, we could make it work. We could do the marriage-and-kids thing. And I could tell everyone that I won at life with my high school sweetheart."

She put a foot on the first step and looked around the yard.

"But when something's not right, it's not right, and no amount of forcing it will make it right. And then you showed up."

"Silas and I aren't actually dating," Maggie interrupted. "We're not anything. Unless fighting is something. In fact, we kind of can't stand the sight of each other right now."

Michelle gave her a small, sad smile. "Sy and I never fought. Maybe that was part of what didn't work. Neither one of us cared enough to fight."

Maggie thought of herself and Dean as newlyweds. They hadn't fought either.

"You showing up here, you taking that safety net away from me, was the best thing that could have happened to me," Michelle announced. "I'd always planned on moving away. Living and working in a city. I want the hustle and energy. Tall buildings and seeing strangers every day. When Silas came into the picture, I just never got around to getting there."

"So you're leaving now?" Maggie asked.

Michelle grinned. "It's about damn time I start living the life I want, right?"

"Never too late," Maggie agreed.

"Anyway, I wanted to thank you. I got a job in Denver. An apartment that I can almost afford. And I'm finally excited about something, you know? I feel like my life is really starting."

"I think the credit belongs to you," Maggie insisted.

"I might have gotten there eventually, but Sy and I always got back together. You took him out of the equation. At least long enough for me to start looking past what I tried to talk myself into wanting. So thank you."

"Then I guess you're welcome. And good luck with everything. New beginnings are exciting."

"Thanks!" Michelle chirped, sliding her sunglasses back on. "Listen, even if you're fighting now, give the guy a chance. He's the best. He deserves the best. And the best is definitely *not* my cousin Arabella."

Maggie didn't know what to say. So she nodded instead.

"Okay. Well, here I go," Michelle said.

"It was nice meeting you," Maggie said.

"You, too. Maybe I'll see you around when I come back for Christmas," Michelle said, with an eyebrow wiggle.

"What took you so long?" Dean demanded when he flung open his door. "You get lost and try to cook the food yourself?"

His room at the inn was a suite with a small sitting area that overlooked rolling green lawn and forest.

"Ha. I had to wait for *your* dumb gluten-free breadsticks," Maggie said, pushing the bags into his hands and slipping off her flip-flops. "And before that, Sy's ex-girlfriend dropped by to say thanks for making their breakup permanent."

"Did she thank you with a boiled bunny casserole?" he asked, already digging through the bags of food.

"No. She was being serious. She's using the opportunity to move out of state."

"Did you tell her you guys aren't even knocking boots because you're too proud to beg?" he asked, leading the way to the striped roll-arm couch. Their YouTube channel was already cued up on the TV.

She picked up her own gigantic salad and followed. She flopped down and propped her foot up on the coffee table. "We're not having sex because I don't want to have sex with some possessive, egotistical, alpha hero."

"Yes, you do."

"Shut up."

"Your toe looks slightly less disgusting," he said, pointing at her foot with the remote.

She glanced down. The bruising had morphed from a dark purple to a nauseating greenish yellow. "Feels mostly better," she said. She hated to admit it, but taking that one weekend off from physical labor had been...nice. She'd caught up on her budget updates, written two blogs, dug further into her research into Aaron Campbell and his wife, and gotten ahead on her social media scheduling.

And she'd actually dragged a lawn chair out onto the lawn for an hour both days and enjoyed the view...with her phone and laptop, of course.

"She wanted me to know that Silas is a good guy."

"So you're thinking he paid her off?" he teased.

She jabbed him playfully with her plastic fork. "No. I'm thinking what kind of guy gets that kind of loyalty from an ex?"

"Uh. Hello?" Dean said, raising his hand.

"We didn't tell people we had been married," she reminded him, scooping up zucchini and corn and tomato with her fork. "Not on the channel."

"True. But you also never complain about your super-gay

ex-husband. Because I'm awesome, and you recognize my awesome-ness. Maybe 'These Boots Were Made for Walking' Michelle just wants to make sure you know how awesome Sly Sy is."

"That's the second boot reference in under three minutes. Where are they?"

He perked up. "There's this disgustingly adorable shoe store at the end of town. Do you think I can pull off cowboy boots?"

She glanced down at his avocado-and-toast socks, pretended to ponder. "I'd need to see them on you," she decided. "Wanna go Saturday?"

He dropped his fork in his salad and sat up with ramrod posture. "Did you just ask me to take you shopping?"

"What? We shop together all the time."

"We *used* to. I'm personally responsible for every cute item in your wardrobe that you left behind in Seattle."

She wanted to argue, but there wasn't a point in fighting the truth. "I could use a few basics," she said. "Plus, I really want to see these cowboy boots."

"Drinks before or after?" he asked, shifting into planning mode.

"During. You have an easier time talking me into things when I've had alcohol."

"Then we're definitely hitting up this place I saw yesterday. They make all their drinks with their own rye whiskey. Maybe we can get a pitcher of mint juleps and then go buy hats," he mused.

Maggie laughed.

"I do think you should sleep with Sy," he said, picking up his iced tea.

"Why?"

"First of all, it would be a waste not to. He's great. He's smart. He works hard. He looks like he stepped off the September page in a calendar of hot guys with rescue dogs. He's nice to his crew. He's not intimidated by your success."

"Maybe that's because he didn't know what YouTube was before I asked him if he'd be comfortable being on it."

Dean sighed in appreciation. "The whole anti–social media thing is kinda hot all by itself. Like he's too busy whitewater rafting and smelling roses to worry about a bunch of strangers online."

"A bunch of strangers online are why we're in business," she pointed out.

"Then there's the whole chemistry thing," he continued, ignoring her. "These smoldering looks of 'I wanna rip your face off' that pass between you guys. And the way he watches you when you're not looking. It's like you're a pretty iced cupcake, and he's a hungry, horny lion ready for his next meal."

She snorted. "That's the most disturbing metaphor you've ever come up with."

"Admit it," he said, poking her with his elbow. "He's your cup-cake, too. Who doesn't want a guy who's easygoing and relaxed on the outside and then BAM!"

Maggie jumped when he slammed his hand on the coffee table.

"I'm here to take care of you, woman, whether you want me to or not," he said in a deep baritone.

"I don't want to be taken care of! I don't like how he thinks he can handle me," she admitted to her salad.

"Magpie, you need someone who can handle you. We *all* need someone who can handle us. The problem isn't the handling; it's when it's not for your own good."

"That doesn't sound accurate. Shouldn't we all be able to handle ourselves?"

"What fun is handling ourselves? It's more fun to handle and be handled."

She wrinkled her nose. "Now you're just being gross."

"Sex is a natural, healthy part of life. Some would argue it's the best part of life. Of course, 'some' wouldn't be you, since you're too chicken to jump the hot guy."

"He wants me to apologize for something that wasn't wrong," she complained.

"What did you do?"

"He thinks I should have called the cops and him or you when Cody and his friends showed up and tried to get in the house."

Dean was suspiciously quiet.

"What?" she demanded. "You didn't give me a hard time about it."

He dug around in his salad. "Maybe that's because I knew it would be a waste of my time."

"You're not saying it bothered you that I didn't call you to come save me."

"I'm saying he's not wrong. It was a dumbass move to walk right up to the strangers trying to break into your house."

"It was fine. Nothing happened."

"Something could have. What's the first thing I did when that drunk white lady hit my Fiat after all-you-can-drink mimosas in Tacoma?"

"You called the cops."

"After that."

"Your insurance company."

The sigh he heaved was dramatic. "After that."

"You called me," she said.

"You picked me up, drove me to urgent care, and then took me straight to the car rental place and made me get a dumb SUV with four hundred airbags."

"All things I'm sure you could have done on your own," she pointed out.

"THAT'S THE POINT!" Dean howled.

"Geez. Dial it down before your neighbors call the front desk! *What's* the point?"

"It meant something to me that you cared enough to show up and be there in my time of trauma. And I bet it meant something to *you* that I called you for help."

Shit.

"People don't bond over small talk and a fancy dinner out," he explained. "They don't bond over nice, normal things. We bond over getting T-boned by Felicias. Or a broken pipe that ruins brand-new hardwood floors. Or divorce or cancer or a house fire or the death of a really great mom." He reached out and squeezed her hand to take the sting out of it.

She took a breath and blew it out again.

"Magpie, when you deal with everything on your own, you're robbing the people who care about you of their chance to be there for you, with you. And that's why you should apologize and have sex with Silas."

"Excuse me. Don't we have a rule about sex with contractors?" she reminded him.

"Don't we make the rules? Doesn't that mean we can change the rules when it suits us?"

"That's not how rules are supposed to work," she said dryly.

He threw his head back against the couch and groaned. "You know how you sound? Bo-ring. Like a little old lady in a pearl-buttoned cardigan tattling on Gladys across the table at bingo night. There is a whole big world out there, little girl. Bigger than houses that need flipping and subscriber counts and amassing piles of cash for what? A rainy day?"

"Are you having a midlife crisis?"

"One of us has to."

"You have the midlife crisis, and I'll have the existential crisis," she volunteered.

"Does that mean I can date a much younger man?" Dean asked thoughtfully.

"How old is Sy's brother, Michael?" She hid her smug smile behind one of the breadsticks. It wasn't half bad.

"How should I know how old he is?" His shrug was careless, but his ears were turning pink again.

"He seemed a little starstruck by you. Of course, I guess we don't know if he's gay or straight," she mused.

"Oh, he's gay," he said with authority. "But newly gay. You know I prefer to jump right in instead of playing gay tutor."

"Huh. That's a shame. He was cute. Seemed like the monogamous, dog-park-on-a-Saturday kind of guy. But I guess if you're too chicken—"

"Listen here, missy!"

Maggie stabbed him with the end of a breadstick. "It sucks, doesn't it, when your mean friend points out when you're possibly being a chickenshit?"

"Point taken. From now on, we'll champion each other's terrible decisions. You stay far away from that sexy landscaper who wants to tear your clothes off."

"And you should definitely avoid a hookup with his adorable brother who definitely goes to the gym and thinks you're gorgeous."

"So glad we agree," he said, pushing play.

Out of habit, they shoulder-shimmied and couch-danced to the short theme song.

"Your hair is a foot longer than it was when we shot this," Dean said.

"It was a month ago, not a year," she reminded him. "I miss your goatee."

"Facial hair is for fall and winter."

"How'd it go with Cody today?" she asked, changing the subject.

He chewed up a mouthful of grilled chicken. "Great. Good kid. Picks stuff up fast. Knows a hell of a lot more about photo editing than I do, and he's got great hookups for royalty-free music."

"Good."

"He's never edited video before, so there's a learning curve. But he did great with shooting. I cut him loose early today because he's got a big test in history or something boring tomorrow. It makes me feel ancient when he mentions high school."

Maggie felt her lips quirk. In many ways, she still felt like a lost twenty-two-year-old looking for answers.

"And get this. I think he's couch surfing. The kid let it slip that his parents don't live in town anymore. I asked around, and it sounds like the dad left town a few years ago, and the mom was wanted for some kind of half-assed identity theft scheme and left about a month ago."

"He's homeless?"

"And practically orphaned. He's your people," he said.

"We're gonna have to do something about that. Good thing I have a seven-bedroom house."

"You can't stay there alone with him."

"What is this, eighteenth-century London? Is my reputation that fragile?"

"I'm just saying. Word gets out that you're shacking up with an eighteen-year-old guy, and people are going to say stupid things."

"Guess you're going to have to move in, too."

"I already started packing. But this means you need to redo some bedrooms and bathrooms stat because I am not bringing my very expensive skin care products into a bathroom with carpet on the walls."

She leaned her head on his shoulder as the camera zoomed in on a pastel pink toilet. "I'm sorry for not calling you. I do need you."

"You're forgiven. Now consider saying it to Silas so you two can stop terrifying everyone on the job."

"I'll think about it."

"I still hate that tile on the bathroom floor," he said, pointing his fork at the screen.

RedHairDontKare: Dean is right. That bathroom floor tile is barftastic.

TomatoWarefare: Maggie just gets prettier and prettier every episode. Also, I want to live in that beach house.

SirFartsAlot: Do we know why Maggie and Dean aren't together? Are they related? They seem like such a good couple!

CulpepperVicky: Maggie come to Culpepper and help me redo my house! I've got tequila!

19

SILAS CURSED AS the dark clouds above them opened with little warning, hurling huge raindrops toward the earth. The crews scrambled to cover tools and materials as the rain soaked them.

A shrill whistle cut through the chaos. "Everybody inside," Maggie called from the door to the sunroom.

"You heard the boss," Silas said. "Move it." The siding and landscape crews filed inside just as a roll of thunder rattled the windowpanes.

"Make yourselves at home, gang. Pizza's on the way," she announced, avoiding his gaze like she'd been doing all week. Her tank top was soaked and clinging to her body. She had a smear of dirt on one bicep and sawdust in her hair. Silas wanted to pick her up and bite her.

"Good thing you got yourselves a new roof," Lewis, the foreman for the siding company from nearby Abileen, said as fat drops slashed at the windows and roared off the roof of the porch.

"Yeah, too bad the gutter folks weren't on the schedule until next week," Dean complained, eyeing the overflowing spouting.

"Shouldn't there be a kitchen around here somewhere?" Lewis asked, observing the still gutted space that they'd all crowded into. The old fridge was plugged in on the wall next to a rickety set of shelves that housed a coffeemaker, paper plates, cups, and a roll of paper towels. A folding worktable acted as a temporary countertop.

Hopeful-looking paint swatches were taped up on the wall where cabinets should have been.

"This room is cursed," Dean told him. "First the cabinets Maggie ordered mysteriously went out of stock. Then the tile for the floor came in wrong."

"It's not cursed," she argued. "It's just completely behind schedule. Two totally different things."

"Maybe it's the ghost of Ava Campbell," Jim said, poking his head into the room. "She might not like you messing with her kitchen. Rumor has it she enjoyed cooking. She'd even send the staff home and cook dinner for the family herself."

"I think Mrs. Campbell's ghost will be very happy with the end result," Maggie told him. "How'd it go upstairs?"

"Both bedrooms are in pretty good shape," he reported. "Hardwood could use some refinishing, but it's not an emergency."

"How about the bathrooms?"

Silas saw Jim wince. "About as bad as yours."

Maggie sighed. "Better focus on those this week. I'll be needing them by the weekend."

Silas wanted to ask what the rush was on bedrooms and bathrooms, but they were still locked in a battle of wills until he was confident that she'd cave. Maybe he looked like a "kicked-back tree-hugger"— his sister's words—but inside, he had a stubborn streak when it came to justice.

"Can I talk to you?" Maggie asked softly, appearing at his elbow.

Victory was his.

"Ah, crap," Elton grumbled, digging for his money clip. "I had next Tuesday."

"I had next month," Travis said glumly.

His mooney-eyed teenage employee should have known better. "Y'all maybe want to shut it?" Silas said, shoving them out of Maggie's path.

"Had what?" she asked, eyes narrowing.

"You two making up," Travis said, even moonier than usual.

She looked like she was changing her mind, so Silas took matters into his own hands and dragged her out of the room, down the hall, and into the newly created powder room behind the staircase.

"Watch the tile. We didn't grout yet," she warned, stepping carefully to the middle of two oversize slate tiles.

He shut the door, looked for the light switch, and found the fixture missing. It was a small space and dark except for the light coming in through a slim, stained-glass window.

Silas leaned against the wall and crossed his arms to keep himself from putting his hands on her.

"I don't know if I want to talk, now that I know there was action on it," she grumbled.

"If it makes you feel better, I had us making up days ago. I had no idea you'd be able to resist me for this long."

She pursed her lips, a gesture he found erotically enchanting. "That does make me feel marginally better," she admitted.

He stayed silent while she ran a finger along the edge of the vanity. She'd gone with a dresser style in here. Painted a dark green with a simple granite top.

"I guess I wanted to say maybe you had a point, and maybe I owe someone an apology. I'm still not sure that someone is you though."

He grinned. "Wow. You're really bad at this."

"Oh, shut up. I still think you're overstepping into areas where you have no responsibility."

"But," he prodded.

"But..." She paused and took a breath like she was working herself up to do something she didn't want to do. "I'm sorry I worried you. And I'm sorry I took unnecessary risks. And just because I'm saying I'm sorry doesn't mean that I want to date you or—"

He stepped onto the tiles in front of hers. "I'm sorry for maybe possibly slightly overreacting and scaring you off with my Fix It Better routine. But I want to be the one you call, Maggie."

"I'm only here for—"

He pressed his index finger to her lips. "I want to be the one you call," he said again.

Those whiskey-warm eyes were wide, and the flutter of her pulse at the base of her neck fascinated him.

"Can I be the one you call? I'll accept it if Dean's the first call. For now. But I want to make the short list."

She hesitated, and it made him hold his breath. "Okay," she said finally, against his finger.

He withdrew it. "Then I'm good. Are you good?" he asked.

She looked at him suspiciously, like she couldn't believe making up could be that easy. "I'm good," she said, then held out her hand.

He grinned down at it. "Darlin', that's not how we seal deals."

The momentary flash of panic and anticipation in those pretty brown eyes when he leaned in tickled him.

"This is how we seal the deal," he whispered.

He nudged her chin higher. She was already parting her lips for him when his mouth found hers. It was supposed to be soft, sweet. Not a blood-stirring mauling. But once again, he'd underestimated his control when it came to touching Maggie.

She clung to the front of his wet shirt like he was an anchor steadying her in the storm. But he was the storm. He devoured her mouth, savored the slide of her tongue against his, and celebrated the way she pressed her body against his. He reached for her ponytail, using it to tug her head back. His blood was electrified as he breathed her in.

Rain pattered hard on the window, and a flash of lightning outside felt like fireworks when the thunder rumbled on its heels.

It's a sign, he figured. All his years of kissing women and she was the first one who made him lose his damn mind in the process.

"Um," Maggie managed when he pulled back.

He grinned down at her, settling his hands on her shoulders.

"Is this how you seal all your deals in Idaho?" she asked, taking a self-preserving step back.

"Only the good ones." He winked.

The house suddenly filled with what sounded like a funeral organ. "What the hell was that?"

"Pizza's here," she said, reaching around him for the doorknob. "What does this all mean?" she asked.

He knew she wasn't talking about doorbells or pizza toppings. "It means we see where this goes."

"It can't go far," she warned him. "I'm not staying."

"My nice crisp five dollars says otherwise," Silas said, opening the door for her. He could already smell garlic and tomato sauce.

"Sy." She stopped him in the hall with a hand on his arm. "It's not a game. I don't want either one of us getting hurt."

He slung an arm around her shoulder and pulled her against him. "I know, darlin'. But it's bound to happen. The sooner you accept that, the sooner we can start havin' a good time. Not getting hurt isn't a good enough reason to not enjoy yourself. You tell me when you're ready."

He gave her another squeeze before releasing her and whistled his way in the direction of pizza and chatter.

They gathered in the front rooms, where the floors had been sanded down and most of the wallpaper stripped. It already felt lighter and brighter in here. And filled with a dozen workers, the house seemed like it was alive.

"Maggie, you ever think about getting some furniture?" Jim asked from his perch on a toolbox.

"How do you watch TV?" Marta wanted to know.

Maggie wandered over to the pizza boxes and selected a loaded slice. "What would I do with a couch and a TV?" she asked.

"Maybe relax for thirty minutes?" Dean suggested from his perch in the bay window across the hall.

"Then who would run the rest of your asses ragged while I had my feet up watching soap operas?" she teased.

Silas glanced around and gave it some thought. The woman was living and working in a construction zone. She was camping under a roof. It sure made it easier to consider circumstances temporary when they were that far from comfortable.

An idea began to take root. A diabolical one.

He got drawn into a good-natured argument with Jim about the high school team's shot at the state wrestling title next school year and let the idea start to bloom.

The rain wasn't letting up, and the play-by-play from everyone's weather apps didn't make any outdoor work likely until after four. The siding crew called it a day and made a mad dash for their trucks. While Silas convened his guys in the dining room to plan for the next day, Maggie wandered by with a bucket of hot, soapy water.

"Anyone seen Kevin?" Silas asked, noticing his dog wasn't around, mooching leftovers.

"Not since he took the pizza crust off my plate," Rudy reported.

Dismissing his crew, Silas stood in the rotunda and called for his dog. But the burly beast didn't come running.

"I think he's upstairs," Dean called out from the kitchen, where he was starting the coffeemaker. "I passed him on the stairs a while ago. He had a pizza crust in his mouth like a stogie."

Silas rolled his eyes and jogged up the sweeping staircase. He poked his head into the back bedrooms on the second floor. It looked like someone was definitely moving in up here.

A loud snore caught his attention from the front of the house.

He found Kevin curled up under the covers on a cot in the middle of the biggest bedroom Silas had ever seen. Maggie's room. Tall, skinny doors led out to a balcony. A deep seat was built into a huge window, framing in the view of river and mountains.

The view was the only thing the room had going for it. The cot was pushed up against a wall where a king-size bed should be. Next to it was a small coffeemaker on the floor. Next to *that* was a painting of Mr. and Mrs. Campbell propped up against the wall. There was a power strip near the bed that housed a variety of chargers and a stack of spreadsheets and blueprints.

The woman even worked in bed.

Kevin gave another enthusiastic snore. His tail wagged under the thin blanket. Silas sighed, snapped a picture, and headed back downstairs.

He found Maggie and Dean in the study at the front of the house.

"Who wants to read a book next to a fire guarded by a gargoyle?" Dean complained, eyeing the fireplace surround currently being attacked by a scrub-brush-wielding Maggie.

It was a rainy afternoon, and Maggie Nichols was hell-bent on not taking advantage of it.

"Who doesn't?" Sy and Maggie said together. She shot him a considering look.

Dean pinched the bridge of his nose. "I'm gonna need you two to spend more time apart. I can only deal with one Maggie at a time."

"Mags, how upset are you going to be if I tell you one of my crew decided to eat pizza and take a nap in your bed?" Silas asked.

She looked up and gave him her first real grin since the fight. It made him feel like some kind of champion. "I take it you found Kevin?"

He showed her the picture.

"Now, that's someone who knows how to use his afternoon off," Dean said behind Maggie's back. He pointed at her and then twirled his finger around his ear. "Don't think you can work me around the clock when I move in."

She glanced at Silas. "Not that you need to know, but Dean and Cody are moving in."

"Kid was couch surfing," Dean explained. "I've got a call in five. I'll be upstairs with a vat of coffee if you need anything."

He waited until Dean was gone before perching on the wide sill of the front window.

"No lecture on letting strange teenagers move in?" Maggie asked.

He held up his hands. "None from me. I asked around. Consensus is he's a good kid from a crap family. Also his grades suck."

"I don't know how much help I'll be with homework," she mused.

"Was this Campbell's study?" he asked, examining the coffered ceiling above.

"I think so," she said as she vigorously scrubbed at the blackened marble surround. "All of his books were on the shelves in here. I boxed most of them up so they wouldn't get damaged, but I read the first one. It was good."

"I liked it," he said. "It had a little bit of everything. Action. Adventure. Romance. Treasure."

She paused her scrubbing. "You read it?"

"I read all of them. I'm from Kinship. A. Campbell is practically required reading here."

She shifted on her knees to get a better angle.

"Watch your head," he warned.

She looked up at the mantel jutting out above her and then froze.

"What? Spider? I can be your hero and trap the long-legged little bastard," Silas offered, standing up.

But she was reaching into the bucket and pulling out a wet cloth. "Not a spider. Not sure what it is." She reached up under the mantel and gently began to scrub.

He got down next to her. There was a perfect circle embedded in the bottom of the mantel.

"It looks like one of the souvenir coins they sell downtown," she noted as the gold finish began to glint through the baked-on soot.

He took the rag from her and worked at the center. "Well, I'll be damned," he murmured.

"Why would Campbell or someone hide a fake gold coin in his study?" Maggie wondered aloud.

"Darlin', there's nothing fake about this gold."

"Are you sure?" she asked, scooting closer to him.

"Just about certain. This is the Wild West, remember? We're born knowing real gold from fake."

"Let me get my camera," she announced. She sounded excited, like a kid just before going downstairs on Christmas morning.

He kept at it until he'd managed to clean off most of the muck and found himself staring at an honest-to-goodness gold coin.

When she returned with the camera, he was flat on his back, staring up at the coin. He heard the click of the shutter and glanced her way.

"Just documenting the find," she said.

He rose up on his elbow and patted the hearth next to him. "Come on down, darlin'."

Shaking her head, she took another picture.

"What was that one for?"

"I might frame it and call it the Playboy Prospector," she teased, joining him in front of the fireplace.

She lay back and wiggled into place so her head was next to his. She was looking up at the coin, but Silas was watching her face.

"I kinda like being in this position with you," he said.

She rolled her head to the side to give him a glare. "Focus, Wright."

"Oh, I am, Mags. I'm focusing on a nice comfortable mattress. Clean sheets. Rain on the window. Your hair spilling out like—"

"Silas. Aren't you the least bit excited?"

"I'm real excited," he promised darkly. He trailed a finger down her neck to the delicate ridge of her collarbone.

"You're terrible," she whispered. But there were goose bumps cropping up on her skin. She extended her arms and framed the coin on the camera screen. "I never found gold before. Matchbooks. Every back issue of *Bikini Babes*. A rat skeleton. But no gold."

She took several shots and then tried a few other angles to catch the raised detail on its surface.

"Now we just need to figure out how to search for gold coin designs. I wonder if a reverse image search would work?" Maggie mused.

"I can do you one better than some online search," he said, patting her leg. "Come on."

He climbed to his feet and helped her up.

"Where are we going?"

"Into town."

*　　*　　*

Fortyflirty: Did anyone else catch the hot, dirty landscaper in the background of Dean's video on FB today? Just me?

JesusLuvsMe39: I HATE HATE HATE the tile she picked for the main bathroom. Ugh! Maggie has lost her touch. This show is basically one giant homage to horrible taste.

Leo4Life: A low maintenance woman who can swing a sledgehammer like that? Marry me, Maggie!

20

THEY LEFT KEVIN snoring in Maggie's bed and headed into Kinship in Silas's truck. She'd changed into clean jeans, a tank, and a soft cardigan that had him fantasizing about her wearing nothing but it and a pair of easily removable underwear.

The rain had slowed to a steady patter on the windshield. It was the perfect afternoon to slow down.

"Got time for a detour?" he asked, pulling up to the first traffic signal at Kinship's town limits.

She frowned. "Detour?"

"My source has something going on this afternoon until two. We've got some time to kill."

"I could have finished cleaning the surround," she complained.

His girl was wound tight.

"Trust me. You'll like this."

"You always say that just before you try to talk me into something I don't want to do."

He slipped his fingers through hers and brought the back of her hand to his mouth. "And you always have a good time once you're smart enough to give in."

She sighed and then perked up. "Five bucks says I won't like it."

"I will take that bet, and maybe I'll be gentlemanly enough to buy you a coffee with my winnings. Now, be a sweetheart and text my mom back and tell her we'll bring coleslaw for the cookout Sunday."

He handed her his phone.

"What do you mean 'we'?"

"You and me, Mags. You and me."

"I don't know what kind of 'see where things go' you're used to. But you can't force me to meet your family."

"You've already met Michael," he pointed out. "That means my moms are not going to be patient for much longer. It's only a matter of time before they just drop by the house. Besides, I already told them I'd bring you."

"Mom or Mama B?" she asked.

"Mom," he said.

Maggie typed up the message he dictated and hit send.

"How often do you all get together?" she asked.

"As a group? Once every week or two. But we mix it up with smaller get-togethers all the time."

She shook her head. "I don't know if I could do that. Have a family obligation every week? I'm just not much of a social animal."

"Says the woman with 999,150 followers," Silas pointed out.

She gave him a small smile. "That's a different kind of social."

"I'll say it is." He turned off Lake Street into the downtown.

"Where are you taking me?" she asked, peering through the rain-spattered window.

"Right here," he said, pulling into a parking space and pointing at the storefront with gray cedar shakes. "Kinship Mercantile," she read from the sign above the door. "I hate it already. You should give me your money now." But he saw the way her eyes lit up when they locked on the cheerfully jumbled window display. Cloud-thin throws and overstuffed pillows with sayings like LAKE LIFE IS THE BEST LIFE perched on a whitewashed oak pedestal table.

"Let's give it a few minutes. Let a man have a fighting chance," he said, reaching over her and opening her door.

It smelled like sage and lemons when he pushed open the glass door of the shop. The swift rush of pride hit him, just like every other time he stepped foot in the Mercantile.

"Nope," Maggie said, shaking her head. "I don't see anything that interests me. I'll wait in the truck." But she was already picking up a stoneware dish glazed the exact color of Payette Lake on a sunny summer day. "Oh. Look at that." She put the dish down and was drawn farther into the store to a rustic curio cabinet showcasing handwoven table linens.

He let her browse and headed toward the register.

"Well, well, well. Look what the cat dragged in—your dead-to-me uncle." Nirina, his baby sister, took after Mama B in the high cheekbones, big smile, and hair-styling creativity departments. She had the Wright eyes, and her skin was exactly halfway between Mama B's dark and Emmett Wright's Irish pale. She was rubbing a ringed hand smugly over her rounded belly.

"Niri, have a heart. I come bearing gifts," he said, stepping behind the counter to give his half-sister a hug.

"I don't want any gift from you unless it's—"

He cut her off and jerked a thumb in Maggie's direction. "I kidnapped my new boss. Thought you might like to meet her."

Niri's eyes widened. The beads of her bracelets clicked when she interlaced her fingers under her chin. "Is that?"

"Uh-huh." He nodded.

"You're the best brother in the universe!" she hissed. Then threw her arms around him for a quick, hard hug. "Holy shit. Okay. I'm gonna get Kayla. Do *not* let that woman leave."

That was high up on his agenda.

Nirina dashed off toward the back office, nimble on her feet for five months pregnant.

He headed back to Maggie. She had one of the airy, featherweight throws tossed over her shoulder, the blue serving dish was tucked under her arm, and she was studying a smaller version of the pedestal table at the front of the store. "Find anything you like?"

"Nope. Not a thing," she said, then looked up at him guiltily. "Ugh. Fine. Here. Hold this. And this." She unloaded everything into his arms and dug into her purse. "Here's your dumb five dollars. Now, go buy me a coffee and leave me to explore every inch of this place."

"You like it?" he asked.

"I want to die here. My headstone will say 'She bought everything.'"

"This is my sister's place," he said with pride.

Maggie tore her gaze away from the table. "Why do you keep introducing me to your family, Sy?"

"Because despite your inherent rudeness, I like you. And I like them."

"You know, I'm worried enough about you managing your expectations about us. I refuse to take responsibility for any misconceptions your family develops," she warned him.

"I take full responsibility," he promised. "Now, come meet my sister Niri. She and her best friend started this place two years ago. At first, we all thought it was just so they could continue spending every second of their lives together. But they've really got a knack for it."

"You can say that again. Sy!" The wonder in her voice had him stopping in his tracks. "Look at that bed." With something close to reverence, she stroked a hand over the rich finish of the bed's carved headboard. It looked almost like a picture frame, with dramatically carved edges around a rattan-looking insert. It managed to look both tropical and French country at the same time.

"Now, that's a step up from a cot," he observed.

"I want it," she breathed.

"Get it. I can think of more than a few reasons to have a big, comfortable bed in that room of yours. Namely, the fact that your cot is gonna get awful crowded when Kevin and I spend the night."

She shot him a downright disagreeable look. "You're supposed to talk me out of it. Remind me that there's a budget and that a stager will have something that fits the room."

"Darlin', you'd have to be blind and plain ignorant not to put this bed in that room. And from where I'm standing, you're neither of those things."

They were made for each other.

"I have to think about it." Her sigh carried with it the weight of responsible self-denial that Silas didn't understand.

He put down her treasures and wrapped his arms around her from behind. "Can't you see it, Mags? It's early morning, and the sun is just coming up. You're waking up with my mouth on you right about here." He dropped a kiss at the base of her neck. She shivered.

He could see it. The way he'd roll over her, covering her with his body. Running his hands over her as she slowly warmed to the day.

"Maggie Nichols, it's a pleasure to meet you." Silas's little sister ruined his vivid fantasy. With great reluctance, he released Maggie and turned to make the introductions.

"Maggie, this is my sister Nirina and her partner / best friend Kayla. Niri, Kayla? Meet Maggie of YouTube fame."

"Hi," Kayla said, handing Maggie a spiral-bound book.

"Are you asking for her autograph?" he stage-whispered.

Niri smacked him in the gut. "Maggie, Kayla and I put together a proposal on how Kinship Mercantile can help you in the renovation on the Old Campbell Place." She'd done that same move in some form or another for two and a half decades. But now his baby sister was all grown up and having her own baby. It made him feel a touch lightheaded.

"I put together a proposal in case our paths crossed," Kayla announced, tapping the paperwork Maggie held.

"And if we hadn't crossed paths?" Maggie asked.

"We'd have shown up at your front door with margarita fixings and a proposal," Nirina said.

"Damn. Maybe I shouldn't look at this without tequila."

"In that case," Nirina said, snatching the proposal back, "we'll see you at your place at seven."

Maggie blinked. "Oh. Uh."

It was nice to see Niri's steamrolling wasn't limited to family. Silas had been on the receiving end plenty of times.

"I guess I'll supply the food then," Maggie said, still looking a little shell-shocked.

"I don't suppose y'all would need a landscaper present to—"

"No!" Nirina and Kayla said together. "Ladies only."

He winced. "It's just that I only recently started kissing this beautiful boss of mine, and I was hoping to get in some more practice."

It was Maggie's turn to elbow him in the stomach. She looked mortified.

"Ooh, sorry, Sy. I'm afraid we can't let our new best friend keep kissing you until we've dissected every single thing about you," Niri said in mock sympathy.

"It's what we do," Kayla agreed.

"I expected you both to be on my side," he complained.

"Just goes to show you how little you know about women," Niri pointed out.

Maggie was laughing now.

"Hey, now! Let's not do any damage to the fine opinion Maggie's been building of me."

"Then I definitely won't tell you that Sy once bet two of his friends he could pee on an electric fence longer than they could," Nirina said to Maggie.

"Nirina Angela, if you want that very expensive designer crib you've been not-so-subtly hinting about since you peed on that stick, you better find some nicer stories about me real fast," he warned her.

"Forget everything I said," she announced, eyes dancing. "Just think of Silas here as Mr. Right."

21

SILAS PACKED MAGGIE'S newfound treasures into the backseat of his truck while Nirina and Kayla waved them off. Maggie had managed to talk herself out of the bed, but only just, and she was already having regrets. Suddenly the thought of another night in the creaky cot seemed unbearable.

"If you're still thinking about that bed, we're going right back in there, Mags," Silas said, sliding behind the wheel.

"No. There's no reason for me to splurge on a bed like that. The cot is fine."

"*Fine?*" he scoffed. "What in life is supposed to be *fine?* That bed makes your cot look like a slab of busted-up concrete."

She wasn't going to admit that that wasn't too far off from how it felt to sleep on the cot.

"I have to be practical. Staging is the last step before listing the property. There's no point in me getting a gorgeous piece of furniture just for me to—"

"What? Use? Sleep in? Have sex with a tall, very smart landscaper in? I find your self-sacrificing deprivation downright depraved."

She smirked. "You would. In comparison, you're practically a hedonist."

"That's the nicest thing you've ever said to me, darlin'."

True to his word, he bought them both coffees at the café. When they came back out, the rain had slowed to a lazy drizzle, leaving the streets and sidewalk shiny. Silas maneuvered the pickup down the block to a cross street and turned right.

"So who's this mysterious source of yours? Are you sure he's going to know something about the coin?"

"Oh, I'm sure. If anyone knows anything, it'll be him. He's a cranky old guy."

Uh-oh. Wait. Odds were there was more than one cranky old guy in town.

"A widower. He volunteered for the historical society. I think he even worked at the Old Campbell Place when it was a museum. He's got an apartment in the senior living place at the end of town."

Maggie cleared her throat. "Does he also wear his pants up to his armpits and hate people who buy old houses to renovate them?"

"You know Wallace?"

"Let's just say I don't know how helpful he's going to feel."

"You're here to see Wallace?" the nurse at the front desk asked in disbelief. "Wallace Pfeffercorn?" she clarified.

"That's our man," Silas said, leaning on the counter. "We've got some business with him."

"Sign in here on the sheet," she said, pushing a clipboard at them. He just lost at blackjack and accused our dealer of cheating, so I hope you don't have your hearts set on him being—"

"Polite?" Maggie guessed.

"*Not* a grumpy pain in the ass?" Silas tried.

"Pleasant," the nurse decided.

"We're both familiar with Wallace's...personality," Maggie assured her.

"Well, then follow me, and may God have mercy," she said with a brisk smile. She led the way through one set of double doors into a spacious dining room. There were tables of varying sizes, all covered with crisp white cloths.

Silas had to jump back when a woman on a three-wheeled scooter zoomed past.

"Hey! I'm scootin' here!" she yelled.

"I told you to slow down in here, Kathryn," the nurse called after her. "Sorry, folks. Mrs. Nolan owned a chain of garages. Now she uses her power for evil and keeps rigging the scooter motors to go faster."

"Later, losers," Mrs. Nolan cackled as she took a turn through another set of doors on two wheels.

"You two are the first visitors Wallace has had in...a while," the nurse told them as she turned down a hallway with doors on one side and a wall of windows on the other.

"I'll let Mama B know," Silas told her. "She'll have volunteers organized in fewer than twenty-four hours."

"The staff would appreciate it," she admitted, opening a door marked LIBRARY and pointing across the room.

Wallace Pfeffercorn was half-hidden behind a stack of old hardbound volumes at one of the tables in the middle of the library.

"Wallace, ol' buddy, ol' pal," Silas said, dragging out the chair across from the man and motioning for Maggie to take it. "How's it going?"

"How does it look like it's going? I'm old. I live with a bunch of other old people. It's the inner circle of hell around here."

"Shhh!" A lady with tight white curls and a Boise State Broncos sweatshirt shushed them with one gnarled finger. She was reading a magazine with a good-looking, middle-aged man on the cover under the headline BILLIONAIRE SEBASTIAN SPENCER TAKES GENEROSITY TO THE NEXT LEVEL. Sebastian wasn't exactly smiling. To Maggie, it looked more like a self-satisfied smirk. But she was biased.

She very deliberately turned away from the woman and her magazine.

"Shove it, Gladys," Wallace grumbled back. "If it bothers you, turn down your dang hearing aids."

"Hi, Wallace," Maggie said as Silas sat down next to her.

He harrumphed in her direction. "What do you want? It better not take long. I've got a nap in fifteen minutes." He closed the book he'd been reading, and Maggie caught the title. *A History of Western Idaho's Influential Families.* There was a legal pad next to him with painstaking notes written within the lines. She saw *Ava Campbell* written in the margin under a question mark and grinned. Her crabby little visitor was already working on research.

"My beautiful friend Maggie here found something at the Old Campbell Place," Silas began.

"Did she chuck it straight in the dumpster or dust it off first?" Wallace sniped.

"Now, Wallace—"

Maggie cut Silas off. "We found this under the mantel, embedded in the wood in Mr. Campbell's study." She turned the camera screen toward Wallace.

He gave it a cursory glance and then stilled. He grabbed the camera from her and peered at the screen first by holding it out at arm's length and then by pushing his glasses to the top of his head and bringing the screen to his nose.

"Under the mantel, you say?" His mustache twitched to the left.

"I thought it was one of those souvenir coins they sell in town," she told him.

"Pretty sure it's real, Wally," Silas said, sliding his arm along the back of her chair.

"I'm curious where it came from and why Aaron Campbell would have hidden a gold coin almost in plain sight like that," she said. "Was it some kind of superstition? Was it handed down in his family?"

"Could be nothing," Wallace said, still squinting at the screen.

"Here," she said, taking the camera and zooming in on the image. She handed it back. "Would you be able to find out anything about the design on the coin?"

He glanced up before looking over his shoulder. Gladys was absorbed once again in her magazine. "Dunno. Maybe," he said brusquely. "If you can get me a real picture of it. Not something on some tiny, useless screen. Maybe I can look into it. *If* I find the time. And *if* you're not going to pry it out of there with a crowbar and take it to the nearest pawnshop," he added.

"I will not pry it out with a crowbar and pawn it," Maggie promised.

"I'll drop off a printout tonight," Silas promised. "Seein' as how I don't have any plans since I was dumped for girls and tequila."

Wallace heaved a sigh. "I guess maybe I could take a look. But don't get your hopes up. It's probably one of those plastic coins some yahoo stuck there with chewing gum."

But Maggie could read him. Beneath that bluster, he was excited. Well, Wallace-level excited.

TerdBurgler57: I call bullshit. No chick that hot can use a nailgun.

DadofTwinGirls: @TerdBurgler57 My seven-year-olds can and will nail your forehead to the carpet.

AlpacaWhisperer: I want more Dean! He's so grumpy and snarly!

CurlzGurl: I wanna be Maggie when I grow up!! Only I want to fix up a beach house and then actually live in it.

SquatGoals: Did anyone catch Maggie's Insta story today? She said they found something amazing in her new house! Guesses? I'm betting voodoo dolls.

22

MAGGIE GAVE THE brace on the table leg a whack until the lock clicked into place.

It wasn't the greatest setup, she thought, glancing around the sunporch. But with the windows open to the breeze, some candles on the paper tablecloth that disguised the paint splatters, and the trio of mismatched chairs, it might look kind of charming and bohemian.

Or her guests would realize that Maggie was a hot mess incapable of living life as an adult with things like matching furniture and dishes that weren't made out of paper and plastic.

At least she had the new serving plate from Kinship Mercantile to class things up. It was in the fridge now with its caprese skewer appetizers next to the store-bought cheese-and-meat tray and pecan pie.

After leaving Wallace to his research, she'd insisted Silas make a pit stop at the grocery store. The man had chuckled his way through the store as she hurled impulse buys into the cart. She couldn't very well serve guests fluffernutter sandwiches.

Coffee was brewing. A pitcher of water was chilling in the now crowded refrigerator. Her jeans were clean-ish. And she'd managed enough time to run the Shop Vac over every square inch of hallway between the front door and the sunporch.

It was as good as it was going to get. Unless maybe she had time to—

The morbid organ of a doorbell echoed menacingly through the first floor. Her time was up.

She took a breath, straightened her shoulders, and headed for the front door.

"We come bearing gifts," Kayla said when Maggie opened the door. She held up a bottle of tequila in one hand and a woven shopping tote in the other. She was wearing cute, lipstick-red pants that cut off above the ankle and a plain white T-shirt with a big, dangly statement necklace.

Nirina was gorgeous in a long magenta dress that brushed the tops of gold sandals. She held the spiral-bound proposal to her pregnant belly. "I vote we skip the small talk and go straight to the part where you give us a tour of this place. It's incredible!"

Maggie laughed, nerves evaporating. "Come on in."

They came inside, bringing warm May air with them. Maggie could almost feel the house's approval as they oohed and aahed over crown moldings and wood paneling and soaring ceilings. They weren't appalled by the dilapidated state of her home. They were enamored with its potential. She felt an instant kinship with them.

Kayla demanded a pit stop in the kitchen, where she began to unload the tote bag on the worktable.

Niri handed Maggie a neatly wrapped package. "Housewarming present from your friends at Kinship Mercantile."

"Better open it now because we need what's inside," Kayla insisted as she unloaded a cutting board, knife, and limes onto the table. The women had clearly been briefed about the state of her kitchen.

"You didn't have to get me something," Maggie said, fingers already plucking at the green ribbon wrapped around the craft paper.

"We're just being neighborly," Kayla told her.

"And we're buttering you up," Niri announced, plunking herself down on a folding camp chair Dean used to watch the coffeemaker do its thing.

Beneath the paper was a plain white gift box. Maggie slipped the lid free. "These are lovely," she said, pulling one of the margarita glasses free. The wide bowl of the glass was bubbled and colored with a blue-green glaze. Utterly festive and feminine. It beat the hell out of the stack of Solo cups she had on top of the fridge, and they'd look perfect in one of the glass-front navy cabinets...if she ever got cabinets. "Thank you so much."

"They're from a glass artist in Boise," Nirina explained. "She's Nez Perce and has this incredible studio in her house."

"Niri is our artist whisperer," Kayla said, squeezing fresh lime juice into a plastic pitcher. "She's the creative spirit. I'm the seductress of spreadsheets and inventory. Which one are you?"

"I guess I'm a little of both," Maggie decided.

"We thought the glasses were perfect for the Old Campbell Place, seeing as how the parties here were legendary," Nirina said.

"Parties?" Maggie asked, eager for more information on the house and its owners. "What kind of parties?"

"The Campbells were famous from the moment they started building this place," Kayla said, taking over the topic. "The fascination got even stronger when Aaron Campbell's writing career took off. Now it wasn't just a man with a big house and a beautiful wife. It was a famous author living in a big house."

"Mr. Campbell made his rounds around town. A shave at the barbershop. Orders at the general store. Checking in on the family jewelry store. Mrs. Campbell, however, was kind of a part-time hermit," Kayla explained.

"No one would see her for weeks at a time," Nirina said, picking up the thread of the story. "Then all of a sudden, she'd emerge from the house and announce she was throwing a party."

"Champagne. Tiered cakes. I heard once the Campbells hired an entire orchestra to serenade a hundred guests on a Tuesday in July," Kayla said.

"Just a random Tuesday," Nirina repeated. "Now, I ask you. Is there a better way to live your life than drinking champagne and listening to a freaking orchestra just because it's Tuesday?"

For a moment, Maggie could see it all as she peered out the window above the sink to the terrace and fountain. Couples swaying to the music. Firelight. Bubbles in the champagne. And the twinkle-eyed Mrs. Campbell from the portrait raising a glass to the mustachioed Mr. Campbell.

"You both know an awful lot of history about this place," Maggie noted.

"History is important," Kayla responded. "The Old West is still new by comparison."

"And you have to admit, famous authors and fancy parties are a lot more fun than bridges being built or battles fought." Nirina had a good point.

"We're programmed to gravitate toward stories," Maggie agreed and dumped colorful salt onto a plate, directed by Kayla. Methodically, she salted three rims.

"A virgin for the preggo," Kayla said, pouring the mixture over ice in the first glass and handing it to her partner.

"There is nothing virgin about me," Nirina said, gesturing at her belly.

"Quit bragging. You know my fear of my virginity growing back," Kayla complained. She opened the tequila and started pouring. "I promise you, Maggie, that we're incredible businesswomen. Consummate professionals."

"But we also love a good time," Nirina said proudly.

With a flourish, Kayla stirred the margarita mixture with a long-handled spoon. "Moment of truth," she said, pouring directly into two glasses. She handed a glass to Maggie and took the other. "To the beginning of a beautiful, successful friendship."

"Cheers," Maggie said. She raised her glass and took a sip. "Oh, that's good."

"Kayla here is a genius when it comes to recipes of any kind," Nirina said proudly. "Now, if one of you ladies can crane my butt out of this chair, we can take our drinks on the road so I can see the upstairs of this place."

"You need that bed," she announced five minutes later when Maggie opened the bedroom door. "It was made for this room. The arches in the headboard are almost a perfect mimic of the balcony doors. And you could repeat it with the bathroom entry on the opposite wall."

It was a great idea that would add drama and personality. Plus, Dean would have a fit about custom bathroom doors. Maggie grinned and took another sip of her excellent margarita.

"I don't know how you walked out of the shop without it," Kayla agreed. "Is it willpower or self-deprivation? Because I could use whatever it is every time I come face-to-face with the bakery case at the café."

"A little bit of both," Maggie admitted. "I don't usually—ever—stage a house until the very end." Besides, if she bought the bed, she'd be compelled to use it. And not just for sleep. Once that line was crossed with Silas, it would complicate things. He would complicate things. She wasn't sure if she was prepared for complicated.

"But you're living here," Nirina pointed out. "Why not enjoy it while you can? If you're not going to live in a seven-thousand-square-foot mansion forever, you might as well enjoy a summer in it."

"Actually, I *am* going to need two beds by the weekend," Maggie mused.

"For staging or sleeping?" Kayla asked.

"Sleeping. My partner and our . . . employee are moving in."

"Cody Moses, right?" Nirina asked.

"News travels fast," Maggie noted wryly.

"I knew things were tough for him, but I had no idea he didn't have a place to stay. Mama B would have stuffed him in Michael's or Sy's old room in a heartbeat if she'd known," Nirina told her.

"You're doing a great thing for the kid," Kayla said, wandering over to the balcony doors and opening them. "He's a really good guy. Just got caught up in family drama and bad luck."

"Pause, please. I need to slobber over this view. This is a straight-up fairy tale right here," Niri announced, joining her friend on the balcony and admiring the view. "Maggie, it would officially be a crying shame if you didn't take advantage of this room while you're here."

And there it was. She'd been waiting for Silas to come up as a topic. "Are we talking about the bed or your brother?" she asked, joining them on the balcony.

"Both," they said together.

"Jinx!" they said in unison. "You owe me a pop!"

"I know you don't know anything about us beyond the fact that we have excellent taste," Kayla began. "But if you want to talk about a certain tall, swoony landscaper, I would not be upset at all."

"And I can give you all the insider info on the man, seeing as how I've known him my entire life," Nirina said, bracing her free hand on her lower back. "But first, we really should talk business."

"Good idea," Kayla said, putting her margarita glass down. "Maggie, we've been in business for two years. Which isn't long, but we've got great taste and deep community roots. We know how important both of those things are to you and your viewers."

"We can connect you with local artisans, hook you up with our interior design expertise, and stage the entire house top to bottom for you at a significantly reduced fee, since you're our new BFF," Nirina said, smoothly taking over the pitch.

"We'd even be willing to work out a discount on any items you decide to purchase outright, like that big, beautiful bed," Kayla said, blue eyes twinkling.

"What's the catch?" Maggie asked, smiling over the rim of her glass. The tequila and female friendship were making her feel warm and relaxed.

"We're just getting our design and staging business started," Nirina said. "As in, you would be our first staging customer."

"The demographics are there. We've got dozens of rental properties out the wazoo in a fifteen-mile radius. Over half of them are on the luxury end. Log cabins. Lakefront bungalows. An entire village of town houses and chalets near the ski resort. If we can get our names out there, in a year, we're going to be able to say a big fat 'I told you so' to every single person who told us we were nuts for setting up shop here," Kayla said.

Maggie recognized the fire, the desire to prove. She also recognized an eye for beauty. Both Kayla and Nirina had them.

"It's a big job," Maggie warned. "I'm touching almost every single room in this place because I can't seem to stop myself."

"We're up to the task," Kayla promised. "We've got furniture artisans, drapery specialists, artists. Niri has a patio furniture hookup. I'm a hell of a threat with a paintbrush. Walls, not canvas."

"Then I'd say you've got yourselves a deal," Maggie said.

Kayla stood stock still, eyes blinking rapidly.

"Uh-oh," Niri whispered to her drink. "Brace yourself."

There was a high-pitched whine coming from somewhere.

Maggie nearly bobbled her drink when Kayla launched herself at her. The redhead wrapped her arms around Maggie and squeezed. That's when she realized where the noise was coming from. The whine was a squeal, and it was coming from Kayla.

"You won't regret this. I swear to you on Niri's unborn baby, you won't regret putting your faith in us. We're going to deliver. And when we're done, it's going to be so perfect you aren't going to want to leave," Kayla vowed fervently.

Maggie patted her awkwardly on the back.

Business tabled temporarily, they talked over appetizers and another round of drinks on the sunporch as crickets and tree frogs did their things in the night air. Nirina told Maggie about Silas as a big brother.

"He's this chill, tree-hugging, earth-loving guy eighty-five percent of the time," she said.

"Ninety-nine percent," Kayla argued. "I've known him since our first playdate in elementary school."

"Girl, please," Nirina scoffed with affection. "Silas has this stubborn, overprotective streak. It's buried deep. But when he gets riled, look out."

"He won't tolerate someone being taken advantage of or someone being put at risk. When he found out that my high school boyfriend with his brand-new driver's license decided it would be a great idea to see if his fourth-hand Dodge Daytona could hit a hundred on the highway with me in the passenger seat, Sy walked right into his house, dragged that boy out of bed on a Saturday, and told him if he ever went one mile over the speed limit with me in the car again, he'd toss him in the river with a boat anchor wrapped around his neck."

Kayla laughed. "I forgot about that. I'll adjust my estimated percentage to ninety."

Maggie winced, recalling her own experience with "the streak." "I may have caught a glimpse of said streak," she admitted. Nirina and Kayla looked at each other and then back at Maggie. "What?" she asked.

"Oh, nothing. Just Sy never got worked up about Michelle is all," Nirina said, smugly admiring her fingernails.

"In all their years of dating, I can't remember them ever really fighting," Kayla agreed.

"It's a sign," Nirina decided.

"You really are your brother's sister." Maggie laughed. "Fighting isn't usually the sign of a solid relationship."

"No, but caring enough to resolve conflict is," Nirina pointed out, tugging on one of her bracelets. "Sy's mama is a therapist, and Mama B is a romantic. Between the two of them, all of us kids were preprogrammed for healthy relationships."

"How did you meet your husband?" Maggie asked, changing the subject.

Nirina filled her in on her secret college romance that blossomed into the early engagement that shocked her family. "People can doubt my ability to succeed because I'm adorable and happy. But that doesn't mean that I'm not going to work my cute butt off, making my dreams come true."

"Cheers to being underestimated," Kayla said, raising her glass.

"Cheers," Maggie echoed.

They stayed for another hour until Kayla started yawning. Maggie walked them to the front door.

"Girl, how are you going to walk away from this house?" Nirina asked her. "I'm already planning where to put the Christmas tree."

"*Tree?*" Kayla scoffed, then yawned again. "This place needs at least six."

"That's true. Maggie, you'd need one on each floor of the turret. Front porch, balcony, bedroom," Niri decided.

"And a big one in the rotunda against the stairs," Kayla volunteered. "Then another in the dining room and a family tree wherever the gifts will go."

"I'll make note of that for the future owners," Maggie said dryly.

Kayla shook her head. "Willpower and self-deprivation."

"I sure hope whatever's next is worth walking away from this," Nirina mused.

As she stood on her front porch and waved off her new friends, Maggie hoped so, too.

Dayana: Any summer vacation plans this year?

23

SATURDAY MORNING, SILAS rapped his knuckles on the wood trim of Maggie's office doorway. She glanced up from whatever she was studying on her laptop, and he caught the way her eyes brightened when she saw it was him.

"Mornin', darlin'," he said, wandering into the room.

"This is a surprise. Don't you have teenage mowers of lawns to harass?" she asked. She had her hair pulled back in a low ponytail. Her feet were bare, but the sneakers and socks she was planning on wearing for the day sat on the corner of her desk. Her shorts were of the yoga variety. Very short and very fitted. Her T-shirt had BUILDING DREAMS emblazoned across the chest.

He approved. The tomboy next door. Just exactly his type.

"Niri and Kayla sent me. I've got the beds you ordered in my truck, and Elton's got the mattresses," he said.

"Oh, that's handy," she said. "Cody showed up with his 'stuff' at eight this morning. All his possessions fit in a backpack and a duffel bag. I know I travel light, but that's by choice. His isn't, and it broke my heart for him."

That news gave Silas a bit of an ache in his chest. He'd be nothing without his family. Without the homes he'd grown up in. The support network four loving adults had worked so hard to build. "Hopefully this will cheer you up," he said, producing the surprise he'd brought her from behind his back.

"Is that for me?" she asked, perking up.

He put the potted plant down on her desk, mostly so he could get his hands on her. "It is. Thought it would look good on that side table you picked up at the shop Thursday."

Maggie leaned in to admire its glossy green leaves in the white ceramic pot. She looked delighted. "It's beautiful. What is it?"

"It's a dwarf citrus," he explained. "Indirect sun is best. You should get yourself a nice little crop of lemons off it."

When she bit her lip, he guessed she was working out the perfect placement in her head. "You didn't have to," she told him. "But thank you."

He nudged her chin up to look at him. And since he felt like it, he slid his hands down her arms to hold her wrists. "I wanted to. And it made you smile. After we put the beds together, I thought maybe we could—"

But his lunch invitation was interrupted by the new resident of the Old Campbell Place, Cody, bursting through the back door. "You guys have to see what Kevin found!" he announced in the doorway before disappearing again.

"Think it's the treasure?" she asked.

"More likely a giant mud pit," Silas guessed. Before she could head for the door, he stopped her and pressed a hard kiss to her mouth. "Morning, Maggie."

Her smile spread like the sun across her face. "Morning, Silas."

"Don't forget your shoes, darlin'," he said, handing them over.

They found Cody in the backyard with the rest of the landscaping crew and Dean huddled around the foundation of the old shed.

"Hell. Please don't be a body," Maggie murmured.

"Would Dean be filming if it was?" Silas pointed out.

"Never know with him," she said.

"Kevin's a daddy," Dean said from behind the digital camera.

Silas knelt down to get a closer look. His big, burly pit bull was curled in a hole at the base of the foundation around two fluffy gray kittens.

"Aw," Maggie crooned. Kevin's tail wagged at the appreciation of his fatherly instincts. "How old are they?"

Silas reached in and gently pulled one of the kittens out. It had thick fur that clumped like a mane around its head. "Probably about six weeks," he guessed, cradling the fur ball to his chest.

He handed the kitten to Maggie and reached for the other one. Kevin belly-crawled out of the dirt after his furry charges. This one mewed at full volume to express his displeasure. The dog whimpered. "Everybody is just fine," Silas promised them both.

Both kittens started to meow, and Kevin was beside himself. "They must be hungry," Maggie guessed. "What can we feed them?"

"Got any canned tuna?" Cody suggested. "We can try to get them to drink the juice until we can get some real kitten food."

"Good idea," she said.

They carried their new charges under Kevin's watchful eye into the house.

"You're not going to use orphaned kittens as a reason to back out on our shopping today, are you?" Dean demanded as Cody and Maggie tried to coax the kittens toward a dish of tuna.

She looked surprised. "Of course not. Our new roommate here volunteered to keep an eye on them while we ponder boots," she said.

So much for stealing her away for lunch, Silas realized. Maybe he could talk her into dinner or—

"Besides," she continued, "Niri and Kayla invited me out tonight. Apparently Niri's mom is headlining at someplace called Cowboy Jake's."

Dammit, Niri.

"Look who's changing from caterpillar to social butterfly," Dean mused, helping himself to some coffee.

Maggie stuck her tongue out at him, and Cody smirked at their byplay.

"I'll run into town and get some fur ball supplies. Then I'll pick you up, and we can head to lunch," Dean offered.

"Perfect. Cody started a list," Maggie said.

"You're going to Jake's tonight?" Silas asked, trying for casual. He'd been hoping for a late lunch date, maybe talking her into swinging by his house and seeing where things went. He had fresh sheets on the bed, a sparkling-clean bathroom vanity, and all of the laundry was where it belonged, where it would stay, since Kevin was with him.

"It was a hard invitation to pass up," she said with a sunny smile. She seemed excited to have friends, and as much as he wanted her attention focused on him, he wasn't willing to be a dick about it. At least, not to her.

While Dean and Maggie completed the feline shopping list and Cody succeeded in coaxing one of the kittens to lick tuna juice off his finger, Silas pulled up his text messages.

Silas: How's a guy supposed to get the girl when his baby sister keeps stealing her away?

Michael: Poor deprived baby.

Taylor: Cockblocked by Niri!

Niri: Are you or are you not going to be at Cowboy Jake's for Mama B's band tonight?

Silas: Now I am. Instead of tempting her back to my clean sheets and Febreze-scented house.

*Michael: You really know how to do atmosphere. *eye roll**

*Silas: *bite me GIF**

Niri: Silas, will you or will you not be dragged up onstage by Mama B for at least one song?

Silas: Probably.

Niri: Imagine how much more irresistible you'll be when you just casually run into her while she's out having fun with friends and then get up onstage and you're all swoony and croony.

Michael: Aren't you too pregnant to have fun?

Niri: You do NOT want my attention on you, Mikey! Not until you have a certain conversation with a certain foursome of parents.

Taylor: What's happening? What's the vague threat about? Do I know? I just had to pull a purple jelly bean out of Sullivan's nose.

Silas: Niri is threatening to set Mikey up with a boy before he tells the moms and dads he's into dudes.

Taylor: Whew! I thought this was something new. Mikey you have GOT to tell the parents!

Michael: Let's turn this back around on Silas for being a whiner who didn't get the girl.

Niri: Listen, my nights out are limited before this baby sitting on my bladder makes it impossible for me to leave my bathroom. You ALL will show up tonight!

Silas: This better not be a diabolical plan to get revenge for that time Mikey and I flattened Jeremiah's tire when we found out you were sneaking out to meet him.

Michael: I would like the record to show that I only distracted Jeremiah while Silas let the air out of his tire.

Taylor: I miss you assholes. I need to move home. And not just so I can dump my children on their aunt and uncles.

A flurry of real estate listings in and around the Kinship area exploded into the chat.

Silas grinned. He loved his siblings. Even if they were assholes.

Elton poked his head into the kitchen. "Maggie, there's a grumpy old guy here to see you. Says it's important."

Maggie locked eyes with Silas. "Maybe someone found treasure after all," she said.

"Hang on. Back up," Silas said as he helped haul Wallace to his feet. "What are you saying?" The man had insisted on getting an up-close-and-personal look at the coin under the mantel. For a round old guy with a cane, he was pretty spry.

Wallace brushed fussily at the creases in his nipple-high pants. "Clean the wax out of your ears, kid! I'm saying that coin matches the description of the coins stolen in the Dead Man's Canyon Stagecoach Robbery."

Maggie's mouth formed a perfect O. "The robbery that inspired the fake gold coins in all the shops in town?"

"The one and the same," Wallace said smugly.

"Where did it happen? What were the circumstances? How can you be sure?"

"I'm not sure. But since you asked..." he said.

"Oh, boy, here we go," Silas whispered.

"What's in your pockets?"

Between the three of them, they came up with some cash and a tube of ChapStick. "Now, let's say this lip gunk is the stagecoach. Part of Benjamin Updyke's stage line, it ran from the Montana gold mines into Boise. Pulled by four of the fastest horses, that particular stage was carrying three passengers as well as four strongboxes. Two of raw gold from the mines, one of gold brick, and one of newly minted coins. All headed for the Basin Bank in Boise."

Maggie stepped closer and watched the reenactment.

"These two dollars represent the hills on either side of Dead Man's Canyon," Wallace said, placing two bills two inches apart. "The coach ran weekly, leaving its overnight stop in Kinship. Dead Man's Canyon was a four-hour ride south of here. Accounts vary, but most agree that the bandit Black Jack McGuire had intel that the coach would be running with more gold than usual. He paid a spy to hang out in Kinship watching for the coach."

"So they could ride ahead and report when the coach was likely to leave," she guessed.

"That's the general consensus. When that coach entered the canyon here," he said, moving the ChapStick between the dollar bills, "Black Jack McGuire was here. His cohorts, Bowman Potter and Samuel Espinosa, positioned themselves here and here on the ridges." He doled out quarters to represent each player.

"Perfect place for an ambush," Silas observed. He'd grown up playing stagecoach robbery in backyards with friends.

"It did the trick. They fired in the air, made a bunch of noise, and managed to get the whip—or driver—the conductor, and the passengers out without killing a single one. No bloodshed. They left the victims in the canyon with water and then made off with the coach, the gold, and all the passengers' possessions."

"Including the Minnie Franklin necklace," Silas added.

"I was gettin' to that," Wallace grumbled.

"What's the Minnie Franklin necklace?" Maggie asked, willing to play the gold star student.

"One of the passengers was the dour-faced Mrs. Minnie Margaret Franklin on her way to San Francisco, where she was meeting her banker husband. In her trunk, she'd packed the gift her father had given to her upon her eighteenth birthday. An emerald-and-sapphire necklace rumored to have belonged to the royal family of Spain. Upon her rescue a few hours later, Minnie Franklin sent a telegraph to her husband saying he had two months to return to Boston or their marriage was over."

"And did he?" Maggie asked.

"He most certainly did. He may have been a banker, but her family was the one who owned the bank."

"Where did the coach end up?" Silas asked, his memory a little foggy on the details.

"The stage was found days later, abandoned outside a silver mine another two hours south. Nothing but scrub brush and canyons for miles in any direction."

"Were the outlaws caught?" Maggie asked.

"Not for that. Reports say they buried the gold and split up, making a pact to come back a year later to recover it," Wallace said, sliding the quarters off in different directions. "Black Jack took a slug to the back of the head after a poker game in Montana. Potter took ill and died on a ranch up north. Espinosa went to prison for a bank robbery in Texas. The law tried to coax the location out of him, but he never cracked. Died from typhoid in prison when he was forty-two. No deathbed confession, much to the disappointment of treasure hunters."

The dog proudly trotted into the room, kittens—dubbed Dolly Parton and Taco by popular vote—on his heels.

"That ain't natural," Wallace observed. Kevin licked his pants and continued his tour of the house with the cats.

"Love is love," Maggie told him.

Wallace harrumphed. "I found this at the library last night before it closed," he said, producing one of several sheets of paper from a zippered folio embossed with the Kinship Historical Society logo.

Silas peered over Maggie's shoulder at the photocopy. It was a page from a book with an illustration of a gold coin. "The coins that stage was carrying were freshly minted in a gold camp in Montana," Wallace lectured. "Now, here's where it gets interesting. Montana was in the midst of a gold rush. Mints that turned raw gold into currency were popping up like them there coffee shops today that set up on the same block. They weren't very regulated, and mistakes were made."

"What kind of mistakes?" Maggie asked.

"Well, rumor has it that the stage that was robbed was carrying a strongbox full of fresh coins made with a dollar dye on one side and a quarter dye on the other," Wallace said.

"An entire strongbox of gold mistakes," Silas mused. He'd never heard that particular bit of gossip. "Where did you hear that?"

"The gunslinger who shot Black Jack swears he took a gold coin off the man. During the poker game, Black Jack was said to have told the players it came from the stage robbery. Used it to up the ante on the last hand and won."

"Where's the coin now?" Maggie asked.

"In a museum in downtown Boise."

"Wait a second," Silas said. "Aren't these mistakes worth more than the actual currency? Like the stamp with the airplane printed upside down."

"You're not as dumb as you look, my boy," Wallace said with what could almost be mistaken for affection. "A mismade coin is called a mule. And that particular mule is valued at around fifty-five thousand dollars today."

Silas let out a low whistle.

"And that's the only coin ever recovered?" Maggie asked, eyes flicking to the mantel.

"The one and only. None of the other coins or bars ever showed up in any law-abiding establishments. People still go hunting in the canyons looking for the treasure today."

He unloaded another stack of photocopies. Each one was a news article about people going in search of the gold. Silas and Maggie paged through. The most recent article was from two years ago when a group of geology master's students, armed with commercial metal detectors and GPS systems, spent two weeks scouring for gold in and around the silver mine where the coach was found.

"None of them got lucky," Silas observed. "And some of them were downright unlucky." He tapped the copy of an article about an unnamed young woman who disappeared in the canyons just south of Kinship in the late 1800s after telling her stagecoach companions she was going to find the gold.

"By the by, you owe me ninety cents for the photocopies." Wallace sniffed.

"I think we can swing that," Silas said dryly.

"First things first," Maggie said. "If this coin is from the robbery, what do we do now? Are there lost-treasure authorities we're supposed to report this to?"

"If you want my advice, which you should," Wallace said loftily, "we need to get that coin out of that mantel. If it matches Black Jack's coin, then we go from there. Either someone brought that coin into Campbell's family's jewelry store and he recognized it or he came across the treasure. If it's the latter, there could be other clues within these walls."

"I'd imagine insurance was paid on the loss," Silas guessed. "So who would the gold belong to?"

Wallace shrugged. "Whoever owns the land most likely."

"Wallace, would you be willing to talk about this, share what you know about the robbery on camera?" Maggie asked.

"Like on the *Antiques Roadshow*?" He schooled his face into disapproval, but Silas heard a note of interest in the man's creaky voice.

"Something like that," she said with a smile.

He harrumphed. "Like anyone wants to listen to an old man like me. Let's get that coin out of there and see what we find on the other side first."

"Mags, how do we do that?" Silas asked.

She blew out a breath and crossed to the mantel. "Best I can tell, it looks like the mantel is in two pieces. This molding here at the bottom is a thin layer with the inlay just a hair smaller than the circumference of the coin. If we pry off the bottom layer, the coin should come right out."

"No time like the present," Silas said.

Five minutes later, armed with a thin chisel and hammer, Maggie set to the delicate work.

"Don't destroy the whole surround," Wallace groused when the tip of the chisel sank into the seam.

"I'm trying real hard not to," she shot back. Tongue caught between her teeth, she carefully worked the wood until the tiny finish nails gave up their purchase. "Sy, can you reach in there?" She nodded toward the gap she'd created at the center of the mantel.

He slid his fingers inside and used his thumb to raise the coin. Triumphantly, he drew it out and held it up. They gathered around him and stared as he flipped the coin over.

"Well, holy shit," Wallace muttered.

HashBrownNerd: Carpet in the bathroom?? Do you know how many decades of pee are in that mess?

Alicia100: Want to earn hundreds werking from house? Checkout vlog here.

PurplePeopleAvoider: I just want to be BFFs with Maggie. She seems like the kind of girl who would eat seven tacos and drink a pitcher of margaritas in one sitting and never get annoying.

24

"WE LOOK GOOD," Dean said approvingly as Maggie approached him in the gravel parking lot. Music of the country variety thumped behind him in the timber building.

"Damn good," she agreed, doing a little twirl in her new jeans and curve-hugging button-down. "I can't believe you went your entire life without those boots."

"I can't believe you went eight months without a damn curling iron," he shot back, plucking at one of the waves she'd worked into her hair.

"The two of us out on the town, dressed to the nines—"

"Closer to the fives," Dean insisted. "The nines do not involve denim."

"Either way, this deserves documentation." She handed him her phone. "You've got longer arms."

He held her phone out at arm's length. "Say one million sub-scribers!"

They both did, and he snapped the picture.

"You better use that beauty filter all over my face," he threatened, looking at the final product.

She snatched her phone back. "Your crow's-feet are distinguished."

"Crow's-feet?" he screeched. "I was talking about the gray hairs highlighted by that stupid streetlight. When did we get so elderly? Have I given you the best years of my life?"

"Saturday night out on the town. About to find out what puts the 'cowboy' in Cowboy Jake's," she said, ignoring him as she typed it out on her phone. "There. Posted. And you're thirty-five. That's not even midlife crisis territory yet. You have to hold off until at least forty."

"Come on, Grandma. Let's go see if this place has any early-bird specials," he said, opening the door of the bar and ushering her inside.

The bar had prime positioning on a low bluff overlooking Payette Lake. Cowboy Jake's was everything a western bar should be. Wood on the walls, sawdust on the concrete floors, barrels and lariats for decoration. There was a stage at one end of the room, a bar with backlit shelves of just about every kind of bourbon imaginable on the other. Between the two were tables crowded with people blowing off steam on a Saturday night and a dance floor in front of the stage.

Music was coming from the sound system, but it looked like a band was setting up on the stage.

"There they are," Maggie said, pointing at Nirina and Kayla, who were waving from a table halfway between the bar and dance floor. She led the way, dragging Dean along behind her.

Introductions were made, and Maggie took an empty chair while Dean headed to the bar to buy a round of drinks.

"How was the store today?" she asked over the croonings of Luke Bryan.

"Good! New shipment of pottery came in today," Kayla said, putting down her white wine. "All blues and greens in a crackle glaze. The dishes would look amazing with your new margarita glasses. Hint, hint."

"I found these sheers in the back. They're hand-sewn lace that screamed 'Hang me in Maggie's bedroom over the balcony doors,'" Nirina added.

"It's true. They did," Kayla said with a nod. "I was there."

"I don't think you have to work too hard to get me back in the store," Maggie assured them.

"We'll start a pile for you," Niri promised. "So, Dean is gorgeous."

"Please tell him that. He's having a moment over gray hair and crow's-feet," she told them.

"We're organizing a watch party for your first Kinship episode at Decked Out," Kayla announced. "The whole town is so excited."

"Hey, boss!" Elton, Sy's right-hand man, ducked down and gave Maggie a smacking kiss on the cheek. "Nice to see you outside of work for once."

"My brother is gonna kick your skinny ass for hitting on his girl," Nirina sang.

Elton grinned at her. "Worth it! Save me a dance, Nichols."

He disappeared into the crowd, and Dean reappeared expertly juggling four drinks. "White wine for Kayla. Club soda with lime for Mama to Be. And beers for the Dream Team," he said, setting a beer in front of Maggie.

"Kayla and Niri were just telling me they're organizing a watch party Monday night for the first episode," Maggie filled him in.

"Did you prepare Silas for his impending fame?" Dean asked. "Viewers are going to eat him up."

"I think Silas is used to being appreciated for his looks and charm," she said wryly. "He'll handle it just fine."

"I appreciate your faith in me, Mags." Sy's voice was unexpected and so close that it had her jumping in her chair. She looked up, and there he was. All six-feet-plus of that boyish charm and hard body. His hair was wet on the ends, and she could smell some magical, manly shower gel that did strange things to her.

"I didn't know you'd be here," she said, unable to control the smile she felt spreading across her face.

He took the chair next to her and held his fingers to his ear. "What's that?"

The man had heard her just fine. But she didn't mind moving in a little closer to repeat the words.

He brushed her hair back so he could lean in and whisper back, "Didn't think I'd miss a chance to show off my dance moves for you, did you?"

His lips brushed against her earlobe, and it sent a delicious shiver up her spine.

"You're crashing Ladies' Night," she told him.

"So's Dean. And Niri's husband will be here in twenty minutes. You look real pretty tonight, Maggie."

Was there a woman out there who could face Silas Wright's charm and walk away unscathed?

"Thank you," she said. "You look..." She let her gaze trail over him, from the tousled angelic curls to that light layer of stubble covering his jaw. Then lower to the T-shirt that hugged all of that ropey muscle. She didn't dare go any lower. Delicious. Sinful. Indecently sexy. "Good," she decided finally.

"Thank you, darlin'."

She could spend a very long time just staring at his mouth and stay completely entertained, she decided, watching as those firm lips of his curved with amusement.

She realized that Nirina and Kayla were watching them smugly and got the distinct feeling that she'd been played. Ladies' Night, her ass.

"Hey, guys." Michael appeared behind Silas, holding a glass of red wine.

"You made it! Have a seat," Nirina said, pointing at the empty chair next to Dean.

Hmm. It looked like they'd both been played. But with Sy's arm on the back of her chair, and his thumb stroking lazy circles over her shirt, she couldn't quite work up to being annoyed.

"I was talking to the dads," Michael said, clearing his throat and looking away from Dean. He pointed toward the bar, where Maggie spotted Morris, her first aid hero, next to a man she guessed had to be Sy's father. He was just as tall but on the rangier side. Where Sy's hair went to blond, his father's was a few shades darker. But there was no mistaking the same gray eyes. The men raised their glasses at them, and everyone around the table echoed the gesture.

"Mama B's playing tonight," Nirina explained to Maggie and Dean. "And my husband better get here quick if he wants to escape her wrath."

"And by wrath, she means disappointment," Kayla said.

"That's Mama B," Silas said, pointing to the stage.

Breonna Wright had the presence for a stage. She strutted across it in strappy gold stilettos, skinny pants that stopped a few inches above her ankles, and a billowing blouse in reds and golds and oranges. Her skin was dark. Her hair was high. Her smile was a beacon.

The crowd broke into spontaneous applause, and all she'd done was walk onstage.

Maggie glanced around the table and saw nothing but unadulterated adoration directed at the woman.

"It's impossible not to love her," Silas said in Maggie's ear.

It could have been her imagination, but she felt like the woman's gaze landed on them in that exact moment.

The band members—a guitarist, bass player, drummer, and keyboardist—settled in around her and started warming up.

"Ladies and gentlemen," Mama B purred into the microphone, "thank you for coming out tonight to spend a little quality time with your neighbors. I'm Mama B, and this is B's Blues. We're here to get your feet tapping and those shoulders shimmying. I want to see you all on the dance floor. You too, Myrtle," she said, pointing to an older woman in sweatpants and a Boise State Broncos T-shirt.

The crowd laughed along with Myrtle.

"Okay, boys," Mama B said. "Let's get this party started."

The band was good. Mama B was better than good. She crooned her way through some country classics—old favorites, judging by the reaction from the crowd—and then worked in a Sinatra number between an R&B classic and filled out the set list with Taylor Swift.

Morris and Emmett stopped by, and introductions were made. Morris reminded Maggie and Dean that they were both invited to the family cookout the following day. When the band smoothly shifted gears into the adorable "You've Got a Friend in Me" by Randy Newman, Emmett bowed low over Nirina's hand and escorted her onto the dance floor.

Maggie felt a little sliver of jealousy, wondering if Dayana and

Sebastian had danced like that at Dayana's wedding. She did what she always did when she saw daughters and fathers and shook it off.

Around the table, between rounds of applause, they talked work and renovations. Nirina's husband, Jeremiah, showed up, and more introductions were made. He was a mechanical engineer trying to get as much work off his plate as he could before he took paternity leave in a few months.

Silas bought the next round and enlisted Maggie to help him carry the drinks. At the bar, he caged her between his arms, her back to his chest. There was something so right about it she was starting to think that maybe it was a good thing she'd shaved her legs that afternoon.

"Hey, Sy," the barback greeted them. He was a big guy with thick silver hair and glasses.

"Hey there, Roy. Heard you were working here," Silas said.

"I miss my machines at the plant, and it sure fucked with my retirement, but this isn't half bad. Either of you know how to make a Cosmopolitan?" he said, reading off the ticket in his hand.

"Vodka, cranberry, Cointreau, and lime," Maggie told him.

He beamed at her. "Thanks. Old Campbell Place, right?"

"That's me," she said.

They were making their way back to the table when Mama B stepped back up to the mic. "Would Silas Wright please report to the stage?"

Nirina and Kayla shared an excited whoop while the rest of the crowd cheered him on. Apparently, this was a thing.

"Get on up there, big bro," Nirina told him, slapping him on the butt when he pretended to balk.

"You sing, too?" Maggie asked him.

He flashed her a wink, gave her shoulder a squeeze, and headed in the direction of the stage.

She sat back down and watched Mama B make room for his big frame on the stage. He traded fresh beer for a guitar and slung the strap over his neck.

Maggie hoped for a Weird Al song. But the way he handled the mic was too smooth, too confident.

"You should see them at Christmas," Michael said, leaning across Dean. "They do a duet that brings the house down."

"Do you sing with your mom?" she asked him.

Michael grinned. "I got none of Mom's vocal talent. But I did inherit her love of stress baking."

"Really? I have a pretty mean apple torte," Dean said. "Maybe we should compare notes?"

Michael's smile widened, and he looked down at the top of the table. "Uh, that would be fun."

The man's shyness was adorable and so not Dean's usual type. But the tips of his ears were a raging inferno of pink. Maybe people didn't always know their type until they were introduced to it, she mused.

"Okay, I guess we're doin' this," Silas said, leaning into the microphone and giving the strings a strum.

"Wooo!" Niri hooted. There were more than a few women in the crowd who echoed it. Maggie couldn't blame them. He looked like he belonged up there. It was yet another turn-on for her. The man seemed to come equipped with an endless supply.

"This one goes out to someone special."

Myrtle stood up and whistled through her fingers at him. Sy's crooked grin found Maggie in the crowd, and they locked eyes.

He counted the band in, and the first bars of "Some Kind of Wonderful" had the crowd erupting in applause and cheers. But she forgot all about the band when Silas opened his mouth. His voice was rough around the edges as it toyed with the notes. His fingers nimble on the strings of the guitar. But it was his gaze on her face that did it.

Maggie felt her cheeks flush, and Kayla reached across the table to grab her hand. The hottest guy in town was serenading her, and she was having a borderline inappropriate reaction to him. In front of his entire family.

"This is the most romantic thing I've ever seen in my entire life," Dean yelled in her ear.

Deputy Mayor Kressley Cho, dressed in a hot-pink business suit, appeared from nowhere. "Honey, no one will judge you if you take him out back and take his pants off."

Maggie couldn't help but laugh. She also couldn't seem to take her eyes off the man. Mama B had sashayed up to his mic, and together they were killing the chorus. When the song ended, their entire table and most of the bar were on their feet cheering.

Silas slipped the strap over his head and handed the guitar back to the band member. Then he leaned in and whispered something in Mama B's ear. Her eyes lit up, and she laughed. He was grinning when he stepped off the stage. His gaze zeroed in on Maggie's face.

She suddenly felt conspicuous and awkward. Unsure of herself.

The crowd was stirred up, and it took him a minute to make it to her. But the second he was close enough, he reached for her and tugged her to her feet.

"That was amazing," she said in his ear.

"Dance with me, Mags."

He didn't give her time to decide or to point out there wasn't any music yet. He just pulled her toward the dance floor. By the time they got there, the band had launched into "Angel" by Aerosmith. One of her favorites. Maggie heard chairs being pushed back from tables as every couple in the bar got up to dance. Silas kept right on tugging her along until they got to the other side of the stage, where the lights were behind them. Shadows enveloped them in the corner. In the cover of the dark, he wrapped her arms around his neck and pulled her closer than was necessary.

The beat was slow, and Mama B's voice was low and velvety.

Maggie looked up and searched those gray eyes for a hint at what he was thinking. She found out when he leaned down to nuzzle at her neck. Her heartbeat thrummed frantically against her ribs when his teeth dragged over her skin.

That jumpy, empty throb was back at her core, reminding her

that she'd gone so long without allowing someone inside. Her breasts ached for his touch. Those strong, rough hands sliding over heated skin. Would he take his time? Would he race her for release? Would he whisper all the words she longed to hear?

She had fantasies about getting on her knees in front of him and begging. Here. Separated from the crowd only by shadows.

"Darlin', if you keep looking at me like that, I might not be able to hang on to my civility," he said in a harsh whisper. He gave her hips a swift pull, and she felt his erection against her stomach. He was hard. God. So damn hard against her. That thick length behind his zipper.

Her breath caught in her throat.

"That's better," he said, his lips coasting over her neck, her jaw. Shifting, he moved one hand to her back, keeping her hips pressed against him. "Is this okay?" he asked, his voice husky as his thumb slipped under her shirt and stroked over her stomach.

She shivered. "Someone might see." She heard the thrill in her own voice.

His grin was deadly, and she knew he'd heard it, too.

"Just keep dancing, darlin'," he promised.

The sigh that left her lips when he flattened his palm against her ribs was very nearly a moan. His thumb brushed purposefully against the band of her bra.

Her body wanted to freeze in place and memorize the feel of his hand on her. But he kept them both swaying at half speed.

"I've been spending an awful lot of time thinking about how it would feel to get my hands on you, Maggie."

"It might have crossed my mind once or twice, too," she whispered.

"I'm gonna touch you now."

Words deserted her as anticipation, sharp as razor blades, flooded her system. Shredding any logic. The second she nodded, that big, warm palm of his slid higher to cup her breast. As her nipple pebbled against the friction, she felt his erection pulse once against her.

The bra, so impractical and not at all supportive, was suddenly her new best friend when his thumb brushed against the thin satin that dipped low over the curve.

"Ahh, Maggie," he breathed against her and squeezed.

Her knees buckled. She wanted to be embarrassed. She was thirty-four years old. This was not her first time running the bases. Enough men had made it to second base that her breasts should have been used to the attention.

But Sy's attention was something else entirely.

It was otherworldly.

His eyes were going sterling as they bored into her, absorbing her every reaction to him. With expert deftness, he slipped finger and thumb under the edge of her bra to find the bud. It tightened at his touch, and she wanted more. So much more.

His voice was ragged against her ear. "My house is clean."

She bit her lip, and he held his breath.

A smile spread across her face. "I shaved my legs."

"Come home with me, Maggie."

Maggie: Just checking in. How's everything at the house?

Cody: Kevin, Dolly Parton, and Taco are asleep on Dean's bed.

Maggie: Weirdest sentences for $200, Alex. That was a Jeopardy reference, just in case you didn't get it.

25

SILAS GAVE HIS front door a kick and, without breaking the lip-lock he had on Maggie, lifted her over the threshold and shut the door. He was dizzy with her. Obsessed with her every reaction to his touch.

"Stay," he managed to murmur as he busied himself stripping her out of her jacket. He threw it in the direction of the recliner. Reveling at the softness of her sweater, knowing the skin beneath was even softer.

"It's Cody's first night at the house," she said between kisses.

"We'll make it up to him tomorrow," he said, toeing off his boots. "I'll buy him a car or an Xbox."

When he reached for her, Maggie took a step back and held up a palm. "You stole my oxygen," she confessed.

He waited, like an engine revving, for her to find her breath, her footing. She was so damn beautiful. He didn't know how he'd survived the drive back with so little blood in his head.

Taking slow, deep breaths, she reached down and slid out of her sexy red platform sandals.

"You good?" he asked, trying his best to tamp down the beast inside that wanted to tear and shred and take. It was a losing battle, one he wasn't sure was worth fighting.

Warily, she nodded. But he saw the need in her eyes. "Yes," she hissed.

It was too much, seeing her need him, witnessing the depth of her want. He was on her in a heartbeat, mouth hard against hers, hands fast and desperate. He boosted her up and swallowed her surprised laugh with his hungry mouth.

When she wrapped those strong, lean legs around his hips, he felt invincible.

His hands and senses full of her, he headed to the bedroom, bursting through the door as if he were being pursued by demons.

"I don't want to stop touching you long enough to get your clothes off," he confessed.

"Then keep touching me while I strip," she offered, giving his jaw a scrape with her teeth.

"You're a very smart woman, Maggie. I want you to know that I respect you. I don't want you to doubt that after all the dirty things I'm going to do to you."

"Less talking, more dirty," she said, yanking her shirt over her head.

He could love her, he realized on the spot. That smart mouth that made his blood sing. Her tentative trust in him. The body that tortured him every day and night since he'd met her.

"Finally," he said, pressing his face to the valley between her breasts. Curves full and round, barely contained by the most useless bra in the history of breast support. The tiny swatch of sheer fabric in the middle begged to be destroyed. He wanted to buy her a dozen of them just so he could tear them off of her.

She felt like magic in his arms. Magic and a desire so deep he knew that once wouldn't be enough. One hundred times wouldn't be enough.

He toppled them onto the bed, pressing her into the mattress and reveling in the feel of her under him. His cock throbbed painfully.

Slow the fuck down, he warned himself. But that voice didn't take into consideration just how many damn times he'd fantasized about this exact moment. Lying here on this bed, hand fisted around his erection, knowing it would never be as good as the real thing.

"Sy," she breathed, rolling her hips against him.

He cupped a hand under each breast and slowly slid his palms higher.

Her back arched, pushing those perfect globes into his hands. He brushed both straps down her shoulders. It was the last gentle move he was capable of because Maggie raised onto her elbows and gave him access to the clasp of her bra.

Finally. His blood seemed to chant the word over and over again as it pooled and pulsed in his cock. He wasn't conscious of dragging the bra off her. But the moment he filled his work-hardened palms with her breasts would be burned into his memory forever. Perfection. Soft, heavy perfection. She fit his hands just right.

Every inch of her was a miracle, a wonder of his personal world.

She let out a ragged moan that he silenced with a kiss. His cock ached as he ground against her. He was hanging on by a thread, the leash on his control was stretched to the breaking point. But he couldn't stop, couldn't slow down. Not now.

His eager thumbs brushed over those rosy, erect nipples. It wasn't enough to just feel her; he needed to taste.

"More?" His whisper was harsh as he trailed teeth and tongue down her neck, over her shoulder.

"Please. Yes. More," she hissed.

Maggie Nichols was begging him for more.

He took a second to admire the way her full breasts fit his hands. Her nipples were a dark, puckered pink that made him think of rosebuds. Breath coming in short pants had those perfect breasts trembling, her heart thundering in her chest just beneath his fingers.

Silas looked her in the eyes as he lowered his mouth to one taut nipple. Her cry when his tongue danced over the delicate peak was music to his desperate ears. Licking, laving, he teased until she again whispered darkly, "More."

He drew the nipple into his mouth and began to suckle. Her legs opened restlessly, and he thrust against her. There were too many layers of clothing to make it anything but a painful, delirious preview.

He cursed the separation, the layers. He wanted her stripped down with nothing between them. Nothing in the way of what they were both chasing.

She bucked against him, and it felt so fucking good. The heat between her thighs required his attention. He released her nipple with a pop. It seemed to strain toward him. Egotistically proud, he moved to the other and repeated the long, hard pulls, reveling as it, too, hardened against his tongue.

It was the whimper clawing its way up her throat that did it. That had him yanking at the fly of her jeans.

She levered her hips up, and he took advantage of the angle, dragging denim and cotton down her legs.

With reverence, he traced a finger over the seam between her folds. "Open for me, Mags," he ordered. When she obeyed, when she dropped her knees, he felt delirious.

"Watch." He snapped out the command and waited until her eyes fluttered open before sinking one finger into her damp, trembling flesh. So wet and hot and tight. She'd be the death of him, but he'd guessed that the first time he laid eyes on her. It was finally time for his hands and mouth and cock to explore all the secrets of her body.

"More, Sy," she whispered.

He gave her more. Harder pulls at her breast, a second, then a third finger in her sex.

She rode his hand with frantic pumps of her hips as he pulled her nipples into his mouth one at a time. Strong and soft. Her body was a miracle of contradictions, and he was going to take his time worshipping each and every one.

"I love touching you, Maggie," he whispered. "I know I'm going to love fucking you."

"You're such a dirty talker," she breathed, then groaned as he thrust his fingers into her even deeper. She was so wet, so fucking ready.

"You love it, don't you, darlin'?"

"Yes." She hissed out the word as he stroked his tongue over her nipple.

"You love hearing how I'm going to pin you to this bed with my cock inside you and ride you hard and deep until you come on me." To emphasize his plan, he ground his erection against her.

"Oh, God. Need to touch you," she panted, fingers frantically reaching for the waistband of his jeans.

Reluctantly, he released her breast and comforted himself by finding her mouth. She worked his jeans open and shoved one hand inside.

The sound she made when she wrapped those long fingers around his shaft had his balls tightening in anticipation.

"Go slow, Mags," he said as she gave him a stroke that had his eyes rolling back in his head. "I'm pretty wound up."

"I don't want slow," she warned before driving him wild by sinking her teeth into his lower lip.

"Then you'd best hang on," he growled. He rose up on his knees and dragged her jeans all the way off. Heavy-eyed and panting, she helped him with his own.

"The red ones," she groaned when she saw his underwear. "I'm so fucking glad you wore the red ones. I've had dreams of these since I saw you in them that first day."

He glanced down. His erection was free of the nuisance of clothing—including the cherry-red boxer briefs. Then her hand was slipping around his length, gripping him tight. All rational thought fled his mind. The only thing left was the *drive* to be inside her, to start pumping into her. It almost made him light-headed.

He levered himself over her, fisting his erection as the blunt crown notched into place. Almost home. She was goddamn quivering around his tip.

"Fuck. Condom."

"Hurry up and find one before I decide to be irresponsible." Her breath came in pants, and the hypnotic rise of her breasts nearly made him forget why he'd stopped.

Blindly, he slapped a hand out for the nightstand. He found the box and emptied most of its contents on the floor but managed to rescue a single condom.

"Oh, thank God," she breathed as he shredded the wrapper.

"Baby, you ain't seen nothing yet," he promised.

He made quick work of the protection and then once again fisted his shaft.

"You better hang on tight, Mags," he warned, lining himself up with her entrance. He let out a guttural groan of triumph as he finally buried himself in her with one hard thrust.

"Silas!"

He held there, sheathed in her fist-tight grip. His toes dug into the mattress, hips pinning her down so he could stay deep.

"Breathe, darlin'," he growled. And when Maggie sucked in a breath and slowly let it out, he slid the final inch home. Finally. She was his.

His senses obsessively cataloged everything there was to know about Maggie in this moment. Sweat-slicked skin, wet folds spread around his cock, round, firm breasts pressed against his chest. Her legs, forced open by his hips, trembled against him. But those long, strong fingers dug into his shoulders as if to hold him inside her forever.

She got impossibly tighter around his shaft, and there was no loosening this time, no chance to catch his breath. He had to move before he lost his damn mind.

It took every shred of willpower to ease out of her, to abandon that wet, hot world he'd just discovered. And as soon as he was out, he needed to go home again. The second thrust was harder than the first, and he told himself he needed to slow down, to ease up, to be gentle.

But she was digging those short nails into his back and squeezing him with those strong thighs. Begging him with her body to take her, to show her what she did to him.

He began to move, slow, measured drives that took him to the very bottom of her. His dick swelled every time she let out one of those breathy little moans.

Breathing in the scent of her hair, he clamped his hands around her wrists and held them over her head. Her body went loose under him, as if she were surrendering to him. And that, he realized, was what he wanted most from her. Here in his bed, Maggie gave up her control to him. He cuffed both of her hands with one of his and reached down to force one of her knees higher, wider. He was enveloped by her, consumed by her.

The angle added a new, exquisite torture to what she was doing to him. He wanted to come. He wanted to let go and mindlessly rut into her until he couldn't take another second of it.

It wasn't until he felt the flutter of her muscles working his cock that he realized he'd done exactly that. Pistoning into her, daring her to take more, to want more.

"Silas," she breathed, "I need to—" She cut herself off with the kind of whimper he'd spend the rest of his life fantasizing about.

"I know, baby. Let it happen."

"But I want more." Her confession damned his soul.

"You'll have it. I'll give you more until you can't take it. Now let yourself go." His command was accompanied by mean, measured thrusts. Grinding into her until she could no longer hide from her release.

The flutter became a wave. And as it built, he brought his forehead to hers.

"Let go, Maggie. Come on my dick." He walked her right up to the edge and then shoved her over with exactly what she needed. His cock bottoming out, throbbing inside her.

She shattered around him. And maybe something in him shattered with her as she rode out her climax in undulating waves that threatened to force his own release.

He wanted to howl at the moon. To beat his chest. He wanted to hear his fucking name from her lips.

"Say it," he said, dragging his cock out of her body before driving it back into her quivering flesh. "Say my name, Maggie."

"Silas!" It was a broken cry, a moan, a prayer.

It was everything he wanted, and he only barely managed to hold himself back. It took every ounce of willpower not to let those seductive squeezes milking his shaft make him come.

"That's right, darlin'. That's right," he said against her ear as he fucked her slowly, thoroughly, wringing every last second of pleasure out of her climax.

Sweat dotted his brow and his shoulders as she went limp beneath him.

It felt so right to be inside her.

"Maggie, baby." His groan was guttural. They were sweaty. Dirty. Deranged for each other. He felt her tongue dart out to taste his neck.

She was coming back into her body now. Hands slid down his back to grip his ass, nails digging in again. When he rewarded her with a hard thrust, her hips rose to meet him, and he could feel that pulse in her core, begging for him to satisfy the renewed need.

"You don't have to hold back, Silas," she breathed. "I won't break."

"You might," he warned her. She had no idea what primitive, selfish cravings she'd unleashed inside him.

"Try me."

The dare, the effect of her words on him, was instantaneous. She'd given him permission to take as much as he wanted as hard as he wanted. Unrestrained, he became a force of nature. He felt an evolutionary drive to make this woman his own. To give her his very essence.

She clung to him as he worked her body closer and closer to the point of no return. They used teeth and tongues on each other as sweat soaked their skin. He couldn't stop the chase, couldn't relish the journey. Because he knew what waited for him at the finish line.

Together, their rough edges created something sharp and beautiful. Something otherworldly and brand-new.

He nuzzled against her ear, whispering the kind of things men didn't say in the light of day. Every dirty promise, every dark confession, every secret fantasy. And she was there with him. Trembling under him. Whispering his name. Chanting "yes" over and over again. He'd unlocked something in her as well as he slammed into her, finding her deepest point and holding fast for a second.

"You feel so fucking perfect," he gritted out. "You're gonna come for me again before I let go."

Roughly, he shoved his arms under her thighs, folding her in on herself. She was secured to him, open and vulnerable. Spread wide. With the change in angle, the head of his dick nudged the perfect spot inside her on every wild thrust. Again and again, he pumped into her. Mating. Rutting. Pillaging. Her nails made his skin sing.

He felt his cock thicken and lengthen as his release became imminent. Wide-eyed, Maggie gasped, feeling it. He rammed into her harder, faster, grunting against her neck. Desperate to find release.

"Come for me now," he commanded. "Don't hold back on me, Maggie."

"Silas!" She wasn't quiet now. And neither was he. When she clamped down on his shaft, he lost his fucking mind on a long, guttural groan. He was coming with her. His entire body tensed as his climax exploded up from the root of his dick just as she closed those hellfire muscles around his cock. It was too much. Not enough. More than he could handle. He poured himself into her as she bucked and begged and came.

Gutted. Hollow. Sated. His orgasm ripped him apart and put him back together again.

Long after she quit quivering around him, he held deep inside her, knowing it still wasn't enough. Knowing he would never be the same.

26

THE MAN WENT from easygoing flirt to savage lover in a heartbeat. Maggie was consumed by Silas Wright from the inside out. Her ears were ringing from the orgasm that hit her so fast, so hard, she was still dizzy.

His cock was still buried in her. His body was pressing hers into the mattress. She couldn't tell if she was being seductively smothered or if her cardiovascular endurance was so poor that two orgasms were the equivalent of a marathon.

Two orgasms that had exorcised every rational thought from her brain. There were no to-do lists, no schedules, no concerns circling when Silas Wright was making her come.

"Am I crushing you?" His voice was muffled by her hair.

"Maybe. I can't tell," she wheezed.

On a sigh, he rolled, reversing their positions. She sprawled across his chest with him still inside her. He was also still reasonably hard.

"How is that physically possible?" she murmured, her finger tracing a shape through his chest hair.

"What?" he asked, brushing his knuckles over one of her nipples. His eyes were closed, and there was a sleepy, smug smile playing at his mouth.

"That," she repeated and squeezed her inner muscles around him.

He grunted and stroked a hand up and down her spine. "That is what weeks of fantasizing about you does to a man."

"That's a lot of fantasizing," she mused. "Did I live up to your internal hype?"

Those gray eyes opened to study her. He slid a hand behind his head. "Baby, you surpassed it. My filthy fantasies have nothing on the real thing."

"So it was good?" she clarified.

He hooked her under the arms and pulled her higher so her breasts were in line with his mouth. "Darlin', I don't know what goes on in that busy mind of yours, but there is no way on this green earth that you could be thinking that was anything but the best sex either of us has ever had."

She relaxed against him and went back to idly tracing shapes on his chest.

"In fact, if I hadn't been so rough with you and hadn't lost most of my body's water content into a condom, I'd go for the instant replay." His tongue darted out to stroke over her nipple.

Her lips curved, and she pressed a kiss to the top of his head.

"Did I hurt you, Mags?" he asked gruffly.

Tomorrow morning, she would be walking like John Wayne after a day on a horse, but she'd wear it proudly. "You didn't hurt me. I wanted it like that," she confessed, suddenly feeling embarrassed.

"I don't know if you noticed, but you let go. You trusted me," he said, sounding smug.

Oh, she'd noticed all right. In the moment, it had felt so right. So good. But now, thinking about it was scaring the hell out of her. She didn't just hand over the reins to someone else. That was exactly how people got hurt.

"Uh-uh," Silas said, giving her a light slap on the ass. "Come out of your head, Mags." He reared up and took her pebbled nipple into his mouth and sucked.

She let out the breath she was holding.

"That's my girl," he murmured. "I'll keep doling out orgasms if it keeps you present."

"I should go home," she stammered. She should go home and overthink everything.

"Oh no you don't. Kevin and Cody are there. Dean's probably

back, too. Now it's time for me to tell you what I think," he said. He shifted her to straddle him, his cock still semihard inside her.

"What do you think?" She wasn't sure she actually wanted to know. There were some things a woman might never recover from.

"I think you're wound so tight in daily life that you need a place where you can let go of all those things you're holding on to. Where you can give that control over to someone else. Where you can be taken care of." Leisurely, he gave her other nipple a lick. "And I think you needing me to take charge was something I very desperately wanted."

She'd been all set to argue until his last admission. "It was?"

"I'm telling you this while you're on top and in charge," he said, giving a teasing thrust.

She loved the way his gaze locked on her breasts, the way his lips parted like he needed to devour her. Maybe part of her needed to be devoured. And maybe part of her wanted to prove him wrong.

"Mmm, you're getting wet again. Aren't you, Maggie?" Reaching behind her, he slipped his fingers down the cleft of her behind. She gasped when they skated over the puckered ring of muscle. And felt something like disappointment when they kept going.

"I should get home to Dolly and Taco," she said, trying to work up the energy to get out of the bed.

Sy's arm tightened around her. "But Dean and Cody are more than capable of keeping an eye on the little monsters. And Kevin's there, too."

"It's weird and adorable that your dog thinks he's a cat babysitter."

"Kevin is a weird and adorable kinda soul," he agreed. His drawl was sleepy, and it made her feel like curling up next to him and going to sleep might not be the worst thing in the world.

She yawned.

"Now, I'm not saying I'd hold you captive, Mags. But I think you're making excuses and trying not to get attached. Which doesn't work for me, seein' as how I'm inclined to make you get attached."

"You don't play fair," she complained.

"Think about that cot you've got waiting for you. That rickety, hard cot. Then there's the matter of breakfast. If you go home, what's for breakfast?"

"Dunno. Coffee and a protein bar probably." She had to go grocery shopping. There was a skinny teenage boy living in the house now. Dammit. She really needed to make things happen with that kitchen.

"I've got homemade granola, yogurt, and fresh berries. Not to mention an entire pack of bacon that Kevin hasn't discovered yet. And my coffee's pretty fucking great."

"You make your own granola?" She groaned. "Ugh. It's like you're some perfect Instagram model #LivingYourBestLife." Sometimes the perfection in others was just plain annoying.

He laughed softly. "If you stay here in this big comfy bed with me, I guarantee you'll like my alarm clock more than your own."

"Your alarm clock is your penis, isn't it?" she murmured into the pillow.

"Only one way to find out. Stay with me, Maggie."

"Why?" she asked. "Besides the five dollars you seem hell-bent on winning from me. Why do you want me to stay?"

"Because I want to wake up with you in my bed. I want to be there when your eyes open. I want the first smile of your day to belong to me. I want to start my day touching you."

The man was a natural seducer.

And she was just stupid enough to fall for it.

She let out a long breath. "Fine. I'll stay. But I want a toothbrush. And eggs to go with the yogurt and the bacon. And I don't want any shit from you when I leave your family cookout tomorrow after an hour and a half so I can catch up on some damn work."

"Anything you want, Mags. You can have it all." She could *hear* his smug smile.

"Why do I feel like I just played into your hands?"

He slid his hands up to cup her breasts. "Because my hands are on you. Besides, you're looking at it all wrong. You don't lose by staying the night."

"Let me text Dean so he and Cody don't think I'm dead in a ditch somewhere," she said.

"How about you text Dean while I go get us some tall waters?" Silas suggested. "Then we can grab a shower."

"Throw in a snack, and you've got a deal."

Once he left, she found her phone on the floor, half under the nightstand.

Maggie: I'm spending the night at Sy's. I'll be home in the morning. If you're a good boy I'll bring you and Cody fancy coffees.

Dean: We'll take two venti lattes with caramel drizzle.

Maggie: Are you ordering two drinks for yourself?

Dean: I'm educating our young friend on good coffee. When he turns 21 you can educate him on alcohol that doesn't come in a plastic bottle.

Dean: Also, did you make Sly Sy turn his hat backward in bed?

Maggie: Shut up weirdo. You and Michael seemed awfully cozy tonight.

Dean: I asked him to dance. He shot me down.

Maggie: Maybe you dazzled him too much?

Dean: Or maybe my gaydar is broken. Or maybe he saw my gray hair and crow's-feet and I scared him straight.

Maggie: Want me to ask Silas?

Dean: DO NOT ASK HOT SILAS ABOUT MY CROW'S-FEET! Or his brother. You bask in the afterglow while I binge-watch BBC murder mysteries and drink age-reversing green juice. PS You need a fucking TV and a couch in this mausoleum.

She sighed and wished there was something she could do for Dean. But everyone had their journey. And it was better to fix things on your own than to accept meddling.

Maggie: Okay fine. Get some sleep so you're well rested and can charm the pants off everyone in his family at the cookout.

"Everything okay?" Silas asked, returning with two tall glasses of water and—sweetly—a stack of peanut butter crackers.

He was still naked and an absolute delight to look at. She hadn't really appreciated the view, being distracted by all those orgasms and all. His tattoo stood out on his left arm, as did the dark tan line at his waist.

"You're really gorgeous," she said, accepting the glass he handed her.

He gave her a wolfish smile. "It speaks to your intelligence that you noticed."

"Where does all that confidence come from?" she asked. "Is it from looking like that?"

"Darlin', I'm surprised at you. Don't you know confidence comes from the inside?"

"Does it? Because from where I sit, you've got an awful lot to feel confident about on the outside," she said, eyeing his muscular thighs and what hung between them.

He sat down on the mattress next to her and gave her bare hip a friendly squeeze. "Confidence comes from knowing that whatever the situation, you know you'll make the best of it. Confidence is certainty in your ability to rise."

Her philosophical landscaper lover.

He took the phone from her. "No screens in the bedroom."

"What if there's an emergency?"

"Then you'll find out about it in the morning," he said, ushering her toward the waiting shower.

"Hey. We found gold today."

He gave her an affectionate slap on the ass. "It was a really good day, Mags."

Dayana: Thanks to you and your beach bungalow kid's room, Keaton now wants bunk beds.

Maggie: He has good taste.

Dayana: I think I know where he gets it. Spoiler Alert: It's not me. Any recommendations for how to keep him in the bed and not falling out of it?

Maggie: Have you considered duct tape?

Dayana: Only every day of his life. Question. What's the real estate market like in mostly rural Idaho?

Maggie: Why?

27

BLAIRE AND MORRIS'S house was a brick two-story on a quiet block at the southern end of Kinship. Cody and Dean climbed out of Maggie's truck and stood on the sidewalk, eyeing the house. Music and voices, a lot of them, carried over the backyard fence.

"Okay. Let's review the game plan," Maggie said, joining them. "These family things can run long and get awkward."

"How would you know?" Dean demanded, crossing his arms. "My family get-togethers are always delightful."

"Are you forgetting that time your aunt Lacey accused her sister of trying to make out with her date to Thanksgiving? There's always a crazy mother-in-law. Or a cousin who picks pockets. Or the creepy uncle." *Or the stepmother who hated her stepdaughter's very existence. Or the reluctant father who was too busy running an empire to care about the twelve-year-old he never wanted.*

"My mom's last family reunion ended early because three of her uncles got arrested fighting over how to grill hot dogs," Cody added.

"See?" she said smugly to Dean. "Okay, boys. How long are we staying?"

"Ninety minutes or the shortest amount of time to still be considered polite," Cody answered.

She gave him an approving nod. "Great. Is everyone armed with their excuses?"

"Finishing touches for tomorrow's episode," Dean answered with a beleaguered sigh.

"Science test to study for," Cody said.

"I need to catch up on all the stuff I didn't do this weekend," Maggie added. "And if none of those excuses work?"

"The kittens," Dean and Cody responded together.

"'Go, team,' on three," she said, putting her hand out. The guys added their hands. "One. Two. Three."

"Go, team!"

Maggie tried to ignore the stumble her heart took when Silas met them at the gate.

"Hey, guys. Mags," he said softly. That achingly familiar naughty smile played on his lips.

She was crushing on the guy she was sleeping with. The guy who was determined to make her stay. Things were going to get ugly.

As if he read her mind, he pulled her in for a soft kiss. Kevin gave a joyful bark.

"Mom! Sy's got his tongue down a girl's throat," Maggie heard Nirina say from the backyard.

"Ooooh!" came the family chorus.

Silas pulled back, grinning. "Ignore them. They're all jerks."

He shook Dean's hand and then gave Cody a slap on the shoulder. "Glad you could make it. My mom heard that you're a fan of potato salad, so she made a quadruple batch."

"Really?" Cody looked embarrassed and thrilled at the same time. It made Maggie's heart hurt for him. Groceries. She would fill that empty kitchen to the ceiling with them. She'd already hit Buy It Now on a big-ass TV and bracket for the room across from her office. She'd ask Nirina where she could get a couch.

"Really. Come on back." Silas led the way, his fingers casually linking through hers. Affection in front of family seemed like they were careening toward a finish line she didn't want to cross.

Big shade trees lined the back of the property. A large deck with a double set of sliding doors held a spiffy grill and a long farm table. It stepped down onto a brick patio lined by raised flower beds with structured plantings. The grass was cut on a precise diagonal.

Everything was orderly and soothingly symmetrical.

The whole family—minus East Coast Taylor—was accounted for in Blaire and Morris's backyard.

In mirrored sunglasses and a flowing orange-and-white dress, Niri sat on the patio just off the deck, feet propped on a wicker ottoman. Her husband, Jeremiah, waved from the grill, where he was watching a woman who looked an awful lot like Silas flip chicken breasts.

Sy's dad, Emmett, and Mama B were distributing wineglasses. Michael walked out of the house with a huge bowl of salad. When he spotted the newcomers, he nearly tripped over his designer flip-flops.

"Starstruck," Maggie whispered in Dean's direction.

"You're drunk on orgasms and don't know what you're saying," he hissed back.

The only person she was surprised to see was Wallace, who was in deep discussion at the table with Morris.

"Mom, I think you're the only one who hasn't met Maggie and company yet," Silas called to the woman behind the grill. With a smile much like her son's, Blaire handed the tongs over to Jeremiah and wiped her hands on the GRILL MISTRESS apron that she wore over navy slacks and a gray sleeveless sweater. She had blond hair pulled back in a no-nonsense ponytail and simple gold hoops in her ears.

"You must be Maggie, Dean, and Cody," she said, coming to greet them. "I'm so glad you could come."

Maggie accepted the offered hand and found the grip cool and confident. "Thank you for inviting us. Wallace, too," she said.

"Rumor has it he hasn't been getting many visitors, so we thought we'd add another place at the table," she said.

"That's nice of you," Maggie said. "I wish we could stay longer. But we have some things to take care of this afternoon."

Silas shot her a look, and she ignored it.

"That's not a problem. We're just happy to have you," Blaire assured her.

"Beer, wine, pops, and waters are in there," Silas said, pointing at a big blue cooler on the deck. "And I'm going to steal Maggie for a second to discuss an important landscaping problem."

Without another word, he towed her through the back door and into the garage.

"What's wrong? Are you mad that I'm not staying, or is there an actual problem?" she asked.

Instead of answering her, he pressed her up against the wall next to a meticulously organized corkboard of yard implements and kissed the ever-living hell out of her.

His mouth was hard and unyielding against hers. His hands settled at her hips, thumbs slipping under her T-shirt to stroke over her stomach. Her legs trembled as her body recalled in exquisite detail last night's pleasure. That morning's flirtation on his back porch over breakfast. She went boneless under his touch.

He pulled back with a growl. "Now that I've got my hands on you, it's a hell of a lot harder to keep them off you," he admitted.

Carefully, he withdrew his hands from her and placed them on either side of her head. He blew out a breath. "I shouldn't have done that."

"Why not?" she asked, still breathless.

"Because now I can't walk back out there," he said.

She glanced down and grinned. He was wearing gym shorts today, which showed off both his muscular legs and his impressive erection. "Oh," she said.

Historically, Maggie hadn't been the kind of girl who got dragged away from picnics because her boyfriend wanted to make out with her. She was the kind of girl who complimented the potato salad and helped wash dishes afterward. She had to admit she liked this version. A lot.

"I guess it wouldn't help if I . . ." She reached down between them and gripped his shaft through his clothes.

"Maggie," he warned, his forehead coming down to rest on hers.

"Oops."

"Don't make me drag you into the backseat of my mom's sedan, darlin'."

It seemed like something he would do. To be on the safe side, she released him and ducked under his arm.

"Do you want me to wait with you?" she offered.

"I don't think that's going to help," he said, eyes steely.

"I'll just go get a drink then and make small talk with your family while you try not to think about how hard you came in me last night."

"Maggie!"

His bark was cut off by her laugh as she closed the door. She felt downright cheerful now and helped herself to a soda—correction, a pop—before taking a seat at the table next to Wallace.

"Have you found anything on Ava's family?" Maggie asked.

He snorted. "Mrs. Campbell's a mystery. I can trace the line forward from her, but not back. The local history books mention her coming from some wealthy European family, but I haven't found anything related to the Dedmans."

"Maybe her family changed their last name when they came to America?" she guessed, recalling her genealogy research in elementary school. The great-great-great-grandfather of one of the kids in her class had gone from the Russian Kohnovalsky to the easier-to-spell Cohen.

She distinctly remembered a classmate, the pigtailed Judy Mc-Donald, asking Maggie where *her* dad was on her family tree drawing. Maggie had gone home to ask her mother that very question, but it was years before she revealed the truth. Years before she realized she was better off not knowing.

Cody and then Emmett joined them at the table.

"How are you feeling about the test tomorrow, Cody?" Emmett asked.

The boy winced. "Okay, I think, Mr. Wright."

Maggie blinked. Sy's dad was Cody's biology teacher? Small towns were so...small.

"Cell metabolism is tough," Emmett sympathized. "You need at least a C on this to keep graduation alive. I think you can do it. If you want, after lunch I can walk you through a quick refresher."

Cody nodded. "Thanks. That would help a lot."

Maggie felt like this was information she should have known. So much for being a cool, informed sort of guardian.

"Are you having trouble in science?" she asked Cody.

He gave a shrug. "More like with school in general."

Before she could extend a vague offer of some sort of help, Blaire announced that it was time to eat, and there was a stampede to the table. Maggie didn't miss the knowing look that passed between Blaire and Mama B when Silas took the seat on her left and slung his arm around her chair. Laying claim.

Conversation began again as food was passed and plates were filled. Dean was sandwiched between Niri and Michael. From where Maggie sat, it looked like Niri was the only one doing any of the talking.

"I read that Sebastian Spencer signed the giving pledge," Morris mentioned to Blaire.

The casual dropping of the billionaire philanthropist's name had Maggie swallowing hard around a bite of chicken.

Dean shot Maggie a sharp look from across the table. She picked up her wineglass and took a healthy swig. Oblivious to her tension, Silas traced tiny circles with his fingers on her back.

"What the hell's a giving pledge?" Wallace grumbled.

"It's when a wealthy person promises to donate the bulk of his or her fortune," Mama B explained.

"Sounds like socialism to me," the old man harrumphed.

Silas laughed. "What it *sounds* like, my crabby friend, is new resources for small businesses to help them grow and adapt. Grants, training, loans to help cover higher hourly wages."

Did every damn person in this town read *Newsweek*? Maggie wondered in exasperation.

"Uh, speaking of businesses," Maggie said, clinging to the segue. "Is there any news on what's happening with the cabinetry plant?"

"The word around town is they're trying to arrange for a private sale, or at least get permission to temporarily open back up to finish the outstanding orders," Emmett said.

"It's a real shame," Blaire said. "Canyon Custom Cabinetry was known for workmanship and quality for decades. Somehow a few greedy people managed to ruin the financial security of half the town's families and run an entire business into the ground."

Maggie dropped her fork as a bolt of inspiration hit her. "I don't suppose there's anyone I could talk to about having the plant design a custom kitchen for the Campbell place?"

"Not in the budget," Dean sang under his breath.

"Eat your potato salad," Maggie warbled back.

"With 999,902 followers, that's a lot of free publicity," Silas drawled.

Risking whiplash, Maggie whirled to look at him. "You memorized my follower count?"

He gave her the flirty eyes and rubbed his thumb over the base of her neck. She tried not to purr out loud. "I might have peeked . . . after Cody showed me where to look," he told her.

Cody snickered. "I was just impressed he had a GIF keyboard on his phone."

"What happens when you hit one million subscribers?" Morris asked.

"It's just a milestone," Maggie said.

"Sounds like one hell of an impressive milestone to me," Emmett added.

Over the ribbing around the table, Mama B clasped her ringed fingers under her chin. "I like you, Maggie," she said with approval. "You've got smarts and heart."

"Start with the deputy mayor," Blaire suggested. "She'll know who you need to talk to about getting you a kitchen."

Maggie found herself grinning her way through the meal as Cody ate enough food for half a high school track team and earned affectionate praise from Blaire, claiming he was saving her from packing up leftovers.

Wallace launched into a ten-minute lecture on Kinship Lodge, which had been torn down twenty years ago.

Morris and Emmett planned out a kayaking day trip, and before all was said and done, they'd invited Cody and Dean along.

It was a genuinely enjoyable meal with a family accepting of its members and outsiders. An utterly foreign concept to Maggie. She felt like an anthropologist exploring a brand-new culture.

"Let me help," she offered, rising with her plate when they'd finished.

"Uh-uh. In this house, the testosterone does the cleanup," Morris insisted, taking her plate.

In less than a minute, Maggie was alone at the table with the women. She smelled an ambush. At least Kevin had decided to stay with her. His big head rested on her shoe.

"You and Silas seem to be enjoying each other," Blaire said, leaning over to top off Maggie's wineglass.

She wasn't picking up on any threatening language from the women, but that didn't mean it wasn't coming.

"You two looked like you were about to go to third base on the dance floor last night," Mama B said with an expressive wiggle of her eyebrows.

A chorus of the Beatles' "A Hard Day's Night" broke out in the kitchen. She could pick out both Dean's and Cody's voices when they joined in.

"That's their cleanup song," Nirina explained.

"We're just having fun," Maggie told the moms, suddenly feeling both defensive and envious. This is what guys didn't get about bringing a woman home to the parents. It said things that weren't necessarily true. Set expectations. Made things weird. Showed girl-friends a glimpse of something they weren't truly a part of.

No matter how old she got, Maggie had accepted that she would always have that longing to belong. To be loved easily and without question. In this moment, the need for it was so keen it took her breath away.

"There is nothing wrong with having fun, sexually or otherwise," Blaire said firmly, letting her therapy degree show.

"Nothing at all," Mama B agreed, refilling Niri's water glass and trailing a hand down her daughter's braids. They shared a look, one so full of familiarity, of love, that Maggie had to look away.

"What's your family like?" Niri asked suddenly.

"You pretty much know," Maggie joked, gesturing toward the kitchen where Dean was helping load the dishwasher and Cody was getting tutored in science.

"That was really wonderful what you did, taking Cody in," Mama B told her.

"No parents?" Blaire asked.

"My mom died when I was in college," Maggie said. "I don't have any siblings." *Not really, at least.*

"I'm so sorry to hear that, sweetheart," Mama B said, reaching over to squeeze Maggie's hand. "How about your father?"

"It's complicated," she hedged, feeling like a major downer on their happy little picnic.

"We know all about that," Sy's mom said, raising her glass in Mama B's direction and winking.

"Honey, you and I wrote the book on complicated," the woman responded with a shake of her head that had her yellow plastic earrings jingling.

Maggie couldn't imagine anything complicated about the Wrights. They were too loving, too accepting of each other to have withstood any real drama. They were the TV family she'd secretly longed for.

"Oh Lord, here we go," Niri said. "It's too bad I'm pregnant with your grandbaby because this girl needs a drink if we're gonna be talking about your scandalous sex lives."

Maggie blinked while both moms laughed.

"We'll spare you the details," Mama B said. "But we weren't always this simpatico."

"But everyone ended up where they were supposed to," Blaire reminded her.

"I fell in love with Emmett while he was still married to Blaire," Mama B confessed. "And let's say that neither one of us acted in a respectful manner to the institution of marriage."

Maggie simultaneously wanted to hear the whole sordid story and wished she were inside on dish duty.

Blaire rolled her eyes. "It was one kiss, Breonna. While we were talking about separating. Not some torrid affair."

Mama B winked at her. "Let me be the bad girl in this story."

"You couldn't be the bad girl if you tried," Blaire said with affection. "Anyway, Emmett and I divorced, and he and Breonna got married. And we made it work."

"With a *lot* of work," Mama B reminded her.

"But eventually, we realized we're stronger together, working toward the same goals, than we ever would have been apart," Blaire explained. "And then I met Morris, and here we are."

"We're not perfect. But we're damn hard workers, Maggie. And what we're trying to say is like recognizes like," Mama B told her. "So whatever you are to our son, you're someone special to us."

Maggie swallowed the lump that had formed in her throat. She missed her mother so acutely in the moment that she felt actual, physical pain.

"You're an incredible young woman," Blaire said, taking her other hand. "What you're doing for the small businesses in this town when they so desperately need it. What you're doing by giving that sweet boy a place to stay and a steady paycheck. You're doing beautiful, good things."

Maggie blinked back tears that welled up without warning. "Thank you." She barely managed to get the words out.

"Y'all need to stop telling people this story," Nirina complained.

"We own our vulnerabilities and our truths," Blaire reminded Nirina. It had the ring of a family motto.

"And we learn to love ourselves no matter what," Mama B said, giving Maggie's hand a reassuring squeeze.

"Y'all aren't terrifying my girl, are you?" Silas called from the open window.

"Are those dishes done yet?" Mama B yelled back.

"No, ma'am," he answered. Maggie could hear the affection in his tone and wondered if he knew how very lucky he was.

28

SILAS PUNCHED THE button on the air compressor, bringing it to life. Kevin barked like a dog possessed. Over the whine of the compressor and rabid barking, he heard a car pull up the drive. Seconds later, Maggie hopped out of Dean's Mini Cooper and eyed him, hands on hips.

"What is that?" she called.

"An air compressor," he said innocently.

Shaking her head, she popped the hatch and started unloading shopping bags. The dog jogged off the porch to investigate. She gave Kevin a smooch on the head and a good scruffing before climbing the porch steps with the first load of bags.

"I know what an air compressor is. What the hell is that?" she asked, pointing at the lump of vinyl slowly taking shape.

Silas rose to greet her, and since her hands were full, he kissed her on the mouth before opening the screen door for her. "That's an inflatable movie screen."

Her lips quirked. "Seriously?"

"Darlin', I'm a man."

"I've been made aware," she said dryly.

"As a man, it's my duty to ensure that all entertainment is viewed on the appropriate-size screen."

"I got a TV. Sixty inches of screen," she argued. "We just have to hang it before the episode airs tonight."

"Already hung," he said, shooing his dog away from the shopping bags. "Got it mounted on the wall, and then we menfolk took a vote. Cody and Dean agreed. If you're having the crews over for an impromptu viewing, we might as well make it a party."

"Ugh. Fine. Boys are weird. I need to unload this stuff before Kevin starts snacking."

"Any more bags in the car?" he called after her.

"A few."

A few bags turned out to be twelve more canvas totes stuffed to the hilt with not just the burgers and hot dogs Maggie had gone shopping for, but also deli meat, bread, pastas, produce, beef jerky, and four boxes of cereal.

He wasn't the only one who'd gone overboard. After the groceries were unloaded, she enlisted him to help her lug two shelving units up from the basement to use as a makeshift pantry in the still-empty kitchen.

He'd just stepped outside to set up the food tables when Dean and Cody arrived in Maggie's truck with a big, manly grill strapped down in the bed. Crammed in with the grill were two oversize armchairs wrapped in plastic. Jim's van pulled in behind them, hauling a trailer with a matching couch.

Maggie Nichols was nesting.

Silas ambled over, thumbs in his pockets.

"Whenever you're done flashing that shit-eating grin around, you can help us unload," Dean joked.

Silas carefully wiped said shit-eating grin from his face. "Looks like you gentlemen have been busy," he observed.

"Where do we start?" Cody asked, eyeing their haul.

"The grill," answered the men.

Less than two hours later, the beer was cold, the grill was fired up, and there were theater-like rows of camp chairs in the front yard facing the movie screen. Bluegrass music poured forth from wireless speakers, and nearly two dozen men and women who'd put in a good day's work ate, drank, and shot the shit with enthusiasm.

"Here you go, Sy," Cody said, handing him a plate of uncooked burgers and dogs. "They're starting to slow down on the food."

Silas fist-bumped the kid and held out the tongs. "You feeling up for some grill mastering?" he asked.

"Me?" Cody looked like he'd just been handed the keys to a Porsche. It made Silas want to make sure this kid got every rite of passage his parents hadn't been around to give him.

"Yeah, you." He was explaining the finer points of the grill and meat cooked over a flame when Maggie fluttered by, nervously checking the coolers.

On her third pass of the food table, Silas snagged her and reeled her in. "Take a breath, Mags."

"Everything's fine. I don't need to breathe," she insisted.

"Everything is not fine," he countered. "It's great. Everyone's having a good time. The food is awesome. And you bought enough beer to last the summer. There's not a single thing that requires stressing over right this second."

She didn't look convinced, so he hauled her into his chest. It took her a beat, but he finally felt the tension drain out of her on a long sigh.

"I've never thrown a party like this before," she confessed.

"What about all those grand reveal parties?" he asked. Every season of her show ended with a big reveal-day party.

"That's all event planners and caterers. All I have to do is show up with my hair done and say stuff on camera. And after your family thing yesterday—"

"What family thing?"

"The cookout at your mom and Morris's?"

"What about it?" he asked, baffled.

"I don't know," she said, sounding ornery. "It was nice. They were nice. Everything was...nice. I've never been to a family thing like that before, and I just want to make sure everyone here has a...nice time."

Between Cody and Maggie, Silas had his hands and heart full.

"You're doing great, too," he told her gruffly. "There's just one more thing you need to do."

"Napkins? I knew I should have gone with something more festive."

He shook his head. "Not napkins, darlin'." He leaned down and snagged a beer out of the cooler at their feet. "You're gonna take this, you're gonna get yourself a plate, and then you're gonna go sit down with me and talk to people."

"What about—"

He shook his head. "Uh-uh. You saw how it worked at Mom's. Everyone pitches in. You're officially off duty."

She tried to pull away from him, her gaze already locked on the tray of cheese slices.

"Yo, Dino," he called.

Dean appeared in the sunroom door, holding a huge mug of coffee. "You shouted?"

"You mind restocking the cheese while Maggie and I grab something to eat?" Silas asked.

"On it," Dean said, disappearing back into the house.

"Now, let's eat," he said, steering her in the direction of the food.

Dusk fell around them as Silas watched Maggie relax, reluctantly, into both conversation and food. Newly minted grillmaster Cody joined them with his third plate and news that he'd earned a B- on the dreaded science test. She'd beamed at him and volunteered to help him tackle his trigonometry homework.

Dean appeared on the porch in front of the screen and clapped his hands for attention. "Five minutes, people! Get your refills now before you all become super famous and have to hire people to get your drinks for you."

Silas grinned amid the ensuing mad rush for beers and second helpings.

Shaking her head, she leaned toward him. "Are you sure you're ready for this?"

"Me? What's there to get ready for?"

"You can't look like you look and act like you act without getting a lot of attention," she warned him.

"I'm flattered, but the only attention I want is yours."

"It can be overwhelming. Even for someone who doesn't know what Twitter is."

"You forget, darlin'. Because I don't have any social media, I'm well insulated from the spectacle."

"Just because you don't hear them doesn't mean people aren't talking."

"Just because people are talking doesn't mean their opinions matter," he countered.

She grinned. "Well, before this episode goes live, consider me your first fan."

He took her hand and kissed her knuckles. "I might not be your first, Mags. But I am your biggest."

She looked at him impishly. "Fan, right?"

"Take it however you want," he said smugly.

"Ugh. You're *the worst*."

He opened his mouth and then closed it again. "Huh. I was going to say I'm *your* worst, but that doesn't work out as nicely as the other thing did."

And then it was too late to say anything more because the screen on the porch came to life and someone handed them each fresh beers.

"We're up," Dean said, from behind the laptop.

The excitement around them was palpable. Silas was already ten shades of proud for Maggie bringing them all together like this, making it feel like they were all a part of something this big, this important.

Their little audience whistled and hummed along with the catchy musical opening and then cheered loudly when Maggie appeared on screen.

"I'm Maggie Nichols, and this is the Old Campbell Place."

While everyone was riveted to the screen and Dean was glued to his phone and laptop, reading out live comments, Silas watched Maggie. She grinned bigger each time she introduced one of the contractors, every shot of crew members at work. She took pride in not just the physical work, but also in the way she told a story. The way she told *their* story. The way she drew people in and made them care.

"Hollywood's gonna be busting down my door," Marta predicted when she was shown in action with a wheelbarrow.

Elton let out a wolf whistle when Silas made his on-screen debut.

"And here come the comments," Dean crowed. "'If Maggie's not dating him, I volunteer as tribute.' 'Hot landscaper guy can mow my lawn any day.'"

"It's a good thing you're not embarrassed by attention," Maggie snickered.

"As long as I've got yours, Mags."

His phone buzzed in the cupholder of his chair and kept right on buzzing.

"The fame circus awaits," she teased.

On a sigh, he opened his messages.

Taylor: Who knew what a dreamy big brother I had? I still think of him as the guy farting on my pillow in junior high.

Michael: Maybe you could sell that story to the gossip blogs. He's getting marriage proposals in the comments!

Niri: OMG! They're shipping Maggie and Sy! #Milas

Michael: I was hoping they'd go with #Saggie

Taylor: Oh my. I might have to bleach my eyeballs after reading some of these comments. There are some thirsty ladies AND gentlemen watching!

Michael: *chugging water GIF*

Silas: I hate you all. Fortunately I'm too famous to talk to any of you losers anymore.

"Mags, what's 'shipping'?" he asked.

"It's when fans push for two characters to hook up," she whispered back.

That he could get behind. Maggie's fans were clearly very intelligent people. "How about 'thirsty'?"

She smirked. "In a nutshell? Horny."

He liked the shipping better, Silas decided.

"I'm concerned my influence is going to corrupt you," Maggie teased, producing her own phone.

"I'm yours to corrupt," he promised.

"Keep your sexytime comments to yourself for a minute," she said, opening her camera app. She stood and began to record their little viewing party. Silas made sure to wink at the camera when she pointed it in his direction.

"Holy shit!" Dean jumped out of his camp chair so fast that it toppled and collapsed. "What's that number?" he demanded, shoving the phone in Cody's face.

"Uh, 1,000,061?" Cody read.

"What?" Maggie asked shrilly.

Silas rescued her phone just before she was tackled to the ground and hugged by Dean and Cody. He hoped to God the video was still recording because this was a moment of magic.

"One million fucking subscribers!" Dean shrieked.

"You guys did it," Cody said.

"We did it," Maggie said, her voice muffled by the aggressive hugging.

Their live audience erupted, and Silas could feel the pride. Each feeling like they'd contributed to the success, each recognizing a personal stake in the game.

"I don't know what one million subscribers means, but it sounds important," Albert from Shitter's Full Plumbing whooped, jumping on the growing pile of bodies.

Maggie managed to crawl her way out of the hug pyramid and make her way toward him, a smile wide and fierce lighting up her beautiful face. Silas tossed her phone aside a split second before she jumped into his arms. He swung her around, lifting her feet off the ground.

"Are you here for this, Mags? Are you breathing this in?"

She wrapped her arms around him, holding him tight. "Yeah. I am."

*   *   *

Megan's RV Life: #HotLandscaperGuy

RetroMama711: In love with this house! And the landscaper!

Starla14: Hate Maggie's hair color. She looks so gross and washed out.

VeggieMarathoner: OMG, I read A. Campbell's book Canyon Secrets when I was in high school! So exciting to be working on a piece of history!

29

SILAS DRUMMED HIS fingers on the steering wheel to the beat of Jimmy Buffett as he turned onto Maggie's lane. The windows were down, the music was up, and the warm breeze carried with it more than a hint of summer.

Even Kevin, not the world's most morning-appreciative dog, seemed in tune with the energy. His ears ruffled in the breeze, tail wagging as the truck neared the house.

This was the kind of day Silas lived for.

He had a plan. He'd made a few calls and run a few early-morning errands before heading up into the hills. He was going to make sure it was a day his workaholic girlfriend would remember, too. Since the episodes of the Old Campbell Place started airing, Maggie'd doubled down on her work schedule, seeming determined to keep things moving.

He also had the distinct feeling she was using it as an excuse to put a little distance between them. It was a song and dance getting her to spend the night with him. She'd only caved twice in the past week, and the last time was only because he said he'd stay at her place.

If she had thought a night crammed into a cot was going to scare him off, she was sorely mistaken. Since childhood, he'd spent half his summer nights camping under the stars. He could handle Maggie's cot if it meant she was wrapped around him.

Only Jim's van was in the driveway so far. Silas parked the truck in front of the garage and climbed out, with Kevin on his heels. He understood Maggie's motives. Self-preservation and all that. What they had going on was scary as shit. It was deeper and wider, sharper and more intense than anything he remembered with anyone else.

The woman was underestimating the hell out of him if she thought he was just going to let her wall herself off. He wasn't going to make it easy to walk away.

It was time to dial up the heat.

He climbed into the bed of the truck, muscled the tree to the tailgate, and then carried it to the side of the garage. Returning to the truck, he reached into the backseat and grabbed the second surprise. The flower bed along the side of the house was deep and shaded. The Japanese maples they'd planted stood sentry over hostas and hellebore, ferns and mosses. He tucked the patinaed copper-blue heron statue into a grouping of columbine and whistled Kevin away from the trash can he was sniffing.

"Let's go sweep our girl off her feet," he told the dog.

Up for the game, Kevin charged toward the house. It was really starting to take shape. The siding—a gorgeous and unexpected dark blue—was done. The windows that had needed it had been swapped for energy-efficient replacements that—miracle of miracles—actually opened, closed, and locked.

Maggie had spent the last two days sanding down the wood trim on the front porch, getting ready to start painting. He'd checked the weather and knew they were in for at least a four-day stretch of balmy, breezy days.

Kevin, in search of his kitten friends, nosed his way through the screen door, and Silas followed.

He found Maggie and Cody in the kitchen. It was a homey scene, despite the lack of appliances, cabinets, and light fixtures. The only progress that had been made was the installation of the French doors, once the right set was delivered...four weeks late. The room was most definitely cursed. But his girl was undeterred.

The upside of not having a kitchen to work on meant that

Jim's crew was finally focused on the en suite bathroom in Maggie's bedroom.

Maggie, with part of her hair pulled up in a tiny, messy knot and wearing the white Bitterroot Landscapes T-shirt he'd given her, leaned over the table, coffee mug in hand, while Cody frowned over an iPad. Two plates with the remains of hardboiled eggs and microwaved bacon sat between them.

"It's perfect already, Cody. You can't shine it up any more," she told the boy.

"I've got ten minutes before deadline," Cody insisted. "I'm just giving it one last look."

"Mornin'," Silas said, stepping into the room and heading for the coffeemaker. Maggie might have been trying to get some distance from him, but she'd also bought him a travel mug that said I LIKE TO GET DIRTY and washed it for him every night.

"Ladies and gentlemen, the world-famous Hot Landscaper Guy," she teased.

Those brown eyes went soft and warm every damn time he surprised her with a gift or a snack or a kiss. And like clockwork, he could see her pull herself back. He knew how to read signs. He also knew how to detour around them.

"Hey, Sy," Cody said without looking up from the tablet.

"English essay?" Silas asked.

"His essay on Campbell's *Canyon Secrets* that's due to be uploaded in mere minutes," Maggie told him with a wink. "Cody's playing perfectionist."

"Said the woman with a six-foot whiteboard that details every step it takes to get a project to perfection," Silas teased.

"Ha. Burn." Cody snorted.

"You leave my whiteboard alone," she said, pointing a finger at Silas. "And you have one minute to upload that paper," she said, moving that same finger into Cody's line of sight.

"Speaking of the whiteboard, Mags," Silas began. "Looks like you're almost two full days ahead of schedule."

"It's all about the momentum," she said, keeping an eye on her watch. "If this keeps up, we might even finish early."

Which would put the house on the market early. Which would put her in her pickup and on the road to her next house early.

Short of sabotage, Silas wasn't going to let that happen.

"Morning, folks," Jim said, sauntering into the kitchen.

"Morning," they chorused.

"You tell her yet?" Jim asked Silas.

"Tell me what? Cody, hit upload, or I'll do it for you," Maggie said.

With a nervous breath, Cody stabbed at the screen and then dropped the tablet on the counter. "It's done. I think I'm going to barf."

"You wrote a great essay. You did the work. Now it's out of your hands, and you've got to let it go. Trust the work to get you the result," she told him.

"If I don't get at least a C, I'm screwed. No graduation. Summer school."

Maggie placed a hand over Cody's. "You are officially cut off from what-ifs. Now, go catch the bus and text me when you get your trig quiz back."

"Yes, ma'am," he said on a groan and walked slump-shouldered out the door.

"Tell me what?" Maggie demanded, taking her mug over to the dish bin that one of the residents of the Old Campbell Place would carry to a bathroom sink to eventually wash.

"Well, you see, Maggie," Jim began. "We have a little tradition around here."

She crossed her arms and raised a skeptical eyebrow. He knew it was going to be a hard sell. "It's a Bonus Day," Silas said.

"Bonus Day?" she repeated. "Are you all asking for bonuses?"

"No. We're giving our crews the day off with pay," Silas explained.

"Why?" Maggie asked.

"It's tradition," Jim said.

"We take the nicest day of the season and—if we're ahead of schedule—we give our crews the day to spend it however they want."

"With pay?"

He nodded. "With pay."

"I don't understand," Maggie said. She looked like she was waiting for a punch line.

"You ever play hooky when you were in school, Mags?" Silas asked.

"Of course not," she scoffed.

"I think I hear a car," Jim said, slipping out the French doors. He mouthed *good luck* to Silas on his way.

"You never wished you were outside enjoying the sun on your face instead of cooped up in a classroom listening to lectures?" Silas pressed, advancing on her until he had her caged between his arms, back to the refrigerator.

"I suppose," she admitted.

"This is us giving our people permission to play hooky. And this is my opportunity to take you on a real date."

"You can date me after work hours," she said dryly.

He grinned down at her. "You sure make me want to kiss you when you're hell-bent on being responsible."

"I still don't know how you talked me into this," she grumbled from his passenger seat.

"I'm very persuasive," Silas informed her.

"I think you hypnotized me with your tongue."

"I appreciate your awe of my oral skills," he said, patting her knee with his hand before taking the exit on the highway.

"I could have gotten started on the porch trim today. I could be skimming some of the ancestry books Wallace recommended. I could be looking for more gold coins around the house."

"Darlin', let me ask you something," he said, changing the subject and derailing her "could have" parade. "What was your favorite thing about the town that fancy beach cottage was in?"

"The hardware stores and lumber yard were both ten minutes from the house. That was convenient," she mused.

"Okay," he said, drawing out the word. "What was your favorite not-work-related thing?"

"There was a great Mexican place a couple of blocks over that had killer queso."

"What about the beach? How was the ocean temp? Was it a good spot for swimming?"

"I didn't really make it down to the beach for anything other than filming. And I know exactly what you're doing, Silas Wright."

He followed the signs and took a left onto a road that cut through thick forest. "I'm taking my girl away for the day," he said, feigning innocence.

"You're trying to make some point about showing me all that Idaho has to offer so I get attached. But I already know. Potatoes. Finger steaks. Bleed Blue. Yay, Idaho."

"I'm planning on you getting more attached to me than the state," he told her, easing the truck to a stop on the berm. "What are you going to do when Cody brings home a B on that essay? Are you going to celebrate the hard work that went into that win or are you going to tell him to forget about it and focus on freaking out over the next grade?"

"Of course we'll celebrate," Maggie said, exasperated. "He's working his butt off to get that diploma."

"You've been working *your* very fine butt off, too. And I haven't seen you bother to celebrate any of your wins. Seems to me like you're too busy trying to get to your next one."

"I celebrate my wins," she argued.

"What did you do when you hit one million subscribers?"

"I had sex with you."

He leaned over and released her seat belt. "You were going to do that regardless of your subscriber count. Now, get your ass out so we can start celebrating."

"We're on the side of the road. Where are we celebrating? In traffic?"

"You're cute when you're crabby." They got out of the truck and Silas handed her a small backpack before shouldering into the heavier one.

"I'm not crabby. I'm behind schedule," she huffed.

He took her hand in his and drew her into the woods.

"You're taking me out here to murder and dismember me, aren't you?" she said, ducking under a low-hanging branch, pine needles brushing her hair.

"This is the Sawtooth National Forest," he lectured as they followed the trail deeper into the scrubby pines. "Watch your step. It gets a little rocky up ahead."

She went quiet, and he let her. There was an anesthetizing peace about being out here, away from modern necessities. It made him focus on his breath. On the earth under his boots. The sounds of forest and river. Birds and squirrels. The patches of sun that filtered down from the canopy above them.

He nudged her ahead of him on the trail when it shrank and waited for it.

"Whoa." Maggie came to an abrupt stop in front of him.

"A punch in the gut, right?" he asked, resting his hands on her shoulders.

"Sucker punched by Mother Nature," she whispered.

The forest opened up, framing an expansive view of rugged mountain peaks of gray and purple and the glimmer of lake water at the base.

"See over there?" he said, pointing over her shoulder at a smaller pool above the lake.

"Yeah."

"Hot springs. There's more of them about half a mile or so to the west. But there's parking and easy trails. These are a better-kept secret."

"How far are we?" she asked.

"About a mile. You up for it?"

"Hell yeah, I am," she said with just a hint of surprise in her tone.

"That's my girl."

They picked their way over downed logs and loose gravel, passing in and out of forest as the trail looped around. By the time they got up to the rocky shore of the blue-green alpine waters, they both had a good sweat going. The lake was small by Idaho's standards, and this one was impossible to get to by car. Which meant they had it to themselves on a late Wednesday morning.

Maggie leaned down and dipped her hand into the water. "Oh my God. It's freezing."

"The lake gets a lot of the melt-off, but the springs up there are bath temperature. I didn't bring Kevin because that tub of lard loves the water, and I didn't want the distraction. If you get what I'm saying."

She gestured at her shorts and tank top. "You didn't tell me to bring a suit."

He grinned and then dropped his shorts to his ankles. "Now what's the fun in bringing bathing suits?"

She let out a scandalized laugh. "*You* want *me* to go skinny-dipping in broad daylight?"

He shucked off his T-shirt, letting it fall next to his shorts. "One million subscribers, Mags. That's a hell of a thing. And what are you gonna do when some other Instagrammer person asks you how you celebrated? Tell them you worked nine hours instead of ten? Tell them you painted a front porch?"

"I'm sure as hell not telling them I went skinny-dipping with Hot Landscaper Guy. It would break thousands of hearts."

"Suit yourself, Mags. You can sit here in the sun and stay dry, waiting for me to take you back so you can pick up a paintbrush or a spreadsheet. Or you can come have a little adventure with me."

"You're diabolical," she said, shaking her head. But those long fingers of hers were plucking at the hem of her shirt. She bit her lower lip.

He slid his thumbs in the waistband of his underwear, tempting her, teasing her.

She looked skyward for a moment before letting out a breath. "Fine. But if we get arrested for public indecency, you're paying my bail."

"Deal."

She stripped off her shirt, and he slid his underwear down his legs.

Boise Banner: SALES OF A. CAMPBELL'S HISTORICAL WESTERN NOVELS SKYROCKET WHEN YOUTUBE STAR REHABS FAMILY HOME

30

THE WATER IN the springs was almost hot-tub hot. It felt luxurious, decadent to just lean back and float. She hoped her sunscreen was up to the task.

She'd managed to hike up the short climb in nothing but a pair of outdoor sandals Silas had magically produced from his backpack. It was the least Maggie-like thing she'd ever done in her life. Watching Silas's spectacular butt flex as he'd climbed the rocks in front of her—because there was no freaking way she was taking the lead naked, thank you very much—was a good enough celebration in her mind.

His confidence was a wonder of nature, she decided, watching him stand there, hands on hips, naked in thigh-deep water.

Of course, his body was perfection. He was strong and lean, tall and sexy. His back was all muscle definition that tapered to the vee of his waist.

But that confidence, that innate knowing, came not from the perfection of his exterior. It came from someplace deeper.

He slipped back into the water and swam toward her, like a shark circling its prey.

She sank lower, as if the waterline would protect her from him.

His hand snaked out and closed around her arm, pulling her to him. It felt like heaven, their wet bodies sliding over each other.

She shivered when he turned her in his arms so her back was to him. He stood her up and walked her to the rocky edge of the spring, where water spilled over and down to the lake twenty feet below.

He held her there, her knees pressed against the rock. Her entire body to the thighs was exposed to the sun. There was nothing but water and light and trees and earth as far as she could see. No one to witness it as Sy's palms coasted up to cup her breasts.

It felt magical. Natural. With just enough danger to make it even more exciting.

She felt his cock stir against the small of her back.

She wanted him here like this. Wild and free. Wet and warm.

"Does anyone ever jump from here?" she asked, eyeing the lake below as his hands kneaded and stroked.

He dropped a kiss to her wet shoulder. "The brave or foolhardy ones, depending on who you ask. It's deep enough."

She bit her lip and peered over the edge again. "I'm up for it if you are."

His hands stilled on her skin. "That lake water down there is cold as hell," he warned.

"I'm feeling foolhardy," she said.

"Well, darlin', then I am, too," he said. He let go of her and helped her up onto the ledge. Warm water rushed over their feet and sluiced down to the emerald-green water below. When he stepped up next to her, Maggie held out her hand, and he took it. "You are the surprise of a lifetime," he told her.

"On the count of three," she said, enjoying the way her heart hammered against her ribs. She felt alive. Awake. "One...two...three..."

He didn't let go. Not when they jumped together, not when they hit water so cold it stole her breath. Not even when they went under, sucked into a world without sound. When they bobbed to the surface together, his hand was still clutching hers.

He let out a whoop of joy and shook his hair back from his eyes.

"Holy shit, it's cold." She laughed, ducking beneath the surface again just for the shock of it. Her body was still hot from the springs, but the cold was stealing it away bit by bit.

"Come here," he said, towing her toward where the hot spring water formed a short waterfall, thundering down into the lake with a cloud of steam.

The force of it pushed them back, but Silas was more stubborn than nature. He maneuvered them behind the curtain of water, where a rock ledge sat back from the cascade. The water was warmer here.

"It's like a secret room," she said, delighted when her voice echoed off the outcropping above them. She braced her hands on the ledge and lifted her upper body out of the water so she could brush her fingers over the sparkle embedded in the wet rock.

She turned, grinning, to look at Silas. One look at his set jaw and hard eyes, and she knew that the easygoing, playful guy was gone. In his place was the hard, hungry man.

"Come here, Maggie," he said. The command was low and raspy. Part of her wanted to escape, just to let him chase her down.

She swam slowly to him and watched his nostrils flare when she paused just out of his reach.

He crooked his finger at her, and there was nothing playful about it. Closing the distance between them, she stood.

Without warning, Silas reached under her arms and boosted her up. Her breasts pressed against his chest, nipples already hard from the cold, reveling in the feel of his hot skin and the brush of chest hair. He wrapped her legs around his hips, his erection pinned between them.

"I don't have a pocket."

Which translated to no condom.

"I'm on the pill," she said, licking water droplets off her lips.

He stilled against her, looking more serious than she'd ever seen him. "Are you okay with me inside you with nothing between us?"

Was she? It seemed like the day for out-of-character adventure. Her body responded with a resounding "Hell the fuck yes." She nodded, wide-eyed and ready to die from anticipation.

"Hang on to me," he said, his voice rougher than the rocks at his back.

She tightened her arms around his neck and buried her face there when he guided his cock to her opening. Her body was revved on adrenaline. She hoped she'd survive it. Then when he fed the first inch into place, she decided she didn't care as long as she could have him inside her.

"No, darlin'. You're gonna look at me," he ordered, his voice sounding strained.

She lifted her head and met his gaze. Those gray eyes had a fire in them. In one swift, short thrust, he slammed himself home.

Her cry echoed off the rock above them as he filled her. They watched each other through heavy lids as he pumped into her while nature flowed all around them. She became part animal as her body gave itself over to the biology, the innate need for him. When he held her by the hips and used his grip to speed the pace, she bowed back.

The edge of the wall of warm water rushed over her hair and down her back as the man moved inside her. Harder and faster. Thick and undeniable.

She was overwhelmed, overtaken by nature. She couldn't wait to get where they were going and, at the same time, never wanted it to end.

When he dipped his head to pull a nipple into his mouth, she hitched her legs higher and reveled in the change of angle. That tight bundle of nerves was exposed, and every brush against the flat of his abs was like lightning in her system.

"Silas!"

"I can feel you getting ready to come, darlin'. Don't you fucking hold back on me."

She couldn't if she wanted to. The only thing her body wanted was to climax.

He was pumping into her relentlessly. All she could do was cling to him. His gaze was fixed on her breasts as they moved with each thrust. With nothing between them, she felt him grow impossibly thicker in her, felt his muscles tense under her hands, beneath her legs.

Every pump was accompanied by an animalistic grunt from his throat. He was so close to coming it made her lightheaded.

"You better fucking come right now," he growled.

The threat worked. Because the second he slammed into her to the hilt, the second she felt the first jet of his release as it loosed inside her, she came.

It was everything. Like fireworks and an earthquake. A tidal wave and a detonation. Her body went off around Silas as he came into her very depths. Part of her knew that her body was made for more than enjoying sex. But in the moment, she felt like she'd realized a beautiful truth, that there was a magic achieved together. A miracle of chemistry and biology and nature.

His shout of victory rang in her ears. Her hips were held in a bruising grip as he stayed buried inside her. Being forced to hold still made the volcanic activity erupting in her core even stronger.

They rode out aftershocks together, arms wrapped tight around each other. Maggie trembled against him as he stroked his hand over her wet hair and whispered sweet words of praise in her ear. He kissed her softly, sweetly. Tasting her mouth and skin with his tongue.

When he finally withdrew from her, her body still felt full and used and oh so good. He drew her to the ledge so she could hang on. When he was sure she was safe, he levered himself up to sit on the ledge.

What a picture he made, his half-hard cock lying heavily against his thick thigh, as if deciding whether to harden again or not. Water droplets clung to his chest and his hair. His stubble was more beard now than it had been two days ago. He looked like he belonged here under the waterfall in the wild.

And for once, Maggie felt like she might belong, too.

31

"YOU JUST WANTED me to buy this so you don't have to spend another night on the cot," Maggie accused him three efficient hours later as the movers assembled the bed rails in her room under Kevin's watchful eye.

She couldn't decide if she was horrified or delighted with the purchase.

"Every other person in this house has an actual bed," Silas argued. "Why shouldn't you have one?"

"You already talked me into it once," she pointed out. And she was having a hard time regretting it when she saw the weathered dark wood of the headboard go up against the cloud gray of the wall. The kittens darted into the room to check on the action and then raced out again.

The buying hadn't stopped there. She'd snapped up a rug, in deeper blues, and twin nightstands with drawers painted a dark gray with absolutely frivolous crystal knobs. Nirina and Kayla had made a gift of crisp cotton sheets in a clean white and a duvet in navy. Then she'd dragged Silas to the furniture store they'd recommended over in Abileen and fallen in love with a deep-cushioned couch and matching armchair for the soon-to-be TV room.

On her way out of the store, she'd gotten Cody's text. An 86 on his trig quiz. The kid had used three exclamation points. She'd hit Buy It Now on the new laptop she'd been eyeing for him. He could use it for school and work rather than her clunky old one, which had to be restarted every hour or two, she reasoned. It was an investment.

Silas had been delighted. Maggie had been mildly appalled. She blamed Bonus Day and underwater orgasms for her out-of-character spending spree.

When the bed was assembled and the cloud of a mattress in place, she tipped the movers and walked them out.

She waited until the van disappeared and then headed around to the side of the house to panic over the lack of work being accomplished. Where the uneven terrace and tumbling retaining wall had been was now an expanse of freshly flattened dirt. The terrace stone, what was salvageable of it, was stacked neatly in the backyard.

The fountain and its four horses, frozen in time, had been cleared of the decade of debris and stood silent and empty. The undertaking seemed more out of reach than on other days.

She blew out a breath and looked at the house. The siding was spectacular, she had to admit. The new windows, with their pops of white and the sharp lines of the grilles, added to the fresh look.

The glass and architectural details on the third floor broke up the dark of the siding. She needed to figure out what she was doing with the third story of the turret. It was too much of a selling point to leave unfinished.

A party, she imagined. With people gathered on the terrace, spilling out of the house from the kitchen and the sunroom. There would be enough room for tables and chairs. Even a dance floor. She could string lights from the house. Guests, dancing or drinking wine, would pause to look up at the lights and then see the expanse of sky beyond, admiring the glow from the windows.

Something tugged at her subconscious. There was something off. Something not quite right. But before she could zero in on it, Silas pulled her attention away.

"You're not thinking about work, are you?" he said, ambling down the porch steps.

"Not on Bonus Day," she lied.

"That's my girl. How do you feel about getting a little dirty?" he asked.

"I feel pretty good about it," she said, linking her hands behind his neck.

"Good. Get your shovel," he said with a wink.

"This is *not* what I had in mind when you said getting dirty," Maggie complained as she helped him drop the rootball of the five-foot-tall Black Hills spruce.

"Help me break up the roots a bit," Silas instructed, reaching into the hole while Kevin romped by, the kittens on his heels.

She did as he asked and then sat back on her heels to admire it. "It looks like a Christmas tree," she observed.

"That's right," he said, swiping his forearm over his brow. "Figured the family tree would go back in the library with the fireplace and all those windows. And this is close enough to the house to run lights to it."

"Your family is obsessed with Christmas trees," she observed, although she couldn't help but think about peering out of the back windows and seeing warm white lights on a snowy December night.

"Between Morris and Mom's twenty-four/seven Christmas carols from Thanksgiving on, Michael's spiked hot chocolate, and Mama B and Dad's nine-foot tree so covered in ornaments and lights you can't see needles, we all go a little crazy over Christmas. I'll hold her straight while you dig," he said.

She worked the dirt back into the hole and patted it down with the flat of the shovel. It was oddly therapeutic, she realized. Putting something in the ground that was going to be appreciated for generations to come.

Silas pulled the hose around. "Let's give her a good soaking," he said, handing her the nozzle and slipping his arms around her waist. She wondered how tall it would be in a year, ten years.

Leaning against him, Maggie squeezed the trigger and watched the water pool at the base of the tree before being absorbed into the fresh dirt. This time it was Taco and Dolly that raced past first. Kevin paused his chase to bite at the water spouting from the hose.

She laughed, and Silas kissed her on the top of the head.

"That should about do it. We'll give her another drink later," he said, taking the hose from her and giving the dog a squirt in the rump.

"What'll we do for the next hour or so before Cody comes home?" she asked slyly.

"I'm about to introduce you to the second-best part of Bonus Day," he told her, leading her toward the back door and up the stairs.

She paused just inside the bedroom door. The room had instantly changed from a temporary camp to an actual bedroom. He'd made the bed when she'd walked the movers out, she noted. The pillows—because six hadn't seemed too crazy in the store—were stacked in a sumptuous pile against the headboard. The duvet was very precisely spread across the mattress, folded over to show the crisp white of the sheets.

"Wow, you really know how to make a bed," she said, unexpectedly delighted at his show of domesticity.

"I'm even better at unmaking it. Now, pick a side," he said.

She blinked. "What?"

"Pick a side, darlin'. Do you want to be closer to the window or the bathroom?"

She had a bed big enough to have a dedicated side.

"What if I want to sleep in the middle?" she asked just to be contrary.

"Then you'll be sleeping on top of me, and I have no problem with that."

"I'll take the window," she decided.

"Good girl. Now, get in."

"Are you really ready for another round?" She was impressed. And a little exhausted. Okay. A lot exhausted.

"No, ma'am. I am not." He shot her that devilish grin. "Don't get me wrong. I'd fumble my way through it for you. But I think we both could use a rest before another attempt."

"You want to take a nap with me?" A nap was something on

Maggie's list of Things Other People with Free Time Do. Like go to the spa or plan meals.

"No Bonus Day is complete without a nap," he insisted, pulling back the covers with a flourish.

She had gone skinny-dipping, jumped off a cliff, climaxed under a waterfall, and gone on a home furnishings shopping spree. Why not add a nap to the day?

"We're not getting in that bed in these clothes," she said, gesturing at her dirt-streaked shorts and shirt.

He gave her that slow, wolfish smile, and her heart said, *Uh-oh*.

His shirt hit the floor, followed swiftly by his shorts.

She had no choice really but to follow suit.

It wasn't a bad way to spend a day, she thought as Silas pulled her up against him. His chest and thighs cradling her while his arm anchored her to him. Hot skin, hard muscle, and the crisp coolness of fresh sheets. He'd left the balcony doors open, and the warm breeze billowed the sheer curtains into the room like ghosts returning home.

An hour later, after she'd rolled over and onto Silas to sleepily demand more, and after she'd fallen asleep again, Maggie awoke with a start. She lay still for a long moment, trying to determine what had pulled her back to the surface.

The house was quiet. Well, as quiet as a 150-year-old mansion got. The kittens had found their way onto the bed and were curled up on Silas. One on his feet and one on his hip. Whatever had woken her, this was a picture that needed taking.

She managed to reach her phone on the new and convenient nightstand without breaking Sy's hold on her. Settling back against him, she snapped a midsiesta selfie of woman, man, and cats. She looked amused and disheveled. Silas, on the other hand, looked like a sleeping god. His hair was tousled. One honey-blond curl fell over his forehead. His lashes formed long, inky lines over closed eyes. Those perfect lips were partially puckered as he breathed slow and deep.

His arm was heavy, draped over her waist, hand cupping one breast. Even unconscious, Silas Wright was a boob man.

No matter what happened, she knew she'd hold on to this day, this memory, this moment in time. Nothing on her to-do list would have been this satisfying to complete, and she wondered if that had been his point.

She could work any day. Every day. But would she remember those days like she'd remember today? Would she treasure those days the way she would this?

How odd that so many of her favorite memories from childhood and adulthood had happened right here in Kinship.

She closed her eyes, and then it hit her. The oddity that had niggled at the back of her mind earlier in the day when she'd been looking up at the bluff side of the house. Her heart rate kicked up a bit.

Easing out of Sy's grip proved tricky. But she managed it without waking him or the kittens. She dragged on her shorts and shirt and jogged downstairs.

She made it halfway down the porch steps before realizing she'd forgotten shoes and, remembering her toe, ran back inside to grab her work boots.

Finally, standing on the south side of the house, she counted carefully. The buzz in her blood got louder.

She hurried back inside and up the three flights of stairs, winding around and around.

On the third floor, she poked her head into the front room with the glassed-in turret and the twin windows that faced the river. Then did the same in the next room. It was smaller, but it had the same two windows on the south wall.

The closets of both rooms lined up with each other. At least, that's the way it seemed. But now Maggie wasn't sure.

Back in the hall, she paced off the distance between the rooms.

"I knew it," she breathed. Excitement bubbled up in her. She found boxes of bathroom tile just off the landing to the stairs and ripped the tops off two of them. When the cardboard was in position, she headed back downstairs and out the front door.

"Silas!" Maggie said, bursting into the room.

He was just starting to sit up, kittens scrambling off him, when she jumped. She landed on him, and to his credit, he caught her.

"You sure know how to wake a man up, Mags."

Hands on his shoulders, she straddled him. "I need you to come downstairs and tell me if I'm crazy," she said breathlessly.

"You're not crazy. But you are sweaty," he said on a yawn.

"I ran up and down a couple flights of stairs. Also, I think my boobs are sunburned," she admitted.

He rolled and pinned her beneath him. "I'll examine them thoroughly in a minute," he told her, then pretended to fall asleep on top of her.

"Very funny, Wright." She gave his butt a hard pinch. "I think I found something."

"Yeah. It's called my ass," he said into her hair. "Which given how much that pinch stings might also be a little sun-kissed."

"Please," she asked, putting a little extra breathiness into the ask.

He sighed theatrically. "You know I can't deny you when you use that voice. But if this is some kind of trick to get me to do work, I'm going to tie you to this bed and leave you here for a week."

"I've got an Abe Lincoln that says you won't regret getting out of bed," she tried again.

"Can't turn down that offer," he mused, easing away. He pulled on his shorts but left them unbuttoned. "This is as dressed as I'm willing to get."

"You're groggy after a nap," she observed.

"Baby, I'm groggy after all the sex you're forcing me to have. Dehydrated, too."

"Poor Silas," she crooned, as she got out of bed. "You need shoes. This is an inside-outside thing."

He shot her a sleepy smile as he shoved his feet into his boots. "I like seeing you excited. It's cute."

"Tell me I'm cute later. I want to hear that I'm smart and not crazy now."

"Well?" She prodded Silas in his bare, romance novel–cover abs.

He scratched the back of his head and squinted three stories up at the cardboard she'd put in two windows. Between them was a single octagonal window. "Could be decorative."

"It could be," she agreed. "But it's not in the closet of the front bedroom. I paced it off in the hallway. I think there's about ten feet unaccounted for."

"Too big for ducting and mechanicals," he observed.

"That's what I thought."

"Maybe it's a passageway that connects the rooms? I've seen them in old houses with rooms that used to be nurseries."

"That's a possibility," Maggie agreed.

"Well, what are we doing down here then? Let's go find us a secret passage."

It took them twenty minutes of careful, dusty searching before Silas found a seam in the back of the smaller bedroom's closet. Their eyes met as he depressed a nearly hidden switch along the molding. There was a distinct click from inside the wall, and then one of the panels sprung toward them.

"Do you want a camera for this?" Silas asked, when she reached for the doorway.

She shook her head. "Not until we know for sure there aren't any corpses or creepy ceramic doll collections inside. Some things shouldn't be commemorated."

"All right. Then let's do this." He grinned.

He hooked his fingers in the opening and tugged. The hinges gave a haunted house–style creak as the door swung open.

"Well, I'll be damned," he said, poking his head in after Maggie stepped over the threshold. She shined a flashlight over the walls.

It was a small room. Barely bigger than ten-feet square, it smelled stale. There was a thick layer of dust covering every surface. One entire wall was buried under shelves of books and thick scrapbooks. There was a wingback chair covered in gold silk in the corner. Next to it was a small table that held a pipe and heavy ashtray. The other wall was covered in framed sepia-toned photos and newspaper clippings.

A thick black curtain hung on the front wall, exactly over where the window in question should be.

Silas distracted her by sneezing three times in rapid succession.

Maggie glanced at him. "Bless you?"

He sneezed again. "Better stop there. These'll just keep going. Allergies."

"You can wait outside," she offered.

"No way in hell, Mags."

"I'll get you an antihistamine with your dinner," she promised and drew the curtain back.

There was the octagonal window. Afternoon light filtered through the dirty glass. Beneath the window sat a small desk, a stack of neatly handwritten pages and a blue-glass inkwell next to it.

She picked up the top sheet.

"Holy crap," she breathed. "I think we found Aaron Campbell's real study. This looks like a book he was working on." There were handwritten notes in the margins. Tidy, loopy script.

"Why hide out up here when there was a perfectly comfortable room downstairs?" Silas asked, skimming the page.

She opened the top desk drawer and peered inside. "Who knows? Writers are weird artistic types," she told him. "I knew a girl in college who ended up writing romance novels. She says she hides in a closet with a bag of fast food to hit her deadlines."

"Wallace is going to have a heart attack over this room," Silas said.

"We'll have to break the news to him carefully," she decided. She turned and watched Silas as he examined the wall of framed photos before moving on to the bookshelves. She cleared her throat.

He glanced up at her.

She held out her hand, palm up. "Five bucks, sneezy."

"I don't have my wallet on me," he said, gesturing at his still unfastened shorts. "However, I've got something I think you'll like better."

"We're not having sex in here. You'd probably have an asthma attack."

"I am capable of thinking of more than just sex, Nichols," he said wryly.

She wrinkled her nose in feigned uncertainty. "Are you?"

"Close your eyes," he ordered suddenly.

She shocked the hell out of both of them by complying.

His fingers skimmed her skin, and something cool and heavy slipped around her neck.

"If you just put some kind of creepy antique BDSM collar on me, we are going to have words," Maggie said.

"Open your eyes."

She did as she was told and looked down. "Holy shit," she gasped. "We need to shoot this."

"We need to rally the troops," he said.

"Guess it'll be dinner for more than just the two of us." She took a step toward the door and then turned back to him. "Silas?"

"Yeah, darlin'?"

She bit her lip. "Thanks for a really good day."

His gaze had gone soft and warm again. He reached out and cupped her chin in his hand. "Anytime, Mags."

They were halfway down the stairs, phones in hand, when they ran into Cody.

"Maggie! We did it—" He took one look at Maggie's braless outfit, the huge antique necklace, and Silas in his state of undress and almost fell backward down the steps.

"Whoa. Okay. Uh. I'll just go then?" Cody averted his eyes from them both.

"No, it's not like that," Maggie insisted. "Stay."

"Well, it *was* like that, and it's going to be like that again, and you're just gonna have to be okay with that, kid," Silas corrected.

Cody chanced a glance at him. His eyes narrowed. "Are you crying, man?"

Silas rubbed his red eyes. "I'm *not* crying. I am sneezing heroically."

Maggie started to laugh and then couldn't quite stop.

"Here's what we're gonna do," Silas decided, putting a hand on her shoulder. "You're gonna call Dean and Wallace. Cody and I are gonna run into town to pick up stuff for dinner. Is that cool with you?" he asked Cody.

The boy nodded, still looking uncomfortable as hell.

"Meet me in the truck," Silas told him before leaning down and kissing Maggie on the forehead.

Michelle: Hey, Hot Landscaper Guy.

Silas: How did you get a preview of my new business cards?

Michelle: Ha! You look like you're enjoying yourself on-screen. The whole project looks amazing!

Silas: Thanks. It's been a hell of a good time. How's Denver treating you? How's your new job?

Michelle: All good here. I'm happy and also happy you're happy if that makes sense.

Silas: Speaking of happy, your mom told Mama B about a certain architectural engineer you met.

Michelle: It's very new and my mom has a big, fat mouth. But yeah. He's pretty great!

Silas: Please accept this "I'm happy for you" GIF as a token of my happiness for you.

Michelle: A GIF from Hot Landscaper Guy??? That Maggie Nichols has changed your life!

32

"A FEW MORE steps," Maggie said encouragingly as Wallace huffed and puffed his way up the grand staircase.

"I don't see why we had to do this before pizza," he complained. The three pies that Silas and Cody had picked up were in the dining room waiting for after the big reveal.

"This better be good. Like stolen-Rembrandt-in-an-attic good," Dean groused from behind Wallace. "I rescheduled a call with a hardware chain for this. Also, one of those pizzas better have a cauliflower crust."

Kevin, unable to contain himself, dashed past them on the stairs and raced into the second bedroom.

"Did you find a dead body?" Cody asked from his position on Wallace's flank, ready to catch the old man if he fell backward. Silas had refused to tell him what they'd found until they all could see it for themselves.

"All these damn stairs," Wallace wheezed.

"This is why the nurses want you to show up to fitness time instead of hiding in the library," she reminded him.

"I'm old! When do I get to just give up and embrace it?" The dog reappeared at the top of the stairs and barked joyfully. All his humans were about to be in the same place at the same time.

"You can decide whether you want to embrace bodily disrepair after you see what we found," she promised.

By the time they reached the third floor, Maggie was feeling giddy. "Silas? Are you ready for us?"

"All set," he called from the bedroom.

"I haven't seen you this excited since you found Marshmallow Fluff in the grocery store," Dean observed.

She clasped her hands under her chin. "You have no idea. Just get your camera ready and follow me."

They followed her into the bedroom, and Maggie rushed over to the open closet door and made a sweeping bow. "Gentlemen, please enter."

"After all we've been through, you want me to go back in the closet? I swear to God, Maggie, if this is some creepy rat skeleton..."

"Less whining. More recording."

Dean heaved a sigh and turned on the camera.

"Can I go in?" Cody asked, excitement clear on his face.

"Yes! For the love of God, yes. Someone come in here," Silas bellowed.

Cody ducked inside. "Holy shit! *Holy. Shit.*"

Wallace, suddenly acting more spry than a fifty-year-old, elbowed Dean out of the way and entered. "Oh my God," the old man wheezed. "It can't be."

Not one to be left out, Dean plowed into the closet and stopped short in the doorway of the secret room. Maggie paused next to him. "Well?" she asked.

"What. The. Hell. Is. This?" Dean demanded, slapping her arm with each syllable without bobbling the camera.

"Ow! It's a secret room full of Campbell family stuff." She grinned over at Silas, who was filming their reactions—hopefully—on her phone.

Kevin ran from person to person to share sniffing and licking.

"Look at the books," Wallace whispered.

"Cool pictures," Cody said, peering at the framed portraits on the wall.

"Is this a manuscript?" Wallace whispered, studying the stack of papers on the desk.

"Looks like an unfinished one," Silas told him.

Dean crammed himself into the room to film every inch of it. Silas wriggled his way out to stand in the doorway with her. Behind the camera, he wrapped an arm around her shoulders and pressed a kiss to the top of her head. Together they watched as Cody, Dean, and Wallace explored the contents.

"Are you guys ready to see the best part?" Maggie asked, unable to contain herself a moment longer.

"There's more?" Dean groaned.

"Cody, how about you open up that drawer in the desk?" Silas suggested.

The kid did as he was told and produced the velvet jeweler's case.

"Well, what are you waitin' for, son?" Wallace asked, popping the lid on the box. Dean tromped forward to get a good look inside.

"Whoa," Cody breathed.

"Holy shit," Wallace announced.

"Guess we'll be bleeping that one," Maggie snickered.

"That's one hell of a statement piece," Dean mused.

"That's no ordinary necklace," Wallace insisted. "That is Minnie Franklin's emerald-and-sapphire necklace, which was stolen during the Dead Man's Canyon Stagecoach Robbery."

Dean screeched out a string of excited curses.

"Yeah, definitely gonna need some editing," Silas predicted.

"Not to be Debbie Downer—"

"Since when?" Maggie teased Dean over cold pizza in the dining room.

He rolled his eyes at her and continued. "This throws a wrench in the show's story line."

It had taken them over an hour to coax Wallace back downstairs and he'd agreed only after they'd promised to box up the first dozen scrapbooks and ledgers on the bookcases so he could start studying them immediately.

The man was eating pizza with his right hand and turning pages with his latex-gloved left.

"How?" Cody asked with interest.

"We've basically confirmed that Aaron Campbell found the Dead Man's Canyon treasure," Dean said. "But how do we tell that story over the renovation timeline? How do we chop it up into bite-size pieces to serve up per episode? How far do we go to prove it to the viewers—minus the conspiracy nuts, of course."

"Of course," Silas agreed while rubbing tiny tight circles with his thumb into Maggie's shoulder.

"How do we wrap it up? What's the big wow ending? Do we get everything authenticated? Who gets to keep it? Does it belong to the original owners or does Maggie own it? Is there more of the treasure left to find in this house? If not, what did Campbell do with it?" Dean asked.

"It fits with the season theme of bringing history back to life," Maggie mused, wiping her hands on her jeans. "But I get what you're saying. We have to figure out how to tell this part of the story."

"I hate to bring this up," Silas began, "but y'all also need to consider what could happen if you go on internet TV and start telling a million people that you found hidden treasure."

"Internet TV," Cody snorted.

Silas threw his crust at him. "Listen here, whippersnapper."

"I think what Sy is trying to say is that we don't want a bunch of treasure hunters showing up here and breaking in," Maggie supplied, slapping the man's hand away from the last slice of pizza on her plate.

"So we wait," Dean said.

Maggie glanced around the table. "I think so. We haven't spilled the beans about the coin yet. So until we can figure out how the story fits into the show, let's keep this between us."

"I won't say anything," Cody promised.

"My lips are sealed," Dean agreed.

"My family is nothing but big mouths. I'm not telling them jack," Silas announced.

"Hate talking to people anyway," Wallace said.

Maggie nodded. "Okay. Then it's settled. Until we know more, we keep all this quiet."

Silas raised his hand. "Question. Until we figure out what's gonna happen with the necklace, can we all take turns wearing it around the house?"

Cody choked on a gulp of Pepsi.

"Dibs! I call dibs!" Dean yelped.

Kevin's big dog head popped up at the end of the table. He eyed everyone with suspicion before lying back down. Taco climbed on top of the dog and curled up. Dolly streaked into the hallway and ran full bore toward the front door.

"On that note," Maggie said, pushing her chair back, "the deputy mayor should be here in ten minutes."

"What did Kressley talk you into?" Silas asked in amusement.

"*We* are going to talk *Kressley* into reopening the Canyon Custom plant so we can get ourselves a kitchen," Maggie said. "So I need you all to be on your best behavior."

Dean's head shot up. "That sounds expensive."

"My goodness. You *have* been busy up here," Kressley announced, pausing to fluff her shiny black hair in the hallway mirror on the second floor. She'd arrived in a plum pantsuit with matching purple stilettos and had pranced her way all over the house after demanding a tour.

"We have," Maggie agreed, stepping over Dolly Parton as the kitten galloped past. "The credit goes entirely to the local crews. They've been incredible. Haven't they, Dean?"

"Consummate professionals," he agreed, gesturing for Kressley to lead the way downstairs.

"Kinship is made up of good people. I'm honored to lead them," she said, peering over the handrail.

"Madam Deputy Mayor," Silas said, appearing at the foot of the stairs. "You look ravishing."

Maggie shot him a hard look. Ravishing? Who talked like that outside of the bedroom?

Kressley beamed at him. "Silas Wright, you are a charmer," she said, swiping a manicured hand in his direction. "I was delighted to hear that your professional relationship with our Maggie has moved into personal territory."

Great. Now she was an "our Maggie."

Cody appeared, cradling one of the kittens.

"Cody Moses," she said, clutching a hand to her heart. "I've heard that you're making great strides at school."

Cody blushed. "Yes, ma'am."

"What a cozy little family you've got here, Maggie," Kressley said, pointedly eyeing Silas and Cody. "Isn't Kinship just the best?"

Small freaking towns.

"Uh, yeah. Let me show you the kitchen," Maggie said, turning her back on Sy's smug face and practically jogging away. It had been one hell of a day. One hell of a long day. And she was ready to curl up in that brand-new bed upstairs for a solid fifteen hours of sleep.

"You're certainly generating quite a bit of buzz for our little hamlet," the woman pressed on, poking her head into Maggie's office as if she were in charge of the tour. "I have it on good authority that Campbell's novels are selling better than they have in the last twenty years."

"Really?" Dean asked.

"The Campbells left the rights to Aaron's novels to the town of Kinship in their trust. They haven't amounted to anything as long as I've been deputy mayor. But with the attention you're bringing with your lovely little show— Oh, dear. I must admit I expected more progress in here." Kressley blinked at the mostly empty room.

"I did, too," Maggie told her. "We've run into one snag after another. But I'm starting to wonder if maybe it wasn't all for a reason."

Kressley spun back to look at her. "What makes you say that?"

"Canyon Custom Cabinetry," Maggie said.

She saw the shrewd spark in Kressley's eyes. She arched a thin eyebrow. "What about the plant?"

"I need a kitchen. The plant needs some visibility to attract a buyer. I thought maybe we could help each other out," Maggie mused.

Kressley tapped a finger to her chin. "Intrigued. Tell me more."

"Let's talk over drinks," Maggie suggested. "Iced tea? Coffee?"

Kressley peered at the tiny gold watch on her wrist. "I really shouldn't this late, but I don't think I could turn down a coffee."

"Now you're talking my language," Dean said, offering the woman his arm. "Right this way."

Thirty minutes later, a caffeinated Kressley was saying her third goodbye.

"I have a good feeling about all of this," she announced, pointing a finger at Maggie.

"I do, too," Maggie agreed, shooing her toward the open front door. Kevin and the kittens had given up running in and out in the middle of the second goodbye and now lay snoozing in the den.

"Oh, silly me! I meant to bring up the opportunity for you to stay in town and renovate the Canyon Country Townhomes. Business has been absolutely dismal for the last few ski seasons since the ski resort renovated."

"Oh, uh...," Maggie looked around wildly for help.

"What a great idea, Deputy Mayor," Silas said with a sly grin.

Maggie kept her smile firmly in place as she elbowed him in the gut.

"We'll have to talk about it," she said.

"Have your people call my people," Kressley called cheerily over her shoulder as she finally crossed the threshold and stepped onto the porch.

33

MAY SEEMED HELL-BENT on exiting Idaho with a summer preview. They had a week straight of hot, sunny days. Business was booming for Bitterroot, and real progress was being made at the Campbell Place. The hardwood floors on the first floor had been sanded, restained, and sealed. The master bathroom was almost finished, and Silas couldn't wait to take his first shower with the lady of the house in the huge, tiled steam shower. The kittens survived their wellness check with the vet. And the unpainted lower kitchen cabinets had been delivered the day before.

Despite all that, Silas had managed to talk Maggie into skipping out of work early and hitting the lake for paddleboarding. Since the discovery of the secret room—and the delivery of Maggie's spectacular bed—he and his dog had spent most of his nights there. There was something about waking up with the "not a fan of cuddling" Maggie wrapped around him like a climbing vine as the sky turned to pink outside those big windows. It felt...right.

He wasn't the only one gravitating to the house and its occupants.

They'd fixed up the front study for Wallace, who showed up every morning at nine as if he were punching a clock. He'd pick up where he left off with his cataloging and research into the third-floor finds. Silas wasn't sure if he was getting used to the man or if Wallace was getting less irate with the world. Either way, the grump was joining them most nights for dinner.

Dean was busy filming both renovations and historical finds and muttering under his breath about the impossibility of telling a story when he didn't know the ending.

They grilled meals and took turns helping Cody study for finals. And it was getting easier to convince Maggie to shut down the laptop and join them in the living room for TV or some quiet reading time. They divvied up the remaining books by Aaron Campbell and were sifting through them, looking for clues.

Silas stepped outside into the humid morning and took his mug of coffee along to check out the in-progress retaining wall and the wider panorama of the gorge below, now that the dead trees had been cut down and hauled away.

Things were taking shape inside and out.

He had a new present for Maggie. She'd loved the copper heron on the side of the house, naming it Henry. He'd taken some of the dried lumber from an old fallen tree and used it to make a series of floating shelves for the bare wall in the front parlor. She'd quickly filled the shelves with a mix of Campbell antiques and new finds.

He held up the comically huge pair of wooden googly eyes that he'd found at a nursery. Whimsical and unexpected. Just like the rest of the house. He put his mug down in the dew-damp grass and set about attaching the eyes to Maggie's favorite tree, a quaking aspen that marked the entrance to the path leading to the under-construction firepit.

Yes. Things were progressing. But unlike the plan for the house, the forward momentum of their relationship went unspoken. For now, they both pretended not to notice that his clothes were finding their way into her closet. Or that he was doing her laundry at his house. Or that they texted about what was for dinner nearly every night like a married couple. They reveled in Cody's slow blossoming from teenage rebel to responsible young adult.

She was pretending that things weren't getting real. That making love until the world stopped was usual, typical. And he was letting her.

It was a problem he needed to tackle sooner rather than later.

So far, the new episodes were doing well. Silas had sat in on a couple of their work meetings, mainly because he liked watching

Maggie when she was in all-business mode. She had a seemingly endless well of energy. He sometimes wondered if he was the only one who saw beneath it. Who caught the slump of her shoulders when she'd pushed too hard for too long. The shadows under her eyes when she got lost in budgets and spreadsheets late at night.

He stepped back and assessed the eyes on the tree trunk. They looked just a little bit ridiculous, and he couldn't wait for her to find them.

Picking up his coffee, Silas gave the tree a salute and headed back toward the house.

Maggie would be dressed and grilling Cody on his plans for the weekend. She'd confessed to Silas that she thought there was a girl in the picture, but neither of them had managed to pry anything out of the kid yet. He made a note to try again that evening and then wondered if he was an idiot for taking it for granted that he'd be here at the dinner table.

Things had the potential to go horribly wrong, and he couldn't quite shake the feeling that some kind of disaster was lurking just beyond the horizon.

On an impulse, he dug out his phone and carefully chose a funny good-morning GIF to send his siblings.

Taylor: I miss mountain time. I've been up for three hours.

Niri: That's the problem with the East Coast. That and the fact that YOUR FAMILY LIVES IN IDAHO.

Michael: Are we shouty caps already today? Wake up on the wrong side of the bed?

Niri: You try waking up 36 times with a baby jumping on your bladder.

Silas: Taylor, I looked at flights from Boston and there's some good deals this summer. Hint. Hint.

Niri: YES! COME HOME!

Michael: You should. I can't quite remember what my niece and nephew look like. What are their names again?

Silas: Chewbacca and Lego Face, right?

Taylor: Thanks, assholes. Way to ruin the surprise. John and I booked tickets for the last week in August. AND IF YOU TELL THE MOMS AND DADS I WILL MURDER ALL OF YOUR FACES!

Michael: The last weekend of August. Didn't anyone tell you? The rest of the family is going to Disney without you. Sorry we'll miss you.

Niri: I'll grab you a pair of the mouse ears if I have time between all of our fun family activities.

Taylor: You are terrible people. If I had any sense at all I'd cancel the flight to Boise and book myself into a spa for a week.

Silas: I guess we could reschedule the Taylor-free Disney trip. Maybe we can squeeze it in before our Taylor-free Alaska cruise instead.

Taylor: *middle finger emoji*

Niri: Okay. Razzing over. I'M SO HAPPY YOU'RE COMING HOME!! I'M CRYING!!

Silas: Me, too. But with very manly tears.

Michael: I'm smiling appreciatively.

Taylor: You guys are the worst. I love you shitheads.

Silas: We love you back, turd breath.

Comforted with the constancy of his siblings, Silas headed inside for more coffee. He was just pouring when the doorbell groaned out a greeting.

"Sy, can you get that?" Maggie called from upstairs.

"On it," he called, heading for the front door. Kevin and the kittens exploded past him.

He opened the door and barely restrained his dog from plowing through the screen into the visitor. A woman with short-cropped dark hair and an exasperated expression on her pretty face bounced a sobbing toddler on her hip.

"They're friendly," he promised as he held the screen open for her. "Come on in."

After a slight hesitation, she stepped over the threshold.

"Kevin, sit."

The dog sat and stared up at the stranger with adoration in his eyes. One of the kittens ran up his back and jumped, sinking its claws into Sy's shorts. It was downright undignified.

"Kevin and Hot Landscaper Guy, right?" the woman said over the wails of the boy in her arms.

"That's right," he answered, holding the screen door open and shooing dog and cats outside. "What can I do for you?"

"Is Maggie around?" she asked.

The little boy spotted him and, with fat tears still rolling down his cheeks, reached for Silas. "Buddy, remember Stranger Danger?" she said with exasperation that tinged toward hysteria.

"Come on in," Silas offered, deciding not to be offended about being called a dangerous stranger. "Do you want any coffee? Water?"

She shook her head. "Just tell her her sister is here."

"Her sister," he repeated. "Okay." On the outside, he made sure he was downright amicable. On the inside, he was feeling a good mad coming on.

He took the stairs two at a time and found Maggie in the bedroom, pulling her daily work uniform of shorts and a tank top over her head.

She had the gall to smile at him and held up her phone.

"Hey! Just catching up on the Silas Wright fan club comments today. SlimShady100 wants to marry you and have your plant babies. Oh, and if you want, you can leave Kevin here today, since you're heading to a new job. It's gonna be pretty quiet around here."

"No, it's not."

His tone caught her attention. "It's not?" she asked.

"Not when the yelling starts."

"What yelling?"

"Me yelling at you for not telling me you have a sister."

She had the audacity to look confused by his anger. "A sister?" she repeated. "Wait. How do you know about Dayana?"

"Well, if Dayana is an attractive, exhausted mother of a toddler, then she's here."

Maggie stood abruptly. "Dayana is *here*?" Now she didn't look surprised. She looked panicked.

"Why'd you lie to me, Maggie?" he asked, crossing his arms.

"I didn't. I mean, not really. We're half-sisters."

"Well, she thinks she's your sister, and she's downstairs."

She scrambled for shoes, eyes wider than the new cat food dishes in the kitchen. "Did she say what she wanted?"

"Not to make this all about me, but I'm a little bit annoyed that I introduced you to my entire family, showed you the skeletons in our closet, and you still lied about even having a sister and a nephew."

"Keaton is *here?*" If her voice got any higher-pitched, Kevin was going to start howling in the yard. Silas stopped her when she tried to brush past him.

"Focus here, Mags. I'm trying to make this about me." It was a joke, but he wasn't feeling very funny.

She lost a bit of the terrified look and focused in on his face. She winced. "I'm so sorry, Silas. I don't have much of a relationship with that side of my family. Dayana and my father—well, we have a complicated relationship."

"I can handle complicated. I can't handle lying by omission."

She blew out a breath.

"I want the story, Mags. Sooner rather than later. And you're not getting an 'I don't want to talk about it' pass on this one." He was hurt. And that annoyed him. By not only *not* confiding in him, but outright lying to him, she'd let Silas know she didn't trust him. And that really fucking hurt.

She nodded. "I get it. I'm so sorry. I'll make it up to you."

"You damn well better," he said, cramming his cap on his head. "Now, get your ass downstairs."

Boise Banner: AUTHOR A. CAMPBELL'S *BOURBON DREAMS* LANDS ON BESTSELLERS LIST AFTER RESURGENCE IN INTEREST

34

THEY WALKED DOWN the stairs together in silence. Silas peeled off toward the kitchen, and a second later she heard the side door open and close. Maggie felt a wave of guilt crash over her as she made her way toward the front of the house.

"Takes a while to find the front door in a house this size, doesn't it?" Dayana said with forced brightness. She was dressed impeccably as usual, in dove-gray capris and an expensive-looking ivory sweater. Her makeup was flawless, even though it wasn't even eight in the morning. But the makeup didn't hide the shadows under her red-rimmed eyes.

Dayana was not a cryer.

Not when she was thirteen and broke her arm falling off a horse at a competition. Not when her father introduced her to an older sister she never wanted. Not even when her parents' divorce had become fodder for the news and gossip blogs.

"You'd know," Maggie said, trying for teasing. The house her half-sister had grown up in had been even bigger. Her current house, one Maggie had never been to, had similar square footage.

"Hi!" Keaton, the three-year-old, was waving violently at Maggie, oblivious to how his mom's face crumpled for a moment.

"Hey, buddy," Maggie said, waving back. He reached for her, and not knowing what else to do, she took him. "Is everything okay?" she asked Dayana, bouncing the squirming little boy on her hip. He had his mother's and grandfather's dark hair. But where Dayana had the cool blue eyes of her Swedish mother, Maggie was surprised to recognize her own brown eyes on the boy's sweet face. She hadn't seen him since he was a baby.

When Dayana looked up again, it was with a tight jaw and fire in her eyes. "No. Everything is most definitely not okay."

"You'd better come on back," Maggie said, gesturing toward the hall. "Let's get some coffee."

As if on cue, Kevin nosed his way back into the house through the screen door, holding it open long enough for the kittens to scamper inside. They were followed by a long-legged, pissed-off landscaper. With his hat on backward.

Even mid–family crisis, Maggie's lady parts took a moment to hum the "Hallelujah" chorus. The man had one hell of a hold on her, and it wasn't lessening at all due to the amount of time they'd spent naked together.

Realizing she was thinking carnal thoughts while juggling her nephew, Maggie thought about paint swatches and grout.

Silas assessed the situation and then grinned at the little boy, who was overjoyedly waving to him.

"If you two don't mind, I'll take Keaton here for a tour. Rumor has it the plumbing crew just showed up with doughnuts," Sy volunteered.

Dayana leveled a look at him, weighing the safety of her child in the care of a stranger.

"Doggy!" Keaton squealed from Maggie's arms as Kevin trotted up and barked.

"One doughnut, no feeding my son to your dog, no dog tongue to the face, and no caffeine," Dayana decided wearily.

"You got it," Sy said, scooping the boy out of Maggie's arms like it was a handoff they'd performed a hundred times before. "Come on, bud. Let's go play with power tools."

Dayana gave Maggie a smack on the shoulder the second Silas disappeared through the front door with Keaton. "Hot Landscaper Guy is even hotter off-screen," Dayana hissed.

Maggie blew out a breath. "I know. It's painful to look at him sometimes."

"Why is he mad at you?" Her sister eyed her shrewdly.

"You can tell?" Maggie was impressed.

"The sparks that flew out of that man's eyes could ignite underwear at ten paces."

It was the truth. "We're kind of seeing each other," she admitted.

"Like 'dinner and a movie, let's see where this goes' or getting naked?"

Maggie was not used to girl talk and felt rusty at it. "Both, I guess? Also, he doesn't know anything about your—our—father. I haven't told him. Or anyone. I mean, obviously Dean knows, but he wouldn't say anything."

Dayana cocked her head and gave her an inscrutable look. "Uh, okay."

"Let's get back to you," Maggie said quickly. "Tell me what's going on."

"Donald's cheating on me," Dayana said over a fresh cup of coffee minutes later. Her manicure had chips in it, and the nails on her index fingers were both chewed down to the quick, Maggie noticed. Day's nail-biting had been another source of constant frustration for her mother. "And you don't look surprised by that."

Maggie winced and nodded toward the French doors. "Let's walk and talk," she suggested. They headed around the house, into the backyard. She'd met Donald on three occasions and had disliked him instantly. There was something smarmy about the guy. And not just because he wore a tie to lounge around his own house on a Saturday afternoon. He gave off a vibe of needing to be liked. Needing to feel respected. Needing to be the most important person in the room. Which was a problem, given who Dayana's father was. No one else could be the most important person in the room if Sebastian was in it.

"Why isn't anyone surprised by that?"

Maggie hesitated. "I don't want to say anything that would cause problems if you two reconcile."

At the back of the yard, they wandered up the long horseshoe curve in the path, and Maggie automatically looked for her favorite tree. Tall and straight, it stood like a lone sentinel just before the path opened into the clearing. Dignified except for the pair of carved eyes someone had affixed to its bark. Another surprise from Silas. The man was constantly surprising her.

And she was constantly trying to keep her secrets from him.

"Maggie, there isn't a chance in hell that I'll go back to that"— Dayana glanced around, making sure there were no impressionable ears nearby. "Narcissistic, grade-A asshole."

"I believe you, and I don't blame you." Maggie led the way into the clearing and noted that Sy's crew had put down the gravel for the firepit.

"Well, now, *that's* a view," Dayana said. She stepped up to where the grass ended and the rocky outcropping began and drank it in.

"It is," Maggie agreed. "So how did this come to a head?"

"I caught him whispering sweet nothings into his phone when he said he was taking a conference call, so I followed him, climbed a fence, and waited until he had his pants down around his knees poolside before spraying them both down with a hose and telling him I wanted a divorce."

"Wow." Maggie was impressed. "What did Dad say?" Their father had introduced Dayana to Donald, having personally selected the man for his daughter. He'd made his son-in-law an executive in the family foundation, and Donald had stepped into his wife's role as senior program officer when she had their son.

Dayana shot her a look. "How should I know?"

"You didn't tell him?"

"I'm sure he already knows. They work down the hall from each other. Besides, he'd just give me the lecture about dignity and the family name. And I am not feeling very dignified right now."

"Wow. Okay. So what are you doing *here*?" Maggie asked. Dayana had friends. Glamorous, wealthy, stylish friends. They sat on boards together and went to galas. They had spa days and went to ribbon cuttings.

"I'd like to be offended by that question," Dayana said. "But I deserve it."

"I don't mean it like that," Maggie fibbed. "I just meant you have a whole life in Seattle. What made you come here to, as Dean likes to call it, Where the Fuck Are We, Idaho?"

Dayana took a sip of her coffee and then sighed. "My entire life feels like a prison cell. I live in a house chosen by a man who knew he didn't love me when he proposed. I worked at a job for another man who groomed me to fit his requirements for the perfect daughter. I'm surrounded by friends in the same situation who are all making it work. Rich husbands cheat. And rich wives are just supposed to accept it. Accept it and redecorate or get a new piece of jewelry."

"That's bullshit," Maggie said.

Her sister nodded. "It is. I can't live with this. I don't need someone telling me how to suck it up and deal with it because the good outweighs the bad or 'what did I expect when I signed up for this.' I'm here because I need my sister."

Maggie didn't know what to say. She and Dayana had always been careful not to refer to each other as sisters.

"I need you because you're not invested in keeping me in line. I need you because I was a shitty sister to you when you came into my life, and it's time to make amends for that. I am done living a life that someone else designed. And the only person I know who can teach me how is you."

"I think I need a drink," Maggie admitted.

"Make it two," Dayana said with a sad laugh. She turned to face her sister. "So, can we stay?"

Maggie blinked. She felt like the time she'd taken a header off the landing into the basement of her first flip. "Here? It's a construction zone. There are people in and out of the house all day long. Plus, there's more than just me staying here."

"I don't care if you have an entire high school marching band that lives in your attic and wakes up to practice at six a.m. I need a change, and I need your help."

Maggie's heart started to hammer in her chest like it did whenever she saw Silas with his hat on backward. But this wasn't the good kind of cardio. This was nerves.

"I'm above begging, but I am not above using my son. Donald hasn't spent a day alone with Keaton in Keaton's entire life. He needs attention. He needs family. *I* need family."

"You're kidding me." Maggie wasn't so much surprised as appalled.

"I wish I were," Dayana said, staring down at the town that had called to Maggie. "I like the vibe here. It's something different."

Maggie *really* needed that drink. Hell. She was going to need another bed.

She helped Dayana unload her bags and dumped Dean with the responsibility of helping her sister choose a bedroom. The second they disappeared upstairs, Maggie went in search of Silas. She found him and Keaton on the north side of the house. Silas was watering the plantings while her nephew chased dog and cats through the wet mulch, squealing with delight. The kid was positively filthy and seemed downright joyful about it.

"I know you're mad at me," Maggie said. "And you have every right to be, but I need advice and I need it fast."

Silas glanced at her and then the hose.

"I wouldn't blame you if you did it," she said, reading his mind.

He put down the hose and crossed his arms. "What's the situation?" he asked.

She filled him in on Dayana's predicament. "So what do I do?"

"About what?"

"Dayana and I don't have that kind of relationship. I barely know her, and she wants to stay here."

He rubbed a thumb over his lower lip. "Do you want to know her?"

"I don't know. I mean, I guess? Is it bad if I admit that I'm pretty comfortable with us not knowing each other? And I've got a lot going on already without adding a sticky family situation into the mix." The weight of it all settled on her shoulders. She felt a rising panic. "How am I going to keep working, keep filming, keep searching for answers about the Campbells, while dating a man who regularly hauls me out of my comfort zone, *and* make time for some kind of family crisis?"

Her chest felt tight, like the stress of responsibility was about to burst out of her rib cage. But an exploded rib cage would set her too far back.

Silas put his hands on her shoulders and squeezed. "Look at me, Mags. You aren't doing any of this alone. And a family crisis is a privilege because it means you have a family to be in crisis with. Your sister—and don't give me that bullshit about half-sister— came here because she needs you. That incredibly dirty little boy needs you."

"I don't want anyone to need me," she insisted. She also wasn't fond of the idea of needing anyone herself.

Keeping Keaton in sight, Silas steered her to the side of the house. He pressed himself against her, and for some reason, his weight calmed her. And that annoyed her.

"I'd like to make it clear that I'm still mad at you."

"Acknowledged," Maggie said, trying not to melt into him.

"But being a good boyfriend doesn't mean only showing up when you're not pissed off," he continued. He leaned down to nuzzle at her neck. "Now, I want you to imagine you're on your deathbed."

"My deathbed? This went dark fast," she said, trying to focus on his words instead of on the way his lips moved against her skin.

"You're the most beautiful hundred-and-five-year-old to ever live," he said. "Are you going to be patting yourself on the back for getting all your chores done on time or are you going to be wishing you'd given yourself more quality time?"

She wrinkled her nose. "I kind of want to say I'd be patting myself on the back."

He pulled away and grinned down at her. Maggie's heart took a funny dip in her chest. It was a completely different feeling from the crushing weight of responsibility from a moment ago.

"God, I'm so into you, Maggie. Even when I'm good and pissed."

"I'm kind of fond of you, too," she stammered.

After another glance at Keaton, who was sitting in a puddle of hose water while the dog licked his face and hair, Silas dropped his forehead to hers. "Take the time, darlin'." His tone was so tender that it made her heart hurt with a want for more. "We can juggle schedules, dates, and to-dos, but you've got a sister who needs you and a nephew who wouldn't mind getting to know his aunt Maggie. You know I'm happy to lend a hand wherever you need me. And Dean and Cody can take over in the areas I'm not equipped to deal with."

"Like anything involving hashtags?"

"Exactly."

She took a breath, blew it out slowly, and then rested her head on his chest. That broad, warm, welcoming chest. His heart beat steadily, comfortingly beneath her ear. "Ugh. Okay. But if this goes horribly wrong, I'm holding you responsible."

"I'd expect nothing less. Now, before you go back in there, call in the reinforcements."

"Reinforcements?"

"Niri and Kayla. Call 'em up. Your sister needs support, and there's none better than girlfriends with alcohol."

"Call Nirina and Kayla. Okay. Got it."

He released her, and she missed his touch immediately.

"Oh, and, Mags?"

"Yeah?" She knew it wouldn't be that easy.

"Pencil me in for that in-depth discussion of why you didn't feel the need to tell your future husband about your family. Tonight."

"I might need reinforcements for that conversation," she said, ignoring the husband bait.

"No, you won't," he said mildly. "Now, I've got to get out to the job site. So you're gonna have to clean up our muddy buddy before his mama sees him."

She started for Keaton but stopped when Silas called her name.

"Maybe you can call it a coincidence that your mama was the first one to bring you here and that your sister showed up here looking for a place in your life. But I see signs."

35

THERE WAS NOTHING like a baseball stadium on an almost summer night, Silas thought. While the women of the family converged on Maggie's place with alcohol, snacks, and sympathetic ears, he had organized a gentlemen's night out. It had started with just him, Cody, and Dean. Then they'd added Wallace to the guest list. When he'd rounded it out with Michael and the dads, Maggie's sister had given the men permission to take Keaton, as long as Silas promised to text her proof of life every hour on the hour.

So there they sat in two rows of green stadium seats, eating more hot dogs and nachos than was healthy and cheering on the minor league Outlaws. They talked work and women—Cody admitted to maybe kinda sorta having a girlfriend—and rated ballpark food while the home team held a comfortable lead.

Silas had picked up on something, either friction or interest, between Michael and Dean and wanted to see what would happen if they spent a little more time together. At the top of the sixth, he handed Keaton over to Emmett and headed to the restroom. His brother caught up to him at the urinals.

"What's your problem?" they both said at the same time.

"Me?" Silas asked, breaking rule number one of men's restrooms and looking his brother in the eye. "You're the one who's looking at Dean like he's a ballpark chili dog one minute and then acting like he's invisible the next."

Michael looked over his shoulder to make sure the topic of

conversation hadn't wandered in behind them. An interesting problem Silas had never considered about being gay. Restrooms were no
longer safe havens to discuss love lives.

"Yeah?" Michael said. "You're the one who's doing a shitty job of
hiding his whole 'woe is me' thing."

"Fuck," Silas grumbled, turning his attention back to the urinal.
"Fine. But you go first."

"I don't know how to do this," Michael said, zipping back up.
"Okay?"

"Do what?" Silas asked over the flush of the urinal.

"Be into a guy. Talk about being into a guy."

Silas zipped, flushed, and met his brother at the sinks. "Pretty
sure it's the same. You flirt. You ask him out. Dazzle him with your
color-coordinated closet and then get married."

"I don't think I'm ready to dazzle anyone with my closet," Michael
said, reaching for a paper towel. "That's pretty much what I told
him at the cookout. I think I just need more time before I get into
a relationship. I barely know who I am, let alone who I am with
someone else."

"Mikey," Silas said, turning the water off and splashing his brother
with his wet hands, "you're thinking it to death. Do you like the
guy? Are you attracted to the guy?"

Again his brother looked toward the door first. "Yeah."

"Then don't waste your time trying to get comfortable first. There
isn't much comfortable about relationships, not if it's a good one at
least. Ask. Him. Out."

Michael puffed out his cheeks and slowly exhaled. "What if he
says yes?"

Silas furrowed his brow. "Then you go out?"

"I mean, this is small-town Idaho. Not San Francisco or New York.
What's everyone in town going to say about two guys on a date?"

Silas dried his hands before putting them on his brother's shoulders. "It's scary as fuck. I get it. But you can't wait for everyone to
be comfortable when it comes to you living your life. You're the only

one who gets to live it. So you might as well do what you want. And if anyone, and I mean anyone, gives you a hard time, you either deal with it or you come get me and I will deal with it for you. You deserve to be happy, Mikey. And anyone who doesn't want that for you is a fucking asshole who doesn't deserve to have a say in your life."

Damn. His motivational speeches were on point today.

Michael cracked a smile as he pushed his glasses up his nose. "You don't suck as a brother."

"Good. You can buy me an ice cream," Silas said, starting for the door.

"Nice try. Now it's your turn. What happened with you and Maggie?"

Deciding it wouldn't hurt to get a second opinion, Silas filled him in as they walked back out to the top of their section.

"Ouch," Michael said when he was done. "Did you ask Dean about it? He'd probably know."

Silas took his hat off and ran his hand through his hair before settling it back on his head. "Nah. I want it to come from her."

"Understandable. So you're scared, then." He said it like it was fact.

"No. I'm not scared. I'm annoyed. Pissed. Justifiably angry."

"Hurt," Michael revised. "You've been opening yourself up to her. You introduced her to your family. Welcomed her into your life. And you've been up front about wanting her to stay when she's done."

"Yeah?" Silas said carefully, sensing there was a trap being laid.

"She's been up front about having no intention of staying."

"So? That doesn't give her the right to lie to me. To our family about being an only child and not having a father."

"Hey, man. I'm on your side," Michael said, holding up his hands. "I'm just saying that if she really believes that she's going to walk away from you and everything here in a few months, maybe she didn't feel safe opening up. And maybe you're realizing how much it's going to hurt if she does walk away."

Silas grunted. His brother had a point.

"Are we being stupid here?" Michael asked. "Isn't this just like all those summer flings in high school and college? All hot and heavy for the season, and then everyone goes back to real life?"

"Not if we convince them to stay," Silas said grimly.

"What if we can't?"

"Maybe I've been feeling a little overconfident in my ability to make her want to stay," he admitted. Maybe that was the root of it. He'd been certain she was meant to be his and hadn't actually considered the idea that Maggie didn't know it. Or worse, would decide to ignore it.

"You're expecting her to give up everything to stay here with you. She's built her entire career around wanderlust. New adventures. Your life, your career—they're both built on roots. Literally." Michael took a breath and glanced at him. "Sy, maybe you don't want to hear this. But you already had one woman hang around town for you for five years, and that didn't pan out. If you're serious about this one, maybe you should be thinking more about what *she* wants and a little less about what you want."

Silas opened his mouth to argue but then closed it again. Kinship was his home. He'd never thought about living anywhere else. Never thought there'd be anything or anyone who could tempt him to dig out his roots and transplant himself.

He'd taken Maggie showing up in Kinship as a sign, especially after learning about her history. But he'd assumed it was a sign for her to stay. Not a sign for him to go.

They returned to their seats, and Silas accepted a sleepy Keaton from Wallace, who had been lecturing the kid on the finer points of the shortstop position. Silas settled the toddler against his chest and gazed at the men around him.

What would his life be like without them down the block or across the hall or waiting for him at Decked Out?

What would his life be like without the roots he'd planted in Kinship?

*   *   *

Darealmvpeen: My female would never be allowed to work outside the home. Especially not with power tools.

BiyatchPleeeeez: @Darealmvpeen. The 1800s are calling. They want your dumb ass back.

36

"ARE YOU SURE they can be trusted with a toddler?" Dayana asked again.

"Day, I think between all of them, including the two who raised children into adulthood, they'll be able to keep up with Keaton," Maggie pointed out as she stuck white tapers into the wooden candelabra she'd found in a shop window downtown when she went hunting for another bed and matching chairs for the dining table that afternoon. At this rate, there would be nothing left to stage when the house was complete.

"He didn't even cry when they left," her sister pointed out. "Another man who doesn't need me anymore. And now I'm being dramatic."

"I feel like you've earned the right to it," Maggie told her, adjusting the forest-green linen chair at the head of the table.

"Well, I feel like I owe you a thank-you and an apology," Dayana said, setting out a platter of shrimp they'd picked up at the market. "I've been a bad sister to you, and making it up to you never translated to more than an item on my weekly to-do list."

The efficiency of it made Maggie think of Dean, and she smiled.

"I'm serious. Look at my calendar." Dayana handed her phone over. Maggie saw tasks scheduled between meetings and luncheons and playdates.

Check in with Maggie.

Send Maggie's birthday card.

Ask Maggie about Thanksgiving plans.

"This looks like effort to me."

As she held the phone, a call came through. The caller ID read DAD. Hastily, she handed the phone back.

Her sister glanced at it, hit ignore, and put the phone down. "You had no reason to feel obligated to take me in. And I am grateful that you were still willing to do it."

"If you're beating yourself up, then I'm going to have to start beating myself up for not making the effort at all. Let's just leave it at you had no reason to come to me," Maggie pointed out. "I wasn't a last resort. You've got resources. You could have kicked Donald out or rented yourself a nice house with full-time help. But you came here because you wanted to. Now, as long as you can handle living in a construction zone, we can see what happens."

She was "seeing what happened" in a lot of areas of her life.

"A clean slate," Dayana said.

"A renovation."

Her sister gave her a wry smile. "I didn't want to share my father with you. It took me a long time before I started to understand that, to my mother, you represented a permanent reminder of the fact that she wasn't enough for my dad. Our dad."

"You know better than anyone that it had very little to do with her and everything to do with him," Maggie pointed out. She added the cheese-and-olive tray to the table. She was getting pretty good at panic shopping for last-minute get-togethers.

Dayana's mother was a beautiful, intimidating woman who didn't hesitate to label someone an enemy. Maggie had been stamped with that title at age twelve.

"She needed us to be a unit bonded against you and your mother. I never bothered picking it apart until years later. I'm sorry for that. I'm sorry for working against you and making sure you couldn't develop a relationship with our dad."

"You're not responsible for anyone else's choices. He could have tried harder," Maggie said lamely as she arranged a stack of napkins. Maybe she could have tried, too. But things still would have ended up the way they did. Accepting that her father couldn't love her the way she'd needed to be loved as a little girl was easier than fighting for that love.

"Why haven't you told Silas who Dad is?" Dayana asked, plucking an olive off the tray and popping it into her mouth. Her phone rang again. This time the screen said DONALD. Her sister flipped the phone over.

Maggie shook her head. "Technically, I'm not allowed to tell anyone, since I signed the NDA."

"What? When? Why?" The genuine horror on her sister's face did something to loosen the knots that had taken up permanent residence in Maggie's chest.

"I thought you knew."

"I most certainly did *not* know," Dayana said.

"It's a long story, and I think our reinforcements are here," she said, hearing Kevin let out a happy bark.

"We *will* talk about it."

Maggie blew out a breath and tried not to think of all the uncomfortable conversations she had to look forward to. This was why she liked her life the way it had been. Simple. Quiet. No one demanding to talk to her all the time.

It was nice having the house full of women for a change, Maggie decided two glasses of wine later. Mama B had shown up with a Crock-Pot full of pierogies and immediately turned on some girl power music on her Bluetooth speaker. Blaire brought four bottles of wine and a huge tossed salad. Kayla and Niri brought margaritas and cookies, respectively.

The occasion felt both festive and solemn as Dayana walked them through the ending of what was supposed to be a fairy-tale life.

"It's okay to want more for yourself," Blaire said, scooping a piece of fresh bread through the olive dip.

Dayana glanced at Maggie. Neither of them had mentioned their family name or how one sister had grown up in luxury. "What if I've always had everything I could have ever wanted? Maybe this is the price I have to pay."

"That's bullshit, sweetheart," Mama B announced. Her fiery, homegrown wisdom was the perfect complement to Blaire's careful, clinical observations. "It doesn't matter if you have a gold-plated toilet. It's not wrong to want a faithful husband."

"I think what the moms are saying," Kayla said, "is that it doesn't matter how much you have, if it's not what you want. You can't just decide to be happy with less than."

The discussion moved on to divorces and attorneys and then what Dayana wanted next.

"I want to go back to work," she confessed. "I mean, don't get me wrong. Keaton is the best thing to ever happen to me. Insert all the other things a modern mother is supposed to say about her child being the center of her universe. But dammit. It's not enough for me. I don't want a three-year-old to be my best friend. I don't want to give up on a career I love just because a human fell out of my vagina."

"Listen up, next generation," Mama B said, pointing her wineglass at each of them in turn. "Babies do not complete you. Babies do not make you a fully realized woman. Neither does a man. That's a truth we all have to learn the hard way."

Maggie's phone vibrated. It was a text from Dean. He'd sent a picture of Silas, hat on backward, watching the game while cradling the sleeping Keaton against his chest.

Dean: If I had ovaries they'd be exploding. Marry this man and have his beautiful babies.

Maggie felt something warm and weird swoop through her chest. She didn't like it at all. She didn't have a biological clock. She didn't have a desire to settle down. She liked her life just the way it was.

"Uh-oh. That's a baby-making look right there," Niri said, pointing at Maggie. "I should know—I had one of those the week before Jeremiah knocked me up. He was playing hide-and-seek with his nieces and *bam*! Pregnant."

"Who needs another drink?" Maggie asked, flipping her phone over. Every woman around the table raised her hand.

*   *   *

The men returned from the baseball game just as the women were getting ready to leave, which meant it was another hour of tours and small talk and nightcaps before everyone who didn't live there was on the road and everyone who did live in the house was settled.

Maggie found Silas on the sunporch, waiting.

"Ready to do this?" he asked.

"I am if you are," she said, bracing herself. He thought this was a conversation about her family baggage. But there was more to it. She wasn't the marrying type. The packing-school-lunches type. The juggling-a-family-calendar type. She'd never even thought about it before. It was time Silas came to terms with that.

"Let's walk," she suggested, grabbing a flashlight from the chest of drawers she had found on a side street in Kinship and refinished with Cody.

The moon was high and bright in the night sky. Lights glowed from Cody's and Dean's windows on the second floor. She glanced up at the window to the secret room and thought about how much she'd rather be in there alone, sifting through someone else's treasures. Then realized that wasn't entirely true.

She'd laughed over delicious food and good drinks with smart women who talked about real things. And now she was taking a moonlit walk with a man who made her question everything she'd always wanted.

She took a breath and a leap. "My dad was married when he met my mother. They were both attending a conference and had a one-night stand. I was the unintended consequence of that night. She didn't tell him about me. Times were tight. Mom was a single parent, and having me derailed her dreams of a high-powered career."

They veered away from the cliff where she'd talked to Dayana today and instead headed in the direction of the barn. Tall green grass whispered in the night breeze.

"She was proud of doing it on her own. That meant crappy jobs and crappier apartments. We moved around a lot until I was twelve and she got a 'real' job. In an office with work in her field. Benefits. Vacation time. It was supposed to be a new beginning. We splurged and took our very first vacation. We came here," Maggie said, stopping in the shadow of the old barn.

She shined her light over the ruin and imagined it as it could be. Silas was silent next to her, listening.

"It was the best week of my life. We had hope. We'd buy a house. She even brought real estate listings with us, and we spent the whole week circling homes and daydreaming."

His hand engulfed hers, fingers intertwining. He seemed to get that it wasn't a happily ever after she was telling him. That understanding, that quiet support, steadied her.

"We drove up here that week and tried to peek down the drive at the house. Mom joked about maybe someday we'd come back here and buy it."

She felt the hitch in her chest. The sad mixed with pride, and for a second, she wished fiercely for things that could never be. "We went home, and Mom started her dream job. Things were great for a few weeks. The paychecks were regular, and she was so proud of herself for providing for us. But I came home after school on a Friday. We were supposed to go to the school carnival that night. Mom was curled up on the couch. Crying."

Silas pulled her into him and held her against his chest. She didn't realize until she felt the dampness on his shirt that tears were slipping down her cheeks.

She swallowed hard around the lump in her throat. "Anyway, that was it. She called him. Told him about me. There was a paternity test. And a month after the results, I met my father."

"Baby," he whispered against her hair.

"She asked him for money, and I didn't realize until it was too late how hard that must have been for her. The next thing I knew, one weekend a month, I was leaving our tiny apartment and getting dropped off in front of the gates to my father's house. My mom was never allowed inside.

"It's embarrassing how excited I was about it," she confessed, still smarting at the memory of the audacity of her childlike hope. "I was finally getting a dad. And bonus, he came with a sister for me. I didn't know that I should be anything but excited to get what I'd wanted for so long. My mom drove me to his house. It was a twenty-two-room mansion overlooking Puget Sound. He had staff. A housekeeper, a cook, a driver. And he had a wife and daughter."

She could still feel the cold disinterest from the stranger who was her father. Still feel the sharp rejection when the stranger's wife told her there was no room at her table for the daughter of a whore. She'd stood there in the Italian marble foyer, and her father left her there to chase after his wife.

"His wife hated the idea of my existence. Understandably. Their daughter, Dayana, had no interest in getting to know me. My father had no idea what to do with a surprise daughter."

Silas held her neck with one warm hand while the other stroked up and down her back.

"I hated going there. I'd lock myself in the guest room and read, watching the clock and hoping time would go faster. At the time, I didn't understand why my mother would have put me in that position. I begged her to let me stay home, and every time she made me get in the car, I told her I hated her."

"Twelve," he reminded her. "You were twelve."

"It doesn't mean it was right. I cringe now, thinking about the pain I inflicted on her just because I was hurting."

To this day, she was ashamed. Worse, she didn't have the opportunity to make up for it.

"After a while, he started to make an effort. But I know his wife punished him for it. There was a workshop in a separate garage on the property. That's how he'd work through his problems. He'd blast eighties rock and tinker. He'd let me sit on a stool in the corner while he built something. Then he started showing me how to sink a screw or sand down a rough edge. Once, when his company was facing a down quarter, I helped him build a bookcase. I still remember the smell of the stain. We finished it, stood it up in that garage, and admired it together."

Silas pulled her over to the stone wall off the barn. He sat down and then surprised the hell out of her when he pulled her onto his lap.

"Keep going," he said.

She took a breath and pressed on. "Our relationship existed only in that shop. Inside the house, I was just a reminder to his wife that her husband had an affair. Their daughter, my half-sister, took her lead from her mother. One of my first weekends at their house, they took Dayana out to dinner for her birthday and left me at the house. They didn't want word to get out that there was an illegitimate daughter. So I ate clam chowder with Mrs. Briggs, the cook."

"'He doesn't belong to you.' That's what Dayana's mother said to me when they walked out the front door."

"Fucking asshole," Sy said succinctly.

"I can see it through her lens. I was the product of a betrayal."

"It wasn't your fault. And her taking it out on you proves more about her character than yours."

"It wasn't my fault," Maggie agreed. "But I was the result."

"What did your father do about it?" he asked.

Her shoulders hunched. "What could he do? My existence was his penance. He had to provide for me but prove to his wife that I didn't matter. He couldn't protect me without further damaging that relationship."

"That's bullshit."

His anger soothed something raw in her. Like aloe on a burn.

"It wasn't all bad," she assured him. "I made friends with the staff. Mrs. Briggs used to take me to a fancy farmers market with her on Saturdays, and she'd make a special dessert. Just for me. When I turned sixteen, my father's driver took me out in the Jaguar and taught me to parallel park downtown. I was so excited and terrified that, to this day, I'm an excellent parallel parker."

He laughed because she wanted him to, and she appreciated it.

"I went. One weekend every month. Until I turned eighteen. That's when I decided I didn't want to have anything to do with him or them. It was a relief for everyone. He paid for my college, at least the years I attended. Something that was hard for me to swallow, but Mom stuck on that. She died when I was twenty-one. A car accident. She had a job she loved finally. With Dad's financial support, she'd moved us into a little house in a nice neighborhood. But it was only home because she was there.

"When she died, I lost my balance. I dropped out and got married. I tried to replace my mom and my father with Dean."

"Twenty-one, Mags. Who knows what the hell they're doing at twenty-one?"

She gave him a smile. "Hardly anyone."

"And look where you are now."

She was enjoying the moonlight on land she'd bought with her own money. His hand slipped under her shirt to stroke the bare skin of her back. It soothed her rough edges.

"Dayana, she made an effort after Mom's accident to, I don't know, get to know me? Acknowledge me? I don't hold it against her, what she did as a kid or a teenager. But I also don't know how to open the doors and let her in."

"And now she's here, knocking on your door."

"And now she's here," she repeated, nodding slowly.

"Neither of you is the kid caught in the middle anymore. You both get to make your own decisions. But that also doesn't mean you have to automatically forgive and forget," he pointed out.

"We're going to see how this goes. Living together in a construction zone during a family crisis. We'll either come out of it sisters or we won't have to remember to send each other birthday cards every year."

"Is your father still in Dayana's life?" Silas asked carefully.

"He is. But he's no longer in mine. He gave me money after Mom died. I wanted to refuse it, but there were medical bills, and I had nothing. Not even a degree. But I did have an idea. So I used part of the money to fix up our little house. I sold it at a profit and bought my next one, learning as I went. It took me four long years, but I finally got to mail him a check for every penny I owed him."

"That must have felt good."

"For about five minutes. Then I realized how much I would have rather had my mom back and a dad who loved me. And after I finished destroying the ugliest laundry room you could ever imagine, I decided it didn't matter who did or didn't love me. Who was or wasn't here. I had myself, and that wasn't going to change."

And it still hadn't. There was a solace and a sadness in that truth.

Silas looked up at the moon and blew out a breath. "Well, damn, Mags. I was countin' on being able to stay mad at you for at least a few more days."

"I should have told you I had a sister."

"You should have. But at least now I understand why you didn't. Can't say I wouldn't have done the same thing."

She reached up and tugged at the ends of his hair. "Thank you for making it easy to tell you."

"I'd like to make a lot of things easier for you if you'd let me, Maggie." His voice was gruff and again it managed to soothe.

"Maybe I'll take you up on that," she said softly.

PotHeadLibrarian: Maggie don't take down the bird of paradise wallpaper in the foyer!!!! At least bring it to me and come hang it in my house!!!

DreemzComeTru: Just me or is Maggie glowing these days? IS THERE A BABY #MILAS???

ReelTalkSmurf: Can we talk about how cute Cody is?

37

JUNE 1 BROUGHT with it real summer temperatures and a renewed energy at the Old Campbell Place. Silas's crew had finished the foundational planting around the house and finished the massive undertaking of clearing brush and nuisance weeds from the remaining acreage. The expanded terrace was being meticulously laid out, mixing in original stone with new like a giant jigsaw puzzle.

The job was enough to keep Bitterroot Landscapes afloat in a down season. Sy would have survived with his crew intact thanks to savings and creativity. But Silas was grateful for Maggie and her big vision for helping even out a tough year.

The pinch of the plant closing was being felt in earnest now as the emergency plan to entice a new buyer had fallen through and the unemployment checks continued to barely cover necessities. Hundreds of neighbors vied for seasonal work with little to no experience. He, like the rest of his family and town, worried about their neighbors. About a mass exodus if they had to move for jobs. About the ones too proud to ask for help.

He didn't like feeling helpless. The second Maggie's deposit landed in his bank account, he made a fat donation to the local food bank after his beloved Mama B mentioned that the shelves were getting bare. His family had taught him to save *and* to share. Because it wasn't right if he went to bed with a full stomach if his neighbor's was empty.

The Wrights built bigger tables.

While he scrambled to swap laundry from washer to dryer in the basement, he thought about tables and solutions. He heard his front door open and the sound of his brother's shiny loafers on the hardwood above. Silas took the stairs two at a time.

"It's not as bad as I thought it would be," Michael said, eyeing Sy's charmingly disheveled living room.

"Haven't been here much," Silas confessed. "But Maggie's place is getting pretty crowded, which is why I invited her to dinner here."

"And then remembered you haven't cleaned in a month," Michael assessed.

It was more like six weeks. But who was counting?

"Which is why I called you. You're the Black Mr. Clean, and I'm throwing myself on your mercy. I have the sheets in the dryer. What do I do next?"

Michael had always been the tidy type. Even as a child, he'd appreciated order and efficiency. His bedroom had looked like a museum to nerdy childhood, with action figures neatly arranged on shelves and books alphabetized on a bookcase that Sy's dad helped him build. Hell, for his fourteenth birthday, Michael had asked for a desk in his room so he didn't have to do his homework in the kitchen anymore. As an adult, the man had a favorite furniture polish, a recipe book on household stain removers, and a robot vacuum cleaner.

And right now, he was Silas's only hope.

"Well, since you're the adult version of Pigpen, I suppose I could offer some assistance," Michael shot back.

"Teach me your ways."

His brother scanned the space. "Your table is buried under six months of paperwork," he observed. "So serve dinner on the deck. What are you having?"

"Steaks, baked potatoes, and whatever green things I can find in the fridge."

"Good. What time is she coming?"

"In two hours."

"Perfect. I have to be out of here before six anyway."

"Have plans?" Silas asked, grabbing his cleaning supplies from under the kitchen sink and piling them on the counter.

"Maybe."

He caught the smile in his brother's voice and looked up.

"Do you have a *date*?"

Michael shrugged, but that half-smile was still there. "Dinner."

"With?" Silas prodded.

He pushed his glasses up his nose. "Dean."

"About damn time. Did he ask you?"

The grin was full-blown now. "Actually, I asked him. And I don't want to talk about it and jinx anything."

"I'll expect a text later," Silas told him.

"You'll be too busy getting Maggie naked on your clean sheets."

"That is definitely in tonight's forecast," he admitted. "But I always have time for your love life."

Michael waved his hands in front of him. "Okay. No more talking about it because it'll just make me more nervous. Let's do a surface clean here in the living room, throw any extra mess in the dining room and shut the pocket door, and focus the deep clean on the bathroom and kitchen. I'll take the kitchen, and you can clean the bathroom while you shower."

Silas wrapped his brother in a sweaty hug and gave him a smacking kiss on his forehead. "You're my hero, Mikey."

Michael extricated himself from his smelly grasp. "It's kind of my superpower." He flipped a roll of paper towels in the air and caught it one-handed. "Let's do this."

Just like they used to on chore day growing up, they cranked the music and got to work.

"How do you keep your place so clean?" Maggie asked two hours later when Silas opened the door for her. "It even smells like lemons in here."

She was wearing a pair of cutoffs that showed off those long, shapely legs and a sexy off-the-shoulder sweater in plain black. Her hair, all russet tones thanks to the sun, was styled in short, tousled waves. She looked casual, sexy, happy.

"Our parents made us have chore day once a week while they all went to brunch. Every time I see a carton of orange juice, I feel compelled to clean the microwave," he fibbed.

"Since you're cooking, I brought flowers and some new finds from the secret room," she said, holding up a box with a bouquet of flowers in it.

He took it from her, put it down, and then did what he always wanted to do when she walked into the room. Silas kissed the hell out of her.

"Wow," she said, eyes wide and bright, when he finally pulled back.

"Preview of dessert," he promised and led the way into the kitchen.

"I don't mean to look a gift penis in the mouth, but you did promise me an actual dessert," she reminded him.

"There's pie," he promised. "I bribed Dad into making it by promising to spend a Saturday in his garden with him. His apple crumb pie is a religious experience, which is why we'll be eating it in bed. After." He gave her his best lecherous look.

She laughed. "After-sex pie. You, Silas Wright, are one-of-a-kind."

He got a mason jar out of the cabinet and handed it to Maggie. "You get our centerpiece organized while I start dinner."

They worked companionably in the tight space of his kitchen and filled each other in on their days.

Silas told her about the client in Abileen who scheduled his crew for the weeding, mulching, and trimming in his backyard when his next-door neighbor was away on vacation. The neighbor was apparently an attractive woman in her early sixties who was into gardening. The client was a recently retired single guy with a black thumb who was working up his nerve to ask her out.

Maggie was making progress in the third-floor bathrooms. The shower surround and new toilet were in place in the hallway bathroom, and the tile and vanity were ready to be picked up for one of the attached baths.

"I got a whole twenty minutes in there this afternoon before Keaton found me, and then Jim needed me for an almost-emergency, and then Dean demanded that I reshoot a one-on-one that didn't have a chorus of circular saws in the background," she told him. "Oh, and in the middle of all that, Wallace wanted to show me sixty pages of Campbell family scrapbooks he had Cody haul down from the secret room."

Plate of steaks in hand, Silas nudged her toward the back door, and they moved their catch-up to the covered deck. "Anything noteworthy in the scrapbooks?" he asked.

"Not unless you count Wallace's commentary on hemlines noteworthy."

While he put the steaks on the grill, she grabbed the box of treasures and two beers before settling in a chair at the small table. "I talked to Dean today," she said innocently, unpacking the box's contents.

He looked up from the sizzling meat. "I talked to Michael today."

They both grinned and left it at that.

He turned down the heat on the grill and joined her at the table. "How did Cody's finals go?" he asked.

"We think they went well," she said, handing him a photo in a protective plastic sheet. It was of three women in gowns staring at the camera. They were in some sort of fancy-looking drawing room, a fireplace and an octagonal window behind them. There was a fourth woman—or girl—dressed in a plain, high-necked gown standing off to the side. "He's nervous, especially about the science exam, since it was comprehensive. But Dayana turned out to be a damn good tutor and helped him cram. Flip it over," she instructed.

Silas did as he was told and saw the inscription written in a tight, loopy scrawl.

The Palmer Sisters and their lady's maid.

There was a name after the word *maid*, but the ink was smudged. It looked like *Ann* or *Anna*.

"Did Cody get his grades yet?" he asked.

"The last three should be posted tonight," Maggie told him. She handed him a page, in its own protective sheet, of the manuscript they'd found on the desk. "He promised to text as soon as he knows. He's scared to death, but I feel good about it. He worked hard."

"Well, get your party hats ready," he said.

She leaned in and gripped his arm. "Do you have inside information? Does your dad know if Cody passed?"

"I may have asked him to hunt down a few of the late graders this afternoon."

She surprised him by jumping out of her chair and throwing her arms around him. "Oh my God. He did it! He's going to be thrilled. Now we definitely have to have a party. Did I tell you I was thinking about throwing a party?"

"You did. And we are. I already asked Mama B if she can make her pierogies."

"We can have it at the house, and now that it's official, he can ask his mom if she'll come." Maggie pulled out her phone to start making a list.

Silas covered the screen with his hand. "Uh-uh. No phones at the table during quality catch-up time," he insisted. He took the phone, stuffed it in his pocket, and returned to the grill to flip the steaks.

"Mean." She pouted.

He pinched the tongs in front of her. "You'll just have to be entertained by me."

"Well, there are *worse* things, I suppose."

He closed the cover on the grill and sat back down. "What am I looking at here?" he asked, picking up the manuscript page again.

She put her beer down and leaned over. "Wallace spotted this. His glasses might be thick, but he's got a good eye for things. Check out the handwriting."

He examined it and then flipped the photo over again. "Looks pretty similar to me."

"Wallace is going to dig into the Palmer family and see if they somehow connect to the Campbells. We're still coming up dry on Ava Campbell. It's like she was the first Dedman or something. The mentions of her family say her father was a banker, but short of scouring every census record for six decades, I don't know how we're going to track him down."

"At least this is a lead. There's got to be some kind of connection to the Palmer sisters if their photo showed up in Aaron Campbell's study. Speaking of which, I finished *Blood on the Moon* on my lunch break. Good book, but I didn't find anything that seemed like it would be helpful. Just a lonely cowboy."

"I'm almost done with *Into the Sunset*, and nothing's struck me as a key to the gold."

They went through the rest of the box's contents, poring over pictures of the Campbells and their children and the newspaper clippings that detailed Black Jack McGuire's death and Samuel Espinosa's arrest.

Silas pulled the steaks off the grill while Maggie grabbed the potatoes and salad.

They talked while they ate. About Keaton's endless exploration of the "big house." About Dayana's first and only conversation with the apologetic Donald. She'd told him that he was welcome to call and talk to Keaton anytime, but any communication he wanted to have with her would go through their attorneys.

Maggie pushed her empty plate away and sighed contentedly. She glanced around them. "I like your place," she said. "It suits you."

"You sound surprised."

"I'm just coming to the realization that I've had eleven houses, and I've never decorated one of them for me," she said, sounding wistful.

"Why not?" he asked, taking her plate and stacking it on top of his own.

"Because they're not mine. I fix them up to appeal to the broadest audience so I can sell them quickly and move on to the next one."

"You seem to be doing okay in the furnishings department," he noted. "Every time I walk through that front door, it looks more and more like a home." It felt like it, too.

"That's by necessity," she said.

"You don't have to need something just to treat yourself," he pointed out.

She smiled, picking at the label on her beer bottle. "But what have I done to *deserve* the treat?"

"You were one of those clean-your-plate-before-you-get-dessert families, weren't you?" he teased.

Her lips quirked. "Maybe. Aren't most people?"

"Mama B always preached that, since life was uncertain, you should eat dessert first."

"Then why did we just enjoy two perfectly grilled New York strips?"

"Because we need the protein to fuel tonight's bedroom activities. And because I didn't want my lovemaking to be overshadowed by the aftertaste of Dad's apple crumb pie."

She laughed. "I can't fault your logic."

He covered her hand with his. "You ever stop and wonder what if life isn't about earning your way to pleasure? What if it's enjoying it when it makes itself available to you?"

"Hmm."

"That was some seriously deep philosophy, and all I get out of you is a 'hmm.'"

"There's another problem that arises if I start buying things for me and falling in love with windows and bathtubs and..." She looked at him. "Other things."

"What's the problem?" he asked.

"Then it hurts to walk away." She was watching him, her expression unreadable.

He decided to lighten the mood. "I bet you five dollars that you're gonna make us do these dishes before we head on into the bedroom for dessert."

She eyed the plates in front of him. "Well, I *do* like clean dishes," she mused. "But I also could use five dollars."

*   *   *

TeddysMom99: The wrong tile! Maggie is right. This kitchen is cursed!

JstKpSwimming: Good thing she has Hot Landscape Guy to comfort her! #Milas4Ever

InternetsCreeper: Rumor mill in Kinship is all over #Milas hookup! We need a confirmation! And an engagement!

38

MAGGIE WATCHED AS Silas dipped a finger into his bowl and then swiped vanilla ice cream over her bare nipple.

"You're insatiable," she said on a gasp when he covered the bud with his hot mouth. Licking first and then sucking. She moved her bowl to the mattress and leaned against the pillows. She felt each long, lazy pull echoed in her sex, a place that felt empty and needy despite the explosive orgasm she'd barely survived an hour before.

He shifted higher on the pillow and pulled her onto her side.

"Your ice cream is going to melt," she said, noting how shaky her voice sounded.

But Silas didn't seem to care about melted ice cream. He was happy to enjoy it.

Once again, she watched his finger dip into the bowl and swirl. Without breaking contact with his mouth, he traced the ice cream over her other nipple. Around and around until a drip gathered at the tip. Only then did he move his mouth to that breast.

His tongue felt like fire as it lapped at her. Her fingers found their way into his hair, and she tugged on those blond curls until he did what she wanted. Fastening his mouth over the bud and sucking.

Impatient now, he grabbed her hips and dragged her on top of him. Reaching up, he closed her hands over the lip of the headboard. She understood his game when his erection prodded at her. It was her turn to ride, with her breasts in his face.

She shifted forward and then down until he was nudging at her entrance.

"You're so fucking wet already," he murmured against her breast. He gave a small, teasing thrust, and she purred when the first inch slid into place.

It was a long, slow slide that had him sheathed inside her.

Their dishes clinked as body weight shifted.

"Ride," he commanded, switching his attention back to the other breast. He gave her an encouraging slap on the ass. She began to move. A slow, steady rock that felt impossibly decadent. His thighs were rock hard beneath her, skin so warm against her.

But slow didn't feel like enough for her. And judging from the grip he had on her hips, Silas wanted speed, too.

Squeezing her thighs against him, she rode faster. His head came off the pillow, and he murmured unintelligible, erotic promises against her flesh. She felt too damn much. Overwhelmed by physical sensations, swamped by feelings and wonder and need.

She moved. She rode. She took until finally he grabbed her hips and held her still, buried to the hilt. Then, on a low growl, he began to pump his hips into her, fast and hard. She could only hold on and take. Her fingers cramped against the wood of the headboard.

But it was building. Building. Building.

A golden glow was melting into the cracks.

Harder. Deeper. Faster. She was at his mercy, and he hammered into her.

Maggie was breaking apart. More pieces. More shards. But that glow was putting them back together. Making them stronger, more beautiful.

It hit her like a sucker punch from a rogue wave. He rode her into the vortex where there was no air, no light. Only release.

Her thighs gripped him as she met her climax.

He jackknifed up, wrapping his arms around her and finding his own climax. He grunted softly, and his body tensed, stilled, and she felt him come inside her. Her own orgasm reincarnated. She let out a broken gasp as he pulled her hips down, held her there. They bucked and ground against each other, riding out each crest.

His breath was hot on her skin, his arms like steel banded around her.

He gave so much of himself to her like this. Taking on her needs. Doing whatever it took to make her happy. How could she walk away from this? How could she move on, knowing this was what she was leaving behind?

Finally, Silas relaxed beneath her, and together they collapsed on the mattress. "I'm never going to be able to eat pie without getting a hard-on again. Family meals are going to be so awkward."

She laughed into her pillow as her body sang with satisfaction.

The phone in the kitchen signaled a message.

They both sat up and stared at the open door, the dark hallway beyond.

"Could be Cody," Maggie said.

"Or my brother."

"Or Dean."

They looked at each other, and both bolted for the door.

Cody: I passed!!! I'm graduating Saturday!!!

Maggie: I TOLD YOU YOU COULD DO IT!

Cody: I got an 89 on my science final.

Maggie: You're a scientific genius!

Cody: And a 92 on the English paper!

Maggie: Hang on. I'm trying to figure out how to order a four-tier cake and a marching band.

Cody: You're so weird.

Maggie: I'm so {insert enthusiastic swear words here} proud of you. You better be proud of you, too!

Cody: I couldn't have done it without you. Thanks, Maggie.

Maggie: I'm not crying. You're crying!

Cody: I gotta go. Dayana and Keaton are taking me and Kevin for ice cream in a minute.

Maggie: Just you?

Cody: We might pick up a girl I know on the way.

*   *   *

Dean: Dinner was good. I had a nice time.

   Maggie: Good??? Nice???

   Dean: What's with the punctuation abuse?

   Maggie: Sorry. Also texting our graduating senior.

   Dean: Me, too. I think we should get him a car.

   Maggie: Excuse me? Tightwad says what?

   Dean: Don't ruin my first moment of generosity by throwing any historical Scrooginess in my face. The kid could use wheels.

   Maggie: Agreed. Let's go halvesies. Think we can find something by Saturday?

   Dean: You find the car. I'll find the giant bow.

   Maggie: Deal. Dayana and Keaton are taking him for ice cream to celebrate right now.

   Dean: I could go for some ice cream.

   Maggie: Just you?

   Dean: I might happen to know someone else who could go for dessert.

Michael: Dinner went well.

   Silas: Your punctuation makes your words sound sarcastic. Went well as in neither of you choked on a chicken bone and needed the Heimlich? Or well as in "I can't find my pants and socks"?

   Michael: Maybe somewhere in the middle. Okay, maybe a little closer to the pants end of the spectrum.

   Silas: Question. How long is too long for a best man speech?

   Michael: Har har. How did your date go?

   Silas: Maggie was impressed with my cleanliness (I tackled her before she could open the dining room door) and I can't find my pants. I've decided to let you tell the electric fence pissing contest anecdote in your best man speech.

   Michael: Really? I thought I'd get more laughs with the time you got trapped under Mary Beth's bed in tenth grade while her parents decided to have the talk with her.

   Silas: Hold on the reminiscing. I'm hearing rumors of ice cream.

Michael: What a coincidence. I'm hearing them, too.

Silas: Are you texting me next to Dean while he texts Maggie?

Michael: Maybe.

Silas: See you in 20.

Michael: Find your pants first.

39

MOTHER NATURE DELIVERED blue skies and puffy white clouds for Cody's graduation day. The football stadium was decked out in balloons and streamers in the school's colors of green and white. Banners from local businesses congratulated the seniors.

"Look over here," Dean insisted, snapping his fingers at Maggie like she was a distracted toddler. They were standing on the far side of the stadium's concession stand while the school's faculty and administration clumped together in their caps and gowns and sunglasses, ready to enjoy a student-free summer.

A whole summer off. Maggie wondered what she would do with that.

"Enough with the pictures," she grumbled. Dean snapped a series of shots while she batted away the tassel that hung in her face. "I can't believe I said yes to this."

He lowered the camera and smirked. "I can't believe you did either."

When the high school principal had cornered her in the aisle at Tanner's General Store and asked her to speak at the graduation, Maggie had been too intent on finding caulk to iterate a firm no. And when the woman had showered her with praise for everything she was doing for Cody, the Old Campbell Place, and young girls in the community, Maggie felt pressured to accept.

So there she was, staring at the rows of metal chairs positioned on the football field for faculty and the future of America, wishing she had ducked into the plumbing aisle instead.

"The kids are all lined up, and the marching band is warming up," Dayana reported. "Last hair and makeup check."

Maggie stood still while her sister reached into her gigantic designer mom bag and produced a travel-size hairspray. She fluffed and then shellacked Maggie's hair. "I see Silas kissed your lipstick off," she noted, handing Maggie a small mirror and a tube of very expensive lipstick. "Try this color."

Since it gave her something to do, Maggie carefully applied the dusky rose color.

"You're not nervous, are you?" Dean asked, snapping a candid shot of the two women. "You speak to an audience of a million every week."

Not in front of them though. Not directly to them. In Maggie's mind, that was a distinct difference. The filter that allowed anonymous users to leave snarky, ignorant comments was also the same filter that cushioned her from the real-time, real-life reactions of her audience.

"Of course not," she scoffed. "I'm just wishing I would have said no so I could enjoy the ceremony. It's a big deal. And instead of basking in Cody's achievements, I have to worry about giving a speech and not saying 'shit' and appalling an audience of grandmas and kids because there's no editing."

"She's totes nervous," Dean stage-whispered to Dayana.

"Am not," Maggie argued.

"Are too," Dayana said cheerfully. She took Maggie's hands in hers. "Nervous is good. Nerves mean it matters to you. Besides, this is a chance to tell the next generation what garbage most of the advice they're going to get is. Tell them what you wish someone would have told you at that age."

Because that wasn't depressing at all. Tell the shiny, happy faces of a bunch of hopeful eighteen-year-olds, "Hang on to your loved ones, kids, because you never know when your mom, your rock, the person who loves you best in this world will be ripped away from you, often without warning."

Yeah. No. She would stick with her generic "work hard and focus on your goals" speech.

The dignified strains of "Pomp and Circumstance" began.

"Well, that's my cue," she said, feigning a smile.

Maggie sat next to Emmett Wright and studied the crowd, spotting Silas immediately. With Cody's parents as no-shows, the man had rallied one hell of a cheering section for the kid. He juggled a squirmy Keaton while Mama B, Morris, and Blaire fanned themselves with their programs. Michael, Nirina, Jeremiah, and Kayla sat on his other side. Behind them were Jim Hines and half of the Bitterroot crew.

She stood when the class marched into the stadium and shocked the hell out of herself when she found Cody, solemn and proud in emerald green, and felt tears start to well up. He looked at her and winked, that half-smile making an appearance.

Emmett squeezed her shoulder. "You did good, kid," he whispered.

Despite the warmth of the sun, Maggie felt goose bumps crop up on her arms.

You did good, kid.

It was something her mom had said to her whenever Maggie managed to make her proud.

The seniors took their seats, and there wasn't nearly enough time for her to calm herself before Principal Richardson was announcing how proud she was to introduce "celebrity Maggie Nichols as our keynote speaker."

She was halfway to the podium before she realized they were clapping. All of them. The students. The faculty. The families in the stands. Off to the side, on the green, green grass, she saw Dean recording away with the camera, standing with a local journalist and representatives from the student newspaper.

She felt a tiny bit like a rock star.

Mechanically, she shook the principal's hand and stepped behind the podium. Cody was full-on grinning now. She could feel the burst of pride coming from the direction of Silas and company. Mama B blew her a kiss.

She cleared her throat and took the leap. "This is where I'm supposed to tell you that hard work and staying focused on your goals is how you succeed," she began as the crowd quieted. "And while that's true, success is only a very small part of life. That's not how you find happiness. Because, at the end of the day, your quality of life is determined by the people you surround yourself with. The significant others, the partners, the sisters, the friends, the team you choose. The people who have your back. The people who celebrate your wins and mourn your losses with you."

She looked at Silas and Dean and Dayana and Cody as she spoke and keenly felt their joy.

"Kinship taught me that." A whoop went up from the crowd, and she smiled. "Maybe it's something you already know. But it's a truth that sooner or later we all forget. And it's one we have to fight to remember."

"Cody Moses," the loudspeaker crackled.

Their section was on its feet, hooting and hollering, when he walked across the field tall and proud to accept that hard-won diploma. The team—okay, fine, the *family*—they'd somehow managed to build was bigger and louder than any nuclear family in attendance. Together they cheered at the top of their lungs while Cody held his diploma up and punched his fist into the air.

It was a win worth celebrating.

"Aw, crap," Maggie gasped as her vision clouded.

Silas, grinning, pulled her into his side and planted a kiss on top of her head.

A teary-eyed Dayana blindly shoved a tissue at her.

Maggie felt like she was one of the parents in the stands. Steeped in the moment. Reveling in the accomplishment of a person they loved dearly.

Kinship's graduating class was mercifully small, and in minutes, they were all on the field, surrounding their graduate and congratu-lating him. When Cody wrapped his arms around her and lifted her off the ground in a wild hug, when he whispered "thank you" in her ear, Maggie knew happiness.

His girlfriend, Jun, the adorable barista from the café, and her parents were welcomed into their raucous circle and introduced around. Maggie noted the not-my-little-girl look in Jun's dad's eye and decided on the spot to invite them up to the house for cake. Then she took the girl's mom aside to warn her that it was a full-on surprise party.

Silas drove them home, celebratory music blaring through the truck's open windows as they brought up the rear of the Campbell house convoy. Maggie covertly texted their ETA ahead to Elton, and when they turned onto the lane, Cody was busy texting Jun.

"Jun said her mom is freaking out that they get to come see the house," he reported, intent on his phone.

"I'll let you give them the tour," she told him.

"Maybe you could?" he asked. "I mean, you could show them around and maybe talk me up?"

"It's your day," she said with a grin.

Silas squeezed her knee and nodded through the windshield. Maggie felt a burst of excitement when she saw what awaited them.

"Speaking of your day," Silas said, bringing the truck to a stop.

Cody looked up and frowned. "Is everyone working today?"

"Nobody's working today," she told him.

Assembled on the front porch decked out with green-and-white streamers and a CONGRATULATIONS, CODY banner were two dozen cheering people. They were all wearing T-shirts printed with Cody's picture that said PROUD OF MY KINSHIP GRADUATE.

"Did you have to with the T-shirts?" he groaned, looking both embarrassed and pleased.

"Oh, we definitely had to," Silas said, sliding out from behind the wheel. "Mags?"

She rounded the vehicle, and as Silas unbuttoned his dress shirt, she stripped the borrowed gown off over her head to reveal their Cody T-shirts.

Mortified, Cody covered his face. "You guys are seriously embarrassing."

Seeming to recognize whose special day it was, Kevin raced up wearing his own T-shirt and proceeded to give Cody a celebratory licking.

Cody trudged toward the porch, pretending to reluctantly accept the accolades.

"Did he see it yet?" Maggie asked, sliding her arm around Sy's waist.

"Not yet," he said, steering her away from the porch. He whistled at Dean and Dayana, gesturing for them to join.

Cody was in the middle of a haphazard receiving line when Silas reached through the car's open window and leaned on the horn.

The guests cheered when the graduate looked over and froze, his expression one of classic shock.

"Now he sees it," Silas said.

"Get over here," Dean called from behind the camera.

Maggie felt like her smile was going to break her face in two as Cody took a tentative step forward and then finally, the reaction they were waiting for. He vaulted over the porch railing and sprinted toward the SUV with the big red bow.

It wasn't new. But it was safe, reliable, and 100 percent paid for.

"Are you serious?" he asked, stopping in front of the hood and staring, his hands in his hair. "You're not fucking with me?"

"We're definitely not fucking with you," Maggie said.

Silas tossed him the keys. Cody stared at them in his hand. "Are you serious?" he said again.

"It's all yours, kiddo," Dayana told him.

He hugged them all. One by one. Wrapping them up in a bear hug and lifting them off the ground. Even Silas, who returned the favor. "Take her for a ride," he said.

As Cody ushered Jun into the passenger seat and zipped around the hood, Maggie blinked back tears.

She'd given gifts in her life. Some of them expensive. Some of them thoughtful. But this was the one she knew she'd remember forever. It delivered joy and freedom. It provided options and opportunity.

"Who's hungry?" Silas called to their guests as Cody drove carefully down the drive, a mile-wide smile plastered on his face.

They grilled burgers—beef, turkey, and veggie—and hot dogs and sat on the terrace, telling stories about high school and college. Cody had a stack of cards and gifts to open and said a sincere thank you to every single person.

Maggie spotted the new arrivals before anyone else and headed them off in the yard.

"Well, well, well," she said as the trouble triplets, with their ripped denim and facial piercings, paused. "You're not gonna break any windows while you're here, are you?"

The boy, who'd grown at least another two inches since they'd met in the dark a few months ago, kicked at the grass with a knock-off Doc Marten. "We'll try to control ourselves," Tommy promised with an impish wiggle of eyebrow.

"Good enough for me," she said. "There's a ton of food over there. Sodas and water are in the red cooler."

"What's a soda?" Lipstick smirked.

Maggie sighed and thanked her lucky stars that *her* smirky teen didn't get mouthy. "Pop," she corrected. "If I see any of you trying to sneak beer out of the keg, I will go zombie apocalypse on you."

"Yes, ma'am," they chorused.

"Now, go say hi to the graduate."

They sauntered into the crowd with feigned teenage confidence.

Maggie took a time out to give Mr. and Mrs. Meng, Jun's parents, a tour of the property.

"You've certainly accomplished a lot in a very short time," Mrs. Meng said.

"It's the only way I know how," she confessed.

Mrs. Meng excused herself to force Cody and Jun to pose for pictures in their T-shirts.

Mr. Meng let out a weighty sigh as he watched Cody slide an arm around his daughter. "A kid who can rally this kind of loyalty must be pretty special," he said finally.

"He really is," Maggie told him. "Listen, I'm not a parent. But I can tell you that there are qualities more important than fancy degrees and family money. I'm guessing when it comes down to it, you want your daughter with someone with a heart of gold who treats her with respect. Who pushes her to follow her dreams, not just his own. He's a good kid turning out to be a good man."

"I guess I can give him a chance," Mr. Meng grumbled. "But one misstep, and I'll make him regret the day he ever met me."

She watched him cross the terrace and strike up a conversation with Cody.

Love took on a lot of forms. She found Silas in the crowd. Easy, since he was a few inches taller than the rest of their guests. He was on the bluff, standing next to Michael as his brother said something to their parents.

Sometimes it meant holding tight and planting roots. Other times it meant loving enough to let go. Maggie wished she knew which was the right choice for her. Holding on or letting go.

She spied Dean coming toward her, two glasses of wine in hand. His expression was odd.

"What's wrong? Are you having a health emergency? Did you eat something weird? Oh my God. We didn't give everyone food poisoning, did we?"

He shook his head, still looking a little dazed when he pushed one of the glasses at her.

"What?"

"I just got off the phone with an executive at the Welcome Home Network."

"Oh boy." She took a preemptive gulp of wine. The Welcome Home Network was the biggest home improvement network out there. It had launched the careers of people like Cat King. "Was it a wrong number?"

"It was not. They have an offer for you. Your own series. Two seasons guaranteed. On the East Coast. It's a Main Street–makeover kind of idea where you'd go into a town and spend a season rehabbing their downtown."

"Holy shit." She took a deeper drink of her wine. She felt like the ground was crumbling under her feet, and she didn't know if she was going to fly or fall.

"The money is generous enough I almost squealed when she mentioned the number. Major advertisers."

"What about our show?"

"They're willing to negotiate. Either you'd use it for behind-the-scenes or you could shoot episodes in the off-season."

She looked around them. At the house. The people. The happy faces.

"This is the big-time, Mags. Forget leveling up. There's nothing bigger."

Her gaze landed on Silas, who had his arms around Michael and Niri as they video chatted with Taylor. "I feel like I'm going to throw up. I don't know if I'm excited or terrified," she admitted.

"Right there with you," Dean said, eyes on Michael's broad smile.

40

JULY ROLLED THROUGH Idaho with heat and sunshine that brought tourists flocking to Kinship, where they cooled off in the lake and river. Silas thoroughly enjoyed the Fourth by forgoing the festivities in town and watching the fireworks on the bluff with Maggie by a campfire. Kevin cowered in a bathtub on the second floor with the rapidly growing kittens keeping him company.

Speaking of rapid growth, Maggie's following had continued to explode in the last few weeks as the Old Campbell Place took shape in each progressive episode. Bitterroot's phone rang constantly with potential clients calling all the way from the Boise suburbs and even across the Oregon border.

Niri and Kayla were thrilled with the interest in the Mercantile, and the whole town seemed to be enjoying an uptick in tourism for the summer.

Life was good. Mostly.

Silas and Maggie spent every night wrapped up in each other, more often than not at her place. Without either of them acknowledging it, she'd made space in her closet for him, and he'd filled it.

The second bay of the garage now held tables of neatly organized tools for both their trades. On clear nights, they'd share beers on the terrace. If it rained, they read A. Campbell novels in companionable silence. He'd been able to talk her into an afternoon on the lake, and they'd even squeezed in another hike and picnic. Then there was the brunch with his family, which Dean attended as Michael's official boyfriend.

His lips quirked as he remembered Mama B's response to Michael's announcement. "Honey, it's about damn time."

As the clock ticked down, days drawing nearer to August and the big reveal party, Silas felt the weight that pressed down on Maggie.

There was still much to be done. Small things. Hundreds of them. Not to mention the kitchen was still an unfinished nightmare of one step forward, two steps back. It was nearing completion through the sheer will of Jim and Maggie.

She was doing what she did best, obsessing over tasks and internalizing the stress of the looming deadline.

Silas hopped off the mower and admired the precisely cut lawn. Except for the fountain—with the new pump on back order—and the maintenance, Bitterroot's work was done here at the Old Campbell Place. The acres on the bluff were now a showcase of natural beauty. Tamed and structured in some areas, like the rose garden and retaining wall. Wild and natural in others, like the grassy bluff trails and beds of wildflowers.

His crew had been divvied up and sent off to new, smaller job sites, where they created beautiful solutions for other homeowners. But they were all counting down to the day of the party, when they could show off their hard work to their families and let loose with friends.

A bloodcurdling scream came from the direction of the house and had Silas glancing up at the blue Idaho sky, asking for patience before heading inside. As suspected, it was Keaton, who had entered an unfortunate screaming phase.

"Perfectly normal part of development," Blaire had insisted when Silas mentioned it. "He's just exploring new ways of feeling important. It'll pass."

Silas had gifted Maggie a pair of noise-canceling headphones to get her through the phase.

He heard another sound. A distinct, horrified "What the fuck" coming from upstairs. He followed the commotion and found Maggie in a sitting room at the back of the house on the second floor, staring in silent rage at the gaping hole in the ceiling.

"What in the hell happened?" he demanded.

"Pipe burst in the bathroom upstairs," Jim said, eyeing the mess of wet plaster on carpet that had been installed only a week ago.

Maggie's eye twitched, and she held two fingers to it.

Uh-oh.

"I don't need to tell you that this is gonna push us back a bit. Couple of days at least for the plumbers, plasterwork, painters, new carpet," Jim said to her, scratching his head, blissfully unaware of the pot that was about to boil over.

"Mags, I need you to take a call with Columbus Paints," Dean said, poking his head into the room. "Holy shit! What happened in here?"

"Pipe burst," Jim said again.

Maggie's eye twitched again.

"Didn't you just lay that carpet?" Dean asked, not noticing that Maggie still hadn't said a word yet. "Never mind. Anyway, I've got a call scheduled at three. They didn't like the lighting in the dining room episode. They felt like the paint color looked off. They want you to shoot something else in the room with different lighting. Also, they want you to repaint the downstairs den in their new Barn Owl Gray."

From somewhere in the house, Keaton let out another blood-curdling scream, and Silas wondered if Maggie felt like doing the same thing.

He saw the clench of her jaw and backed out of the room. Figuring he had a window of about ten minutes, he jogged into the still unfinished kitchen, grabbed the sandwich fixings, and went to work. The lower cabinets had been installed and painted. There was a delay—shocker—with the countertops though, so they'd been living with plywood surfaces.

He had everything packed in a small cooler and stowed in the truck with two minutes to spare when he heard one of the painters yell down from the third floor.

"Has anyone seen Maggie? Cats got in the paint again. We got yellow paw prints all over up here."

One of the cats in question ran past him on the stairs, feet and tail streaked yellow. Silas found Maggie, sledgehammer in hand and a wild look in her eyes, still standing in the ruined sitting room on the second floor.

"I'll take that," he said, plucking the hammer out of her hand. "Your presence is required outside."

"I don't have time to deal with another crisis right now," she said slowly, carefully.

"Is Maggie in the house?" someone else yelled. "We got a problem."

She reached for the hammer, murder bright in her eyes.

The window had closed. On yet another toddler howl, Silas dropped the sledgehammer on the ruined carpet and dragged Maggie down the stairs. They made it out the back door without being spotted, and he skirted the side of the house at a run with her in tow.

"Get in," he said, opening the passenger door of his truck.

"I can't leave. I've got fifty-seven emergencies happening at the same time in there," she insisted, pressing her fingers to her temples.

He picked her up, dropped her on the seat, and shut the door.

She was pissed, but not unhinged enough to jump from a moving vehicle, so he started the engine and took off down the drive.

"Silas, I don't know what you're cooking up, but I have shit I need to take care of. In case you didn't notice, we're officially two days behind schedule."

"Oh, I noticed. But how many days will you end up behind if you start swinging at painters with a sledgehammer?"

"I wasn't going to hit anyone with it," she scoffed. "Maybe I thought about how good it would feel, but I wasn't going to actually do it. Probably."

"I sure wouldn't blame you for it, but you going to jail and all would really put the job behind."

"Why do kids scream like that?" she asked, still wearily rubbing her temples. "Keaton sounds like his arms and legs are being ripped off, and when you go running in to find out which body part was severed, he just smiles like it's all a game."

"Kids are jerks."

"And Cody showed up half an hour after curfew last night and then acts like I don't know exactly what he was doing in the backseat of the car *we* bought him," she continued.

"Get it all out, Mags," Silas advised. "Otherwise you'll go geyser on someone or decide to add French doors to nowhere on the third floor."

"I've got two weeks to finish and stage this place for the damn party."

He wisely chose not to point out that she was the one who selected the date and could probably just as easily change it.

"I still don't have a kitchen. How many things can go wrong in one room?" she railed. "I mean, are the ghosts of the Campbells mad at me? Am I cursed?"

"Probably not, but I can see how you might feel that way," he said, navigating into town.

"I should have my next project lined up by now. Or at least I should have an idea of what I'm going to do next. I was supposed to squeeze in another house by Christmas."

Silas bit his tongue. If he called her out on talking about moving on, when he felt like it was a team decision at this point, she might hit him with a shovel. And if he pointed out that maybe she wasn't real estate shopping because part of her was thinking seriously about staying, he couldn't be sure that she wouldn't pack a bag and be gone by morning just to prove him wrong.

"Why are we at your house?" she asked as he pulled into the driveway and drove around the back of the house to the garage. "Silas Wright, if you try to get me to take a nap or have sex with you right now, I will post your phone number on my next episode."

"I'm just picking something up," he promised. "Stay put."

He left her in the truck with the engine running and picked up the kayak and paddle.

"No. Nope. No way," she said when he threw it in the bed of the truck and strapped it down.

He climbed in behind the wheel and threw the truck in reverse.

"I'm not getting in that thing. Not when I have a thousand things to take care of."

"You're getting in it if I have to tie you to it," he said cheerfully. "You have one thing to take care of today. That's yourself."

"Don't start giving me that 'you can't pour from an empty cup' bullshit," she snarled.

"A word of advice—don't ever say that in front of my moms or they will corner you and spend a week lecturing you on self-care."

He made a left and a right before pulling into the lot at the boat launch.

"I can't believe you right now," she said, crossing her arms. She sat there stubbornly as he unloaded the kayak, the cooler, and lugged both down to the water.

She had her arms crossed over her chest when he opened her door.

"Take me back to the house."

"Nope," he said, reaching across her and releasing her seat belt. "Come on, slugger." He plucked her out of the vehicle, dragged a life jacket over her head, and threw her over his shoulder.

"I am going to kick. Your. Ass," Maggie growled, enunciating each word.

He dropped her neatly into the boat, handed her a paddle, and kissed the hell out of her. She bit him on the lip—hard—but he kept right on kissing her. It didn't take long before she forgot her mad and kissed him back. He teased her with teeth and tongue until she was limp and glassy-eyed before breaking the kiss.

"I'll pick you up downstream," he said, taking his hat off and plopping it on her head.

"I don't have my phone!"

"Good."

She looked at him like he'd just told her he burned down orphanages for fun. "What if there's an emergency?" she demanded.

"There's a walkie hooked to the cooler. Channel twelve if you run into any trouble. I'll answer."

"I meant what if there's a *work* emergency."

"Maggie, unless the house burns down or someone accidentally chops their leg off with a circular saw, there's no such thing. I'll pick you up downstream."

"How? Where?" She was holding the paddle upside down and frantically stabbing at the water with it, trying to force the kayak back on land. It was adorable.

"You can't miss it." And with that, he shoved the kayak into the current and watched her float away.

"You are in so much trouble," she shouted as she disappeared around the first bend.

41

"HOW DO YOU steer this stupid thing?" Maggie asked no one as the river hurled her downstream. Silas was going to regret sending her to her death. She'd make sure of it. She'd haunt his ass.

"Uh-oh," she said as the blue-green waters of the Payette River lined her up with a big, wet boulder that stuck out from shore like a menacing monster, crushing novice boaters for their insolence.

"Oh, no," she chanted, thrusting one end of the paddle into the water. "Oh, shit." It didn't so much turn her away from the looming boulder as spin her around backward.

She braced for the impact, holding her nose in preparation for being tossed into the churning waters.

The impact was more of a bump, and the water, she realized as the kayak lazily turned with the current, was more meandering than churning.

Okay. So she wasn't dead. The world didn't end. But she *was* still mad.

The nerve of Silas Wright. To literally drag her away from work like she couldn't take care of herself. Like she was some poor, fragile, stupid little girl who needed her hand held.

Comfortable in her grumpiness, Maggie flopped against the padded seat and looked up. There was a cloud above her, above the forest on both sides of the river, that looked distinctly like a white, fluffy penis.

It was hard to hold on to the mad while looking at a cloud penis. She reached for her phone, thinking she could send Dean a picture. Then she remembered it was somewhere back at the house that she'd been abducted from and got mad all over again.

"I can sit and float in my rage or I can learn how to use this thing and get back to work and murdering Silas faster," she said to the yellow butterflies that silently flittered around a flowered shrub onshore.

It took her a few minutes, but she was pleased with how easily paddling came to her. She no longer felt like she was going to flip over every time she shifted her weight.

"Let's do this," she said with grim determination and dug one end of the paddle into the water and pulled.

She lasted ten minutes of hard paddling before she was sweating and in need of a break. Her arms and shoulders burned, and she made a note to search upper-body workouts online. If she ever got kidnapped and thrown in a kayak in a river again, she wanted to be able to last longer than ten minutes.

The water was a deeper green here. On whatever the right side of a kayak was called, the river cut around the base of jagged cliffs. To the left, lush forest blocked out any hint of civilization.

It was just her and the river. And that deer drinking from the shore, she noted. She held her breath as the current carried her past the doe. Its tail flickered white, and it watched her, waiting to see if Maggie revealed herself as a threat.

"I'm nice. I promise," she whispered.

The deer seemed to believe her and went back to drinking.

"Oh my God. Is that a fucking bald eagle?" She watched the bird swoop low, talons dipping into the river less than fifty yards in front of her. When it rose again, there was a shimmering fish in its grasp.

"Okay. I get it, Nature. You're awesome," she said dryly. "That doesn't mean that I have to drop everything to come out here and appreciate you."

Her stomach growled. She'd probably burned through a lot of extra calories holding her rage inside, Maggie guessed. She remembered the cooler and hauled it out of the footwell.

There was a bottle of sunscreen in it, and grumbling about not knowing how long she was going to be in the sun, she slathered a layer on before poking through the rest of the contents in the cooler.

The man had packed her a sandwich, two bottles of water, a Pepsi, and a piece of cake left over from Dayana's small but festive birthday celebration earlier that week. The napkin had a handwritten note on it.

Float. Think. Be. And if you still feel like hitting me with the paddle when you get to Jeb's Pull Out (you can't miss it), I'll hold still while you swing.

Even when he wasn't with her, the man was still trying to tell her what to do. She was going to have to fix that. It had been too easy to let him maneuver her into this accidental relationship. He'd distracted her with orgasms and hiking and his loud family. Then managed to weasel his way into her life.

Hell, they had conversations about things like what to make for dinner and choosing between college or a gap year for Cody. They took turns doing the laundry and swinging into town to run errands.

The man had tricked her into a full-blown relationship.

She reached for the sandwich but then reconsidered. Revelations like that made it an eat-the-cake-first kind of day.

Maggie ate her way downstream. She had to give him credit. Silas knew just how she liked her fluffernutter sandwiches. Cracking open the soda, she carefully propped her feet on top of the kayak's body and leaned back.

The river meandered around another bend, and she spotted a cozy timber cabin on an emerald rise of grass. Near the shore, there was a couple sharing a lazy moment in a hammock, a wine bottle open next to them.

The man raised his glass to her, and Maggie held her Pepsi aloft.

They looked relaxed. Happy. Completely content to be doing nothing. When would she feel like she'd earned the pause? How many houses would it take? Subscribers? Dollars in the bank?

Would her very own show on a network make her happy? It was bigger than she'd ever dreamed. She'd read the basics of the offer about a dozen times so far. There was so much to it that it took her breath away. She and Dean hadn't had a real discussion about it. Not since he'd been spending most of his free time with Michael.

Maybe it was smarter to stay the course. Decline the offer—politely, of course—and find her next property.

She glared down at the soda—because she was allowed to call it a soda in her own damn head—and wondered if Silas had managed to spike it with some of his philosophical leanings. She *liked* working hard. *Liked* accomplishing. *Liked* setting goals and marching after them single-mindedly.

But does it make me happy? asked a tiny voice that should have been easy to ignore.

She thought about happy and reached back into her memory banks.

The hot springs with Silas came to mind. That ticklish drop when she jumped, free-falling into the alpine lake below. The heady combination of contentment, anticipation, excitement when he wrapped his arms around her. The way he managed to surprise her again and again in small, thoughtful ways.

Cody's graduation. The pride when he held up his diploma, the shock and joy when he realized the car was for him.

Watching Dean and Michael explore something so new and so tender.

Margaritas and shopping with Dayana, Niri, and Kayla.

She went back further.

Her father. Standing up the bookcase they'd built together. His half-smile. His hand on her shoulder. "This is really great work, Maggie," he'd said. "You have a lot of talent, but it's the work ethic that's most important."

She went back again. Further still. And remembered.

This river. Her mother's laugh coming from behind her as they wrestled against the current in a tandem kayak. The sun hot on her face and the cool spray of the water as it spilled over the rocks in front of them. Maggie had been temporarily terrified as the current careened them toward the shelf of rocks.

"Mom!"

"Just hang on, Mags! Don't try to control it. This is where it gets fun!" her mom had called back.

They'd shot right between two of the biggest boulders Maggie had ever seen in her life, which to be fair, growing up in Seattle hadn't exposed her to many boulders.

There was a second of weightlessness as the water carried them over and through. And then that tickle in her belly as they dropped. Landing with a splash and a whoop. She'd felt free as she listened to her mother's damp laughter.

Her heart ached with the memory. She hadn't had enough time with her mom to make up for the hateful teenage years. To reassure her mom that, no matter how painful the choice had been, she'd made the right one.

"Miss you, Mom," Maggie whispered up to the blue, blue sky.

How much would she miss Silas? The thought came out of nowhere. If she stuck with her plan, if she sold the Old Campbell Place and moved on, how would she feel about packing up and driving away from Silas Wright?

She could picture it—the man, the myth, the pain in her ass getting smaller in her rearview mirror as she drove toward...what?

Just what was she really looking for?

What was around the next corner that was going to be better than Silas?

What about Dayana and Keaton? They'd gotten comfortable in their temporary arrangement. Would they go back to Seattle? Would Dayana hire help and go back to work between appointments with her attorney and battles over the prenup?

And Wallace. The man was still a grump by anyone's standards, but he'd found a purpose with her, with the mystery of the Campbells. What would he have when she was gone?

Cody, too. He said he'd come with her, and that could work. But was it what he really wanted? He'd grown up in Kinship. He'd fallen in love in Kinship. He'd found his place there. Was he just choosing her because he felt he owed her? Like Dean had.

What if?

Maggie let her self drift and daydream a bit. Playing with what it would feel like to go. Weighing what it would mean to stay. To wake up every morning in that big, beautiful bed in that big, beautiful house on the bluff.

Would she be rolling over to kiss Silas good morning? This thing between them was so new. How could she be sure it would last? That these past few months were a foundation for something completely different?

Maybe she could figure this out if she treated the situation like she was trying to decide between two houses on the market. Weigh the pros and cons. Do the research. Make the right choice.

Again she thought of the jump, the free fall.

She floated drowsily, basking in the sun and silence. Going with the literal flow.

The hero of the A. Campbell book she was reading shimmered into her consciousness. Cody had written his English essay on *Canyon Secrets*. In it, the good-hearted bandit who found the gold only took half, hoping that another worthy soul would find the rest.

Something sparkled in her brain, and Maggie sat up. She thought about the secret room. The pipe. The news clippings and photos. There was something there that she'd missed. Something important.

But before she could focus in on it, a rock outcropping caught her eye. It had been spray-painted yellow and orange, neon colors that stood out from the vibrant green everywhere else. Sloppy block letters spelled out JEB'S PULL OUT. MORE THAN A BIRTH CONTROL METHOD.

There, on the concrete ramp, stood a hipshot Silas Wright. Arms folded across his chest. Legs braced apart like he was ready for a fight. And there was that stomach drop. She'd almost gotten so used to feeling it every time she saw him that she didn't bother defining it for what it was.

"Well, I'll be damned," she muttered to herself as she paddled in the direction that she'd gone and fallen in love with.

42

SILAS REGARDED MAGGIE with suspicion as the truck bumped down the lane. The woman hadn't swung at him with paddle or fist. Instead, she'd kissed him hard and fast right there on the boat launch and then remained eerily silent on the drive back to the house.

She seemed more relaxed than when he'd dragged her out this morning. Her shoulders were no longer rubbing her ears. But she appeared to be lost in thought and kept shooting searching looks in his direction, like she was trying to figure out a puzzle.

He hoped what she found at the house would loosen her tongue a bit so he'd at least know what she was thinking.

"You ready to go back in there?" he asked when he pulled in behind Cody's SUV.

She stared at the front of the house like she was seeing it for the first time. "Yeah. I am," she decided.

"Okay then," he said when she hopped out of the truck and headed toward the front porch. Kevin burst out of the woods behind the garage, his lower half covered in mud. The kittens scampered after him, blissfully muddy from head to tail.

"For fuck's sake. Can't you all stay out of trouble for five whole seconds?" Silas demanded. He'd already lost nearly a pint of blood during each of the baths he'd given the fur balls that morning.

Kevin, avoiding his father's disapproval, barreled after Maggie. Silas waited for the yelling to start, especially when his damn dog decided to shake off half of the mud all over the front porch and windows and Maggie.

But she merely reached down and squished the dog's face between her hands before giving the undeserving mutt a kiss.

Silas wondered if sunstroke could lead to irrational calm. He'd ask his stepdad.

He caught up with her in the atrium, where the painters had spent nearly two hours cleaning lemon-yellow cat prints from the stair treads.

"You didn't hit your head while you were on the river, did you?" he asked.

She frowned and started up the stairs. "I hit a rock. I guess a boulder," she said. "But that just dented your kayak, not my head. Why do you ask?"

"No reason," he said, trying to get a good look at her pupils.

"Why's it so quiet in here? Everyone's cars are still out front."

"Listen," he said. "Before you go upstairs, there's something you gotta see in the kitchen."

He expected a fight or a comment about what else could possibly have gone wrong. But she gave him neither. She simply followed him down the hall to the kitchen. He paused in the doorway and then stepped back to make room for her.

"Holy shit," she said.

"Surprise!" Jim, Cody, Dean recording the whole thing on camera, and the rest of the crew shouted.

Maggie took in the finished kitchen in one long, lingering look. Silas had to admit that she'd been dead right on the blue for the cabinets. A step brighter than navy, it gave the room just the right vibe. The white quartz counters were a classic choice and kept the room bright and clean. The appliances were finally where they belonged, including the range under its cheery, hammered-copper hood. The plastic had finally been removed from the widened doorway between the kitchen and dining room. They'd even hung the pendants over the island for her.

"Now, the paint's a little wet, and there's no grout on the back-splash yet," Jim explained. "But it's a hell of a lot more done than it was this morning."

"This is the most amazing surprise," she said, putting her hands on her hips and drinking it all in.

"Figured you can't sell a house without a kitchen," Jim said.

"Kinda hard to live in one, too," Cody pointed out.

"You've outdone yourselves," Maggie said. She looked over her shoulder to where Silas leaned in the doorway. He winked at her.

Someone popped a bottle of champagne while someone else started doling out plastic cups. Maggie tested drawers and doors—all soft close—and admired the stools that Kayla had dropped off only an hour ago. The seats were wrapped in a warm cognac leather that reminded Silas of Maggie's eyes.

"A toast to Maggie's white whale," Jim said, lifting his cup. "There were times we thought it would never happen, but when it came together, it was magic."

"Cheers!"

"Wow. I am cooking in here tonight," she announced.

The workers packed up for the day, riding high on the surprise. And after Maggie took half an hour to herself examining every inch of the kitchen, she went upstairs, where Silas waited for her in the bedroom.

"You thinking about tackling the sitting room?" he asked neutrally.

She shook her head. "Jim let it slip that they finished my bathroom, too. I want a shower." She stripped off her clothes and padded naked to the bathroom.

He followed her, barely noticing the white tile floors and the white marble counters atop natural wood vanities. The huge soaker tub was set just so in the enlarged window.

He put his hand on her forehead. "Are you feeling feverish?"

She gave him a slow, gut-punch of a grin and shook her head. "Nope. Are you?" She reached up and slapped her hand to his brow. "You feel kind of warm. Maybe you should take the rest of the day off."

With that, she reached into the shower and turned on the water.

He returned to the bedroom and waited for her on the bed, wondering if giving Maggie Nichols time and space to think was the worst thing he could have done. But when she opened the door, fresh-faced and smiling, he forgot what it was he'd been worrying about.

She dropped the towel to the floor, and he forgot his own damn name.

Silas awoke sometime later, thoroughly confused as to the day and time. And what had rendered him unconscious. Then he remembered naked, wet-from-the-shower Maggie. Who, after rocking his world in the middle of the afternoon, had disappeared from bed.

He found her in conversation with Veronica, the plaster master—as she'd been dubbed by Jim's crew—in the sitting room. The mess of soggy plaster and ruined carpet had been hauled out that morning shortly after Silas kidnapped her.

"Like I said, it's a real good thing this happened when it did," Veronica said to Maggie. "It made the plumber open the wall up there to check the old couplings, and he found another bad one. Would have been a whole lot worse."

"I'm glad it played out this way," Maggie agreed.

"Should have this patched and repainted in two days. Carpet guys are already scheduled for the day after that."

"I appreciate it," Maggie said.

"Forgot your shirt there, Sy?" Veronica smirked at him in the doorway.

He glanced down and realized he was wearing only shorts. Unzipped ones at that. He turned away from them and zipped his fly.

Veronica winked at him on her way out. "Looks like you had a nice afternoon."

Maggie reached up to brush a hand over his hair. "You look exactly like you just had sex," she observed.

"I did just have sex. Why did you leave?"

"I had a few things to catch up on, and you were so cute snoring—"

"I do *not* snore," he said, offended.

"Okay. You were so cute whistling through your nose I didn't want to disturb you."

"So you're not mad anymore? About this." He pointed at the ceiling. "About me kidnapping you and forcing you onto the river?"

She cupped his cheek and gave it a gentle pat. "Why would I be mad about that? It gave me a lot of time to think about a lot of things."

That had been the point. But now he was wondering if he'd overplayed his hand.

"So everything's fine?" he asked warily.

She nodded, looking thoughtful. "I really think it's going to be." She gave him another pat and then headed for the staircase. "Dean?" she called.

"Maggie?" Dean yelled back from what sounded like the third floor.

"Marco!"

"Polo!"

Silas chased Maggie up the stairs, and Dean met them on the landing.

"I need to put a GPS tracker on you in this damn house," he complained. "It's like a continent."

"Before you say anything, I know I missed the call with the paint people," she began.

Dean waved it away. "Forget about it. I took the call, listened to their demands, and then I exercised our right to cancel the contract."

Silas saw Maggie's eyebrows skyrocket. "I'm sorry. Did you say you canceled the contract?" She looked shocked but not outraged.

"They were too nitpicky with their demands. They can't glue strings to you and play you like a puppet. It's not authentic. Plus they pissed me off. So we're out some advertising dollars. But we don't have to jump through any damn hoops anymore. I think it was worth it. But you can yell at me if it'll make you feel better."

Silas watched as Maggie threw her arms around Dean. "Thank you," she said. "Thank you for getting me and having my back."

"I also had a talk with Cody about keeping his word and not

impregnating girls, especially after he recently managed to gain their parents' respect."

"I helped with that," Silas said, wanting his credit.

Maggie peeked over Dean's shoulder at Silas and reached for him. She pulled him in for a group hug. "Thank you *both* for getting me and having my back."

"What did he do?" Dean wanted to know.

"I kidnapped her and threw her in the river," Silas said.

"And *that's* what unleashes Zen Maggie? I always thought it would be a combination of a head trauma, alcohol, and maybe a massage or a really great pair of shoes," Dean said.

"It might have been the fluffernutter I packed her. I nailed the peanut butter ratio," Silas told him.

"You're ruining our very nice moment," she warned before releasing them.

"Sorry," they both said.

"Now I need to go deal with some things. I trust that you can entertain yourselves?"

"I've got an empire of Hot Landscaper Guy lovers to thrill with a behind-the-scenes interview on getting dirty with fertilizer on Insta," Dean said grandly. He pointed at Silas. "And then I have a date with your brother."

"I guess I have an asshole dog to wash," Silas said, shoving his hands in his back pockets. Still feeling unnerved. Something had changed in Maggie, and he needed to figure out what exactly that meant. "I can pick up some groceries for dinner tonight, since we're cooking," he offered.

"Sounds great. See you later," she said, rising on tiptoe to brush a distracted kiss over his cheek.

Silas washed the dog and managed to hose the worst of the mud off the cats as they sprinted by. Then he fixed the timing belt on the mower before talking Cody into driving him into town so he could keep an eye on the kid's driving habits.

They picked up the groceries and swung by the hardware store before it closed to get Maggie a new drill bit to replace one she'd misplaced. And since they were there at the counter, Silas bought two little succulents in hammered-copper pots that would like the light in the kitchen and play off the range hood.

By the time they got back to the house, it was almost seven.

Cody took the groceries into the kitchen and started to unpack them with Dayana while Silas went in search of Maggie.

He found her—with Kevin and the kittens, of course—in her office, behind her laptop on the same paint-splattered worktable. She was wearing the noise-canceling headphones and peering intently at the screen.

Silas started to lean in, planning to snap her out of her trance with a kiss on her neck, when he read a few lines of the document she was looking at.

"Maggie, what the hell is this?"

She jumped and yanked the headphones off. "You scared the crap out of me," she said, minimizing the document.

"Is that an offer from the Welcome Home Network?" he asked, his voice low and calmer than he felt.

Silas felt like he'd been sucker punched.

He'd just assumed that he'd win. That she would fall for him like he'd fallen for her. That they'd stay—preferably—or go together.

Yet here she was making plans for *her* future. Not *theirs*.

"They offered me my own show," she said.

"When?"

"On Cody's graduation day."

Silas put his hands on his hips so he wouldn't be tempted to strangle her. "You've been sitting on this offer for a month, and you didn't think to mention it to me?"

"It was unexpected. I didn't even know if it was something I'd be interested in," she said. "It's on the East Coast. At least two seasons."

He looked at the whiteboard. Her timelines were to an end, and she'd filled the empty space with demographic stats on what looked like two towns.

He heard Keaton's little feet making their way toward the kitchen.

"Where's Sy?" Keaton sang.

His chest hurt. Physically hurt. She was weighing her options, and from the looks of the research, she wasn't even considering what he thought was the best choice. Him.

Couldn't she see they'd started to build something here? Something real. Something that felt right.

"So you're deciding between another house or a show with a network?"

"Among other options," she said vaguely.

He crossed his arms over the ache in his chest and stared her down.

"Just because I don't want you making decisions for me doesn't mean we're not in a relationship," she said, getting a bit of fire in her eyes.

"If the situations were reversed, I would have brought all of this to you. I would have asked you your opinion because you know what's most important to me, Maggie?"

She remained silent.

"You. These aren't just my decisions anymore. They're our decisions." It was coming out wrong. But he didn't care. He needed to be part of the process, needed her to trust him to listen to her. But maybe that was asking for too much.

"I live the way I do for a reason. I don't have to take other people's feelings into consideration."

"Are you even taking yours into it?" he demanded. She sounded pissed off and just a little bit scared, and he hated it.

"Silas, you're the one who wanted me to have a little time and space to think. And I thought about a lot of things on that water. A lot of those things scared the hell out of me. So I'm doing what I do, weighing my options, doing my research."

"Are you even going to stay long enough to find out how Campbell found the gold? What he did with it all? Do you even care? What about Cody? And Wallace? Your sister? Were you even going to ask me to go with you?" he snapped. The ache in his chest was getting worse, blooming bigger by the second.

"Sy," she said, hurt in her voice, "you mean a lot to me—"

He held up a hand, cutting her off. "Save it."

"Hey, Sy, what do I do with the chicken?" Cody called from the kitchen.

"Get the marinade out," he called back. "I'll be there in a second." He turned back to Maggie, who looked like she'd had the wind knocked out of her. That made two of them. Couldn't she see what they were building together? "Look, I'll stay and help you cook dinner tonight because I'm selfish enough that I want to be in that memory of yours. But after dinner, I'm leaving, and I'm not coming back until the party."

"Why?" She looked shocked.

Good. He didn't want to be alone in that.

"Why?" he repeated on a humorless laugh. "Because I've been building us into something you don't think we are. A relationship. A partnership. You'll get the time and space to decide if what you really want is to continue going solo."

Those molten brown eyes went wide on him. "What if I don't want to stay?" she asked, her voice trembling just a bit.

"Then I'll go with you, if you let me. But you need to decide if you've got room in your life for me. And, darlin', I take up a lot of space."

"You can't give up everything to follow me. That's how resentment grows. That's how you start stalking exes on Instagram and having FOMO meltdowns over farmers market hashtags and engagements." Her voice was hushed, but the panic rang through clearly.

"You are everything to me, Maggie. Do you hear me? The fact that you think I'd give you up over geography? What do you think we've been doing here?"

"Having fun. I *told* you. I *warned* you from the start," she said defensively.

"I know you did. But actions speak louder than words. I've got more damn clothes than you do in your closet. You bought my dog a bed for your office."

"Your roots are here," she argued. "You can't just rip them out and go if I want to."

"They're planted deep, and that's why they'll survive no matter where I am. It's you, Maggie. I've been waiting for you. Make the decision. Don't just do what you've always done and call it a choice."

43

THEY COOKED BALSAMIC chicken with oven-roasted vegetables and ears of bicolor sweet corn loaded with butter and salt to a group-curated playlist that covered everything from Dua Lipa to The Smashing Pumpkins and Earth, Wind & Fire.

The kitchen—her kitchen—was filled with people she loved, but Maggie was having a hard time enjoying it, knowing that she'd hurt one of them so deeply.

They gathered around the dining table to eat off real dishes and catch up on the day as the world outside the window went pink and orange. Afterward, with the dishwasher making its maiden voyage, they gathered on the terrace to enjoy Popsicles and beers.

While Keaton put on a show for the adults, running from one end of the terrace to the other with the cats and Cody giving chase, Silas wandered over to the fountain. Maggie felt herself drawn to him. She intertwined her fingers through his and squeezed, hoping she hadn't ruined this. Not with everything that she'd realized today.

He returned the squeeze and brought her knuckles to his mouth.

She loved him. Fiercely. And that scared the hell out of her. She thought there wasn't anything worse until the sun set. Then Silas said his goodbyes, collected his dog, and drove home.

"Where's Sy going?" Dayana asked, approaching her with a glass of wine in one hand and a Popsicle wrapper in the other.

"He's giving me some space," Maggie said evenly.

Dayana shot her a "have you lost your damn mind?" look. "Did you ask for space?"

Maggie shook her head. "He saw me looking at property listings and an offer from a network."

"You're leaving?" Dayana asked, dark eyebrows skyrocketing.

"I don't know," she said honestly. "I always leave. I always move on to the next thing. This is the first time I've even thought about a 'what if I stay.' But I don't make decisions like he does. He jumps. I weigh options, outcomes, consequences." She paced the tile she'd spent hours researching.

"Because you want it to be right."

"Yes! Exactly! He can't just demand that I commit to him on the spot. He can't possibly understand the consequences of a decision like that," she complained. "He acts like it's easy to just go for it. But he's not even considering how resentful he might get if he comes with me or how resentful I might get if I decide to stay."

"Hold it. This sounds vaguely familiar," Dean mused, joining them near the fountain. Cody followed him.

"It should. You resent choosing me over Will. I shouldn't have made you feel like it was your job to keep me happy or make things up to me. And you," she said, pointing at Cody. "You say you want to come on the road with me. But you're eighteen years old. Do you even know what that entails? How do you know you really want to or that you won't change your mind six months into it? What if you get homesick for Kinship?"

"Uh, then I come back?" Cody said, looking at her like the answer was obvious.

"Most decisions can be undone. Minds can change," Dayana pointed out.

"Are you going to change your mind and go back to Donald? You came here to get away from it all. What will you do if I put up a FOR SALE sign and decide I'm going to rehab a house in Arizona or Kansas?"

"I came here because it was time we got to know each other as sisters," Dayana told her. "And no, I'm not changing my mind about Donald."

"We're all responsible for our own choices," Dean told her. "I'm responsible for choosing not to settle down with Will, and thank God I did. Because look who I'm joining for a night of good wine around a firepit tonight? I could have missed out on Michael if I'd settled. But I chose. I made the decision. You didn't force me into it or cast some spell shackling me to you."

"Should we be offended that Maggie thinks we're all incapable of making our own decisions?" Cody asked everyone.

"Yes," Dean and Dayana agreed.

"Maybe you should think about what's best for you instead of worrying about what you think is good for everyone else," Cody suggested.

"He's wise beyond his years," Dayana observed.

"He gets that from me," Dean announced proudly.

They grinned at each other.

"Part of Maggie's problem is she's constantly searching for stability in an unstable world," Dayana posited.

"That makes sense," Dean agreed. "She lost her mom so young and without warning. It makes her feel like everything can change in a heartbeat, so she clings to things like plans and goals and timelines to feel like she has control."

"Life can change in a heartbeat," Maggie said firmly. *It had.*

"And this relentless pursuit of financial security," Dayana added. "Can you imagine what it was like for her, driving up to our father's megamansion once a month? Being forced to spend time with 'family' who looked at her as some kind of interloper? Again I apologize for being an asshole. So she's built a fortune on her own and substituted a million subscribers—strangers—as stand-ins for the family she deserves."

"It's a wonder she's not more screwed up," Cody said.

"I'm sitting right here," Maggie said dryly.

"Good. Then you'll hear us when we tell you you've built a life around clinging to the memory of one parent while rejecting another. Neither of which is necessarily wrong or even weird, given the situation," Dean added when she opened her mouth to argue. "But at some point, don't you need to put down the expectations of your parents and figure out what you want for yourself?"

"I'm going for a walk," Maggie announced.

Maggie walked the property, following the trails Silas had blazed through the years of neglect. And when she still didn't have the clarity she craved, she drove into town.

It wasn't until she pulled into the parking lot of the senior living facility that she realized why she was there.

After a minute of small talk with the nurses at the front desk, Maggie found herself knocking on Wallace's door.

He answered in pajama pants hiked up to his ribs. "This better be good. It's the middle of the night."

It was eight thirty.

"Sorry it's so late," she apologized. "Can I come in?"

"Do what you want," Wallace grumbled and tottered back to the recliner he'd vacated.

She followed him inside to a roomy apartment. The living room had a TV over an electric fireplace. There was a small kitchenette and a table with chairs for six. She wondered if he'd ever had anyone sit around the table.

"Why do you live here?" she asked him. "You're healthy. In good shape. You don't have to be in senior living."

"You sound like you think you know the answer. Why do you think I live here instead of alone in a house?"

She thought about the first time she'd come here. He'd been doing research in the library, grumbling at other residents when he could have just as easily cracked the books in his apartment. He chose to come to her house, with the noise and the dust and the cats and the people, nearly every day to wade through books and papers and mementos that he could have taken home with him.

"Because you're substituting residents and staff for real family," she guessed. The man was lonely. Worse, he was grumpy about being lonely.

"Think you're so smart," he grumbled with no real heat.

"I think I'm lonely, too," she admitted. "And I think I keep busy so I don't have time to think about how lonely I am."

"Eh. Boohoo." He snorted.

Noticing the only personal memento in the space, she picked up the framed photo on the mantel.

"Who's this?" she asked.

"Florence. Not that it's any of your business," he harrumphed, angling to the side to see the TV screen.

"Who was Florence?"

Wallace let out a long-suffering sigh and, with dramatic reluctance, turned off the *M*A*S*H* rerun. "You're not here to ask about Florence."

"I'm here to discuss a couple of hypotheses with a top researcher," she countered. "Who was Florence?"

"Florence *was* my high school sweetheart. She *is* a retired librarian over in Aberdeen who married a good-for-nothing insurance salesman after I hemmed and hawed too much over asking her to marry me."

"Was he really good-for-nothing or are you just saying that because he got the girl?"

"Everyone else seemed to like him," he admitted. "But I don't think he gave her everything she deserved."

"Would you have?"

"Does it matter? I had my head shoved too far up my ass trying to make the right decision. I was worried it was too soon, that I didn't make enough to support the two of us, let alone a family. I needed more time to get my ducks in a row."

"And she didn't want to wait?" she guessed.

"Those romantic types have it in their heads that it's better to jump in and figure things out later."

"And us practical types want to have a plan with all the angles considered."

"Nothing wrong with that." Wallace bristled. "So I waited a couple of years and married someone else. Nice gal. Smart gal. But she wasn't Flo. We had thirty decent years together."

"Are thirty decent years good enough to make up for the fifty great ones you could have had with Florence?"

"You're dumber than you look if you have to ask that question."

"I have to decide whether or not I'm willing to make room in my life for a man who takes up a whole lot of space," she confessed.

"It would change everything you do."

"It would," she agreed. "Are you glad you didn't ask Florence to marry you? Was it the right choice?"

The man rolled his magnified eyes behind his lenses. "I took the safe path. I wanted security. I wanted to avoid making mistakes. Hell, I wanted to study history and work for the National Archives. But on paper, it didn't make sense. There wasn't any real money in that. Not enough to raise a family on. So I went to school for accounting. Job security and all that crap. I punched my clock for that plant for forty-three years. I saved my paychecks, lived a comfortable life. I played historian on the weekends. Turns out, it didn't matter, since Regina and I never had a family to support."

"Do you regret it? Any of it?"

"You're asking an old man to look back on his life's choices and tell you if you're about to make a mistake."

"Well. Yeah."

"My life ain't yours. My regrets—whether they exist or not—aren't yours."

She had expected as much. But still had hoped for a magic bullet.

"Okay. Next hypothesis. I think we've been looking at A. Campbell all wrong." She saw it in his cagey expression. Wallace had already gotten there, and he hadn't said anything to anyone.

"Say it," he insisted.

She took a breath. "I think A. Campbell was Ava Campbell, not Aaron."

"Not much of a stretch of the imagination there, considering the evidence," he said.

"The handwriting on the manuscript in the secret room that matched the captions on the photos. The fact that Aaron's pipe was next to the armchair, not on the desk. The fact that Ava Campbell would disappear from the public eye for long stretches of time. Possibly about the same length of time it would take to finish a manuscript," she recapped.

"Not to mention the romantic story lines in the books. They had the fingerprints of a woman all over them."

"I missed that one," Maggie confessed.

"Don't beat yourself up. You're too busy chasing the almighty dollar and losing your mind over paint swatches and sandpaper."

"If that weren't the truth, I'd take offense." The only reason she'd managed to come up with the theory was because Silas had dumped her in a kayak with nothing to distract her. That time, that stillness, had unearthed a lot of things that still required some excavating. The fact that Silas knew that was exactly what she'd needed was one of the things requiring excavation.

"I also think I figured out where Ava Dedman Campbell came from," she said.

"What are you saying, girlie?"

She laid it out for him, walking him through it. When she was done, he gave a noncommittal hum. "Might have a hell of a time proving it."

"I think it might be easier than we think. There's this thing called the internet."

"You and your internets and your Facey Tweets," Wallace barked.

"Leave my Facey Tweets alone. They might be all I end up with."

"So you still want to keep working on this even though you've been making all this noise about leaving and your big-deal network offer?"

"How did you know about that?"

He shrugged, all innocence. "I may have accidentally borrowed your computer a couple of days ago."

"How did you know my password?" she demanded.

"You talk out loud a lot when you have those headphones on."

Maggie shook her head in surprise. "Facey Tweets," she snorted. The cagey old goat.

"Well? You staying on?"

"I'm here until we have a last chapter," she promised.

44

SILAS OPENED HIS door and then thought about closing it in his visitors' faces. His mother read the intent and bustled inside, looking cool and fresh in gray linen pants and a white sleeveless sweater. Mama B followed with a devious smile and a swirl of her full skirt in blues and yellows.

Kevin was much more enthusiastic about their visitors. He pranced back and forth between the women, lavishing them with licks.

"Are we really doing this?" Silas groaned as his moms made themselves at home on the couch he'd just vacated.

"Blaire, do you smell that?" Mama B asked, spreading her skirt out and tucking her feet up under her on the cushion. She was clearly settling in for the long haul.

"I do, Breonna," Blaire said, nudging the greasy pizza box he'd left on the floor with the toe of her sandal.

"It's the smell of a crisis that could have been avoided with a little awareness and effort," Mama B said, adding a tsk-tsk at the end.

"I'm not in crisis," he argued. "I am fine. I get up and go to work every day just like I always have."

"Why is every pair of underwear you own piled in your dining room doorway?" Blaire asked innocently.

"That was Kevin." Silas pointed an accusing finger at the pit bull curled on the couch between two of his favorite women. The dog had also left the refrigerator door open overnight. He'd awoken to room-temperature beer and old ketchup. He hadn't gotten up the energy to hit the grocery store.

"Sit down, Silas," Blaire said in her therapist voice. She gestured toward the recliner that was buried under the debris of the Pouty Life, as Taylor and Niri dubbed it anytime one of the siblings was down after a breakup. This was Sy's first personal foray into the Pouty Life.

He picked up the pajama pants and empty takeout bags and iPad he'd not been able to find for three days and tossed it all on the floor.

Kevin whined as if to say "You see what I've been dealing with?"

Both moms instinctively gave the dog comforting pats.

Mama B produced a bottle of bourbon from her Mary Poppins purse.

"I'll get the glasses," Blaire volunteered.

"Oh, geez." He sighed, collapsing into the chair. Something squeaked beneath him. Kevin's ears perked up. Silas shifted and pulled the squeaky toy hammer Maggie had given his lug of a dog out from under his ass.

Just looking at it made him feel like crap. He threw it in the direction of the hall. Kevin hurled his bulky body to the floor and raced after it. He returned, squeaking and chewing proudly. He shoved the hammer at Silas and gave a playful growl.

Silas had been tag-teamed before by the moms. They all had at some point when their lives seemed to be slipping into crisis. Some of the talks had been heavy. Like when he and Michael had been called to the couch at twelve to learn why it was safer to be white after dark than Black, why there were different rules for boys brought up as brothers, and why it was Silas's job to use his privilege to call out the unfairness of it—*especially* to adults.

There had been other talks. While the dads handled the Mechanics of Sex talk for the boys, the moms had hit them all with consent, respect, and mutual gratification. When Nirina came home at twenty-two with an engagement ring and a stranger, there had been talks. When his sister Taylor dropped out of her premed program and switched to a business major, the moms had road-tripped to her school, knocked on her dorm room door at 5:00 a.m., and hashed things out over diner pancakes and coffee.

It wasn't that the moms wanted to control their decisions, Silas knew. It was that they wanted to make sure their kids were making those decisions with all of the information. Taylor's switch to business had been the right call, and the moms were happy to support her. Nirina's fiancé-turned-husband had held up to the mom tag team but had also agreed that running off and getting married fresh out of college after knowing each other for a grand total of four months wasn't the best foundation. The moms had helped the young couple find their first apartment and walked Niri through the conflicts that arose during the next two years.

The alcohol was a new addition and a nice touch.

Blaire returned with three freshly washed glasses and zero comments on the state of his kitchen.

Mama B poured, and Blaire handed him a glass. "Go ahead," she said.

These conversations always began with an uninterrupted monologue from the kid about their take on the situation. Usually an enthusiastic defense of whatever stupid choice they'd made. Once the kid finished and was feeling confident in their self-righteousness, the moms gently and systematically destroyed them.

"Can we just skip to the part where you tell me that I was wrong?" he asked, taking a swallow of bourbon.

"There are no shortcuts in life that get you to where you want to be," Blaire reminded him.

Silas rested his head against the chair and sighed. They wouldn't leave until he gave them what they wanted. His tattered, bruised heart on a platter.

"Fine." He sighed and polished off the rest of his drink. He held out the empty glass, and as Blaire poured, he began.

"And then she insisted that if I came with her, I'd just end up resenting her for ripping out my roots or some other landscaping metaphor." Silas was on his third bourbon on an empty stomach, and things were getting a little blurry.

Not blurry enough that he missed the look his moms exchanged.

"Okay. Let me have it. Tell me how I'm the one who screwed up." He was feeling pretty confident that most of the blame could be laid at Maggie's work boots.

"Silas, how does Maggie make decisions?" Blaire asked. She was keeping up with him on the bourbon count. Mama B had switched to tea halfway through his explanation.

"She overthinks things to death. Does her research. Compares possibilities. Makes lists."

"Smart," Mama B commented.

"Data obsessed," Silas said.

"Do you feel good about the data you provided her?" Blaire asked.

"I didn't provide data. That's not how I decide things. I go with my gut."

"So you gave her a romantic ultimatum, and then you were surprised when she didn't jump into your arms?" Mama B clarified, one hand in her hair.

He could smell a setup.

"Shouldn't she know by now that she wants to be with me?"

"And by 'by now,' you mean shouldn't she realize that she wants to enter into a long-term relationship with the man she met three months ago?" Blaire asked. There was no judgment in her tone, but the question itself felt like it was loaded with it.

"What are you saying? That all mutual decisions should be made her way? That doesn't seem fair." He reached for the bottle and poured himself another. Then he topped off his mom's glass.

"Relationships are like anything else that's worthwhile. They're damn hard work," Blaire explained.

"Hard work?" Silas frowned. "You make it sound like I've never done a day's hard work in my life."

Mama B leaned forward and, with love in her eyes, said, "Honey, you've had a lot of things come real easily to you. Just because you work hard and play hard doesn't mean you've had to try hard to get what you wanted. Until now."

"I'm not sure how insulted I should feel."

"Do you remember when you tried out for the soccer team in high school?" his mom asked.

"Vaguely," he said.

"You'd never played the game. But your friends were on the team," she continued. "You were a starter by the end of your first season."

"A natural talent," Mama B added.

"There's nothing wrong with being a natural," he complained, feeling defensive.

"Of course not, honey," Mama B said. "The only time it's a problem is when *everything* comes natural. The first time you brush up against something that doesn't come easily makes it feel like you should just walk away, give it up."

"What did it take to get Michelle to say yes to your first date?" Blaire asked.

"Michelle? I don't know. I guess I asked her out. Or no. Wait. She asked me out." It was a little cloudy.

"And every time you two broke up, what did it take to get back together?"

Silas shrugged. "I guess one of us would text. Ask if the other wanted to hang out or meet for drinks."

"And you didn't live happily ever after with Michelle," Blaire noted. "You spent five years give or take in a comfortable limbo."

"Easy. Simple. Uncomplicated," Mama B observed.

"None of those words apply to Maggie Nichols," he complained.

"Maybe that's one of the things you like about her. She challenges you, and I think you challenge her, too," his mom suggested.

"Maybe." He was still feeling a little too raw to agree.

"And maybe while Maggie has to decide whether or not to take a leap of faith to choose you, you have to be willing to *try* to keep her," Mama B said.

"That's what I've *been* doing." He thought about the gifts, the surprises. Whisking her away to play. "She needs time to slow her damn brain down and the space to step back and look at the big picture. And that's what I'm giving her."

"Is it possible that you two just aren't speaking the same language?" Blaire asked.

"I think that's damn clear," he complained. "Why can't we just figure it out as we go?"

"*You* can. *She* can't," Mama B told him. "If you were being wooed, you'd rather have a grand romantic gesture," Mama B explained. "Maggie would rather have the research done and the case presented to her."

"You're giving her the time and space, but you're also expecting her to do all the research and fill in the blanks on what a life with you would look like. You're asking her to choose *for* you. That's not fair to her."

And through the bourbon haze and the frustration, things suddenly became clear.

"Well, fuck."

"I'll drink to that," Blaire said.

"Cheers, my dears," Mama B said, raising her tea.

"Do either of you know how to use that PowerPoint thing?" Silas asked.

45

MAGGIE GAVE PASSING consideration to throwing up but decided that wouldn't get rid of the nerves, and she'd get too sweaty and ruin her makeup. Instead, she tiptoed to the stairs, hoping to stay invisible to the rest of the house for the next few minutes.

Downstairs, the caterer had commandeered the kitchen and dining room.

On the second floor, Dean was instructing Cody on the finer points of tying ties.

She made it to the third floor and, before she ducked into the spare room, overheard Dayana and Keaton in a serious discussion about why pants were important when socializing.

The big day was finally here, she thought, crossing to the closet and stepping over the velvet rope—Dean's idea—into Ava Campbell's garret.

She and Wallace had decided to keep their theories and some proof to themselves until after the party. It was all happening today. No doubt Dean would complain about having to recut episodes.

She had spent four hours shooting with him today, walking through every inch of the house and grounds before it was filled with guests.

There would be the preparty toast to her crew and the expected one-on-one later tonight, but that was it for the rest of the night.

Usually, she was feeling the hum of excitement about her next project. Usually, she was ready to move on to the next fixer-upper. But there was nothing usual about this house, this episode, this decision.

Maggie had made one. Had technically made it that day on the river, not that Silas had given her a minute or a reason to tell him. Despite the fact that her gut and her research had agreed, she still found herself wishing fervently for a sign. But plans were in motion with or without the universe's input.

She sat at Ava's desk and imagined that she could catch the scents of pipe tobacco as Aaron quietly flipped through manuscript pages while his wife's pen wrote out new, beautiful stories. They'd known everything about each other and still wanted to share the same space. She'd loved him enough to let him into her sanctuary. He'd loved her enough to keep her secrets. Together, they'd built not only this house and a legend, but they'd also created a fascinating partnership.

Maggie peered out the octagonal window. Kinship was framed in it. Like a treasure map marking the spot. Only this town wasn't sitting on top of a stash of gold. It was the gold. The Campbells had made their place here. They hadn't waited for an invitation or tried to conform to an existing aesthetic. They built a wild and wonderful home and life on top of the bluff without apology or acquiescence. Ava wanted to write but had no luck being taken seriously as a woman author. So her husband gave her his name, his power.

He didn't want her to change, to conform to his or anyone else's standards. He supported her like a partner.

Maybe that was the sign she'd asked for. Though, in Maggie's opinion, it could have been a bit more in her face. If the universe dealt only in subtleties, it was no wonder so many took wrong turns on their maps.

There were a few minutes before the chaos began, before the crews and their families arrived. Before *he* arrived. Just the thought of Silas had her nerves reappearing. This time she didn't bother pushing them aside or burying them under a to-do list. She let them exist and realized maybe it wasn't the worst thing in the world to feel.

There was one last thing she wanted to do before opening the front door. She gave the room a final look, making sure everything was in order, and then returned to her bedroom to retrieve her own personal good luck charm.

She could hear voices and vehicles outside by the time she ducked into the first-floor study. Dean was out there instructing everyone to not look at the "damn camera, people."

"There," she said, placing the photo of her mom grinning in the direction of Kinship's lake on the mantel exactly above the gold coin, which had been temporarily tucked back into its hiding place. "Now you have a front-row seat to everything, Mom. I hope you're proud. I really want you to be proud."

She heard the celebratory pop of a champagne cork and then another coming from the kitchen.

"Maggie?" Cody was standing in the doorway, looking impossibly dapper in a shirt and tie.

"Hey," she said with a smile at the rush of pride she felt for him.

"They're ready for you out front," he said, shoving his hands in his pockets.

"You look great," she said.

He beamed down at her. "Thanks," he said, smoothing a hand over the tie. "Think Jun will like it?"

"She'll love it," she predicted.

"Maggie!" Dean yelled from outside. "Get your ass out here!"

"Guess we should go," Cody said.

"One second. I'm really proud of you, Cody. And I guess I just want you to know that. Whatever you decide to do with your life, I know it's going to be great, and I want you to know I have your back."

He cleared his throat and seemed keenly interested in the tips of his loafers. "Thanks, Maggie."

A chant had started outside. "Maggie! Maggie! Maggie!"

"One other thing. I hope this isn't weird, but I love you." She said the words in a rush. "Okay. Let's get out there."

"Wait. I, uh, guess I kind of love you, too," he confessed.

She gave him a brisk nod and tried not to blink. "Cool."

"Yeah. Cool."

Some joker rang the doorbell, and the gothic organ music made them both laugh. He held out his hand, and she accepted it. "Let's go."

Things were going to change when she stepped out on that porch, and she was suddenly ready to take the plunge. With a fond backward glance at the photo on the mantel, Maggie stepped into her future.

Dean met her on the porch. A bow-tied Kevin sat at his feet, basking in the attention.

The cheer that went up from the men and women assembled in front of the house was deafening. Dean had hired a local film crew to help, since it was a big shoot with so many moving parts. Two camera people buzzed around, shooting different angles.

"You ready?" Dean asked her.

"Yeah. I am."

The waitstaff marched out, trays of champagne held aloft. Maggie accepted a glass and only then did she let her gaze roam the crowd.

She found Silas immediately. She always would. Because there was something that connected her to the tall, handsome landscaper staring at her. And she just had to accept it. She felt the buzz between them. The frustration. The need. The hurt. The way he looked like he was ready to devour her. The way she felt ready to be devoured.

"That's everyone," the head server whispered to Maggie as they headed back into the house with empty trays.

She smiled and took a breath. "This is the first community celebration in this house in decades," she began. "It's not going to be the last. And that's because of each and every one of you. Thank you for every hour, every drop of sweat, every effort you gave to uncover this hidden gem. You took rubble and ruin and made it into treasure."

Several someones in the crowd whooped.

"We're awesome!"

She laughed and raised her glass. "To the Old Campbell Place. May its future be even more storied than its past."

The men and women assembled—the painters and plaster workers, the landscapers and plumbers—raised their glasses. But she only saw Silas, that dangerous half-smile playing on his lips.

"Cheers!" the crowd roared.

"Now let's get ready to party!" she yelled over the celebration.

He didn't come to her in the ensuing chaos as close to fifty tradespeople dispersed to show off the work they'd done to their families. And she didn't seek him out either. But she got the sense that they both knew it was inevitable.

Maggie was swept into a conversation with Kayla and two of Cody's teachers and then was handed off to Jim to meet Mrs. Jim. It went on like that for at least an hour until Dean waved her into the sunporch. "This is Jeanie Lacruz from Atwood Publishing."

"It's nice to meet you," Maggie said, shaking the woman's offered hand.

"The pleasure is mine. I hope you don't mind me practically crashing your party," Jeanie said.

"The more, the merrier," Maggie told her, scanning the terrace, looking for Silas. She found him in conversation with his dads and Roy from the plant.

"I must confess. I come with ulterior motives. My company is the one that holds the publishing rights to A. Campbell's books. They've been experiencing a revival of sorts because of you. The town is going to be very happy with the royalties for the last quarter," she predicted.

"That's good to hear."

"Have you ever considered writing a book?"

Maggie blinked. "A book?"

"You have an innate talent for discovering and showcasing potential. Atwood Publishing does plenty of nonfiction titles a year. I'm confident we could find a market for a design book by Maggie Nichols."

"I'll let you two talk," Dean said, bowing out politely.

Behind Jeanie's back, he mimed a freak-out.

"That's an interesting proposition, Jeanie," Maggie confessed, doing her best to keep a straight face. "And I think I've got something else that might make your night."

Ten minutes later, her head was still spinning when Dayana approached. "Don't hate me," she said.

"Oh God. Did Keaton flush another action figure? Did you try the plunger?"

"It's not a plumbing problem. It's Dad."

Maggie frowned. "Is he okay?"

"He's here."

"Here?" Maggie parroted. "As in Kinship?"

She winced. "As in in the study. I invited him without consulting you, and you can be mad at me later."

"Day! Why would you do that?" Maggie felt panic clawing its way up her throat. She wasn't mentally prepared to see her father. She hadn't seen the man in years. They'd barely spoken in a decade.

"You two need to talk," Dayana insisted.

"I'm kind of busy here," she said, gesturing at the party happening around them. "What if someone recognizes him?"

"That's part of what you need to talk to him about," Dayana said, pushing her down the hall.

Maggie's heart thumped harder the closer they got to the study. She wished she had Silas to hold her hand or to drag her away and throw her in the river again.

But there was no Silas waiting for her in the study. Only her father. Billionaire investor and philanthropist Sebastian Spencer. He was tall and trim. His dark hair showed more salt than it had the last time she'd seen him. He was dressed casually in slacks and a shirt with the sleeves rolled up. But the clothes still screamed wealth.

He was holding Keaton in one arm and the photo Maggie had placed on the mantel only an hour before in his other hand. He looked up, the smile freezing and then dimming just a little as his gaze roamed her face.

Dayana took her son and gave him a loud kiss. "Come on, little man. Let's get you a snack while Grandpa and Aunt Maggie talk. Talk nice, you two." She gave them both a pointed look before she left the room.

Maggie didn't know what to say, and frankly, she didn't feel like the burden of hospitality was on her, since her sneaky sister had done the inviting.

Sebastian was the first to break the silence. He turned the photo to face her. "Your mother was a beautiful woman."

She looked away. There was something so odd about her father, a man she barely knew, looking so tenderly at an image of the mother she'd loved so desperately. She focused on the framed needlepoint she'd returned to its place of honor above the fireplace.

WHERE IS THE ADVENTURE IN FINDING ONESELF IF ONE USES SOMEONE ELSE'S MAP?

Next to it was an old topographical map. Both had been here the day she purchased the house. On the mantel. Above the gold coin...

"Maggie?"

Sebastian was looking at her expectantly.

"Sorry. What?"

He put the photo back on the mantel. "I'm sorry to drop by unannounced like this."

"It happens more often than not in these parts," she said wryly.

"I know you're busy, and I understand that tonight is important to you, so I'll keep this short." He sounded all-business now, and it annoyed her.

"You don't have to worry. I haven't told anyone you're my father."

He looked pained. "That's actually why I'm here. Dayana told me about the NDA."

"What do you mean she told you about it?" she asked.

"I'm embarrassed to say that I had no idea that Rebecca, my ex-wife, forced you to sign something like that."

"You had no idea?" she repeated slowly.

"Did you wonder why I didn't present it to you? Why it wasn't my attorney in the room?"

"Of course not. I assumed you didn't want to deal with it. With me," she said, still clinging to what she believed to be true. That she was unwanted. Unloved. Unwelcome.

He grimaced, and she noticed the lines around his eyes were deeper now. "I can't blame you for thinking that.

"After I turned your trust over to you, you essentially vanished from my life. You stopped returning calls, stopped accepting invitations."

"Because I thought you made me sign the NDA swearing I would never tell anyone that you were my father!"

"I'm not here," Dayana insisted, stepping into the room. She had a bottle of scotch in one hand and two glasses in the other. "And I'm not saying anything other than my mother is a cold, single-minded person who hurts people for sport." She put them down on the desk that stood between father and daughter and left.

They both stared at the bottle.

"Rebecca told me you were finished with me because you got your money. That your trust was all you wanted from me."

"I *never* wanted your money," Maggie said, her voice shaking. She sat because she would start throwing things or making new holes in walls if she let herself think too hard.

"I understand that now," Spencer said gently. "I started to believe it when you sent that check to me. It was a gift, Maggie. Not a loan."

She closed her eyes and covered her face with her hands. "I wanted to prove that I didn't need you. That I didn't need a father who didn't want me."

"You are so much like your mother," he said wistfully.

"I didn't know that you two knew each other beyond . . . well, me."

"I loved her."

His confession had Maggie uncovering her face and reaching for the scotch. "I think I need this."

"Make it two," Sebastian said.

She poured heavily, and they sipped in silence for a moment.

"My marriage was rocky when I met your mother at that conference. I'd brought up the idea of separating a few weeks before, and Rebecca had agreed to move into our apartment downtown. In my head, it was a done deal. I met your mother. This bright, beautiful, intelligent, caring woman with this energy. This zest for life. It was intoxicating. We spent the entire conference together."

Maggie stared over his head at the picture. The picture he painted was exactly how her mother would have liked to be described.

"When I got home, Rebecca was still there. She insisted we give things another try."

"Have you ever watched the TV show *Friends*?" she asked.

"We were on a break," he said wryly.

She snorted into her whiskey.

"I called your mother. Told her I was going to try to make my marriage work. She wished me luck."

"And that's the last time you spoke until you found out you had a twelve-year-old daughter," Maggie said, filling in the blanks.

He surprised her by shaking his head. "I knew about you. She called to tell me she was pregnant and that, not only was she not asking for any kind of support, but she was refusing it. She didn't want her daughter to grow up feeling like an obligation or a rich man's castoff."

"And that hurt you," she guessed, surprised.

"Deeply. I would have left Rebecca. I would have married your mother, gotten her a job, a nanny, whatever she wanted. But her rejection of me, of what I could give, hurt. I allowed the hurt to dictate my reaction. I gave her exactly what she wanted. Nothing. Shortly after that, Rebecca told me she was pregnant. So I focused on the family that chose me. And here we are."

"I had no idea," Maggie said.

"Apparently, this is why communication is important."

She smirked. "Who knew?"

"Your mother was a very stubborn woman. I hope you don't take offense if I say I see a lot of her in you."

She thought of Silas. "You wouldn't be the only person here to make that observation."

"Rebecca and I divorced last year," Sebastian said.

"I, along with the rest of the world, know that," she told him, thinking of the tabloids reporting on the settlement.

"I can lay the blame with her. I can say that she played off both our insecurities to keep us from forming a bond. But in the end, I am your father, and I didn't fight hard enough for you. You deserve better, Maggie. A lot better. But I hope that maybe we can stop thinking in terms of owing debts and making up for things, and perhaps we can start over. Without anyone else running interference."

She nodded. "Except maybe Dayana."

"Except maybe Dayana," he agreed. "I should go."

"You can, uh, hang out for a while," she said. "Dayana and Keaton would love that. There's a lot of food out there, and the band is just getting started."

He nodded. "I'd like that.

"I thought the Midtown Mansion was my favorite. But this?" His gaze roamed the room. "This is incredible."

Well, holy shit.

"You watch my show?" she asked.

He nodded and looked both proud and embarrassed. "Every episode."

"Dad?" she said, as he moved toward the door.

He stopped.

"Do you remember the bookcase we built?" she asked.

His smile was slow but warm. "Of course. It's in my office."

He walked out, leaving Maggie with her spinning head.

"Maggie?"

She looked up and found Blaire standing in the doorway. "Listen, if you have a book deal or a surprise parental confession for me, I think I've already hit my quota," Maggie told her.

Blaire smiled and took the chair next to her. "Dayana confessed everything to Silas and me outside. She's vacillating between thinking she did exactly the right thing and worrying that she just ruined all the progress you two have made together."

"She told you that?" Maggie was impressed.

Blaire pointed a finger at herself. "Therapist face. It makes people want to open up and spill all their secrets."

"Thank you for coming to check on me," Maggie said.

"I had to have Breonna put Silas in a choke hold to keep him out. I figured since you two haven't had a chance to talk yet, him running in to confront your father wouldn't be as helpful as he thought it would be."

"Oh boy." Maggie took another sip of her drink.

"Are you okay?"

Blaire was right. There was something about her face, the lack of judgment, the presence of sincere interest, that made Maggie want to spill her guts. But she owed those guts to Silas first.

"I am. At least I think so. It's been an overwhelming party so far, and it's not even dark yet."

"Is that your mother?" Blaire asked, pointing to the photo on the mantel.

"It is. That picture is actually the reason I bought this place," she confessed.

Blaire got up to look at it.

"She brought me here on a vacation when I was twelve. We were here for a week and had the time of our lives," Maggie explained.

"Kinship has that effect on people," Blaire said, picking up the frame and examining the picture more closely.

"We spent the whole week making up stories about the people who lived in the big house on the hill. I've always kept my eye on real estate here, and when this house came onto the market, I just knew. I guess it felt like one of those signs that Silas is always talking about."

Blaire was still staring at the picture.

"Is everything okay?" Maggie asked. She really didn't think she could deal with another crisis or revelation.

Blaire looked up, her smile bright and her eyes damp. "Oh, honey."

46

"DON'T DO ANYTHING stupid, Sy," Dayana warned as Silas watched Sebastian Spencer step outside, hands in pockets, surveying the scene on the terrace.

"I never do stupid things," Silas insisted. Kevin gave his clenched hand a nudge with a cold, wet nose, offering doggy comfort. The billionaire philanthropist was too casual for his liking. In Sy's opinion, the man should be groveling, earning forgiveness and generously providing apologies.

His anger was a living, breathing thing. It seemed fundamentally wrong to him that everyone around him was enjoying themselves while the man who had deeply scarred Maggie, the reason they were all gathered, was perusing appetizers.

"What about that time you tried to do a handstand on the bridge railing over Strawbridge Creek?" Michael asked.

"For the one millionth time, it's 'crick' not 'creek.' You've lived in Idaho since you were seven. Get it right. Secondly, I was eight when I did that. This is different. I'm not going to dislocate a shoulder doing this."

"Probably not. But you might get your pants sued off," Nirina pointed out before turning to Dayana. "You probably shouldn't have told him. There's no way he's not going to do something stupid in the name of defending his lady's honor."

Dayana groaned. "I couldn't help it. I just started word vomiting to Blaire. I didn't know he was eavesdropping."

"You pushed me out of the way so you could talk to her," Silas pointed out.

"He didn't make Maggie sign that stupid NDA," Dayana said. "My evil mother did that, and you can rest assured she will be punished."

"What NDA?" he snapped. Kevin wasn't a fan of confrontations and slunk off to hide under the buffet table.

Her eyes went big and she took a step back. "Oops. I thought she'd told you."

The list of things Maggie hadn't told him was getting longer and longer. "Dayana, *what* NDA?" He felt like his head was going to explode.

"Let's maybe all just take a breath," Dean suggested.

But Silas was locked on and stared Dayana down until she cracked.

"My mom thought she was protecting the family by having her lawyer draft a nondisclosure agreement. By signing it, Maggie agreed to never admit to anyone that Sebastian Spencer was her father. I didn't know about it until I came here. And my father had no idea until I told him. My mother set it up to make it look like she wanted nothing to do with our dad anymore once Maggie got access to her trust."

"Oh, shit," Nirina whispered. "That's diabolical."

Silas made a move for the house, but the siblings formed a wall in front of him.

"He didn't know, Sy," Dayana said, pleading with her eyes.

Even if the man hadn't known, he'd still made Maggie feel unwanted. Still allowed her to be a stranger in his home. Sebastian Spencer deserved to—at the very least—get punched in the face and then be made to feel like shit.

"Punching out your girlfriend's billionaire father in front of all of these witnesses and cameras on her big night is a terrible idea," Michael told him, reading his mind.

"Then I will wait till tomorrow," Silas said through clenched teeth.

"Uh-oh, incoming," Niri hissed.

Dean and the rest of the siblings very deliberately stepped between Silas and Maggie's father. "Mr. Spencer, what brings you to Idaho?"

"Dean, it's good to see you again," Sebastian said, offering a handshake.

"Sebastian Spencer?" Silas elbowed Dean out of the way. Then came up short when Michael jumped in front of him.

"Mr. Spencer, can I just say that the giving pledge—" Michael's greeting was cut off when Silas lifted his brother by the elbows and moved him out of the way.

"You try to pick me up, Silas Andrew, and I will kick you in the balls so hard your male children will be born with limps," Nirina said, taking up the sentry position between the two men.

"I'm missing something," Sebastian said.

"Everybody stop protecting both of these two grown men from suffering the consequences of their actions," Dayana insisted.

"It's what family does," Michael said, returning to stand shoulder to shoulder with Nirina. Dean hurried to stand next to him, completing the wall.

"Dad, this is Silas. Maggie's boyfriend. At least, he is if they can get their heads out of their asses long enough to make up. Silas, this is our father, Sebastian, who is aware that he has a lot of years of mistakes to make up for," Dayana said, making the introductions.

"Wow. Hot Landscaper Guy." The man looked delighted. Silas didn't want him to look delighted. He wanted the man who had abandoned Maggie to look punched in the face.

"Your daughter is an incredible woman, and you're a goddamn fool for walking away from her," Silas said, hands fisting at his sides.

"I would have to agree on both counts," Sebastian said.

It wasn't good enough. He was calculating the odds of getting around or at least over the human wall in front of him when his mother's summons had them all turning.

"Silas!"

"You're in trouble," Niri sang under her breath.

"You behave or I'm getting that kid a drum set," he threatened, pointing to his sister's belly.

"Go," Michael said, steering him in the direction of Blaire.

"Fine. But until I come back, I want you to make sure Spencer has zero fun. Throw drinks in his face. Slap appetizers out of his hand. If you even catch him starting to dance, I want you to pants him."

"It's good to see that your vengeance has remained at the middle school level," Michael said.

"What's wrong, Mom?" Silas asked when he reached her side.

His unflappable mother took him by the hand and dragged him into the house. "You need to talk to Maggie. She's upstairs."

Fuck.

"Is she okay?"

Blaire smiled, but her eyes were clouded with tears. "She's great," she promised.

"Are *you* okay?" he asked.

"I'm great, too," she said, squeezing his arm. She led him to the rotunda and stopped at the foot of the stairs.

"Any last-minute advice?" he asked.

She cupped his face in her hands. "I love you, and I'm so proud of you."

"That's not advice," he told her through smooshed cheeks.

"I trust you to know what to do to be happy," she said.

"And that's too vague for advice."

She smiled up at him. Her eyes glittered with tears. "Thank you for being exactly who you are. I will never doubt your signs again."

"Are you really okay? Did someone put something in your drink?"

"I'm wonderful," she promised. "Now go find your girl. I'm going to go slow dance with Morris on the terrace my son built."

"Okay, weirdo." She released his cheeks. "I love you, Mom."

"I love you, Silas."

He took the stairs slowly, uncertain of what waited for him above. Instinct told him Maggie wasn't on the second floor, so he climbed to the third. There was a faint glow visible from the doorway of the guest bedroom. The closet door was open, and the velvet ropes were set aside.

"Maggie," he said, stepping into the secret room. She looked beautiful, ethereal. And maybe a little crazed. God, he loved that about her. He loved every fucking thing about her. Even the parts that drove him nuts.

"Silas."

Yeah. He especially loved the way she said his name.

She reached for his hands, and when he held them out, she towed him farther into the room. She'd lit candles.

Candles were a good sign, right? She wouldn't light candles to break up with him. Unless the overhead light had malfunctioned, and she needed the candles. But still, there were other more convenient ways to break up with people.

"Have a seat," she said, gesturing toward the armchair.

He sat. "Maggie, I—"

"Me first," she said. "Please. I have something for you."

Nude photos? Something to remember her by? Shit. If it was a forwarding address, he was going to go downstairs and get very, very drunk.

She handed him a roll of papers. "These are for you," she said, pulling the desk chair over and perching in front of him.

He removed the blue rubber band and watched her face while he unrolled them.

She was biting her lip, her hands clenched in her lap. She didn't look devastated, but he could definitely smell fear.

He turned his attention to the plans in his lap. "Is this your barn?" he asked, studying the blueprint. It looked like she was planning to renovate the entire structure with storage and garages on the lower level, workshop space on the main floor, and office space in the hayloft.

He flipped to the next page.

It was a plan for a greenhouse.

"You'd mentioned before that if Bitterroot could grow some of its own perennials and annuals, it would add up to some serious savings over the years. Plus Kinship doesn't have its own nursery, so it would mean more jobs."

He looked up at her. "Hold up. You're not giving me this place as a parting gift, are you?"

She looked horrified. "No! I'm asking if you'll move in with me. Officially. Here. In this house. To stay."

Maggie Nichols looked like she was about to puke.

"Don't you want to go?" he asked gently.

She shook her head. "I've been waiting my entire life to find home. And I found one. I *made* one. Here. With you."

Those teary brown eyes murdered his soul. It took everything he had not to grab her and crush her to him.

"Baby, I'd go with you," he whispered.

"I know. I know you would if I asked you. But the thing is, I don't want to go. I want to stay here and go kayaking and hiking, and I want to sleep late on Sundays. I want to wrestle for mattress space with a pit bull and two stupid cats."

He was gutted.

And thrilled.

And crushed.

And so fucking happy.

"Maggie, what about your show? What about everything you've built? What about the East Coast offer?"

"What about *us*? I can still do my show, *if* that's what I want. Apparently, I can also write a book. Or renovate a ski resort or...well, anything I want. But what I want most of all is you and this house. I want to fill this house with the family we choose, the family we make. I want to be here next to the fireplace when you string lights on that Christmas tree in the backyard."

His heart was beating faster, as if he were in the front car of a roller coaster chugging up that first big hill. It wasn't fear. It was the thrill of a new adventure.

"You matter to me so much that I have to take the leap. I have to step into the unknown and try. I'll do things wrong. I'll get into funks. I'll argue with you and work too hard. But I will also love you as intensely as I do anything."

He dropped the sheets of paper to the floor and grabbed her. "Are you sure? Be sure, Maggie." He couldn't quite grasp that all his dreams were coming true.

She nodded and gave him a sweet, watery smile. "I'm staying. Even if you're too stubborn to date me. I'll make it awkward as hell at the general store and Cowboy Jake's. I'll probably still be invited to your parents' house for cookouts and brunch. You can still have the greenhouse, the barn. But I'll charge you an astronomical amount of rent to remind you every month or so that you could have had me, too."

"You about done?"

"About. I just need you to turn the last page."

He bent down and picked up the sheets he'd dropped. Then he grinned. There, taped to the last page, was a crisp five-dollar bill.

"You win," she whispered.

He dropped the papers and reached into his pocket. "Maggie Nichols..."

"Holy shit. Are you seriously about to overshadow my grand gesture?" The hand she brought to her mouth was shaking.

He paused, midkneel. "You're damn right I am."

"Don't you *dare* propose. I haven't even told you about the sign. About Ava and Wallace. And my dad. You deserve to know everything before you do whatever crazy thing it is you're about to do."

"After," he said, sinking down to one knee and holding the ring that had been burning a hole in his damn pocket since he'd arrived. "Maggie Nichols, will you do me the great honor of putting up with me for the rest of your life? Will you let me love you? Will you be my wife and partner and best friend?"

"Dammit! That's a lot nicer than five dollars and a dumb greenhouse," she whispered, eyeing the diamond solitaire.

"Maggie, say yes right now or I won't be responsible for my actions."

"Can I say yes and still not hold you responsible for your actions? Because I'd really like that."

He surged up, lifting her high and wrapping her legs around his waist.

"Wait, Silas!" Her laugh was breathless. "There's something you really need to know."

"Did you murder a bunch of people for money?" he asked.

"No."

"Then I think it can wait."

"My mom loved your energy," she said.

He stilled. "What?"

She pointed to the picture he hadn't noticed until now. The framed one she kept in her bedroom of her mom laughing.

"Look at the picture, Silas," she whispered.

He picked it up rather than putting her down because he wasn't ready to be without Maggie Nichols in his arms for a good, long time.

"She's beautiful," he told her.

"Look at what she's smiling at," she insisted.

He looked closer, and the recognition dawned slowly. "Wait. Is that—"

"It's *you*. You can just barely see your mom's profile behind her," she said, tapping a finger to the glass. "I didn't want to get in the lake because I couldn't see the bottom. I couldn't see where I was walking or what was coming. And my mom pointed to a boy charging into the water with a battle cry. He'd run up and attack that water with a cannonball or a front flip. Even a terrible cartwheel. It was you. She was looking at you."

His throat was closing up. The image was blurring before his eyes. "My cartwheels still need work," he said.

"My mom said, 'Maggie, that's the way you do all the best things in life. You just run and jump and hope for the best. Just like that boy.' Just like you, Silas."

"How?" It wasn't the right question, but it was the only one he could come up with.

"It's our sign. I've been carrying you around with me since I was twelve years old," she told him.

And then the time for words was over. Their kiss went on and on, spiraling out in time. Reaching both backward and forward until he knew that his life wasn't just his own. It was Maggie's, too.

"I love you, Silas." They were just words. But coming from her mouth, he felt them like a spell.

He kissed her again, loving her with his mouth. With the promises he whispered, the breath he shared with her, they let themselves love.

"We should get back downstairs," she whispered against his shoulder a long while later.

He stroked his hand down her back. "I guess that wouldn't be the worst idea." He still had one surprise left for his girl.

"I missed you," she confessed as they both searched for her underwear.

"I missed you, too, Mags."

They heard the click of toenails on hardwood and glanced toward the door of the closet. A wet nose wedged itself in the crack, and suddenly there was Kevin, a caterer's apron dangling from his mouth. The dog's eyes widened, and he froze.

"Busted, buddy," Maggie teased.

Silas groaned. "You thieving butterball."

Kevin, carefully avoiding making any eye contact, backed out of the doorway and trotted away before either of them could steal his treasure.

It was dark by the time they made it outside. Disheveled and so damn happy. Silas had lipstick not just on his collar, but right down the placket of his shirt. Maggie's hair couldn't be tamed, so she'd pinned it back from her face. But it didn't matter because she kept staring down at the diamond that glinted on her left hand and beaming.

They were so wrapped up in their own happy that it took a solid minute before they realized everyone was shit-faced.

"We're gonna need to tell everyone the news all over again

tomorrow. This is getting dangerous," Silas complained after he pried Emmett's and Mama B's faces off of Maggie when they tried to take a "kissy face selfie" that lasted two minutes too long. Blaire had gone in for a hug and ended up putting the happy couple in headlocks. Morris was asleep at one of the tables. The grinning Michael announced that he was "sho happeeeeee" for the seventh time, and the sober Nirina gleefully recorded the chaos on her phone.

Silas managed to find Elton at the bar. "It's time," he said to the man who was juggling four cocktails.

"I'd guess it's about nine?" Elton said, tilting his hand to look at a watch that wasn't there and dumping two of the cocktails on his pants. "Ah, man!"

"Focus. It's time for the fountain," Silas said, taking the rest of the drinks from him and handing them to Cody's girlfriend's parents as they tangoed by to a song that was much slower than the one the band was actually playing.

He got Elton in place—and put him in a chair in case the man's balance deserted him—and headed over to the band. The band leader gave him the nod and cut off the song as Silas took the stage.

"Excuse me for interrupting the festivities, everyone," he said into the microphone. "But I just asked a very special lady to marry me, and since she had the good sense to say yes, I have a little surprise for her."

There was yelling, catcalling, and even a playful "boo" from Wallace's neighbor Gladys, who kept winking at him.

He found Maggie in the crowd. A wide-awake Keaton on her hip and Dayana's arm around her waist. She was beaming at him, those brown eyes full of a happiness he'd never seen there before. One he wanted for the rest of his life.

He loved her. Fiercely and forever.

"Hit it, Elton," he said.

Almost on cue, the first plume of water shot up and out of the fountain, followed by a second and a third.

The crowd cheered wildly. But he kept his gaze on Maggie. She clapped a hand to her mouth and watched as the Campbell Fountain came back to life. He met her in the center of the terrace, plucked her nephew from her arms, and gave the boy a loud kiss on the head before turning him over to his mother.

"It's amazing," Maggie told him over the din of the crowd.

Then he picked her up in his arms and marched toward the fountain.

"What are you doing?"

"Tradition, darlin'," he said, stepping over the stone lip of the fountain into the water.

"You are the most ridiculous romantic," she said, cupping his face in her hands as a few hundred gallons of water misted around them.

"'S not a party till someone's in the fountain," Dean yelled, dragging Michael into the water with him.

"Dean is going to be so pissed he ruined his shoes," Maggie observed from Silas's arms.

"Is that Wallace?" Silas asked incredulously. "Who's he dancing with?" he asked, nodding toward the edge of the patio where Wallace, in his high-waisted pants, was slow dancing with a woman in a pink dress. The man was all but unrecognizable because of the thing his mouth was doing under his bristly mustache.

Wallace Pfeffercorn was smiling.

"That's Flo, Wallace's high school sweetheart," Maggie said airily.

"You sure know how to throw one hell of a party, Nichols."

She grinned at him and tightened her arms around his neck. "Imagine what the wedding will be like."

He gave her a spin and then set her down in the water. "By the way, this is a conversation for a later date because I fully plan to spend the rest of the night necking with you, but the bridle on this horse has the date of the coach robbery etched into it," he said, taking her hand and running it over the stone of the statue.

"You're kidding!"

"I am not. Each horse has a different date. This one's the robbery. Those two are the Campbells' wedding day and the date this house was completed. Not sure what the third one marks. It's between the robbery and the wedding day."

Maggie grinned. "I think I have an idea," she confessed. "But I'd rather neck with you for the rest of the night. We've got a whole lifetime to talk."

"I am the luckiest man who has ever danced in this fountain," he said.

"Look!" she breathed, pointing up. He caught it as it streaked across the night sky before winking out of existence. A shooting star, bright and bold.

"Well, I'll be damned," he whispered.

"Do you think it's a sign?" she asked.

"I most certainly do. I think your mom is here, looking down and feeling awfully proud," he told her.

She nodded, eyes glistening. "Yeah?"

"And it looks like your dad's here, too," he said, leading Maggie to the side of the fountain where Sebastian stood, looking apart from everything.

He held Maggie's hand out to the man. "Be good to her," Silas warned.

When Sebastian Spencer toed off his trillion-dollar loafers and stepped into the fountain to dance with his daughter, Silas took it as another sign.

47

"GOOD MORNING," MAGGIE sang as Dean, followed by Michael, slumped into the kitchen. "Who wants breakfast?"

Dean hissed at her and went straight for the coffeemaker. Michael eased himself onto one of the stools at the island and rested his forehead on the countertop. "Uhhhhhh," he groaned.

She slid the last pancakes off the skillet and onto the plate. "We've got eggs—"

"I will vomit all over this kitchen," Dean warned, slipping on a pair of sunglasses and taking the stool next to his boyfriend.

"Ugh. Make her stop," Michael groaned.

"Pancakes, bacon, and hash browns," she continued, undeterred.

"Morning, kids," Silas said, entering the kitchen with his arms full of grocery bag totes. "I brought sports drinks, ibuprofen, and fixin's for Bloody Marys." Kevin and the kittens jogged into the room on his heels. They did a lap around the island before racing through the open terrace door.

"What kind of evil villain are you, expecting us to drink *more*?" Michael said to the countertop.

"Give me a sports drink and the pills, and nobody gets hurt," Dean said, his face buried in a giant mug of black coffee.

"I'll take a Bloody Mary," Maggie chirped.

"Why are these monsters screaming?" Michael groaned.

"Did you get to retell them the good news yet?" Silas asked Maggie, leaning in to give her a kiss.

"Not yet," she said, melting against him.

"Oh good. They made up," Dean said dryly.

Michael raised his hood and pulled the strings so tight that only his nose and mouth were visible. "Yay."

Dayana slunk into the room, a piece of paper stuck to her cheek, and moaned dramatically. "Has anyone seen Keaton?"

"I got this," Silas said. He crossed to Maggie's sister and peeled the paper off her face. "We left you a note last night. Your dad took Keaton to the inn for a sleepover."

"Oh. Good. I didn't dream that part," Dayana said, shuffling toward the coffee.

"I've never been this hungover in my life," Dean moaned.

"He says that every time," Maggie told Silas.

"Why are we here and not hibernating for the ten months it's going to take for me to feel normal again?" Michael rasped.

"Because these jerks have something 'important' they want to talk about," Dean said.

Maggie started another pot of coffee while Silas took the bacon out of the oven.

"I hate everything," Dayana rasped.

"The benefit to spending parties having sex instead of enjoying the open bar," Silas whispered to Maggie.

"We're so smart," she told him. Her thumb found the band of the engagement ring, and she couldn't hold back the smile.

Cody bopped into the room. "Hey, guys!"

"Get out!" they roared as one.

Maggie cut him off at the door. "Don't listen to them, but do memorize their faces. This is what a hangover looks like after thirty."

"It's not pretty," Cody observed.

"Come over here and say that to my withered, dehydrated face so I can throw up on your shoes," Dean said.

"I'll help," Michael volunteered.

Cody grinned.

"Wait a minute. Shoes," Dean said. "Something happened to my shoes last night."

"You can dole out the sports drinks and headache meds," Silas told Cody. "We've got a lot to talk about."

"Knock knock!" a familiar voice called from the front of the house.

"Is that...?"

"It can't be. He sounds too—"

"Cheerful?"

"Human."

Wallace poked his head into the kitchen. His mustache twitched when he got a look at them all. "What the hell happened to all of you?"

Maggie held up her hand. "Sy and I got engaged."

"I remember that part," Wallace huffed.

"You did?" Michael sounded confused.

"Congratulations. We'll celebrate later," Dean offered.

"Much later," Dayana agreed.

"Sounds like a real Campbell party," Wallace said, rubbing his palms together.

"What's with this guy?" Dean demanded. "Where's his snarly face and mean stage whispers?"

"Maybe he got some," Silas suggested.

All of the heads, including the hungover ones, whipped up to study Wallace's face. He wasn't smiling, but his perpetual frown was absent.

"Florence?" Maggie asked gleefully.

Wallace schooled his features into his usual disdain. "A gentleman doesn't kiss and tell."

"Yes, we do," Silas, Dean, Michael, and Cody said together.

"Let's table this and focus on what's important," Maggie said.

"We get it. You guys are engaged. I'll be happy for you three days from now when I'm sure my head isn't going to snap off my neck," Dayana groaned.

"I'm talking about the fact that we are pretty certain that A. Campbell was actually Ava Campbell, who is not a descendant of some wealthy European family but is in fact Anna Potter, granddaughter of

Bowman Potter, one of the men who robbed the stagecoach in Dead Man's Canyon," Maggie announced. "Anna allegedly disappeared in Dead Man's Canyon when she went looking for the gold. Only, I think she didn't disappear. I think she came out of the canyon with the gold and a new name."

It didn't get the reaction she'd hoped for. Silas handed her a Bloody Mary to make up for it.

"Good for her," Dayana murmured into her coffee with zero enthusiasm.

"Is there a reason for your theories or are you currently drunk?" Dean asked.

"Well, as you all know, it started with the gold coin in the mantel. It happens to match the only other recovered coin from the coach robbery," Maggie said.

"Yeah. Fast-forward beyond that," Dayana said.

"In the secret room, we found some clues—including an unfinished manuscript in Ava's handwriting—that hinted at her being the famous A. Campbell instead of her husband," Maggie continued.

"That's cool," Cody said, helping himself to a plate of food and shoveling it into his face.

"We were also able to trace Bowman Potter's lineage forward and found an overlap with Ava Campbell's descendants. We're waiting for some of that DNA testing for confirmation," Wallace put in.

"Does anyone else think the earth is spinning faster today?" Michael asked.

"Maybe you should tell them the part about Ava only taking half the treasure and leaving the rest," Silas suggested.

That perked them up.

Dayana raised her face out of her coffee mug. "Huh?"

"Are you saying there's half of a treasure out there in some canyon?" Dean asked wearily.

"Yes!" Maggie said. "From what we can surmise, Anna worked as a lady's maid for a wealthy family in Boise. Her grandfather Bowman must have left a clue or told her where the gold was. Because in

1895, she was reported missing by the local newspaper after a young woman matching her description told fellow stagecoach passengers that she was going on a treasure hunt. We think she not only found the gold, but that she took half of it, reinvented herself, and met Aaron Campbell shortly after."

"Less enthusiasm, please," Dean told her.

"Okay. If all of this is true, I don't suppose Ava/Anna Whatever-Her-Name-Is left a treasure map?" Dayana asked, attempting to open a bottle of green sports drink and then giving up and handing it to Silas.

"As a matter of fact," he said, unscrewing the top and pointing at Maggie.

She reached behind the island to grab the topographical map she'd stashed there. "We think she did."

"I know you guys think you're being cute, but really, the Vanna White routine makes me want to murder your faces," Michael told them.

"If I wasn't convinced my head was about to split in two right now, I would laugh. Because that was fucking funny, and it makes you even more attractive than your good looks and top-shelf hygiene," Dean said earnestly.

"If I hadn't thrown up less than ten minutes ago, I'd kiss you," Michael told him.

"Back to me and Vanna," Silas insisted.

"A needlepoint and this topographical map hung side by side in the study, above the mantel with the gold coin in it," Maggie said.

"So? Ow," Dean grumbled when Wallace elbowed him in his haste to load up a plate.

"We really should have done this in the afternoon," Silas told her.

"Or tomorrow," Dayana suggested.

"Well, you're all already here. So now you can eat grease and listen to how smart we are," Maggie insisted.

"Ugh. Fine." Dean groaned.

"The needlepoint said 'WHERE IS THE ADVENTURE IN FINDING ONESELF IF ONE USES SOMEONE ELSE'S MAP?'"

"It sounds like a meme on Pinterest," Dean complained.

"Except we think it was a clue," Wallace said, helping himself to a fresh cup of coffee before joining Cody at the breakfast nook.

"Next to it was this pen-and-ink sketch of some Idaho topography," Silas filled in. "Land that just so happens to neighbor Dead Man's Canyon, specifically."

"I hate to be a wet blanket," Dean began.

"Since when?" Maggie shot back.

"I kinda thought that was your thing," Cody said, going back for seconds.

"You're both dead to me," Dean said. "Wouldn't the gold belong to whoever owns the land?"

"That's the best part," Silas said, winking at Maggie. "If you'll look closely at a much later date when you don't feel like barfing bile and liquor on our major clue, you'll notice that it matches up with the sixty acres that the Campbells left in a trust to the town of Kinship."

"Hang on," Michael said, picking his head up off the countertop. "Are you guys really engaged?"

"Why do you think Anna/Ava only took half of the gold?" Dayana asked with one eye closed.

"Cody, what happened when the main character in *Canyon Secrets* finds the gold?" Maggie asked smugly.

"Can't you just tell us?" Dean moaned. "Are these theatrics necessary?"

Cody's eyebrows winged up. "The cowboy main character finds the gold and only takes half of it. He doesn't need it all, and he hopes that someone who needs it will benefit from it," he recited.

"Is anyone going to get to a point in this century, or can my boyfriend and I go back to bed?" Michael demanded.

"I love that you can finally say 'boyfriend,'" Silas told his brother. "Welcome to the family, Dean. If you cause my brother a moment of suffering, I will destroy you."

"So noted. Same goes for Maggie. Blah blah blah," Dean muttered.

"Understood," Silas said, grinning.

"Back to the gold," Maggie announced brightly. "Since the land is still in the trust, and since the bank's initial claim was paid by insurance, any gold found on it would technically belong to the town."

"Really?" Dayana asked now with both eyes closed.

"Really," Wallace said.

"If Anna/Ava took half of the gold, that means there's still half to find," Maggie explained.

"How sure are you?" Michael asked.

"We're not certain," she said.

"But we have a real good feeling about it," Silas told them.

"I brought a shovel," Wallace added.

"You're 'shovel sure'?" Dean asked.

"Yes." Maggie nodded emphatically. "So, who wants to come with us?"

"Now?" Dayana moaned.

"Why wait?" Wallace said.

"If half of the gold is still there, what's the harm in leaving it there for another seventy-two hours until I'm human again?" Dean wondered.

"Okay. So Cody and Wallace are in," Silas said, swiping a piece of bacon off the plate. "Who else?"

Maggie winced. "Well, there's one other person I should probably call."

48

"MAGGIE, IS NOW a good time to talk to you about my idea of having you personally renovate the Canyon Country Townhomes?" Kressley Cho asked as she adjusted the angle of her beach umbrella. The ice in her glass rattled and made Maggie want to hit the woman with the shovel she held with blistered hands.

"Now's not a great time," she said, gasping for breath. Her lower back was screaming from two hours of fruitless digging. This particular canyon with its whistle-pig holes and spindly trees and stupid, big rocks hadn't even warranted a name on the map. But she was certain it would have a name by end of day.

"Maybe you could grab a shovel and help, Madam Deputy Mayor," Silas suggested, climbing out of the ninth hole he'd dug. He leaned down and dragged Maggie out of hers. "Drink break," he insisted.

"Why am I the only one digging?" Cody complained.

"Because your back is twenty years younger than mine," Silas called from the striped lawn chair he'd collapsed into.

The August sun cast a special kind of swelter over the land as mirages blurred the landscape of dust and scrub brush.

"This was a stupid idea," Maggie said. The cold water in her canteen chased the grit from her throat.

"Not stupid," Silas insisted, dragging his sweaty, dirty T-shirt over his head and dumping water over his chest.

"Definitely not stupid," she murmured, admiring the show.

"Are we on a break, people?" Wallace demanded from under his Panama Jack hat. He gave his face and mustache a sassy spritz with a spray bottle.

"Are you on some kind of deadline?" Silas asked, refilling his tumbler with water from the cooler.

"As a matter of fact, I invited Florence to dinner tonight."

"We're in the middle of a treasure hunt," Maggie complained. "How the hell are we supposed to find the treasure and get you back to Kinship for dinner in time?"

"Don't forget you also have to cook dinner," Wallace insisted.

"What?" Silas asked. "Where is this dinner you're hosting?"

"The Old Campbell Place, of course. Where else?"

"I'm gonna bury him in one of these holes," Maggie whispered.

"I'll help," Silas said, throwing his shirt in the back of his pickup.

"Yoo-hoo!" Kressley called, waving with an iPad. "I'm working on the press release. Who wants to hear it so far?"

"Press release for what?" Cody asked.

"For finding the gold, of course. Here's what I have so far," she said, clearing her throat. "Kinship Idaho native Deputy Mayor Kressley Cho solved the century-and-a-half-old mystery of the Dead Man's Canyon stage robbery after discovering a historic trove of gold."

"New plan," Maggie said. "I'll hit her with a shovel, and you take Wallace."

"Deal," Silas said.

While Wallace and Kressley bickered over the wording and Silas forced Cody into a hydration break, Maggie picked up the photocopy of the topographical map for the hundredth time.

She scanned the area, noting the outcroppings above them. The map had led them to an offshoot of Dead Man's Canyon, barely a mile from where the bandits had taken the stage. It was a centuries-old streambed that had run dry ages ago, now scattered with scrubby trees and huge, dusty boulders. It was just inside the boundary of the sixty-acre plot the Campbells had purchased in 1910.

"What am I missing?" she muttered to herself.

She took her shovel and climbed the short incline behind their dig site, thinking to get a better look at the lay of the land. She'd reread the scenes in *Canyon Secrets* half a dozen times that morning. But Ava hadn't left any additional clues in her words.

The air buzzed with the sound of insects, the slow, steady beat of shovels attacking the ground beneath her.

"Okay. I'm a bandit. I've got four strongboxes of gold. Where am I going to put them? Mrs. Campbell? Mom? A little help?"

When no signs from the universe arrived with fanfare, Maggie took another drink from her canteen. The water dribbled down her chin and splashed onto the boulder beneath her.

She wouldn't have seen it with the dust covering it. That's how she'd tell the story for years to come. That accidental splash of water landing at just the right spot in that entire canyon? Well, it had to be fate.

"Silas? Can you come up here a second?" she called.

"Be right there."

"This is no time for you two to take selfies," Kressley reminded them. "We have holes to dig."

Sy's long shadow came into view as Maggie crouched down and dumped more water onto the surface of the boulder.

"Is this a make-out break?" he asked. "Because I might need some deodorant first."

"Oh, we'll be making out," she assured him. "But first, I think I found a sign."

He joined her in front of the broad, flat slab of rock, and she pointed to the wet spot.

"Well, I'll be damned. That looks just like Ava's pretty little octagonal window," he mused.

"Which looks just like the one in the picture of her as a lady's maid. I think it's a sign," she told him.

"'Course it is," Silas said with confidence. "Let's dig."

It took them ten minutes of focused digging, their shovels and backs working in tandem. And then Sy's blade hit something.

"That didn't sound like rock to me," he said.

Maggie grinned. "That sounded like metal. Should we get the others?"

"Let's make sure it's something and not nothing before we haul Wallace up here," he suggested.

They dug more frantically until the first box came into view.

"Well, it's heavy as fuck. Either there's gold in there or someone melted down a buncha antique bowling balls," he predicted.

"Holy shit. Holy shit," she said as she helped him brush away the dirt and loose rock. "Wait a second. It's a lockbox. We need a key, unless we want to use our shovels to destroy an artifact."

"Hang on a second," he said, reaching into the hole. He scooped dirt away from the underside of the box. "Aha." He produced a small leather pouch. "No destruction necessary."

"You are so sexy right now I almost want to have my way with you instead of opening this box."

"Why not both?" Silas said, slipping an old-fashioned brass key from the pouch. "You do the honors."

Maggie wiped her palms on her dirty jeans and blew out a breath. She lay down on her belly and finagled the key into the lock. "Are you ready?"

Silas lay down next to her and put his hand on her ass. "Now I am."

It took some work and some muscle, but the key turned, and the lock opened.

"I'm so excited I feel like I might barf," she whispered.

"Don't barf on the gold," he said. "Barf around the gold."

"Let's do this together," she suggested, taking one corner of the lid.

"You're just saying that in case we unleash some centuries-old mummy curse opening this box."

"Well, now I am," she said dryly.

"Hang on," he said, putting his palm on the lid. "What do you think of October?"

"You want to wait two more months to open this thing?" she asked.

"No."

"Okay. Then I think October's a nice month," she decided. "Cooler weather. Fewer bugs."

"Good. It's settled." He patted the box. "We'll get married in October."

"*This* October?" Maggie temporarily forgot about the gold.

"I think the thirteenth has a nice ring to it," he mused, brushing knuckles over her cheek. She felt the dirt transferring onto her face.

She swallowed. "That's my mom's birthday," she whispered.

"Imagine that," he said, nudging her chin up.

"I love you, Silas." She barely got the words out before his mouth closed over hers. Before her heart sang. Before her body vibrated with the rightness of it all.

"I want you." His words caused tremors in all the right places.

"Let's go home," she whispered.

"Maybe we should open this box first," he said with a smug grin.

"Oh, yeah. That. On the count of three. One, two, th— Holy shit, Silas Wright, you sure know how to show a girl a good time."

He gave her a celebratory slap on the ass. "Just imagine what I can do with the rest of your life," he said, shoving his hand into the coins that glittered in the afternoon sun.

In the corner of the box, Maggie spotted a scroll of paper tied with a leather cord. Carefully, she withdrew it and worked the knot free.

"Silas!" she said, smacking him.

"What?" he asked, turning to face her, two gold coins for eyes.

"Listen to this. *I, Anna Potter, do solemnly promise I took only what I needed and will do only genuine good with what I take.*"

He let the coins fall from his face. "It's just like the book."

"Wow," she whispered.

"What are we gonna do now?" he asked her.

"You mean besides plan a wedding in two months?" she said with a grin. "I've got a few ideas."

"Are they any good?" Silas teased.

"That depends. How do you feel about getting everyone their jobs back?"

"Damn, I love you, Maggie Nichols."

"Five bucks says I love you more," she told him, closing the distance between their mouths.

"Prove it," Silas whispered, just before their lips met.

Thanks to the remaining gold and a sizable investment from Sebastian Spencer, Kinship was able to purchase Canyon Custom Cabinetry and reopen as an employee-owned company.

Maggie and Silas got married at the Old Campbell Place on the most beautiful October 13 on record. They went on to have two kids, Ava and Bowman, because in their words, "Cody deserved a big, messy, loving family." Kevin and the cats are deliriously happy.

Michael and Dean got married on the terrace at the Old Campbell Place the following summer. They have a little girl named Campbell.

Silas got his greenhouse and eventually made Elton and Marta full partners in Bitterroot Landscapes. He turned down an offer from the Welcome Home Network to star in a show called Hot Landscaping.

Maggie's book Building Dreams *stayed on the* New York Times *bestseller list for nineteen weeks. She's working on another book when she's not rehabbing the entire Canyon Country Townhomes development from top to bottom. She semiretired from her YouTube fame, releasing only one episode a month. She now has three million followers.*

Kayla and Elton finally went out on a first date, which lasted forty-eight hours. They decided not to have kids and instead spend three months every winter traveling.

Dayana's divorce was finalized. She decided to stay in Kinship and accepted the position of chief financial officer at the plant. She met a nice guy with two little girls, and they're taking their time getting to know each other. She has no idea that he bought a ring for her the day after their first date.

Cody took a gap year before going off to art school. After graduating with honors, he rejoined Maggie's company and is planning to propose to Jun once she's done with dental school.

Wallace finished Ava Campbell's last manuscript, and it hit the New York Times *bestseller list. The royalties on Campbell's backlist paid for the Ava Campbell Park, created on the land where the gold was found. Wallace went on to write a book about Mrs. Campbell and dedicated it to his family: Maggie, Silas, and Cody. Maggie cried when he gave her a signed copy. He and Florence finally got married and honeymooned in Branson, Missouri.*

Sebastian Spencer bought a modest cabin on the lake and hired Maggie to renovate it. There's nothing modest about the eight-bedroom luxury villa now. But there is a special bookcase in the living room. The whole family spends every Christmas afternoon there.

Taylor moved her family back to Kinship so she wouldn't miss out on anything anymore.

Folks in Kinship still call Maggie and Silas's house the Old Campbell Place.

ACKNOWLEDGMENTS

Special thanks to the following:

- Mr. Lucy for his boundless patience, big heart, and excellent beard.
- Agent Mark Gottlieb at Trident Media Group for his wheeling and dealing.
- Grand Central Editor Alex Logan for thinking I'm funny.
- Editor Jessica Snyder for making my rough draft less rough.
- My readers for having excellent taste in books.
- My author pals for their commiseration about how damn hard it can be to write a book.
- Tacos.

ABOUT THE AUTHOR

LUCY SCORE is a *Wall Street Journal* and #1 Amazon bestselling author. Small-town contemporary rom-coms are her lady jam, and she enjoys delivering the feels with a huge side of happily ever after. Her books have been translated into several languages, making readers around the world snort-laugh, swoon, and sob. Lucy lives in Pennsylvania with the devastatingly handsome Mr. Lucy and their horrible cat. In her spare time, she enjoys sleeping, drinking copious amounts of coffee, and reading all the romance novels in the universe.